D1005837

DOWN A DARK ROAD

Center Point
Large Print

Also by Linda Castillo and available from
Center Point Large Print:

Among the Wicked
The Dead Will Tell

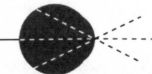

DOWN A DARK ROAD

Linda Castillo

CENTER POINT LARGE PRINT
THORNDIKE, MAINE

This Center Point Large Print edition
is published in the year 2017 by arrangement with
St. Martin's Press.

The text of this Large Print edition is unabridged.
In other aspects, this book may vary
from the original edition.
Printed in the United States of America
on permanent paper.
Set in 16-point Times New Roman type.

ISBN: 978-1-68324-500-1

Library of Congress Cataloging-in-Publication Data

Names: Castillo, Linda, author.
Title: Down a dark road / Linda Castillo.
Description: Center Point Large Print edition. | Thorndike, Maine :
    Center Point Large Print, 2017. | Series: A Kate Burkholder novel
Identifiers: LCCN 2017025822 | ISBN 9781683245001
    (hardcover : alk. paper)
Subjects: LCSH: Burkholder, Kate (Fictitious character)—Fiction. |
Amish—Fiction. | Murder—Investigation—Fiction. | Large type books. |
BISAC: FICTION / Mystery & Detective / Police Procedural. | FICTION
/ Mystery & Detective / Women Sleuths. | GSAFD: Mystery fiction.
Classification: LCC PS3603.A8758 D69 2017b | DDC 813/.6—dc23
LC record available at https://lccn.loc.gov/2017025822

For my husband, Ernest
Always

ACKNOWLEDGMENTS

Researching and writing a novel is a monumental undertaking and I owe thanks to many people who generously shared their knowledge, time, and expertise with me. As always, I'd like to thank my publisher, Minotaur Books, and all the wonderful people who bring the books to fruition. Charles Spicer. Sally Richardson. Andrew Martin. Jennifer Enderlin. Sarah Melnyk. Kerry Nordling. Paul Hochman. Kelley Ragland. Marta Ficke. April Osborn. David Rotstein. Martin Quinn. Joseph Brosnan. Allison Ziegler. Lisa Davis. You guys are my dream team and I'm so pleased to be part of your publishing family. I also wish to thank my friend and agent, Nancy Yost, who just happens to be the best in the business. Many thanks to the fine professionals at the Ohio Bureau of Criminal Investigation for the fascinating tour and for answering my crazy author questions without so much as a blink. Thank you to Wally Lind, retired Senior Crime Analyst and police officer, and founder of the Crimescenewriter email loop, for answering my questions about hostage negotiations. I also want to mention that I took much literary license in the depiction of several law enforcement agencies. Any procedural errors and creative embellishments are mine.

PROLOGUE

Two years earlier

He waited until the children slept. It was his final kindness. Give them a few more hours of peace before he took from them the thing they loved most. Before he shattered their innocence forever. Took something from himself he would never get back.

He didn't have a choice. Not now. He'd made the decision months ago, after spending a hundred nights tossing and turning beneath sheets damp with nervous sweat. He'd decided to kill her as he lay next to her, listening to her breathe, her body soft and warm against his. Even as the thought of having her again titillated that dark part of him that had spiraled out of control so long ago he couldn't recall.

He parked midway down the lane, walked the hundred or so yards to the house. The smell of rain hung heavy in the air, wet earth and growing things. Thunder growled in the distance, a beast prowling the countryside, hungry and snuffling the air for blood. He crossed the wet grass of the side yard, traversed the sidewalk. It was the same track he'd taken a thousand times before. Tonight would be the last.

He let himself in through the back door that

was never locked. Standing in the mudroom, rain dripping to the floor, mud and gravel sticking to his boots. Darkness all around. Propane refrigerator hissing from its place in the corner. Around him the house slept.

He found the shotgun in its usual spot, leaning against the wall, next to the coatrack. His hands shook as he picked it up. Breaking it open, he checked for shells, found it loaded. He started toward the kitchen. The lingering aromas of coffee and this morning's cornmeal mush and maple syrup.

Lightning flickered as he crossed through the living room. A snapshot of familiarity. How many times had he sat here with her on that eyesore of a sofa, piled high with homemade pillows etched with the silly stitching she was so fond of? The memories tore at him, and the now-familiar grief moved heavy and bittersweet through his chest.

Boots silent against the hardwood floor. The steps creaked as he started up them. On the landing at the top, dim light slanted in through the window at the end of the hall. The three bedroom doors stood open. His feet whispered against the rug as he went to the first, where the boys slept. He reached for the knob with a gloved hand. The latch clicked when he closed it. He went to the girls' room next and stood in the doorway, hearing the soft purr of a child's snore.

He lingered, regret echoing inside him despite his resolve because he knew after tonight it would be lost.

No time to dwell. He'd weighed his choices, made his decision. The only one he could. It was him or her. He'd chosen his life, his future. A dark curtain fell over his emotions, snuffing them out, and he pulled the door closed.

The master bedroom was at the end of the hall. Door open a few inches like it always was, so she could hear the children if they woke during the night. Stupid, fretful woman. Using his free hand, he pushed open the door the rest of the way. The silhouette of the bed beneath the window. Too dark to make out details, but he had an image of it in his head. Cheap knotty pine, yellowed with age. Threadbare sheets that smelled of laundry detergent and sunshine and woman. He had an image of her, too. The way she looked up at him when he was inside her. The way she sighed when he came. The sound of her laughter when it was done . . .

There was just enough light filtering in for him to discern the lump of her body beneath the quilt. The faint scent of kerosene from the lantern hovered in the air, and he knew she'd stayed up late reading, the way she always did.

A flash of lightning lit the room and in that instant he saw himself with her, their bodies arching and entwined, and he had to choke back emotions that threatened to strangle him. His conscience told him it didn't have to be this way. They could be a family. A real family. But he knew that was only the fear talking. He had too much at stake and far too much to lose.

He swallowed the bile that had crept up the back of his throat. The fear crowding his chest, making it difficult to breathe.

"I'm sorry, baby." His heart was beating so hard he didn't know if the words were a thought or if he'd actually spoken them aloud.

He stopped a few feet from the bed and raised the shotgun. His body quaked as he raised the stock to his shoulder. Set his eye to the sight. He'd been handling rifles since he was thirteen years old, and for the first time in his life the muzzle trembled. Sweat gathered between his shoulder blades as he leveled the sights center mass. Finger on the trigger. Deep breath, slowly released.

The explosion rocked his brain, scattered his thoughts, shook his resolve. Her body jolted, did a quarter roll. Right leg stiffening, then relaxing. Then she went still.

Dear God, what had he done?

His heart was running like a freight train. Emotion threatening to put him on the ground. The smell of blood rising, a primal stink filling the room, threatening to drown him. Time to walk away. Never look back. Forget if he could.

Lowering the rifle, he backed away.

"Datt?"

The voice jolted him, a lightning bolt coming through the roof and lighting up every nerve in his body. Adrenaline fired in his gut, spread in a hot rush to his limbs. He spun, raised the rifle.

"What are you doing?" the child asked.

He opened his mouth, but no words came. He stared at the little round face and all he could think was that she was going to ruin everything . . .

The whites of her eyes flicked and he knew she was looking at the bed where her mother lay dead. "I want Mamm."

He lowered the rifle. "She's sick. Go to bed."

"I'm scared."

"It's just a storm." He motioned toward the door, his hand shaking violently. "Go on now."

Turning on her heel, she padded barefoot toward her room. A tiny figure clad in white. An angel with fat little hands and baby hair.

He raised the shotgun. Tears squeezed from his eyes as he leveled it at her back. Finger snug against the trigger. No choice. Dear God, help him . . .

He pulled the trigger.

The firing pin snicked against the primer, the sound barely discernible over the pound of rain against the roof. Disbelief punched him. He

11

lowered the shotgun, stared at it, incredulous that it had betrayed him.

Vaguely, he was aware of the girl letting herself into her bedroom. The click of the latch as the door closed behind her.

Panic wrapped gnarly fingers around his throat and squeezed. He stood there, a maniacal laugh trapped and choking him. He weighed his options, tried to decide what to do next. But it was too late to act. Time to go.

Taking a final look at the bed, he backed from the room, bumped into the door. Then he was in the hall. Shotgun at his side. The knowledge that he'd screwed up hammering at the base of his brain.

Go back, the voice inside his head chanted. *Finish it. Kill her.*

By the time he reached the steps, his entire body shook uncontrollably. Breaths labored as if he'd run a mile. The voice at the back of his brain urging him to go back into the bedroom and finish it.

Coward, whispered an accusatory little voice. *Coward!*

He took the steps two at a time to the living room. Boots heavy against the floor as he crossed through the kitchen. A sound of anguish tore from his throat as he reached the mudroom. Lightning flickered outside the window as he set the shotgun in the corner where he'd found it.

Thunder cracked, like the final shot that hadn't come.

And the ground shook with the knowledge of what he'd done—and what he hadn't.

PART I

❦   ❧

That's all we may expect of man, this side
The grave: his good is—knowing he is bad.

—Robert Browning,
The Ring and the Book

CHAPTER 1

The Tuscarawas covered bridge is a Painters Mill icon. In spring and summer, tourists flock to the little-used back road for photos, for lunch with the grandkids, or just to spend a few minutes strolling the ancient wooden structure to ponder who might've walked the very same spot a hundred and fifty years earlier. Couples have been married here. Children have been conceived. High school yearbook photographs have been snapped. The Amish regularly set up their wagons on the gravel pullover to sell baked goods and fresh vegetables to *Englischers* anxious to fork over their cash for a sampling of the plain life.

I've passed through the old bridge a thousand times over the years, and I'm ever cognizant of its beauty, its historic significance, and its importance to the tourism segment of the town's economy. The magnitude of the latter echoed loud and clear in Mayor Auggie Brock's voice when he called me earlier this morning. In addition to the bridge being a favorite of locals and tourists alike, the place has recently become the target of graffiti artists and home base for a multitude of other illicit activities. I know that by the end of the day I'll have the town council breathing down my neck.

I park in the gravel pullover, take a final swig of coffee, and shut down the engine. As I get out of my city-issue Explorer, the *whooit-whooit-whooit* of a lone cardinal echoes among the treetops of the hardwoods that flourish in the greenbelt of the Painters Creek floodplain. Through misty shafts of sunlight, I see the footpath that leads down to the water's edge.

My boots crunch through gravel as I approach the bridge. Shadows envelop me as I start across it. The smells of ancient wood, the muddy dankness of the creek below, and new spring foliage greet me as I traverse the structure. Pigeons coo from the rafters above, their droppings marring the sills of the half dozen windows that run the length of it.

I'm midway across when I spot the graffiti. A tinge of indignation rises in my chest at the utter mindlessness of it. It's the usual fare. *Fuck you. Eat me. Panthers suck.* (Panthers being the name of the high school football team.) There's even a swastika. All of it haphazardly spray-painted in colors ranging from royal blue to safety orange. To my relief, there are no gang symbols. That's one segment of the criminal element that hasn't reached Painters Mill despite the recent emergence of a booming meth trade.

I cross to the nearest window and look down

at the creek fifteen feet below. The moss-green water swirls as it meanders south. I see the silver flash of a sunfish. Large stones a few feet beneath the surface. The olive-green hues of the deeper pools in the center of the creek. I know the depth there because eighteen years ago, I jumped from this very window on a dare. I walked home in a soaking-wet dress and stinking of creek water. Mamm didn't understand why I did it, but she allowed me to change clothes before my *datt* came in from the field. She knew that sometimes his punishments were too harsh for the crime.

A pigeon takes flight as I reach the opposite end of the bridge, the high-pitched whistle of wings harmonizing with the birdsong in the forest. I turn and look down the length of the bridge. Beyond, my Explorer bakes in the sun, the engine ticking as it cools, heat tendrils rising off the hood like steam from a cup.

I should be baffled by the advent of graffiti in such a revered, bucolic place, but I'm not. I might've grown up Amish, but I was not as separate from the rest of the world as my parents wanted to believe. I was certainly not immune to bad behavior. For a short period of time, I was one of those mindless, angry teens, bent on making my mark—any mark—however self-defeating or destructive.

I stroll to the center of the bridge, look up at

the rafters where a huge red swastika grins down at me. I shake my head in disgust, imagining some drunken idiot standing in the bed of a pickup truck, a can of spray paint in hand and a head full of rocks. Whoever did this wasn't in any hurry; they took their time and reached places that required some effort.

I continue on to the other side of the bridge and I can't help but wonder about all the things this place has witnessed over the years. When I was a kid, my *grossmuder* told me some places have memories. At the time I didn't have a clue what she was talking about and I didn't necessarily care. Only now, as an adult, do I appreciate her wisdom.

As I pass by one of the windows, my eyes are drawn to the dozens of initials carved into the ancient oak beams and planks. Most of them have been painted over multiple times. A few of the initials are familiar to me. My own, along with those of my one-time best friend, Mattie, are there somewhere, though for the life of me I can't remember where.

I'm standing at the window with my elbows on the sill when the sound of an approaching vehicle draws me from my reverie. Straightening, I glance over to see the mayor's Cadillac coupe pull up behind my Explorer. The driver's-side door opens and the mayor struggles out and slams it behind him.

Leaving thoughts of the past behind, I start toward him. "Morning, Auggie."

"Hey, Chief." Mayor Auggie Brock is a corpulent man with hound-dog jowls and eyebrows invariably neglected by his barber. He's wearing a JCPenney suit with a lavender shirt that's already wrinkled and a tie I wouldn't wish on anyone.

"Sorry I'm late." Holding a tall coffee cup from LaDonna's Diner, he enters the bridge. "Got caught up in a council meeting already. Would have ended an hour ago if Janine Fourman hadn't gone on about this graffiti problem. The woman can talk a blue streak."

Thinking of Councilwoman Turner, I frown. She and I have gone a few rounds over the years and not a single one of them was pleasant. "You have my sympathy."

He stops next to me. I can smell the coffee in his cup and the Polo aftershave he slapped on after his morning shower. He's a scant inch shorter than me and looks as harried as a fox surrounded by hounds.

"The director of the historical society was there, too, Kate. Needless to say, she was not a happy camper." Looking past me, he gestures so abruptly some of the coffee squirts from the opening of his cup. "Did you see all of it?"

"Kind of hard to miss."

He slants me a look as if trying to decide if I'm

21

messing with him. Which I am. Usually, even when we're dealing with some unpleasant topic or problem, I can drag a smile out of him. This morning he doesn't bite.

"For God's sake, *swastikas?*" he says. "Who the hell does stuff like that?"

"Young people with too much time on their hands." I shrug. "Too little responsibility or guidance or both."

"Don't kids have jobs anymore?" He strides to the window and gestures at a particularly vulgar carving. "Kate, we just spent eight thousand dollars painting this bridge for the second time in three years. We don't have the budget to do it again. The folks over at the historical society are shitting bricks."

"I understand," I say diplomatically.

"We've got to put a stop to the graffiti. I mean, for chrissake, the elementary schools bring little kids here for field trips. Can you imagine a kindergartner seeing some of those four-letter words? I didn't know what that word meant until I was in the army. Good God, some six-year-old starts talking like that and we'll probably get sued and then where will we be?"

"Auggie, we might be able to get some volunteers out here to paint over the damage," I offer. "I know some of my guys would show. We can get this covered up."

"It's those little shits out at the Maple Crest

subdivision," he grumbles. "Those high school kids have no respect. I think we need to make some kind of stand here, Kate. Some kind of concerted effort to catch them."

"I could sic Pickles on them," I say. My most senior officer, Roland "Pickles" Shumaker, has a reputation for taking a hard line with anyone under thirty. It was a running joke up until a year ago when he handcuffed a twelve-year-old boy for tossing a pop bottle out the window of a moving vehicle. The boy just happened to be the grandson of Councilwoman Fourman, who failed to see the humor.

"You can't be—" Realizing I'm kidding, he bites off the words and gives up a chuckle. "I'm glad one of us has a sense of humor about this."

"I can step up patrols. Work with County, persuade Sheriff Rasmussen to do the same."

"That's a start, Kate. I want those little bastards caught. I want them arrested. Forty hours of community service ought to show them the error of their ways. Let's see how they like spending their Saturdays out here painting over swastikas."

I consider pointing out the fact that the last time I caught someone out here defacing the covered bridge—a senior at Painters Mill High and a football player to boot—the boy's parents lodged a complaint and eventually the charges were dropped. But I don't mention it. It's part of being a small-town cop. It's my job to arrest people for breaking the law. The rest is up to the courts. I'd just as soon stay out of any back scratching that happens along the way.

Making a sound of irritation, Auggie crosses to one of the ancient oak beams and slaps his hand against the wood. "Could you imagine driving all the way from Columbus for some wholesome sightseeing and instead getting *that?*"

"There are quite a few teenagers out here just about every weekend," I tell him. "I'll park an officer down the road at that little turnaround. If we can catch them in the act and make an example of them, it'll stop."

Even as I say the words, we both know it will be me who parks down the road and stays up all night. My small police department consists of only four full-time officers, including me. Pickles is getting on in years and went part-time last summer. That's not to mention my budget, which leaves me no funds for overtime. And even if we're lucky enough to catch some numbskull artiste in the act, chances are—if he or she is a juvenile—Judge Siebenthaler will cave when the parents complain.

I make eye contact with Auggie. "I wouldn't be doing my due diligence as chief if I didn't remind you that a budget for OT would be helpful."

He makes a face I can't quite decipher. "I know you're operating with a skeleton crew, Kate. You know I'm in your corner. I've been trying for years to get the council to increase your budget. Rest assured, I've got the bean counters working on it."

That's one of the things I like about Auggie Brock. While he is a political animal, I know he cares.

"In the interim," he says, "let's get some volunteers out here."

I nod. "I bet Jim over at the hardware store will donate the paint."

"Good thinking," Auggie says. "Jim and I are in Rotary together, so let me get with him on that."

My phone chooses that moment to erupt. I check the display. Curiosity sparks when ODCR pops up on the screen. The Ohio Department of Rehabilitation and Corrections.

"I gotta take this," I tell Auggie.

He looks at his watch. "I've got a meeting, anyway."

"Don't forget to talk to Jim." Giving him a wave, I turn away and answer with, "Burkholder."

"This is Jerry Murphy, Chief Burkholder. I'm the deputy warden out at Mansfield."

The Mansfield Correctional Institution is a maximum-security state prison about a hundred miles north of Painters Mill.

"What can I do for you?" I ask.

"There was a security breach involving an

inmate last night," the deputy warden tells me. "You're on our notify list, Chief Burkholder."

A notify list contains the names of individuals— law enforcement, officers of the court, witnesses that testified during trial, family members, and victims—that are to be contacted when the status of an inmate changes. For example, when an inmate is paroled. I suspect this call has nothing to do with a formal discharge.

"Who?" I ask.

"Joseph King."

The name impacts my brain with a solid punch that leaves me breathless. I was eight years old when I met Joseph. He was Amish and lived on the farm next to ours. My older brother, Jacob, and sometimes my sister, Sarah, and I would meet Joseph and his two brothers after our chores were finished. There was a wooded area and a creek between our farms—prime real estate for a group of bored Amish kids.

Joseph was full of mischief, a born explorer, and a master teller of tall tales. He was funny and ornery and always ready for fun and games. Even with our many chores, we somehow always found time to play. Cowboys and Indians in the woods. A swim in the deep part of the creek. When I was nine, Joe set up a baseball diamond in a paddock, and I learned how to play baseball. In winter, we'd meet at nearby Miller's Pond to skate. When I was ten years old, Joseph taught me how to play hockey. I was competitive for an Amish girl—a trait that was frowned upon by my *datt* and brother. Not Joe. He liked me all the more because I was a tomboy, a sore loser, and I never shied away from a little rough-and-tumble.

I was twelve when I fell in love with him. It was an innocent Amish-girl crush, but to me it was a mile wide and as deep as the ocean. I never told a soul; not even my best friend. It was my secret, and I held it tightly. But it was the first time I had my breath taken away by a boy. It was my first bittersweet taste of love, and it was as powerful and formative as my first steps.

Joseph's *datt* was killed that fall when a drunk driver plowed into his buggy. He stopped coming over, and I didn't see him much after that. But I heard the stories. The rumors that said he'd lost his way. He'd lost the light in his eyes and opened his heart to some waiting darkness I had no concept of. They said he'd traded his happy-go-lucky persona in for a new model of brooding—and sometimes rage.

Two years ago, I received word that Joseph King had shot and killed his wife in their farmhouse while she slept. I'm not easily shocked, but I had a difficult time believing that the boy I'd once known could partake in such a vicious act. I'd actually been tempted to go see him, but life intervened and I never got around to it. I followed the media blitz of a trial. In the end, he was convicted of first-degree murder and sentenced to life in prison.

"Chief Burkholder? You still there?"

The deputy warden's voice jerks me from my reverie. "Yeah." I mumble something about our connection. "What happened with King?" I ask.

"He escaped custody sometime after headcount last night and as of this time, we've not been able to locate him."

I almost can't believe my ears. It's rare for an inmate to escape. There are too many layers of security and even more in the way of checks and balances. Without help from the outside, it's an almost impossible feat.

"I was on the notify list?" I ask.

"That's correct," he replies. "He's got ties to Painters Mill."

After Joseph's conviction, I remember hearing that his five children went to live with his wife's sister here in Painters Mill. "Rebecca and Daniel Beachy adopted them."

"Since the kids are living near your jurisdiction, we wanted to give you a heads-up in case he tries to make contact. We'll be notifying Holmes County, too." He pauses. "I understand you're part of the Amish community there."

"I used to be," I tell him. "I know where the Beachys live. They don't have a phone, so I'll drive over and let them know about King."

"Appreciate it."

"Has King made any threats against any of them?" I ask, knowing that when kids are involved, emotions can run high.

"Not that I know of," he tells me. "That doesn't mean he won't try to make contact. Or harm them or the family. From what I've heard, Joseph King is a cold-blooded son of a bitch."

The words disturb me more than they should. In some small part of my brain, I still think of him as the footloose boy who couldn't bring himself to scale a fish without first knocking it unconscious.

"We've got a BOLO out with the highway patrol. Richland County Sheriff's Department is all over this. We got dogs on scene. I suspect BCI will get involved, too."

Which means that my live-in lover, BCI agent John Tomasetti, will be getting a call, too, if he hasn't already.

"Can you text or e-mail me a recent photo of King?" I rattle off my e-mail address.

"We're blasting his mug shot to all law enforcement agencies in the four-county area, including Cuyahoga."

"I appreciate the heads-up."

"You bet."

I disconnect and slide my phone back into my pocket, troubled. I haven't seen or heard from Joseph King in twenty years, but I heard the stories. Not only from the Amish, but from law enforcement as well. Evidently, King was a troubled man with a marriage on the rocks, a litter of kids he didn't want, and a loose interpretation of his marital vows.

I vividly recall the day I learned his wife had been found dead—and Joseph was arrested and charged with first-degree murder. I couldn't believe the kid I'd known—the one with the toothy grin and big laugh—could do something so horrific. But no one knows better than me how profoundly life can change people—and that too often those changes are not for the best.

I'd wanted to talk to him, ask him myself if he'd done it. But I knew it was only that tiny part of my heart that remembered what it was like to be thirteen years old and in the throes of my first crush. The part of me that was loyal to a fault and still believed people were fundamentally good. I never went to see him.

I did, however, follow the investigation and trial. Joseph King, his wife, and their five children lived on a small farm near Middlefield, Ohio, which is about two hours northeast of Painters Mill. The night of the murder, King claimed to have gone fishing on Lake Erie. Since his destination was too far to travel via buggy, he'd paid a local Yoder toter to drive him to a cabin. During the night, someone walked into his unlocked home, picked up his shotgun, and shot his wife in her bed while their five children slept across the hall. Come morning, the children discovered their mother's body. Two days later, Joseph was arrested and charged with murder.

Throughout the trial, Joseph proclaimed his innocence. He claimed to love his wife and swore he'd never harm her. No one believed him. His temper was common knowledge around town. Worse, he had a criminal record that included two domestic-violence convictions. His prints were on the shotgun and the shells. One of his jackets, found at the scene, had gunshot residue on it. No one at the lake remembered seeing King at the cabin. The crime scene was a virtual smorgasbord of evidence—both circumstantial and physical—and the prosecutor offered up every juicy morsel.

The trial lasted three weeks, a spectacle that drew tourists from as far away as New York. In the end King was convicted of first-degree homicide and sentenced to life in prison. He maintained his innocence right through the day he was led from the courtroom in shackles. No one believed him, including me.

The case was high-profile not only because King was Amish but because of the level of brutality—and the fact that the children were in the house at the time of the murder. It brought to light the reality that domestic violence transcends culture and religion. And it drove home the fact that all the warning signs had been there, but for whatever reason everyone missed them, including law enforcement, family, and the Amish community.

Naomi King had been just twenty-nine years old. A pretty Amish mother whose life was cut short by a jealous, controlling, and sometimes violent husband. A family destroyed, countless lives ruined, and for what?

Graffiti forgotten, I walk to the Explorer, slide behind the wheel, and call dispatch.

My first-shift dispatcher, Lois, answers with a perky "You didn't throw Auggie off the bridge, did you?"

I can't help it; I laugh, and the cloud that had been hovering over me dissipates. "I need you to call everyone in for a quick meeting."

"This about that BOLO for Joseph King?"

I shouldn't be surprised that she's already heard; news travels fast in a small town. And with the police radio, it's not unusual for my dispatchers to know things before I do.

"Meeting in an hour." I tell her about my conversation with the deputy warden. "I'm going to head over to the Beachy farm to let them know."

"ODRC think he's coming here?"

"I don't think so, but the family needs to know he's out, and we need to cover all our bases just in case."

CHAPTER 2

I call Holmes County sheriff Mike Rasmussen on my way to the Beachy farm.

"You calling about Joseph King?" Mike begins without preamble.

"Is everyone a mind reader?" I mutter, and then say, "I'm on my way to talk to Rebecca and Daniel Beachy."

"Good. I think it's probably best if you're the one to talk with them since you know the language and whatnot. Every time I've been out there, they just sort of nod their heads and ignore everything I say."

"It's that whole separation thing, Mike. They hear you just fine; they just pretend they don't."

"Must come in handy."

I chuckle. "Did ODRC mention how King escaped? I didn't think to ask when I was on the phone with them."

"I just hung up with the sheriff up there in Richland County. From what I understand, King sawed through some kind of steel plate, crawled through an unsecured plumbing tunnel to the roof, and then rappelled to the ground using a rope made from sheets."

"Never underestimate the power of ingenuity,"

I say, my mind working over the information. "Do they think he got help from someone?"

"He didn't saw through that steel plate with his toothbrush."

"Someone inside?"

"The sheriff wasn't real forthcoming."

Even though he can't see me, I roll my eyes. "You going to put a deputy out at the Beachy place?"

"I'll step up patrols, Kate. I don't have the manpower to cover their farm twenty-four seven."

"Mike, I'm perpetually understaffed."

"Look, if I was facing life in prison, I sure as hell wouldn't come down to Painters Mill. I'd get as far out of Dodge as possible."

"Canada?" I say.

"Or Mexico."

"Unless he wants to see his children."

He sighs. "People do get touchy when it comes to their kids."

The words ring uncomfortably in my ears. "I'll let you know how it goes with the Beachys."

"I appreciate that."

"Let me know if you hear anything else."

"You got it."

Rebecca and Daniel Beachy live on a dirt road three miles outside Painters Mill proper. Their farm is sandwiched between the heavily wooded floodplain of Painters Creek to the west and a checkerboard of soybean, hay, and corn fields to the east.

I'm not unduly worried that Joseph King will show up here. I've got a pretty good handle on the Amish community; King is probably well aware that he doesn't have any friends, English or Amish, in Painters Mill. With every law enforcement agency in the area actively looking for him, chances are he'll be apprehended quickly. Still, I worry. Rasmussen is right about people and their children. King's kids could be a powerful draw. That's not to mention the fact that King was Amish. Even ostracized, the urge to return to the only thing he knows could be strong.

I pass by an overgrazed pasture to my left and the dark woods that run along the creek to my right as I idle down the lane. The farm is isolated, which could also be attractive to a man on the run. Chances are the Beachys don't have a phone. If something happened, they wouldn't be able to call for help.

Following the driveway around a bend, I end up on the back side of the house. I park behind an ancient manure spreader heaped with wood shavings, muck, and straw. Beyond, there's a tumble-down barn with peeling white paint and a rusty tin roof. Next to it, a massive silo gazes out over the property like some aging sentinel. In the side yard, an old-fashioned clothesline holds a mishmash of children's clothes—dresses and trousers and shirts—all hung neatly and flapping in the breeze.

I get out of the Explorer and wade through a dozen or more fat red chickens pecking the ground and make my way to the back door. Before I can knock, the screen door swings open. A little boy of about six years of age gapes at me with wide, impossibly blue eyes. He gives a single yelp and takes off running toward the barn with a lumbering puppy in hot pursuit.

"Levi! Go help your brother give that dog a bath!" a female voice calls out from inside. "He smells worse than that old boar!"

The words make me smile. My own *mamm* only had three children, but we were a handful—especially me—and she used to bark out orders like a boot camp sergeant. I catch the door to keep it from slamming and find myself staring into an unsettlingly familiar set of brown eyes. *Joseph's eyes,* some long-buried remembrance whispers. They belong to a boy about eight or nine years of age. He's standing in the mudroom, straw hat, blue work shirt, trousers rolled up to skinny knobby knees, revealing dirty bare feet.

"Hi." I offer a smile. "I'm Kate. Are your parents home?"

Never taking his eyes from mine, he calls out,

36

"*Mamm! Mir hen Englischer bsuch ghadde!*"
We have a non-Amish visitor!

I step aside and the boy blasts past me, making his escape through the door.

"Can I help you?"

I turn my attention to the Amish woman standing in the kitchen doorway, a red-and-white-checked towel in her hands. I guess her to be in her mid-thirties. She's wearing a light blue dress with a white apron and *kapp*. She's small, barely over five feet tall, with dark brown hair and eyes. A buttermilk complexion and a smattering of freckles on a turned-up nose.

"Mrs. Beachy?"

"*Ja.*" Her eyes sweep over my uniform. "What's wrong?"

I identify myself and show her my badge as I step into the mudroom. "I'd like to talk to you and your husband for a few minutes. May I come inside?"

Concern tightens her expression. She starts toward me. "Has something happened?"

"It's about Joseph King," I tell her. "Is Mr. Beachy home?"

"Joseph? Has he been hurt? Has he—"

Her words are cut off when a tall Amish man emerges from the kitchen. He's clad in typical garb—blue work shirt, dark trousers with suspenders, and a flat-brimmed straw hat. I estimate his age to be around forty or so.

"What happened to Joe?" he asks.

No smile for me. He doesn't acknowledge his wife as he brushes past her to confront me.

I tell them about the call from the prison. When I finish, they both fall silent, their expressions troubled.

"*Eah is am shpringa,*" the Amish woman whispers. He's running.

I nod. "Yes, he is."

"You think he's coming here?" Daniel asks. "You're here to warn us?"

"I don't know where he'll go," I say. "The police are looking for him. But I thought you should know, so you can stay alert and keep your family safe."

"The children." Rebecca's hand goes to the collar of her dress. Her fingers flutter nervously over the fabric. The couple exchange a look.

They're spooked, I realize. After everything I've heard about King, they should be.

"Is there a place we can sit and talk?" I ask.

Daniel motions to the door. "*Dess vayk.*" This way.

Rebecca leads us to a big country kitchen with cabinets painted seafoam green, off-white Formica countertops, and a pitted porcelain sink. It's a typical Amish kitchen, large and plain and cluttered with the tools of everyday living. An old-fashioned percolator coffeepot sits upside down in a dish drainer. A Dutch oven rests atop the stove. There's a bottle of vitamins on the windowsill. A rosemary plant flourishes in a terra-cotta planter. A lantern sits in the center of a rectangular table draped with a checkered tablecloth and surrounded by eight chairs.

When the three of us are seated, Daniel says, "You're the one who used to be *Amisch*."

"Yes." I don't miss the flash of disapproval in his eyes. But it's fleeting and tempered with curiosity. We're not here to talk about me or debate my decision to leave the fold. I turn my attention to Rebecca. "Naomi was your sister?"

She nods. "She married Joseph when she was just eighteen. He was still on *Rumspringa*. And so handsome. But there was a darkness inside him. And anger, I think. I tried to tell Naomi that something wasn't right with him. But she was crazy about him. All she talked about was getting married and starting a family. She couldn't wait to have children. She'd loved them so . . ." She breaks off, shaking her head.

"You were close to your sister?" I ask.

"Especially when we were younger. After she married . . ." She shrugs. "Things . . . changed."

"How so?" I ask.

"We didn't approve of him," Daniel says flatly. "Especially later."

His wife presses her lips together and continues. "Daniel and I visited them as often as we could.

39

Especially after the babies came. And of course we always saw them at worship."

"How was her relationship with Joseph?"

"At first, everything seemed okay. Naomi said he was a good husband. I could see for myself he was good with the children. He yelled at them a lot, but . . . I just thought he was strict." Another shrug. "Some men are just that way, you know."

"He was good to her when others were watching," Daniel interjects.

I keep my eyes on Rebecca. "And when no one was watching?"

"There were . . . problems," Rebecca tells me. "Joseph had a weakness for alcohol and a temper to boot."

Bad combination, I think. "Was he abusive to her?"

"The police arrested him for it," Daniel replies.

"Did he hit her?" I press.

The couple exchange another look and shake their heads. "He was careful not to let anyone see that side of him," Daniel tells me.

"But we think he was cruel to her." Rebecca's voice falters. "Mean, you know."

We fall silent. Through the open window, I can hear the children playing outside. The puppy barking. A rooster crowing from someplace nearby.

"Did either of you visit Joseph in prison?" I ask.

Daniel shakes his head. "After what he did to Naomi, we washed our hands of him."

"When's the last time you saw him?" I ask.

"The trial," Daniel says.

"We wanted to believe him at first," Rebecca tells me. "He seemed heartbroken that Naomi was gone. But . . . there were just too many bad things against him."

"He was a *leeyah*." Liar. Daniel grimaces. "What happened . . . it was . . . *gottlos*." Ungodly. "What kind of man wants his wife gone? What kind of man kills in cold blood?"

"We prayed for him up until the end," Naomi says. "We didn't want to believe Joseph could do such a thing."

"We still pray for his soul, but we're done with him," Daniel says.

"*Er is ganz ab*," Rebecca whispers. He was out of his mind.

"Has he had any contact with the children?" I ask.

"No," Rebecca replies.

I look at Daniel. "Does he want to see them?"

"Throughout the trial," he tells me, "Joseph claimed to miss them. He seemed desperate. He wanted to see them. We always made an excuse." The Amish man shrugs. "After what he did . . . Finding their mother the way they did. It was so bad."

"How are the kids doing?" I ask.

41

"Better," Rebecca tells me. "They miss their *mamm*, of course. Crazy as it sounds, they miss their *datt*, too."

"Do they understand what happened?"

Daniel shakes his head. "We thought it best not to tell them." He shrugs. "Maybe when they're older."

Tears gather in Rebecca's eyes. "Can you imagine? Your *datt* killing your *mamm*? *Mein Gott*." My God.

"Shush now," Daniel tells her, as if sensing the approach of some emotional storm. "They've adjusted, they way kids do. We keep them busy. With work. Worship."

"They're happy here with us, I think." Rebecca smiles, but tears shimmer in her eyes. "Naomi is surely watching over them from heaven. Keeping an eye on all of us."

"The two of you probably know Joseph better than anyone." I divide my attention between them. "Did he ever mention escape?"

"Like I said," Daniel replies, "we haven't seen him since the end of the trial."

Realizing that sometimes people know things and don't even realize it, I try another approach. "Do you have any idea where he might go?"

Daniel tightens his lips. "To hell, maybe."

"Do you think he might come here?" When they don't respond, I get more specific. "To see the children?"

When Daniel speaks, his voice is reverent and low. "You were raised Amish, Kate Burkholder. You know that forgiveness is our way." He ducks his head slightly, not proud of what he's about to say next, but deeming it too important to remain unsaid. "None of the Amish here would raise a finger to help Joseph. Not after what he did. To his wife. His children. To all of us. He has no friends among the Amish."

"What about English friends?" I ask.

"I wouldn't know about that," he tells me.

The sound of children's laughter from outside fills the silence. It's an innocent, carefree sound that only serves to remind us of all the things that have been taken away from them, of what's at stake.

"I'll be stepping up patrols in the area," I tell them, "especially here around the farm. The sheriff's department, too. Just in case Joseph shows up. I want to make sure you and your family stay safe."

"We don't need the English police," Rebecca replies. "God will take care of us."

Daniel's gaze slides to mine and he gives me a minute nod. "*Ich hab nix dagege.*" I don't object.

I know what the answer to my next question will be, but I ask it anyway. At the very least, I have to plant the seed.

"Do you own a firearm, Mr. Beachy?"

"I have an old muzzle-loader," Daniel replies. "An antique that belonged to my *grossdaddi*."

Our gazes lock. An unspoken understanding passes between us. Nothing else needs to be said. I'm well aware that the Amish are pacifists. They believe it is a sin to take a human life regardless of the circumstances. But the Amish are human, too; I know from experience that the will to survive—the need to protect yourself and those you love—trumps religion.

"Will you do me a favor and keep it loaded?" I ask.

Another barely discernible nod.

"Do either of you have a cell phone?" I ask.

"We have no need for such things," Rebecca tells me.

"The payphone on Hogpath Road is more than a mile away," I tell her. "If Joseph shows up, you'll have no way to call for help." When they say nothing, I add, "You've got the children to think of." I reach into my pocket and hold out a cheap cell phone I picked up at the Walmart in Millersburg. "In case there's an emergency." I give a casual shrug. "No one's using it. I've got my cell number, nine-one-one, and the sheriff's department number programmed in already."

"We do not need a phone," the Amish man maintains.

"If you were to look away for a second, I could accidentally leave it on the counter or maybe

44

drop it into the drawer. You could just forget about it."

My words are met with a smile from both of them, but they shake their heads. "We have God to watch over us," Rebecca repeats. "He will take care of us and the children."

Rising, I cross to the counter and set down the phone. I then extend my hand first to Rebecca and then Daniel. "Thanks for your time."

As I walk back to my vehicle, worry follows me, like a rash at the back of my neck that's starting to itch.

CHAPTER 3

I've just settled behind the wheel when my phone vibrates against my hip. I glance down at the display and smile. "I take it you got the call?" I begin without preamble.

"I'm on my way to Mansfield now," John Tomasetti tells me, referring to the prison from which Joseph King escaped. "We're going to be assisting Richland County."

Tomasetti is an agent with the Ohio Bureau of Criminal Investigation and works out of the field office in Richfield, Ohio, which is half an hour north of our farm in Wooster. We met in the course of my first big case five years ago—the Slaughterhouse murder investigation—right here in Painters Mill. We became involved in the course of that horrific case. Early on, things were pretty rocky between us. That's what you get when you throw two damaged individuals—cops no less—into the midst of a high-stress case. Tomasetti had recently lost his wife and two children. My frame of mind wasn't much better; I had personal ties to the case—ties that came within a hair of destroying me and nearly cost me my life. Somehow, we overcame all of it.

Of course, life is never without complications. Fraternization is frowned upon by most law enforcement agencies, including the Ohio Bureau of Criminal Investigation and my own small department. That's especially true when our jurisdictions intersect. Even though we're not working together directly, we'll need to be cautious.

"What's the latest on King?" I ask as I turn onto Hogpath Road.

Tomasetti reiterates what I'd already learned from Sheriff Rasmussen earlier. "I talked to the warden about an hour ago. King was in his cell for the nine P.M. headcount. He got out sometime after that. No one knows how he circumvented the fence alarm. Perimeter patrols were on duty, but no one saw shit. Next headcount wasn't done until three A.M. so it's possible King got a six-hour head start."

"Any indication where he might be headed?" I ask.

"According to the warden, it rained up there last night. The ground was soft and muddy. First guys on scene found tracks that headed northeast from the prison. There's a wooded area there, so King may have been looking for cover. Richland County Sheriff's Department brought in dogs, but they lost the scent at the highway."

"You think someone picked him up?"

"Or he jacked a vehicle."

"Who the hell picks up a guy wearing prison clothes?"

47

"An idiot," he mutters. "Or someone who knew he'd be there and was waiting."

"If he had help in the form of tools, he could've gotten his hands on street clothes, too. Or maybe he had someone stash them someplace for him."

"A lot of possibilities," he says on a sigh.

"Which highway is that, by the way?" I ask.

"State Route 545 is just east of the facility. Meanders northeast."

"Toward Cleveland," I add.

"Good place to get lost if you want to. From there, it's a short skip to the Canadian border."

"Tomasetti, if he has a vehicle he could be anywhere."

"If it was me, I'd get as far away from the prison as possible, then I'd concentrate on getting to my destination."

"Any word on whether he might've had help from someone on the inside?" I ask.

"That's what we're looking at now. Going to interview all the officers who had contact with him. We're going to look at visitor logs. If he had any visitors, we'll be talking to them." He sighs. "From what I hear, King's a handy guy."

"Most Amish men are. That would explain how he cut through that steel plate."

"Evidently, he worked at a production shop at the prison where parts are cleaned and deflashed for Honda. I don't know what kinds of tools the inmates have access to, but I'll find out."

"So he may have pilfered some tool from the shop."

"Or someone could have smuggled it in," he replies. "A visitor."

"Or a corrections officer."

"We're going to be checking all of that."

I pause, take a moment to get my words in order. "Tomasetti, I knew Joseph King. I mean, when we were kids. They lived next door to us for a while."

"Small world."

"Especially when you're Amish."

"You have some insight into what he might be thinking, Kate? Where he might go?"

"It was a long time ago. I haven't talked to him in over twenty years." We both know how much can happen—how much a person can change—in that length of time.

"He was a good kid back then," I say. "A typical Amish boy, until his *datt* was killed in a buggy accident. I think he was fourteen or fifteen years old."

"Tough age to lose a parent."

"It changed him. That was when he started getting into trouble. Shortly after that, the family moved to Geauga County and I never saw him again."

"I understand he has family in Painters Mill."

I recap my conversation with Rebecca and

49

Daniel Beachy. "They don't want anything to do with him."

"You believe them?"

I've considered the possibility that they lied to me; that they may have, in fact, helped King. Or they've offered him shelter. But I don't think that's the case. "The Amish may be forgiving, but after what he did . . . I suspect he knows he doesn't have a friend in the world here."

"The big question now is whether he'll try to make contact with his children."

"Surely he knows that would be foolhardy. Every law enforcement agency in the state is looking for him."

"He's not exactly father-of-the-year material anyway."

"And what's he going to do with five kids?" I say. "Throw them in the backseat and take them with him? I don't think so. They'd only slow him down."

"And the older children may know enough to either hate him or fear him. My bet is he's on his way to Canada."

"Going to be an interesting case."

"Things are always more interesting when you're involved," he says.

"I'm glad you feel that way."

"I'd feel even better if you'd do me a favor and keep your eyes and ears open for this son of a bitch."

"Count on it."

• • •

Ten minutes later I walk into the Painters Mill police station. My first-shift dispatcher, Lois, mans the front desk, headset hugging her overprocessed curls, the switchboard humming a steady tune. As is usually the case, my third-shift dispatcher, Mona, has found an excuse to stay past her usual clock-out time. As chief, I'm obliged to give her a hard time about it. Today, I'm secretly pleased she's here, because I have a job for her.

"Chief!" Putting a caller on hold, Lois rises and waves a dozen or so pink slips at me. "For God's sake, you'd think Charles Manson had escaped."

"Probably going to get worse before it gets better." I pluck the messages from her hand as I pass by her desk.

"Something to look forward to," she mutters.

Mona falls into step beside me. "The guys are all here, Chief."

I slant a look her way. "Working kind of late this morning, aren't you?"

"I thought you might need an extra hand in light of the Joseph King situation."

"You know I can't pay OT, right?"

"It's okay." She offers a sheepish smile. "To tell you the truth, I didn't want to miss out on the excitement. Or the experience."

I shouldn't be such a pushover; payroll laws are explicit and strict. Still, I can't help but smile.

51

Mona recently graduated from the local community college with an associate's degree in criminology. Much to my good fortune, she doesn't mind the graveyard shift. One day, she's going to be a fine police officer. Budget permitting, I hope to be the one to hire her.

"You know I appreciate that, right?" I say.

Her smile augments into an all-out grin. "I thought you might want these." She shoves two file folders at me. "The first one contains everything I could find on King previous to the homicide. The second file is everything I could get my hands on with regard to the homicide of Naomi King. I'm still waiting to hear back from Geauga County Records. I'm running copies of the mug shot for the rest of the guys now. Oh, and I set up the half podium in the war room."

"War room" is a term only Mona could have coined for our storage-room-turned-meeting-room. I use it occasionally for our weekly briefings, storing unused or broken furniture, and archived file boxes.

A glance at the clock above the coffee station tells me it's already after noon. "I'll be there in five." I lift the file. "Going to take a quick look at these first. Can you let everyone know?"

"Rounding them up now." She pivots and starts toward the reception area.

"Mona?"

Swinging around to face me, she raises her brows. "Yeah, Chief?"

"You, too," I tell her.

She dazzles me with another grin, and again I'm struck by the unencumbered love she has for her job. That she's only twenty-four years old and life is one big adventure. She's not yet accumulated the kind of baggage most cops own after a few years. And in that instant, I feel . . . old.

"Roger that," she says.

In my office, I slide into the chair at my desk, open the file, and find myself looking at the mug shot of Joseph King. The boy I'd once known has grown into an attractive man. He's still got that boy-next-door face and dark, puppy-dog eyes. The same eyes I looked into a thousand times as a kid. In this particular photo he still bears the typical Amish "bowl" haircut and a beard that reaches past his collar. There's a trace of a smile on his lips, but the twisting of his mouth doesn't jibe with the angst in his eyes.

The mug shot was probably taken the day of his arrest—regardless of any protests because of his religious beliefs, if he had any left. I can tell by his expression he's not taking the situation seriously. Not yet, anyway. I've seen the reaction before. People who've committed serious crimes believing—even after they're arrested, booked, and jailed—that some miracle will happen and the whole thing will go away. They think some-one will step forward and rescue them. The cops will come to their senses and realize it's all a big mistake.

I bet he's taking his situation seriously now.

"Joseph, what the hell happened to you?" I whisper.

I leaf through the remaining pages, refreshing my memory, looking for new information. Thirty-six-year-old Joseph King, his wife, Naomi, and their five children, ages ranging from three to ten years, lived on a small farm near Middlefield, Ohio. On the morning of May 11, twenty-nine-year-old Naomi King was discovered by her children, lying dead in her blood-soaked bed. The oldest child, Becky, ran to a neighbor's farm, over a mile away, and called police.

According to the children, King had gone fishing at Lake Erie. He arrived home a few hours after the grisly discovery, at which time he was detained and interviewed by the Geauga County Sheriff's Department. The Amish man claimed no knowledge of the murder. Ultimately, King was released. He took his children to stay with relatives while the police processed the crime scene. But as King's criminal record came to light—and the stories about his rocky relationship with his wife emerged—he quickly became a person of interest.

The Geauga County Sheriff's Department

confiscated a shotgun found at the scene. The CSI was able to capture the tread of a single shoe print. A bloodstained jacket found in a hamper was also sent to the lab for testing. When the police interrogated King a second time, the timeline of his alleged fishing trip didn't quite align with his previous story. Forty-eight hours after Naomi King was discovered dead, a warrant was issued for his arrest. Sheriff's deputies picked him up at his farm and arrested him in front of his children, who were placed with relatives.

According to the prosecutor, sometime between three and five A.M. King returned to the farm, entered the residence, and shot his wife as she slept. The murder weapon was a shotgun owned by King; his prints were all over it, and all over the shells. The jacket found in the hamper was determined to belong to King and tested positive for gunpowder residue as well as Naomi King's blood. The evidence was damning—and it didn't end there.

Those who knew the Kings claimed their marriage was rocky. Joseph had a temper; he was abusive and had a record of domestic violence. Combined with the physical evidence, it was enough to make a case against him and take the case to trial.

I turn the page, find myself looking at a statement written by one of the social workers who interviewed the children. The oldest, Becky, who'd been ten years old at the time, reportedly heard "thunder" during the night, but she didn't get up and the children didn't find their mother's body until morning. Upon making the gruesome discovery, all five of the children ran screaming from the house.

Next is the autopsy report. The coroner states that Naomi King died from a single gunshot wound to the abdomen sometime between one and five A.M. A devastating wound that killed the twenty-nine-year-old mother instantly. The coroner ruled the cause of death as massive trauma from a gunshot wound. The manner of death was homicide.

I glance through King's abbreviated criminal case history. Two DUIs. Drug possession. Marijuana. Meth. Battery upon a public servant, for which he was convicted and served time. Most disturbing, however, is the smattering of domestic-violence calls and arrests in the months before Naomi was killed, two of those calls ending with convictions. I sigh in disgust, suspecting there were dozens more instances no one would ever know about. Physical and psychological abuse that Naomi King suffered in silence.

When you're Amish you don't call the English police. Most Amish women do have a support system—either family or female members of the community or even their preacher or bishop—but that's not always the case. Some Amish women have no one to turn to. Nowhere to go. Far too often issues like domestic violence are glossed over, dressed up to look like something else, or ignored.

Closing the file, I head toward the war room. My small force of officers is already assembled. At twenty-seven years of age, T. J. Banks is the rookie of the group. He's lounging in a green paisley task chair, thumbing something into his smartphone. Word around the station is that he's got a new girlfriend, and this time it's serious.

Next to him, Chuck "Skid" Skidmore, resident practical joker and smartass extraordinaire, is embroiled in a retelling of a PIT maneuver he performed while involved in a high-speed chase back when he'd been a patrol officer in Ann Arbor. I'm pretty sure there's some embellishing going on. Judging from Mona's face, I'm pretty sure she knows it.

"Pickles" is sitting across from T.J., sipping coffee with a reverence usually reserved for fine whiskey. He has over fifty years of law enforcement experience on his résumé, a good deal of that time spent working in an undercover capacity. He's the oldest officer to ever serve Painters Mill. But you won't catch him admitting to his age, which, according to his personnel file, is seventy-five years. He dyes his hair to cover the gray and stays in damn good physical condition. This afternoon, he's wearing a crisp uniform and well-worn Lucchese boots that glisten with polish.

But it's the attitude more than anything that keeps him young. He doesn't take any shit from anyone, including me. Pickles might look like some kindly grandfather, but rub him the wrong way and you'll quickly figure out he's got a titanium spine and a tongue capable of laying open even the toughest of shells.

Sitting at the head of the table, Rupert "Glock" Maddox is scrolling through his phone, smiling at something, probably photos of his kids. He's got two now and a pretty wife named LaShonda. A former marine with two tours in Afghanistan under his belt, he's a solid cop, the first African American officer in the history of the Painters Mill PD, and my go-to guy when I need something done right.

I step behind the half podium set up at the head of the table. Mona has taped a chalkboard-size road map of Holmes County behind me and left a marker in case I need to spotlight a specific area. She also set up the mike, but I don't need it, so I flip off the power. News travels fast in a small town; I can tell by the way everyone's looking at me that they already know why we're here. I want to make sure they have all the right information.

"I got a call from ODRC this morning," I tell them. "Sometime last night, convicted killer Joseph King escaped from Mansfield. Amish male. Thirty-eight years old. Last seen at nine P.M. The next headcount was at three A.M., so we have to assume he's had a six-hour head start. The Richland County Sheriff's Department brought in dogs, but evidently they lost his scent at the highway northeast of the prison."

Turning, I indicate the area on the map. "It's believed King reached the highway here, so law enforcement is operating under the assumption that he has access to a vehicle—jacked or stolen or else someone picked him up. If he had help from someone on the outside, we also have to assume he's had a change of clothes and, more importantly, that he may be armed.

"Normally, we wouldn't get involved in something two counties away, but King's got family ties in Painters Mill. His five kids are living with his deceased wife's sister and her husband, Rebecca and Daniel Beachy, out on Left Fork Road, that dirt track off Hogpath." Again, I turn to the map, and I use the marker to circle the general location of the Beachy farm.

"I know the place," Pickles says. "Clarice bought a quilt from her a couple years back."

"You expect King to show up here?" Glock asks.

Looking at the map, I take a moment to

consider the logistics of the prison in relation to Painters Mill. "Most of the law enforcement I've talked to believe he's likely on his way to Cleveland or possibly the Canadian border. Still, we have to be prepared in case he tries to make contact with his kids."

"Any bad blood between him and the Beachys?" Skid asks.

"Not that I'm aware of," I tell him, "but you never know what's in someone's mind. With the kids involved we need to be prepared."

I look at Mona. "You have those photos of King?"

"Hot off the press," comes Lois's voice from her place at the door, where she's been listening in on the meeting while keeping an eye on the phones in reception.

Mona is already up and out of her seat, mouthing a thank-you to her counterpart and then passing the photos to the rest of the team.

I glance down at my notes and continue. "Joseph King is six feet one inch in height. Two hundred pounds. Dark brown hair. Brown eyes. Full beard. He was last seen wearing a prison-issue blue jumpsuit. White sneakers. Possibly a gray hoodie. Be aware that he may have changed his appearance by now."

"Easy enough to shave a beard," T.J. comments.

"If he *keeps* the beard and gets his hands on

60

Amish-type clothing," Pickles drawls, "it might be even *more* difficult to recognize him."

"You're not suggesting that we start profiling the Amish, are you, Pickles?" Skid spouts off.

Chuckles erupt around the table.

Leave it to Skid to go there.

I jump in before they can take it too far. "King is from Geauga County," I tell them. "His main connection to Painters Mill is the kids."

"Was he close to them?" Glock asks.

I recap my visit with Daniel and Rebecca Beachy. "It's my understanding that King did not have a close relationship with his children."

"Do they know what he did?" T.J. asks.

"Parents did not tell them." I shrug. "But people talk. Kids may have heard something."

"You think he might try to harm them?" Glock asks.

"Don't like the sound of that," Pickles growls.

"If King, for whatever reason, blames his sister-in-law or her husband for his woes, if he condemns them for taking custody of his kids, if he believes they interfered in some way or helped the police . . ." I shrug. "I suppose it's possible."

"Or he might go to them for help." Skid spreads his hands. "Money. Clothes. Safe haven."

"I got the impression he won't find much in the way of help from the Beachys," I say. "I think King knows that."

"So he'd be foolish to risk his neck coming here to Painters Mill," T.J. says.

"Still, we have to be vigilant and take every precaution." I scan the faces of my officers. "In the interim, I'm going to talk to the mayor about overtime. Volunteers?"

T.J. raises his hand. "I'm in."

Skid grins. "Gotta impress the new squeeze with all that cash."

I smile. The population of Painters Mill is just over 5,300, a third of which is Amish. With the sheriff's department operating with a skeleton crew owing to budget constraints, we pick up a lot of slack and take county calls as well as those in Painters Mill proper. But my small force has been stretched thin for years. With vacation time and sick days at a premium, I'm unduly grateful T.J. has a penchant for overspending and a new girlfriend to impress. He's my OT go-to guy.

I turn my attention to Mona. "Will you contact ODRC and see if they have a list of people who visited King while he was in prison?"

"You got it, Chief."

I scan the faces of my small team. "There are multiple law enforcement agencies actively searching for King. BCI, State Highway Patrol, Richland County. Holmes and Geauga Counties are on alert. Our department is pretty much on the periphery of the operation. I suspect it's only a matter of time before he's apprehended.

Still, we need to keep our eyes open and stay alert."

I page through the papers in front of me, looking for the most recent schedule for the department. "Who's on tonight?"

"I'm on now," Skid tells me.

T.J. pipes up. "I come on at midnight."

I smile at them. "I'll buy the doughnuts."

CHAPTER 4

There are a thousand places a wanted man could take refuge in northeastern Ohio. The countryside is a plethora of vast forests, small towns, and farmland with dozens of abandoned houses, barns, and silos sprinkled throughout. There are roadside motels and campgrounds where a man could hide out for days and no one would be the wiser.

It's three A.M. and, as of the last update I received from ODRC, Joseph King is still at large. BCI set up a tip line and a steady stream has trickled in; so far none have panned out.

Painters Mill sleeps like the dead as I idle down Main Street. The storefronts are darkened, the lights dimmed. Some of the awnings have been folded down, the shutters or blinds closed up tight. It's a clear night—I can see the stars and a sliver of moon—but lightning flickers on the horizon to the west, and I know by dawn we'll have storms. I consider stopping in at the police station to say hello to Mona as I drive past, but I want to get out to the Beachy farm, where T.J. is keeping an eye on things.

I just left the Butterhorn Bakery. The place isn't open at this ungodly hour, but I happen to know that the owner, Tom Skanks, arrives at

2:30 A.M. to start the doughnuts. I found the front door unlocked and Tom at the rear prep kitchen, pulling his first batch of apple fritters from the oven. I reminded him there's a convicted murderer on the loose and suggested he keep his front door locked, at least until King is apprehended. He gave me a baker's dozen on the house for the good advice. T.J. is still young enough to appreciate the sugar and fat.

I pick up my radio. "What's your twenty, T.J.?"

"I'm parked in front of the Beachy farm, Chief."

"Any activity?"

"Bull got frisky with one of the cows a little while ago."

"I guess at this hour, we're not too picky about our entertainment."

"You got that right. To tell you the truth, I'm starting to feel like a voyeur."

I laugh. "Stay put," I tell him. "I'm ten-seven-six."

A few minutes later I pull up beside T.J.'s cruiser and lower my window. His windows are already down. I suspect he's using the cool night air to stay awake. "I didn't wake you, did I?"

He grins. "I'll take the fifth on that."

I glance toward the darkened farm. Set back a hundred yards from the road, the house is barely visible through the trees. I don't see any lights in the windows. As a whole, Amish country is incredibly dark at night. There are no streetlamps or porch lights and there isn't much in the way of headlights or taillights. Even with a police officer parked at the mouth of the lane, it would be easy for someone to slip by and not be seen.

"I drove around the block a couple of times earlier," T.J. tells me. "Didn't see a soul, but honestly the farm could be approached from any direction."

He's right; I looked at the aerial map earlier. "We can only cover so much area." I pass him the bag of doughnuts. "I'll take it from here."

He looks into the bag. "Damn, Chief, apple fritters from the Butterhorn Bakery are like cop heroin."

"Try not to OD."

"Tall order when I have thirteen of these suckers in striking distance."

"Get some sleep and I'll see you tonight."

Giving me a mock salute, he pulls onto the road and drives away.

I watch his taillights until he makes the turn onto Hogpath Road; then I shift my attention to the Beachy house. It's a big farmhouse with a lot of windows. The front yard and pasture are heavily treed, which not only blocks my view, but throws the entire area into shadows. I can just make out the hulking silhouettes of the barn and silo behind the house.

It's a pleasant night, cool and humid, so I leave

my window down and turn off the engine. A chorus of crickets and spring peepers from the swampy area near the creek rides on the breeze. Aside from the cattle in the pasture, there's no movement anywhere. The storm to the west is closer now. Distant thunder rumbles and for the first time I smell rain. Keeping one eye on the house, I flick on the radio for some music and slink down in my seat.

I'm watching the cattle, wishing I'd kept one of those apple fritters for myself, when Mona's voice comes over the radio. "Chief, I got a ten-seventy." Code for a fire.

Sitting up, I snatch up the mike. "What's the twenty on that?"

"Abandoned barn next to Amos Yoder's place out on Dogleg Road. RP said the whole structure is on fire and burning like hell."

The word "abandoned" flutters in the forefront of my mind and refuses to settle. "You call the fire department?"

"They're en route. I thought you might want to head out there."

I reach for the ignition and start the engine. But a prickly sensation on the back of my neck keeps me from putting my vehicle in gear. Amos Yoder's place is only a couple of miles away; I can't help but think that a fire would be the perfect distraction to draw a cop away from her post.

"Dispatch T.J., will you?" I say. "He's still up. On his way home."

"Chief?"

"I'm out here at the Beachy farm. I'm going to stick with it a while longer."

"Roger that."

I rack the mike.

Keeping in mind that someone could approach the farm from any direction, I put the Explorer in gear and pull onto the road.

Chances are, Joseph King is in Canada by now. But experience has taught me to listen to my gut. I don't like the timing or the proximity of the fire. If King has access to a vehicle and has traveled to Painters Mill, he could have set the blaze to divert the attention and resources of law enforcement so he can get to his children.

The Beachy farm comprises sixty acres of forest and pastureland and a couple of plowed fields. It's bordered on three sides by township roads. The fourth side is the greenbelt that runs along Painters Creek. If I wanted to approach the farm and remain unseen, that would be my first choice.

Punching off my headlights, I make a U-turn and head toward the greenbelt. There's just enough moonlight for me to navigate without running off the road. I roll down my windows, listening, but the only sound comes from the crunch of my tires on gravel. I make another turn, using the trees to guide me. I pass by a beat-up guardrail that spans a wet-weather creek. In the periphery of my vision, I notice the glint of something on the other side of the ditch. I stop, pull my Maglite from the seat pocket, and shine it out the window. The beam illuminates a dark sedan parked on the other side of the ditch, well off the road, just a few feet from the trees that demark the beginning of the greenbelt.

Keeping my eye on the vehicle, watching for movement, I pull onto the shoulder, shut down the engine, and get out. The volume of the spring peepers is deafening now. Maglite in hand, I close the door quietly and cross to the sedan. It's a newish Buick LaCrosse. I set my hand on the hood, find it warm to the touch. I hear the engine ticking as it cools. No sign of the driver. I shine the beam into the interior, front and back seats. No one there. Nothing on the seat or floor. The keys are gone.

I go around to the rear, illuminate the license plate, and hit my lapel mike. "Ten-eighty-five." Keeping my voice low, I utter the code for an abandoned vehicle. "Township Road 102. I need a ten-ninety-nine." I recite the plate number, so Mona can check to see if the vehicle has been reported stolen. "Buick. Four-door sedan. Blue."

"Stand by."

"Any word on that fire?"

"Fire department is on scene. Structure is a total loss."

"Anyone hurt?"

"Negative."

"Call me back on my cell, will you?" I ask.

"You got it."

Flicking off the flashlight, I turn my attention to the woods, trying to get a handle on the prickle at the back of my neck. The trees are thick with patches of undergrowth and bramble. Fingers of fog rise from the damp ground. The Beachy farmhouse is less than a quarter mile away, but the woods are too thick for me to see it. Still, it would be an easy hike for someone if they parked here and cut through.

I walk back to the road, keeping an eye on the tree line to my right. From thirty yards, I spot a gap in the trees. I traverse the ditch, sinking up to my ankles in mud. I go up the incline on the opposite side. Sure enough, it's an old path tangled with overgrowth. Probably left over from last summer when people parked here and walked to the creek to wade or pick raspberries that grow in profusion along the old fence line.

Flicking on the Maglite, I check for tracks, but the ground is a mosaic of dead leaves and yellow grass left over from winter. A few yards into the trees, I realize there's enough moonlight for me to follow the path without mishap, so I turn off the flashlight and continue.

Where's the driver of the Buick? Did someone have car problems and call a friend to pick them up? That's the only legitimate reason for that car to be here. The thing that's making me nervous is that it appears the driver went to some trouble to park out of sight, driving through the ditch and risking getting stuck in the mud.

My phone vibrates against my hip. I dig it out. Mona. "What do you have?" I ask.

"Vehicle came back stolen," she tells me. "Out of Richland County. Reported this afternoon."

A chill scrapes up my back. Turning around, I start back toward my vehicle. "Get T.J. out here. Ten-forty." *Expedite.* I set my hand on my revolver, my eyes striving to penetrate the darkness all around, my every sense on high alert. "Get County out here, too. I'm on the two-track off Township—"

The ambush comes out of nowhere. One instant I'm striding down the path toward my vehicle, the next I'm knocked off my feet. No time to react or break the fall. I hit the ground hard. Left shoulder grinding into the earth. The left side of my head strikes something hard and bounces off. My attacker comes down on top of me with so much force that the breath is crushed from my lungs. My left cheekbone sinks into mud, leaves and twigs scratching my cheek. Dirt in my mouth. In my ear.

A hundred thoughts rush my brain. My attacker

71

is male. Heavy build. Strong as hell. Aggressive.

Rough hands shove my right shoulder to the ground. I'm facedown, arms grappling like a crab. Defenseless. Shit. *Shit.*

"I'm a police officer!" I twist left, try to throw him off balance, get my arms and legs under me. The toes of my boots dig into mud and slide. I can't get my knee up.

He jams his knee against my back, grinds it into my spine. A hand clamps the back of my neck like a vise, fingers squeezing hard enough to cause pain; he shoves my face into the ground.

"Don't fight!" he says. "Don't fight!"

"Get the fuck off me!" I twist right, bend my leg at the knee, reach for my sidearm. "Get off!"

Using his other knee, he crushes my triceps. Pain zings down my arm all the way to my pinkie, and I end up with a handful of mud and grass.

"Hold still," he grinds out. "Just shut up and listen."

Recognition kicks in my brain. Something inside me sinks. I know that voice. It's deeper now, tinged with high-octane stress, underscored with panic. But I'd recognize it anywhere. Closing my eyes, I bite back a curse. If I could've managed in that instant, I would have kicked myself. Hard.

You screwed up, Burkholder.

For the span of several heartbeats the only sound comes from the quick in and out of our breaths. Then I say, "What the hell do you think you're doing?"

He goes still. He's straddling me. I feel his entire body trembling, the wet heat of his sweat soaking into my shirt.

"Joseph, get the hell off me," I say.

He doesn't move, doesn't respond. I read hesitation and confusion in the lack of response. He recognized my voice, too, but he doesn't know what to make of it.

A thousand thoughts rush my brain. I'm not sure how to handle this. How to handle *him.* I'm trying to figure out if I can somehow use our past to convince him to turn himself in when he speaks.

"Katie Burkholder."

He says my name with a familiarity I don't appreciate. Especially when I'm facedown in the mud and his knee is grinding into my spine.

"I heard you were a cop."

"I don't have to tell you you're in serious trouble, do I?" I tell him.

"I'm aware."

My mind races with what to say next. I remind myself I haven't seen or heard from him in over twenty years. We may have been close as kids, but that was a lifetime ago. It may as well have been a hundred years.

"I figured you'd be on your way to Canada by now," I tell him.

"Thought about it."

"Why didn't you?"

"Got some business to take care of right here."

"What business is that?"

He doesn't respond.

"Your kids?"

No answer.

I'm seriously uncomfortable, wet with mud, his fingers clamped hard around the back of my neck. His knee is grinding into my back with so much force that my legs are tingling. "Get off me."

He shifts his weight and the pressure subsides. I try to rise, but he stops me. "Not so fast."

"Let me up. Right now. We need to talk about . . . what's going on here. About your situation. Get things figured out."

He surprises me by laughing. It's a tense, strange sound in the woods in the dead of night. His hand falls away from the back of my neck. He eases his weight off another degree, but doesn't get off me. Shifting, he reaches down and yanks my .38 from its holster. "I'll take this."

I close my eyes, rest my cheek against the muddy ground. "Joseph, you don't want to do this."

"You going to behave yourself if I let you up?"

"I'm going to try to talk you out of this."

"I reckon I can handle that." In one smooth motion, he moves off me and rises.

I roll, snatch up my cell, and quickly get to my feet. We're facing each other, breaths elevated, adrenaline zinging between us. There's just enough light for me to see his silhouette. He's standing four feet away, my .38 pointed at me, center mass.

"You got another gun on you?" he asks.

"No."

"Don't lie to me. I don't want to have to kill you."

"I'm not armed."

"You alone?"

"For the moment." Cautiously, hoping he doesn't notice, I drop the cell into my pocket.

It's too dark for me to read his expression, but I'm pretty sure he's frowning. "What does that mean?" he asks.

"I was on the phone when you ambushed me." I'm shaking all over. My legs. My hands. My heart is drumming hard against my ribs. I take a deep breath, let it out slowly, trying in vain to calm myself. I'm aware of increased traffic coming over my radio. "In a few minutes this place is going to be crawling with cops."

He looks around and sighs. "Nothing I can do about that."

I take a step toward him, hold out my hand for my weapon. "Give me my sidearm. Right now."

"Don't be an idiot."

"Joseph, it's not too late to end this. Turn yourself in. Please. I'll help you."

"As much as I like the idea of your helping me, I don't think I'll comply."

"Whatever you have planned, it's not going to work."

"You have no idea what I have planned."

Considering the circumstances, he seems calm, but then Joseph was always cool under pressure. He's almost *too* calm. But I know how quickly a situation can spiral out of control.

"You came back for your children?" I ask.

"Among other things."

"Other things like what?"

I can't see his face, just tiny pinpoints of light from his eyes. "I didn't kill my wife," he tells me.

Dread curdles in my chest, a sour, sickening sensation. I don't know the particulars of his conviction. But I've read enough to know he's lying. To avoid setting him off, I engage him. "Let's talk about it. I'll listen to you. If I can help you, I will."

He stares at me, saying nothing. Even from four feet away and in near-total darkness, I feel the intensity pouring off him. A different kind of alarm flutters in my gut. I have no idea how long he's been here. If he's already been inside the house. I don't know what his intentions are. What he might've already done . . .

"I didn't kill her," he repeats. "I don't know how they got all that evidence for the trial, but I didn't do it. I'm not going back to prison for something I didn't do."

"This is not the way for you to help yourself." I motion toward the revolver in his hand. "The gun is going to make things worse. Or get you killed."

He shrugs. "There are worse fates."

"I don't believe that. Neither do you."

"You don't believe it because you haven't spent the last year in prison."

I struggle to get a read on his frame of mind, straining to see his face in the darkness, his eyes. "Joseph, don't do this. Please. Give me the gun. Let me help you. You know I will." I deliver the final sentence in *Deitsch.*

"Been a long time since I heard *Deitsch.*" He cocks his head slightly. "Never thought I'd miss the sound of it."

Frustration builds in my chest. Sighing, I look down at the ground, then at him, aware that my cell is vibrating. "Do you realize how serious this is?"

"I know exactly how serious it is."

"You can't take a cop hostage and expect anything good to happen. Joseph, they'll kill you. Do you understand that?"

"Yeah, I got it."

The initial rush of adrenaline is beginning to subside. My hands are steadier, my brain clicking back into place. "Did you start the fire over at Old Man Yoder's place?"

"I guess it worked, didn't it?" he says.

"Have you been inside the Beachy house?"

"For a little while."

"Are the children all right?" I ask. "Rebecca and Daniel?"

"Of course, they're all—"

"Datt?"

I startle at the sound of the high-pitched voice coming at us from the general direction of the farmhouse. I glance down the trail and see a branch rustle. Feet crunch over dried grass, getting closer. In the moonlight, a small figure emerges from the darkness. A little girl. Five or six years old. She's wearing a plain white nightgown. I can't see her feet, but I think they must be muddy. She's a tiny thing with long brown hair and big brown eyes set into an angel's face.

"Sadie." Joseph stands rooted in place, as if an electrical current has come up through the ground and delivered a thousand, paralyzing volts. "I told you to stay inside."

"You said you were coming right back." The little girl stops a few feet away, her eyes on me. "Who is she, Datt?"

I give King a warning look. "Don't bring them into this," I say quietly. "Please. This is between me and you now. Send her back to the house."

78

"Too late," he mutters, and starts toward the child, holding the gun down at his side, keeping an eye on me.

The little girl goes to him, crossing right in front of me, close enough for me to discern her child scent. Nightgown swishing, feet slapping the ground, she runs to her father and throws her arms around his legs.

"I thought they might take you away again," she says.

He ducks his head as if the words cause him physical pain. "I'm not going anywhere."

"I'm scared."

"Don't be scared. Everything's going to be all right."

She falls silent for a moment, and then: "Levi said since God sent you back to us He might send Mamm, too. So I came out to see for myself if maybe she was here, too."

Even as she says the words, I imagine her eyes skimming the forest, as if she's expecting her long-dead mother to step out of the shadows and announce her return. Something shakes loose inside me at the notion. I can't see her face, but I know it's filled with a child's innocent faith—a faith that will undoubtedly be ripped from her young heart all too soon.

King sets his hand on her back and for the first time he takes his eyes off me. "She's not coming back."

She peels her face away from her father and turns in my direction. "Who is the *Englischer*, Datt?"

"A policeman," he tells her.

"Is she going to arrest you? Take you away from us again?"

"No." I feel King's eyes on me. "I think she's going to help us."

"Really?" the girl squeaks.

"Really." He rises to his full height. "We have to get back to the house. Quickly now. Come on."

Easing the girl away, he shifts the revolver toward me and motions with it in the direction of the house. "Keep your hands where I can see them," he says quietly. "Don't make me do something I don't want to do. Do you understand?"

I nod and we set off at a brisk pace.

We've only walked a few yards when in the distance a police siren begins to wail. I don't know if it's the fire department and is related to the barn fire—or if Mona followed through and dispatched T.J. and Holmes County after our communication was abruptly severed.

"Joseph, you need to think about the consequences of what you're doing. Once law enforcement realizes I've been taken hostage, that you've taken the children and the Beachys hostage, the situation is going to escalate and—"

"I sent Daniel and Rebecca packing," he cuts in. "I don't want them here. I don't need them—"

"Every police agency within a hundred miles is going to jump into this," I tell him. "Someone is going to get hurt." When he says nothing, I add, "You're putting your children at risk. Exposing them to—"

"You never did know when to stop talking. You still don't." He tilts his head toward the house. "Walk."

I continue toward the house, aware that another siren has joined the first, an unsettling harmony that echoes among the treetops like the promise of something dreadful to come.

CHAPTER 5

The activity on my radio intensifies on the short walk to the Beachy farmhouse. Evidently, when my conversation with Mona was cut off abruptly without explanation—and when I failed to respond to her attempt to reach me—she must have assumed I'd run into trouble and put out a county-wide emergency dispatch.

Good girl, I think, and I catch a flurry of codes coming over the airwaves as King, the little girl, and I traverse the muddy, overgrown path to the house.

Investigating abandoned vehicle . . .
Came back stolen.
Exited vehicle . . .
. . . radio check . . . officer in trouble.
Ten-thirty-nine.
I'm ten-seven-six.

Other than the hiss and crackle of the radio, we walk in silence, single-file with the little girl in the lead, me in the middle, and King behind me. I can only assume my revolver is leveled at my back, which doesn't give me much in the way of options. I have no idea what the situation is inside the house; I don't know if he's telling the truth about Rebecca and Daniel—if they were harmed—or if they're helping him.

But it's the five children that worry me most. If Joseph King is cold-blooded enough to murder his wife in her bed with the children in the house, God only knows what else he's capable of. Even if he has no intention of harming them outright, they are no doubt in danger. How will he react when he realizes they are the perfect bargaining chip?

We ascend a grassy incline, climb over a split-rail fence, then cross the wide expanse of yard. We take a narrow, broken sidewalk to the rear of the house and King motions me up the concrete steps to a small porch. Before the little girl reaches the door, it swings open. The little boy I met earlier in the day thrusts a lantern at us. His eyes widen at the sight of me. "Oh." Big blue eyes dart to his father. "Datt?"

"It's okay," King says, and then to me: "Get inside."

I obey, aware that he's right behind me. That he's still gripping my .38.

"Who's the *Englischer*, Datt?" the boy asks.

"A policeman," he replies. "She's going to help us."

I enter the mudroom. A row of windows to my right. Jackets and summer straw hats hang neatly on wood pegs to my left. There's a wood bench against the wall. Six pairs of boots lined up on the floor beneath it. Chunks of mud all around. A rug at the doorway to the kitchen for wiping feet. The boy goes into the kitchen and I follow.

It's the same kitchen I visited when I talked to Daniel and Rebecca to warn them about Joseph King. It seemed sunny and benign then; the place seems menacing tonight. The big table is occupied by three more children, one boy of about eight, who I'd met when I was here before, and two pre-teen girls, their faces illuminated by a flickering lantern. All of them are clad in nightclothes, telling me they were roused from sleep.

The youngsters stare as I enter the kitchen, their eyes wide and apprehensive. They're mature enough to realize something is wrong. Smart enough to know their long-lost *datt* isn't here for a visit.

From where I'm standing, I can see into the dimly lit living room. There's no one there. No sign of a struggle. No trace of Rebecca or Daniel Beachy. A thread of worry goes through me. I look at Joseph. "Where are Rebecca and Daniel?"

"I told you," he says. "I asked them to leave."

A thin layer of relief slips through me, but it's tempered by the thought that he could be lying. That he could have harmed them—or worse.

"*Sitz dich anne.*" King's voice cuts into my thoughts. Sit down.

By the light of the lantern, I get my first good look at him. The years have not been kind to

Joseph King. His face is hardened and gaunt, his cheeks are hollow, his mouth is pulled into a grim line. His brown eyes are flat and expressionless. He's still wearing his prison-issue clothes. His trousers are caked with mud up to his knees. The gray hoodie is torn at the pocket. His sneakers are covered with mud. His left hand is bleeding, old blood already crusted over, but it doesn't appear to be a serious injury, and he doesn't seem to notice.

He motions toward the table. "Sit down, Katie. Now."

Moving slowly so as not to spook him, I go to the table, pull out the nearest chair, and sink into it. The older boy goes to the counter and lights a second lantern. The little boy who answered the door is bent over a bowl of cereal, eating intently. The youngest, Sadie, has returned to a mug of what looks like hot chocolate. The rise and fall of multiple sirens outside adds an eerie countenance to what should have been a benign scene. Interestingly, the children don't appear to be fearful of their father. Because they've been protected from the truth? Or is the child-parent bond so unshakable that they're able to accept his presence and rationalize the circumstances of his return?

I make eye contact with the oldest girl. She's about twelve years old with dishwater blond hair and hazel eyes. "*Wie geth's alleweil?*" I ask, letting my eyes touch each of them. How goes it now?

"*Miah sinn zimmlich gut.*" We are pretty good.

The answer comes from Sadie, who met us in the woods. She's animated and social and I'm touched by her sweetness. She lifts the mug and slurps the last of the hot chocolate.

All the while my police radio is going nuts. Both County and my own department are requesting a response from me. They know I'm in trouble. The problem is they don't know exactly where I am or what's happened, just that I was in the proximity of the Beachy farm.

"I'm Kate," I tell the children. "I'm a police officer. What are your names?"

"I'm Sadie." The little girl holds up her hand and spreads her fingers. "I'm five."

The boy next to her, the one who answered the door, slides in next to me. "I'm Levi and I'm six." He proffers a shy smile, revealing two missing front teeth.

I look at the girl across the table from me. She's about ten years old with curly brown hair and a gap between her front teeth. "My name's Annie."

I let my eyes slide to the girl next to her. The oldest child is on the cusp of adolescence and very pretty. "How about you?" I ask.

"I'm Becky."

I look at the boy sitting at the end of the table. He looks startlingly like his father. I guess him to be eight or nine. Brown hair and eyes. Blunt-cut bangs and the typical bowl-shaped haircut. His skinny chest pokes out. "I'm Little Joe."

"It's nice to meet all of you," I tell them in *Deitsch*.

They stare at me, their eyes flicking from me to their father. They're wondering what happens next. The older kids know something isn't right. They're wondering why their *datt* is home after being gone for so long. Why he woke them in the middle of the night and pulled them from their beds. Why he's wearing such strange clothes that are dirty and torn. Why he asked their aunt and uncle to leave. Poor little things . . .

"How does she know *Deitsch*, Datt?" Sadie asks.

"I used to be *Amisch*," I tell her.

Levi, the little boy with the missing front teeth, pipes up, "How come you're not *Amisch* anymore?"

"It's kind of complicated," I tell him.

"Oh." But his brows go together, as if he's trying to figure out some hidden meaning.

King has turned his attention to the window, using the revolver to move the curtain aside. Watching for movement outside. According to the codes coming over my radio, they've found my vehicle. Rebecca and Daniel have been located. Holmes County, as well as my own department, has arrived on scene. I wonder if Tomasetti has gotten the call.

King drops the curtain, his expression grim, and strides to the table. "Looks like your cop buddies are here," he tells me.

I set my hand against the radio strapped to my equipment belt. "I need to let them know I'm okay. That'll calm them down. Buy you some time." I look at the children. Five innocent little faces tinged with a wrenching combination of anxiety, excitement, and hope. They're staring at me. Counting on me to help them and keep them safe.

I look at Joseph. "We need to figure out how to end this so no one gets hurt." I motion at the kids. "Especially them."

He sends a pointed look to the pocket in which I dropped my cell. "Call the police, Katie. Tell them you're here. With me and the children. Tell them we are all fine." He raises my .38. Finger inside the guard. "Let them know I'm armed and they're not to come inside. Do you understand?"

"All right."

But a new layer of trepidation slips through me. While I'm glad law enforcement has arrived on scene, I have no idea how King will respond to the added pressure.

Keeping my eyes on his, I reach for my cell,

wipe a smear of mud from the touchscreen, and thumb in the speed dial for dispatch. Mona picks up on the first ring.

"*Chief!* I've been trying—"

"I'm okay," I cut in, not sure how long King will let me talk. "I'm inside the Beachy house with Joseph King. His five children are here with us. Everyone's okay."

"Okay. Okay."

"Are Daniel and Rebecca Beachy all right?"

"They're being interviewed now. They're unhurt, just upset."

King jabs the revolver at me. "Tell them I'm armed and they're not to come in."

Nodding at him, I relay the information.

"Is he right there, Chief? Listening?"

"Roger that."

"Are you in danger?"

"Probably." I hesitate. "But . . . it's not imminent."

"So this is a ten-ninety-three?" she says, using the ten code for hostage situation.

"That's affirm."

"I notified County. Is there anything else I should do?"

Before I can respond, King leans close and yanks the phone from my hand. "That's enough."

He hits the END button with his thumb and tosses the phone onto the table. "They'd better not try to come in."

"They won't," I assure him, hoping I'm right. Initially, the situation will fall under Sheriff Mike Rasmussen's jurisdiction. The first thing he'll do is call BCI for assistance. BCI will bring in a negotiator.

A burst of activity crackles over my radio. I glance at King, wanting to respond, to let my counterparts know I'm fine and that, for now, the situation is calm. But he snatches the lapel mike from where it's clipped to my shirt and drops it to the floor.

I rise abruptly. "I need that to communicate."

Leveling the revolver at my chest to keep me at bay, he crushes the mike beneath his shoe, grinding it into the floor. "Sit the hell down," he snaps.

Annie begins to cry.

I lower myself back into the chair, glance in her direction. "It's okay," I tell her, but my voice isn't very convincing.

King looks at her, and blinks. The flash of emotion on his face is so fleeting I might have missed it if I hadn't been looking right at him. An instant of softness tinged with regret or maybe pain. And in that instant, I know that while he is a violent man, a drug user, a murderer even, there's still something human, something reachable inside him. *He cares about his children.* That's knowledge I can use to my advantage. To manipulate him. Make him listen to reason.

The realization is cold comfort tonight, because I know that sometimes love—especially a desperate, hopeless, unreciprocated love—can be lethal. If Joseph King can't handle it, he might decide to end it all—and take everyone in the house with him.

"Everything's okay, Annie," he tells the girl.

She hiccups. "We're not supposed to yell or cuss."

"I'm just . . . tired," he says softly. "Stop crying now."

"Maybe it's past your bedtime, Datt," Sadie says thoughtfully.

A smile whispers across his mouth. "Maybe I'm not the only one, no?"

The little girl looks down at the empty mug in her hands. It's obvious she's exhausted, but she shakes her head. "I'm not sleepy, Datt. Not at all. I want to stay up and help you and Katie get things figured out."

King's brows arch. It's an astute remark for a five-year-old child. She's repeating what she's heard, and I'm reminded that children see and hear more than we realize.

Reaching out, he musses her hair. *"Die zeit fer in bett is nau."* The time to go to bed is now. King addresses the oldest girl. "Becky, take the little ones upstairs and tuck them in, will you?"

91

"*Avvah, Datt, vass veyya shtoahri zeit?*" Sadie cries. But Datt, what about story time?

The words are spoken in perfect Pennsylvania Dutch, her voice as high-pitched as a toy doll's. She's got a smear of chocolate on her cheek and she's clutching a raggedy, faceless doll to her chest. Despite the circumstances, I'm completely charmed.

"Okay." King brings his hands together. "*Shtoahri seahsht un no shlohf.*" Story first and then sleep.

Looking relieved to be excused from the table, Becky rises and starts for the stairs. In a flurry of scooting chairs and stampeding feet, the four remaining children make a mad rush for the door and clamber up the stairs.

I turn my attention to King. "They're frightened," I tell him.

He gives me a sour look. "Can you blame them? They don't know what to make of all this. Wakened in the middle of the night by a father they haven't seen in two years." He shrugs. "I'm practically a stranger to them. And who knows the things people have told them? About what happened with their mother. About me."

"I talked to Rebecca and Daniel," I tell him. "They didn't tell the children anything."

I can tell by his expression that he doesn't believe me. "I didn't kill Naomi," he says.

I don't respond. Instead, I hold his gaze,

looking in vain for some shred of conscience I can call upon to convince him to release the children, but there's nothing there. "It's obvious you still love those kids very much."

"Of course I do," he says irritably. "They're my children."

"I know you don't want them hurt."

"I'm not going to hurt them."

"You've put them in an incredibly dangerous situation." I motion toward the window with my eyes. "There are a dozen cops with guns outside. All they know is that you're a convicted killer and you're holding these kids hostage."

"Nothing I can do about that."

"You can end this. Release the children. Give yourself up. Joseph, if you don't, someone is going to get hurt. You or me or one of those sweet kids."

"People have already been hurt," he snaps. "My wife is dead. My children have been taken from me. I've been imprisoned for something I didn't do."

I look closely at him, wondering if he's delusional or medicated, but I see no indication of either. Has the stress of the last two years—the trial and incarceration—sent him over the edge of some psychological precipice?

"Joseph, they've already lost their mother," I say quietly. "Don't take their father away from them—"

"Don't take their father away?" he says angrily. "Are you kidding me? I've not seen my children for two years!"

"You're alive."

"Alive?" He laughs. "That's not a word I would use to describe my existence."

"This is not the right way to go about changing it."

He looks down his nose at me. "Look at you. Sitting there all smug. So smart like some do-gooder. Judging me. You know *nothing*."

"I know you don't want those kids to be hurt."

He slants me an assessing look. "You always were a persuasive one. Strong-willed. *Too* willful, according to your *datt*."

"Joseph, I'll help you. If you'd just—"

"Maybe too many years have passed. Evidently they've taught you how to be a good liar."

"I'm trying to save your life."

"Save your breath," he says nastily.

Through the open kitchen window, a renewed chorus of sirens reaches us. Emergency lights dance on the wall. Joseph goes to the window and looks out. I can't see anything from where I'm sitting, but I imagine there are dozens of law enforcement vehicles parked on the road in front of the house. The sheriff's department has probably set up roadblocks and a perimeter around the farm, blocking anyone from entering or exiting. In the back of my mind I wonder if Tomasetti knows where I am. I wonder how worried, how upset, he is.

"Joseph, those cops out there will kill you." I send a pointed look toward the flashing lights. "Please. I don't want this to end that way."

He turns away from the window and looks at me for the span of a full minute before speaking. "I loved my wife, Katie. I love my children. I didn't do the things I've been accused of."

"Then do the right thing," I say quietly. "Release the kids. I'll stay with you. I'll help you. We'll work through this together."

He starts toward me, eyes intent on mine. For an instant I think he's going to drag me to my feet and punch me. I brace, but he only pulls out a chair and sinks into it. He leans forward, puts his elbows on his knees, close enough for me to smell the fear sweat and stale breath, but I don't shrink away. His eyes are bloodshot and filled with intensity as they search mine.

"I didn't kill my wife," he says urgently.

I stare back, wondering if he has any idea how often law enforcement and prosecutors and judges hear those words, and that they're almost always a lie.

He scrubs both hands over his face, then looks at me over the tips of his fingers. "You don't believe me."

"What do you expect? You break out of prison.

Jump me in the dark. Take your children hostage—"

"I did what I had to do."

"Joseph, this is not the right way to go about convincing anyone you're innocent."

"Then how?" he roars. "Go back to prison where I'll be silenced and forgotten until I die? I didn't murder my wife, Katie. With God as my witness, I didn't do it!"

"So appeal your case."

"I did. It was denied."

"What do you want from me?" I snap, adding a hefty dose of attitude to my voice.

"A little faith! Your trust. Your help, damn it!"

I stare at him, realizing he unquestionably believes what he's saying. If I can somehow capitalize on that, work it to my advantage, lead him to believe I'm an ally, I might be able to talk him into releasing the children.

"All right," I say after a moment. "I'll look into your case. But if we're going to do this, it's got to be a two-way street. You have to work with me."

He scowls. "Work with you how?"

"Release the children."

"No!" He slams his open hand against the tabletop. "They are *my* children! I want them here with me!"

"Joseph, listen to me. I'm a cop. I can help you. I can look at your case. The evidence. Transcripts from your trial. If there's something there, I'll find it. I'll find it and I'll make sure it gets to the right people." It's not true; I have no intention of looking at anything related to his case. But I've no compunction about lying to him if it will end this and keep those children safe.

He looks at me like he wants to put his hands around my throat and squeeze. "You think this is some kind of *joke?* You think you can sit there and lie to me as if I'm some kind of fucking *half-wit?*"

"That's not what I think."

He stares at me for so long and with such intensity that sweat breaks out on the back of my neck. He looks desperate and dangerous, like a man at the end of a very short rope. "What happened to you, Katie?" he says with a quiet belied by the dark rage in his eyes.

"I grew up," I say firmly. "Something you didn't quite manage."

He sinks against the back of the chair, looking strung-out and exhausted. For the span of a few minutes neither of us speaks. I study the tabletop between us and listen to the rumble of an engine outside, the occasional bark and hiss of a police radio, the rise and fall of an approaching siren.

"I'll be the first to tell you I wasn't a good husband to her," Joseph says after a moment. "God knows she deserved better. I was a shitty father. An unreliable friend. I was a cheat,

97

a liar, and a thief. I have a temper and I have a weakness for booze. I'm not proud of any of it." He raises his eyes to mine, his gaze burning. "I'm a loser. *But I did not fucking kill her.*"

I stare back, assuring myself I'm not swayed. But for an instant, looking into his eyes, I catch a glimpse of the Amish boy I once knew. A thousand memories rush at me, a hail of spears sinking into places that are startlingly tender. The time he swam into a rain-swollen creek to save a stray dog from drowning. The day he got his ass beat by two bullies who'd pulled the underpants off a special-needs Amish girl. The time my brother started a fire in a shed and Joseph took the rap because he knew Jacob was in for a whipping.

"Joseph, do you have any idea how often cops hear that? Come on. I wasn't born yesterday and neither were you. You have to give me *something.* Some kind of evidence or proof or at least a theory."

To my shock, he offers a statistic instead. "According to the National Registry of Exonerations, since 1989 two thousand convicted people have been exonerated."

"You've been reading up."

"Desperate times . . . and a decent library."

"All right," I say. "You have my attention."

He gives me a lackadaisical smile. "You're quite the tough customer, Katie Burkholder."

I ignore the comment. "Let's start with this: If you didn't kill your wife, who did?"

"I don't know. The one thing I do know is that he's still out there." He sighs. "I always believed someone would figure it out. Find the truth. I never imagined it going this far."

"What was the motive?" I ask. "Why would someone kill an Amish woman? A mother of five?"

"I can't answer that. *I don't know.* Naomi was always . . . the good one. Everyone loved her, including me." He gives a wan smile. "I'm the one everybody wanted to kill. Yet here I am."

The words reverberate in the silence of the kitchen, punctuated by the sounds of the police presence outside. The chirp of a police radio. The occasional blast of a siren. A voice coming over a loudspeaker.

"I know how all of this sounds," he says.

I give him a hard look. "Crazy? Delusional?"

"Desperate. Far-fetched." His mouth curves, but the smile does nothing to mask the sheen of bitterness in his eyes. "The cops said I had drugs and it was true. They said I was drunk; they were right." Something lights up in his eyes, some dark emotion that's both hot and cold at once. "But I have never struck my wife. Never. And I did not take her life."

I've heard a hundred variations of those words and not once have I believed any of them. I don't want to believe them now. But there's something in the depths of his eyes that beckons me to listen, to look deeper. Am I biased because I grew up with him? Because he influenced my life in such a significant way? Or is it possible there's some shred of truth to his words?

"You can't fight the charges like this," I tell him. "Not by holding me and your kids hostage. You can't do that. It will not help your cause."

Another silence, steely and brittle. We sit across from each other, staring at the tabletop. It's so quiet I can hear the spring peepers outside.

"I always knew you'd make something of yourself," he says after a moment. "I always knew it would be something . . . big and important."

"I don't see how you could have known such a thing," I tell him. "I didn't."

He surprises me by laughing. "I bet Bishop Troyer wasn't happy about it."

"He had no say in the matter." When he raises his brows, I add, "I left when I was eighteen."

He nods, thoughtful now. "How are Jacob and Sarah?"

"They're both married. I have nephews and a niece."

"But no children for you?"

I say nothing.

"Are you close to them?"

"Not like we were." The old pain burgeons, but

I shove it back. I've been estranged from my brother and sister most of my adult life. I've reached out to them several times since I've been back in Painters Mill, but because I left the fold their responses were tepid.

"I don't think we'll ever get that back," I say.

"It's a sad thing," he says. "You were close once. I'm sorry you lost that. I know how much family means."

I don't respond. I don't want him inside my head or knowing too much about me. I don't want him to know how much those tattered relationships hurt when they slipped away.

He gives a resolute nod. "So are you any good at what you do?"

"Good enough."

"Good enough to find the person who killed Naomi?"

I don't know what to say to that, so I remain silent.

"You look the same," he says after a moment.

Now it's my turn to laugh, but it's a short, uncomfortable sound. "I hope not."

"The same only . . . better."

"You were always good at dishing out the compliments," I tell him. "Especially when you wanted something."

"And you were always good at breaking the mold. Still are, aren't you?" He doesn't expect an answer and so I say nothing.

He stares at me as if seeing me for the first time. Scrutinizing me, as if my sitting here at this table with him is somehow shocking.

After a moment, he speaks in a low voice. "As fucked up as all of this is . . . I still wondered if it would be you who came tonight."

"It's my jurisdiction."

"I'm glad I got to see you again."

A softness unfolds inside me, an uncomfortable mix of nostalgia and melancholy, the latter because the sweet boy I once knew took a wrong turn somewhere along the line and more than likely there's no coming back.

He laughs abruptly. "Do you remember that time the pigs got out of their pen and it was just you and Jacob and I to round them up?"

Despite the situation, I find myself smiling. I tell myself that reminiscing might help me gain control of the situation, soften him up, get him to come to his senses, but that's not completely honest, because in that instant he's the old Joseph I once looked up to. The Amish boy I was half in love with and loyal to till the end.

"Must have been a dozen pigs running around," I say.

"Rooting up the garden. Gobbling up all the corn and tomatoes."

"Not to mention Mamm's peonies."

"We got an earful about that, didn't we?" He

barks out another laugh. "You and I trapped that big sow between the barn and the silo."

I surprise myself by laughing, too. It's such an inappropriate, out-of-character reaction that I set my hand over my mouth to smother it. Chief of Police Kate Burkholder would not be laughing with this man, a prison escapee and convicted murderer. But thirteen-year-old Katie with her unfettered sense of humor and reckless heart would laugh until tears streamed from her eyes.

"You climbed onto her back and tried to ride her back to the barn," I say.

"She bucked me off halfway there."

"You never were a very good rider."

"She was so traumatized she ran all the way back to the pen."

Our laughter commingles, overriding the sounds of law enforcement outside, the weight of the situation. And for the span of several seconds, we're teenagers and our biggest problem is how to finish our chores so we can go swimming in the creek, or to the woods for a game of hide-and-seek.

Reality intrudes when my phone vibrates on the table. I glance down at the caller ID, but I don't recognize the number. Evidently, Mona has passed my number on to the sheriff's department or BCI. More than likely, they want to know what the situation is. What King's intentions are. If he's armed. If anyone has been hurt. I let the call go to voicemail.

Sobering, I make eye contact with King. "Sooner or later I'm going to have to answer that."

"I know." The last remnant of his smile fades, and for the first time, he looks frightened. *"I didn't kill her,"* he whispers, the softness of his voice making the words somehow more powerful.

I stare at him, suddenly angry with him for putting me in this position, for expecting me to believe him when my every instinct is warning me not to, for asking me to do something I don't want to do.

"I need more than just your word," I say.

He tightens his mouth. "Will a witness do the trick?"

CHAPTER 6

Disbelief wells inside me. "A witness? Who?"

"Sadie."

My last vestige of hope sinks. The disappointment that follows is bitter and deep. "You know what, Joseph? I've heard enough." I rise abruptly, but he reaches out, sets his hand on my arm.

"Sit the hell down and listen to me," he hisses.

"Let go of me."

He surprises me by obeying.

I sink back into the chair. "Joseph . . . *Sadie?*"

"She saw a man come into the house that night," he tells me. "She *saw* him, Katie. In the hallway, outside our bedroom. He had a shotgun in his hands."

I'm not sure what to make of his assertion. What does he possibly hope to accomplish? I read enough about the case to know the kids were in the house the night of the murder. It's common knowledge. What kind of man drags a five-year-old little girl back into such a nightmare scenario?

"That's ridiculous." I keep my voice level, but I hear the hard ring of anger in it. "Investigators and a social worker with Children Services interviewed those kids. All of them. Multiple times.

Any knowledge of the crime would have been uncovered in the course of those interviews."

"It was."

"I don't believe you."

"She told them what she saw. But because of her age no one took her seriously."

"Joseph, she was three years old."

"I know how old she was!" he shouts.

"A child that age would be considered an unreliable witness."

"You have to understand something," he tells me. "Sadie is not like most children her age. She's . . . wise beyond her years. Mature for her age. Smarter than me. Naomi, even. This child of five . . . Katie, she already knows her mind."

He's right about the girl. I discerned her keen intellect within a few minutes of meeting her. For a five-year-old, she's extraordinarily self-assured, poised, and well-spoken. That said, the murder of her mother was two years ago; Sadie was only three years old at the time. Mature or not, she is an unreliable witness.

King doesn't seem to notice my skepticism. "Naomi and I knew Sadie was different when she was still practically a baby. We used to call her our little *aldi hutzel.*" Old woman. "She does not make up stories or tell tall tales," he says. "I swear to you, Katie, I believe she saw the man who shot and killed Naomi."

"How did you find out about it?"

"I didn't until I was already in prison. No one bothered telling me," he says darkly. "Sadie confided in Becky, my oldest. But Rebecca and Daniel wouldn't let the children visit me. So Becky wrote me a letter. I'm sure you know the people at the prison read all the incoming mail. This one got through."

"Did you tell your attorney?" I ask.

"Of course I did," he says crossly. "I was certain her testimony would exonerate me. Maybe help the police find the man responsible. It gave me hope." He shakes his head. "My attorney petitioned for Sadie to be interviewed."

"And?"

He sags against the chair back, deflated. "They said she was too young to be reliable. The psychologist and social worker agreed. And they were afraid another interview would cause her further emotional trauma."

I nod, saying nothing. Any cop who's investigated a case involving child abuse or exploitation by a parent or guardian knows children will say or do anything to protect them. A traumatized child who's lost a parent will likely turn to the other parent, even if the surviving parent has been cruel. In addition, kids who've experienced emotional trauma sometimes create fantasies to help them deal with it.

It's a protective mechanism, and I've seen it more often than I care to recall.

"Do you have the letter?" I ask.

He shakes his head. "They took it. The correction officers. They came in one night and searched my cell for contraband. I'd hidden it in my Bible. When I came back, it was gone."

My phone erupts again. I glance down at it, see Holmes County Sheriff on the display.

"They need to know everyone's okay," I say.

"Answer it. Make it so I can hear."

I hit Speaker and answer with, "Burkholder. You're on speaker."

"Kate, this is Mike Rasmussen. Mona tells me you're in there with King and there's a hostage situation. Is that correct?"

Rasmussen and I have worked together on a handful of cases over the last few years. He's a good cop with a level head and nearly twenty years of experience under his belt. He doesn't rattle easily. I can tell by the tone of his voice he's rattled now.

"That's correct," I tell him. "Joseph and his children are here. Everyone's okay."

"He's armed?"

I look at Joseph and he nods. "That's affirm." In the back of my mind I wonder if the Beachys keep a rifle in the house.

"Kate, are you in imminent danger?"

"No."

"Is Mr. King listening?"

"He's right here, sitting across the table from me."

"All five kids there?"

"Yes."

He pauses, stymied because he knows King will hear whatever he has to say. "Mr. King?"

"I'm right here."

"Any chance I can talk you into coming out here to talk to me?"

"No."

"What about the kids? Will you send them out? I'm sure both of us want to keep them safe, make sure they don't get hurt."

"They stay with me."

"Mr. King, I don't have to tell you this is a very serious situation, do I?"

"I know how serious it is," the Amish man replies.

"It would be prudent for you to put down any weapons you have and come out to talk to me. I promise to listen."

"Not going to happen."

"What is it you want?" Rasmussen asks.

Looking annoyed, King nods at me to answer. I interject, "Mike, he wants us to look into the murder of his wife. He says he didn't kill her."

"All right." The pause that follows tells me he's ruminating the statement, trying to think of a

109

way to use it. "Is there anything I can do to help bring this to an end?"

"I'll let you know." King snatches the phone off the tabletop and ends the call.

"Joseph, this is so not the right thing to do," I tell him.

"What else is there?" he growls.

"There are a dozen cops out there with guns. More on the way. SWAT, too, probably. A negotiator. This is not helping your cause."

Shooting me a dark look, he rises and stalks to the window and parts the curtains to peer outside. The butt of my .38 is sticking out of his waistband. In the back of my mind I wonder if I could get to it before he stopped me. Red and blue lights flash on his face from the law enforcement vehicles parked at the end of the lane. He stares at them a moment, then drops the curtains and returns to the table.

"How many?" I ask.

"Too many to count." He drops into the chair.

"They're not going to go away."

"I don't expect they will."

"Joseph, they'll kill you. I don't want that to happen."

Sending me a withering look, he rises abruptly and strides to the living room. At the base of the stairs, he looks up at the landing and shouts, "Becky, bring Sadie down here!"

The girl shouts something unintelligible.

110

He reclaims his place at the table.

"Please don't bring her into this," I say.

"You still don't believe me."

"Joseph, what do you expect? What do you—"

"I expect someone besides me to care about the fucking truth!" he roars.

Movement at the door draws my attention. My heart sinks when the little girl steps into the kitchen. She's wearing her nightgown and hugging that tattered, faceless doll to her side. No one bothered to wash her dirty feet before she went to bed, and the mud has caked. I can tell by the crease on her cheek that she'd been sleeping. Still, she's happy to be back down here with us.

Behind her, the older girl—Becky—sets her hands on her younger sister's shoulders. "Why are all those police cars parked on the road, Datt?" she asks.

"That's for me to worry about, not you," King tells her.

"Levi is upstairs at the window. He's scared."

King sighs. "Tell him to get away from the window and go back to bed. Close the curtains, too."

She nods. "Okay."

"Katie and I need to speak with Sadie for a few minutes. I'll bring her up when we're finished."

Bowing her head slightly, her eyes flicking to me and then back to her father, the older girl backs from the room and pounds back up the steps.

Sadie goes to her father, climbs onto his lap. "Can I have hot chocolate?"

King takes her into his arms—a natural, practiced move despite his having been away from her for two years. "You already had hot chocolate."

"It was good. Maybe I could have another one."

There's a smile in his eyes when he looks at me. "She's a good negotiator, no?"

For the child's sake, I smile. "I can see that."

"You remember Katie from earlier?" King asks. The little girl nods.

I'm a couple of light-years out of my element when it comes to dealing with children. I'm not a mother and I don't spend as much time as I should with my niece and nephews. I do, however, know that all children are innocent. They're trusting and forgiving and vulnerable. Those things seem especially true for the Amish.

"Katie is going to ask you some questions about what happened the night Mamm went to be with Jesus," King tells her. "Do you remember that?"

"I remember." The little girl's open expression falters.

"I know it's scary, but Katie's a policeman and she might be able to help us figure some things out. It's important, so I want you to answer all her questions as best you can. Do you understand?"

Her foot starts to jiggle, but she nods. "Yes, Datt."

He pauses as if to take a moment to get his words in order and then asks, "Do you remember telling Becky about what happened that night?"

Another nod.

"What did Becky do after you told her?"

"Her face turned red and she cried."

His expression softens. "What else did she do?"

"She wrote a letter."

He looks at me. "If you want we can talk with Becky after we're finished here."

I nod, but I don't want to be part of this. I don't want to bring yet another child into this. And I'm not convinced either girl will bring anything new to the equation.

He turns his attention back to his daughter. "Sadie, I want you to tell Katie what you saw the night Mamm went to heaven."

The little girl hugs the faceless doll more closely against her and snuggles against her *datt*. She looks exhausted and scared and I feel a rise of anger that her father would put her through this.

"What's your doll's name?" I ask, hoping to ease her anxiety.

"Dottie."

"That's a pretty name." I offer a smile I hope is

reassuring. "I used to have a little hen named Dottie."

The child grins; she thinks I'm pulling her leg, but she's game, a good sport. "I have a rooster," she tells me. "He's white with a big tail and his name is Bobby Doo. Becky hatched him from an egg."

"Good thing you didn't eat that egg for breakfast."

She giggles.

Silence descends, so I reach out and run my hand over her doll. "I bet you and your brothers and sisters miss your *mamm*."

She gives a big nod. "Sometimes Annie still cries at night. Levi, too."

"That happens when you miss someone." I glance at King and he nods for me to keep going. I turn my attention back to Sadie. "Can you tell me what happened the night your *mamm* went to heaven?"

She bites her lip, looks down at the doll, saying nothing.

It's wrenching to see this little girl struggle to find words no child should have to utter. It's a helpless feeling because I have no way of knowing if she did, indeed, see anything that night. Or if her father coached her and asked her to lie for him. All I can do at this juncture is gently dig and listen.

I give her a moment and then ask, "What

do you remember about that night, sweetheart?"

"I heard thunder."

"What did you do?"

"Me and Dottie got up."

"Do you take Dottie everywhere with you?"

She looks at the doll and scrapes at a stain with a tiny fingernail. "When I'm allowed."

I wink at her to let her know it's okay. "What happened after you and Dottie got up?"

"We went to go pee wee."

"What did you see?"

"*I* didn't see anything."

I glance at Joseph, confused. If he's relying on this kid to save his neck, he's in for an epic fail.

He nods at his daughter. "Go on."

"Not me. *Dottie.*"

"Oh." I nod. "What did Dottie see?"

"A man."

"Do you know who he was?" I ask. "Was he someone you'd seen before?"

She shakes her head.

"What was he doing?"

"Standing outside my *mamm* and *datt*'s bedroom."

"Did he see you?"

She nods vigorously. "He looked . . . funny. His face was shiny and red. He told me to go back to bed."

"What did you do?"

"I told him I wanted Mamm."

"What happened next?"

Of all the questions I've asked, this one garners the most powerful response. Sadie seems to curl in on herself. Make herself smaller. As if she's trying to sink more deeply into her *datt*'s lap. Hiding behind the doll.

"He told me Mamm was sick. Me and Dottie started to go back to our room and he raised the long gun like he was going to shoot us. I heard it click, but he must've been playing."

A slow, seeping horror moves through me. Does she understand what she's saying? Is it the truth?

I glance at Joseph, but he's staring at her intently, stone-faced and pale.

"What did you do?" I ask, turning my attention back to the child.

"I went to my room."

I let the words settle and then ask, "What did the man look like?"

"An *Englischer.*"

Of course that's the way a little Amish girl would describe a non-Amish man she didn't recognize. "What color was his hair, sweetie?"

"Brown like mine, only short."

"Do you remember what color his eyes were?"

She shakes her head. "I didn't really see his eyes."

"How big was he?"

"Big."

I glance at Joseph. "Bigger than your *datt*? Or was he smaller?"

"About the same, only fatter."

"Do you remember what he was wearing?"

Her brows knit; then she shakes her head. "Just regular *Englischer* clothes."

I'm so engrossed by her demeanor, her utter certainty about what she saw, the conviction with which she tells the story, I find my earlier skepticism starting to crumble. The story is too elaborate for a five-year-old to make up. There are too many details for her to recall had she been coached.

Still, I make an effort to shake her up. "Is it possible the man *was* your *datt*?"

Across from me, King makes a sound of annoyance. I ignore him and I don't take my eyes off the child.

"It wasn't my *datt*."

"Are you sure? I mean, it was dark, right?"

"My *datt* was fishing."

That, she was told. I continue pressing her. "Maybe he forgot something. His fishhooks maybe, and he came home to get them."

It doesn't elude me that all the while Joseph sits quietly, making no attempt to intervene or influence her.

"But the man didn't *look* like Datt," the girl insists.

"Really? What was different about him? I

mean, you said you didn't see the man's face, right?"

"I saw it. I mean, a little, when he looked at me, but . . ." Her smooth little brows furrow. "He wasn't Datt."

She's not rattled, but thinking this through, I realize. Not trying to remember forgotten lines. Not looking to her father for guidance. *She's remembering what she saw . . .*

"He didn't have a beard!" she exclaims. "And he didn't wear suspenders."

"What did you do next?" I ask.

"Me and Dottie went back to bed."

I stare at her, mentally picking at her body language, her facial expression, the words she spoke with such earnestness. The only thing that comes back at me is the guileless expression of an innocent child.

"Sadie," I say, "you're not in any trouble. But I'm going to ask you a very important question and I need for you to tell me the truth. Okay?"

"Okay."

"Did anyone ask you to tell me this? To say you saw a man in the house the night your *mamm* went to heaven? Or did you really see him?"

"It's what I really saw."

"Did you tell anyone else about it?"

She looks at her *datt.* Not for direction, I realize. But for permission to tell me the truth. He gives her a nod.

"The social lady and her friend."

I glance at Joseph, raise my brows.

"Children Services," he clarifies.

I nod, turn my attention back to the girl. "Anyone else?"

"I told Becky. At first she said it was just a marenight."

King interjects. "Nightmare."

The little girl grins. She knows "marenight" isn't a real word, but she enjoys saying it and the attention it garners from her *datt*. "Becky got sad and worried. She cried and she never cries. She wanted to tell Datt, but no one would let her because he was sent away. We didn't know what to do. Aunt Becca told us little kids aren't allowed to go to the place where Datt was staying." She lowers her voice. "That's when Becky wrote the letter."

King addresses me. "I was to have no contact with the children. So Becky signed her aunt's name instead of her own and the letter got through to me. I recognized her handwriting so I knew it was from her."

"Sadie, you're a brave little girl." Reaching out, I touch Sadie's cheek with my fingertips. "Thank you for answering all my questions."

"Are you going to help us so my *datt* can come home for good?" she asks.

"I'll see what I can do."

CHAPTER 7

Ten minutes later I'm sitting at the kitchen table. Sadie's troubling account of the night her mother was murdered replays in my head like the trailer of some low-budget horror flick. Joseph King sits across from me. The red and blue lights flashing against the curtains and adjacent cabinets serve as a constant reminder of the situation. He made coffee, but neither of us has touched our cups.

"Sadie is a smart little girl," I tell him.

"Took after her *mamm*." He offers a self-deprecating smile and once again I'm reminded of the boy I once looked up to and knew so well. "She's no liar."

The notion that some mysterious *Englischer* came into the house that night and shot Naomi King while she slept goes beyond far-fetched. There was a shitload of circumstantial and physical evidence against King. It was common knowledge among law enforcement—and the Amish community—that the marriage was rocky. King had been convicted of domestic violence on two previous occasions. He was a known drug user and a man with a temper. It was the kind of pressure-cooker situation that all too often ends badly.

But I can't discount what I heard from that little girl. The fervor—the utter certainty—with which she spoke made an impression. Is it the truth? How can a five-year-old tell a huge, frightening, detailed lie with such natural, unrehearsed conviction? Either she's a natural-born liar or she was telling the truth.

. . . he raised the long gun like he was going to shoot us.

God knows I'm no expert on kids. I do know they are capable of deception. Especially an intelligent child who is loyal to a parent, smart enough to see the big picture—and shrewd enough to know how to get what she wants.

Is it possible the man in the hall was, indeed, King and Sadie somehow blocked it out? Did she make up some fantasy to exonerate him, if only in her own mind? Or maybe it's not as complicated as that. Maybe she was disoriented after being wakened abruptly from a deep sleep. Maybe King *had* been wearing English clothes. Maybe the girl was so accustomed to seeing him in his Amish garb, she mistook him for a stranger.

That doesn't explain her assertion that the intruder was clean-shaven. At the time of his arrest King wore the full beard customary of a married Amish man. How did she come up with that detail? Was she simply mistaken? Was it her child's imagination? Or had she been coached?

According to police reports, the children

discovered their mother's body the next morning around eight A.M. Death due to a shotgun blast would have been gruesome. Is it possible Sadie's skewed recollection of events is the result of psychological trauma? Was she so traumatized her mind *invented* the stranger because she simply couldn't accept the truth?

Maybe. Maybe. Maybe.

I want to condemn Joseph for dragging his five-year-old little girl into this mess. Put him back in a cage with the rest of the animals that maim and murder and steal. The problem is there's a part of me that doesn't believe the girl was lying. That puts me in an untenable position.

"You're a son of a bitch for bringing her into this," I say.

He doesn't look up. "I know."

We fall silent again, thinking, thinking. My phone rings. We don't look at it this time. I don't answer.

"I don't know what to make of her story," I tell him.

He finally makes eye contact with me. "I wasn't there that night, so I do, obviously. She's telling the truth and no one listened to her."

"If you're lying to me, I swear to Christ I'll bury you."

"I'm not lying."

I pick up the mug and sip cold coffee. "Did Naomi have any enemies?"

Joseph stares at me, a kaleidoscope of emotions churning in his eyes. "No."

"Any disputes? Had she recently argued with anyone? Neighbors? Friends? Family members?"

He shakes his head. "Everyone loved her. She was . . . good, Katie. Better than me. Too *good* for me. She was . . . everything I wasn't."

"Were you faithful to her?"

His eyes flick away. "No."

"Who was she?"

"Just . . . a woman in a bar."

"Her name," I snap.

"I don't remember." He shakes his head. "Not even sure I asked."

"Did you hear from her again? I mean, afterward?"

"No."

I think about all the gnarly repercussions of infidelity. An angry husband. A scorned lover. The list is seemingly endless. "Is it possible *you* were the target?"

I can tell by his expression the thought hadn't occurred to him.

"Answer the damn question," I say firmly. "Did you have any enemies? Jealous husbands? Pissed-off lovers? Any ongoing disputes? About money? With neighbors? Anything?"

"I rubbed a lot of people the wrong way, but I don't think I pissed off anyone to the extent that they'd want to shoot me or my wife."

"What about drugs? You got busted with pot, didn't you? Meth? A lot of unsavory individuals involved in that crap. Did you owe drug money to anyone? Did you double-cross anyone?"

"Look, I bought pot a couple of times. Small amounts, mostly. But it was a pittance. Less than an ounce. I paid cash." His mouth tightens. "Look, I know you don't want to hear this, but the other drugs the cops found in my buggy? The meth? It wasn't mine."

I slap my hand down on the tabletop. "Stop lying to me! For God's sake, Joseph, can you just tell the truth! I'm trying to help you! I don't care about the drugs at this point. I want to know about the *people* you dealt with. We both know what kinds of people involve themselves in the drug trade."

"I did not keep company with drug dealers," he tells me. "That's the truth, Katie. Never spent more than thirty or forty bucks and always in cash."

A tense silence ensues. I find myself watching the red and blue lights dancing on cabinets, a new sense of pressure coming down on top of me. I look at Joseph and my eyes fall upon the butt of my .38 sticking out of his waistband. Two things strike me at once. I'm not afraid of him. And I want the truth. All of it. Even if it's something I don't want to hear.

"Do you trust me?" I ask him.

He stares at me a long time before answering. "Yes."

"Do you want my help?"

"You know I do."

I hold out my hand. "Give me my sidearm. Right now. Give it to me."

He doesn't move.

"Give me my pistol and we can walk out of here together. I'll make sure you're treated fairly while I look into your case. You have my word."

His mouth curves, but any semblance of a smile is obliterated by the agony in his eyes. "Ah, Katie."

"Don't say that to me," I snap. "Don't look at me that way. Goddamn you."

"I can't give you the gun. That would leave me defenseless."

"Joseph, for God's sake, I'm offering to help you. Don't screw this up."

"I'm not going to leave my children. I'm not going back to prison."

"Do you know what's going to happen to you if you continue with this . . . this hopeless farce? They're going to kill you. One of your kids could get hurt in the cross fire. The cops do not mess around when there are hostages involved. Is that what you want?"

He looks away, shakes his head. "No."

I point to the window where police lights glint off the curtains. "The cops have probably already

125

brought in SWAT. A negotiator, too. They've been trying to call. If you don't talk to them, if you don't strike some kind of deal, they'll storm this place. I'm talking tear gas and flash-bang grenades. If one of your kids gets hurt it's going to be on you."

"I have no control over what they do." He brushes his hand over the pistol's butt. "I'm not going back to prison. If that's the only thing you can offer, I might as well put a bullet in my head now and get it over with."

"Then let the children go!" I shout. "Let them go."

His eyes hold mine. "The only person I'm going to let walk out of here is you."

"For God's sake." I throw up my hands in frustration.

My cell erupts. King gives me a nod. Blowing out a breath, I pick up. "Burkholder."

"This is Curtis Scanlon with BCI," a male voice tells me. "Everyone all right in there?"

My memory clicks. Curtis Scanlon is a hostage negotiator. I don't know him personally, but I'm familiar with his reputation. He's one of the best negotiators in the state of Ohio. Perhaps the entire Midwest. He's handled dozens of hostage situations statewide and is well known in law enforcement circles. He's got the voice of a radio personality. His manner of speaking is calm, yet affable. He's competent. Reasonable. He's as

126

charismatic as any Hollywood heavyweight. Rumor has it he's received marriage proposals from fans who've seen him on TV.

"Everyone's fine," I tell him.

"Can you talk?"

"Yes. Mr. King is right here at the kitchen table with me."

"Good. Good. Kitchen. Got it. He's armed?"

"Yes."

"Long rifle? Handgun?"

"Both."

"All right. Thank you." A thoughtful pause ensues. "Do you know what he wants?"

"He wants the police to take another look at his case. The evidence. His conviction. He says he didn't murder his wife."

"I understand. Do you think he'll talk to me?"

"I can check." I offer the cell to King. "Curtis Scanlon is the negotiator. He's good, Joseph. He can help you."

His eyes holding mine, Joseph takes the phone. He's taken it off speaker. I'm sitting close enough to hear Scanlon speaking, but I can't make out what's being said. Joseph listens dispassionately. He probably doesn't realize it, but Scanlon is already gathering information. He's getting a feel for King's personality, his frame of mind. Figuring out what makes him tick. Looking for weaknesses. In the back of my mind I wonder if he's ever dealt with an Amish person. . . .

"That's not what I want," King says after a moment. "I didn't kill my wife. I've spent over a year in prison for something I didn't do. I don't want to compromise. The children are fine."

After a few minutes, he removes the phone from his ear. Scanlon is still speaking. For a moment we listen to the drone of his voice, and then King disconnects.

"What happened?" I ask.

"*Ich bin sei geshvetz laydich.*" I'm tired of all his talking. "Your smart guy isn't so interested in the truth. Only in resolving this *his* way."

I'd been hoping that Curtis Scanlon, with all his charisma and experience, would be able to convince him to lay down the gun or at least release the children.

"Give him a chance," I say. "Joseph, he can help you. Listen to him."

He tosses the phone onto the table between us. "The only one who can help me is you. Katie, you know me. You—"

"I don't know you," I cut in. "Not anymore. The Joseph I once knew would never do anything as stupid and dangerous as this."

"Put yourself in my shoes!" he shouts. "What would you do?"

"I'd go through the proper channels."

"Yeah, that's you all right. Miss Proper Channel." He leans back in the chair, crosses his arms over his chest. "The Katie Burkholder I used to know was a rebel. She knew right from wrong and she wasn't afraid to stir the pot."

"We're not kids anymore," I snap.

Another silence falls, tense and uncomfortable. I feel the minutes slipping away, the opportunity for a positive outcome fading with every tick of that silent, invisible clock.

"I always knew you'd grow up pretty." He follows up with a half smile.

"How can you say something so flippant when you're an inch away from getting yourself killed?"

"That bothers you."

"If it's all the same to you I'd rather no one get killed."

"No, I mean when I tell you you're pretty."

I stare hard at him. "You are your own worst enemy. You always were."

He doesn't argue.

After a moment, he motions toward the door. "I'm going to let you go now."

I should be relieved. He's going to let me walk away from this. No one was hurt. I'm loath to leave the children behind, but I don't think he'll harm them. And I'll have the opportunity to do my job and try to resolve this with the help of my counterparts outside.

"Do me a favor?" I ask.

He frowns at me.

"Keep the kids away from the windows." I set

my hand on the phone and slide it across the table to him. "When Scanlon calls, do not hang up on him. Talk to him. Work with him. He is your lifeline."

He starts to protest, but I stop him. "You owe me that, Joseph. I'm going to look into your case. Don't forget that."

He picks up the phone and puts it in his pocket without looking at it. Rising, he motions toward the door. "You can go out through the front."

CHAPTER 8

As Joseph and I pass through the darkened living room, I feel eyes on me. I glance up, toward the stairs, and see Sadie and Rebecca sitting together on the top step of the landing, hands gripping the rails, watching me. I want to wish them good night, but Joseph and I continue on and the chance is lost.

We reach the door. The flashing lights of the emergency vehicles parked at the end of the lane dance and skitter on the opposite wall. King has taken my pistol from his waistband and grips it in his right hand. His finger is outside the trigger guard, but even in the dim light I can see that his knuckles are white, his hand shaking.

He opens the door. His eyes scan the porch, darting to the shadows cast by the juniper and trees in the yard, going finally to the ocean of vehicles beyond. "Must be a couple dozen vehicles out there," he says quietly.

I stop next to him. "There's still time to end this."

"You never were one to give up easily. Even when you were wrong." He turns to face me, his eyes searching mine. "But then that's one of the things I always liked about you."

"Now that I'm a cop, maybe you're not quite so fond."

"I'm still fond of you." The shadow of a smile passes over his lips as he raises his finger as if to scold. "You're the same, whether you want to admit it or not. You haven't forgotten who we were."

I stare at him, feeling watched and exposed, standing in the doorway, his face a scant foot away from mine. I want to think it's because an army of my counterparts with binoculars and night vision are camped out a hundred yards away. Or maybe it's the thought of a sniper with Joseph in the crosshairs. But neither of those things are the reason why my heart is pounding. Or why I suddenly can't seem to get enough oxygen into my lungs.

"We never talked about the way things were between us," he tells me.

I shrug. "We were kids."

As I stand here, looking into a face I once knew so well, I'm shocked to realize some small part of me still remembers that knockout punch of my first crush.

"Joseph, this isn't the right way to do this," I tell him, surprised when my voice is breathless. "I don't want to see you hurt."

He doesn't respond, just continues to stare at me, his eyes roaming my face. "You never married, Katie?"

"That's none of your business."

A sudden grin and he braces a hand against the

jamb behind me. I know an instant before he leans close that he's going to try to kiss me. A farewell kiss? Or something more final? Whatever the case, it's inappropriate. I turn my head an instant before his mouth would have made contact with mine. Instead, his lips brush my cheek and linger. I'm aware of the warmth of his face against mine, the scrape of his whiskers, the realization that he's trembling, his breaths are quickened. It's not a chaste kiss, but neither is it overtly sexual. Just a tidal wave of something melancholy and bittersweet laced with the knowledge that I'm a fool for caring about any of it.

Raising my hand, I set my palm against his cheek and ease him away. "Cut it out."

"You remember," he says thickly.

"I remember you're full of shit."

"That's my Katie." He studies me a moment as if debating and then steps away. "Whoever he is, he's a lucky man."

I glance toward the road, then back to him. "Goddamn you for doing this."

"Find the truth, Katie Burkholder."

I step onto the porch and turn to him, surprised to find that my legs are shaking. My heart pounding a hard tattoo against my ribs. Quickly, the adrenaline ebbs into something else. Something final, uncertain, and unbearably sad. There's nothing left to say.

"Joseph . . ."

He melts into the shadows of the living room. "Get out of here," he says. "Go on."

I turn and descend the steps to the sidewalk. Even as I walk away, the ties to Joseph King and the children wrap around me and pull taut. I have no idea how long I was inside. For the first time in what feels like hours, I can breathe. The night air is cool and humid against my face. As I walk toward the gravel lane that will take me to the road, it occurs to me that I should have called Scanlon to let him know I was coming out. All it takes is one overzealous trigger finger to take out a cop with friendly fire.

I reach the lane and go left toward the road. A sea of emergency lights ahead. Dust floating in the glare of a hundred headlights. The rumble of a diesel engine and at least one generator. I'm walking blind. I raise my hands to shield my eyes, and I call out, "I'm Chief of Police Kate Burkholder! I'm coming out!"

The hairs at the back of my neck prickle uneasily as I draw closer. I envision the crosshairs of the sniper's scope on my chest, and I call out again.

A spotlight sweeps toward me. In the glare, I see the bulky silhouette of a man in tactical gear rush toward me, equipment jingling, boots thudding against the ground.

"Kate Burkholder?" he shouts.

I raise my hands to shoulder level. "Yes."

"Keep your hands where I can see them."

I know it's protocol, but still I'm perturbed by the order.

He reaches me and takes my arm with a gloved hand. He's armed with a tactical rifle. A Kevlar vest. Protective helmet and face shield. He's breathing heavily. SWAT, I think. Through the face screen I see he's young, probably not yet thirty, and high on a mix of testosterone and adrenaline.

"He didn't booby-trap you or anything, right?" he asks.

"No, he didn't. I'm unarmed."

"Are you injured in any way?" he asks as he walks with me toward a massive RV emblazoned with Licking County Sheriff's Department. "Do you need an ambulance?"

"I'm fine. I need to talk to whoever's in charge."

We reach the mobile command center vehicle. Behind it, two Holmes County cruisers block the road. An SUV from Geauga County Sheriff's Department. A swarm of cops from half a dozen jurisdictions rush around, speaking into their cell phones or shoulder mikes. A television news van is parked behind a line of orange cones roped off with yellow tape, several people are setting up lights and equipment, and I realize this situation is big news. Not only are we dealing with a barricaded gunman and hostage situation, but the perpetrator is Amish. That makes for sensational airtime no matter how you cut it.

The SWAT officer escorts me to the door of the mobile command center and opens it. Yellow light floods out, blinding me.

"I've got Burkholder," he calls out.

"Kate!" comes a familiar male voice from behind me.

I swing around to see John Tomasetti and Holmes County Sheriff Mike Rasmussen jogging toward me. I see the sharp edge of concern on Tomasetti's face. Rasmussen looks just as grim. They're running now. Rasmussen is usually pretty laid-back; tonight his face is slicked with sweat, his eyes jumping. But it's Tomasetti I can't look away from. As he closes the distance between us, I descend the steps, and the rest of the world falls away.

"Are you all right?" Urgency burns through the restraint I hear in his voice. For an instant I think he's going to break our self-imposed rule of conduct and embrace me. Or maybe tear into me for getting myself ambushed in the woods. Instead, he runs his hands over my arms, taking my hands and squeezing them briefly before releasing me.

"I'm okay." I look from Tomasetti to Rasmussen and back to Tomasetti. "I'm fine."

"What happened?" Rasmussen asks. "We got a

136

call from dispatch. Got worried as hell when we found that stolen vehicle and no one could get you on the horn."

Sighing, I tell them about being accosted by King. "He took my radio. My phone. He's got my sidearm."

"Shit," the sheriff mutters.

"Kids okay?" Tomasetti asks.

Silently cursing Joseph, I nod. "They're fine. They have the run of the place. In bed for the night. I don't think they understand exactly what's going on." I pause. "Rebecca and Daniel Beachy are all right?"

"They walked out about the same time you went in," Tomasetti replies.

"SWAT's on scene," Rasmussen says. "I've got three deputies on perimeter, but we're stretched thin."

"Incident commander is Jason Ryan with BCI." Tomasetti motions toward the RV. "He wants to talk to you."

I'm still trying to get my feet under me, put everything that happened into some kind of perspective that doesn't have to do with a troubled Amish boy or the misplaced loyalty of the girl I'd once been. This is a hostage and barricaded gunman situation. The lives of five children are at stake. I can't let my past relationship with Joseph King affect my judgment or decision making.

"Chief Burkholder."

I turn to see a large, grim-faced man standing in the doorway of the command center. He's wearing dark, creased slacks with tactical boots. A white shirt and tie peek out from the front of a navy blue windbreaker embellished with the BCI logo.

I cast a look at Tomasetti. His eyes are already on me. I'd wanted to spend a few minutes with him, but the opportunity is gone. The man is already coming down the steps.

"Jason Ryan. BCI." He extends his hand to me and we shake. His grip is too firm. Two quick pumps and release. Dry palm. "Are you all right?" he asks. "Anyone hurt in there?"

"I'm fine," I tell him. "Everyone inside is fine."

"Good. Good." But I can tell he's in a hurry to get down to business; he wants the lowdown on Joseph King. "I'd like to debrief you inside if you have a few minutes."

The "if you have a few minutes" was thrown in only as polite-sounding window dressing. I don't have a choice in the matter. I suspect Ryan is the kind of guy who will be your best friend when he wants something. If you've screwed up, he'll be the first one to cut you loose.

I know what's coming next. They need intelligence. They want to know King's frame of mind. What he's thinking. What his demands are. What's going on inside the house. The level of danger for the hostages. How I walked into it. A thousand questions from a dozen sources crammed into a small period of time.

"Of course," I tell him.

He motions toward the stairs. "Watch your step. We've got coffee if you want it."

Tomasetti follows us inside.

The trailer is cramped and smells of pressed wood, new carpet, and coffee, all of it laced with an odd blend of aftershave, sweat, and hot electronics. To my right is the control room chock-full of high-tech gadgetry. Left is a good-size table surrounded by six chairs, a tiny kitchen with a sink and coffeemaker. Beyond, I can just make out the lighted dash of the cab.

I'm aware of Tomasetti touching my arm as I take one of the chairs. Sheriff Rasmussen sits next to me. Tomasetti and Ryan sit across the table.

The door swings open. The vehicle rocks slightly as a fourth man enters. Short and trim in stature, hostage negotiator Curtis Scanlon is neatly dressed in blue jeans, button-down shirt, and tie beneath a BCI windbreaker. A headset with a mouthpiece is clamped over his head. Expensive haircut. Precision goatee. No sidearm. I guess him to be in his mid-forties.

He crosses to the table and sticks out his hand. "Curtis Scanlon." He says his name as if he likes hearing it. His eyes are on me, so I reach out and we shake. "Glad you're here and in one piece, Chief. We need to get a read on this guy."

Curtis Scanlon is a legend among law enforcement. He's a talented negotiator with a solid reputation and instincts that seemingly never steer him wrong. He's got a track record of successfully talking down even the most unstable and violent hostage takers. Two years ago, he worked a case in which laid-off factory worker Raymond Lipscomb took his girlfriend and her newborn twins hostage in a Cleveland apartment building. Lipscomb was suicidal and threatened to "take his family to hell with him." Scanlon spent forty-two hours on the phone with him with no breaks and no sleep. He engaged Lipscomb, discovered little things that made him tick. They talked about fishing. They talked boats. Outboard motors. They argued lures versus live bait. Scanlon had some fresh fish sent in from a local restaurant—he delivered it himself. In the end, Lipscomb surrendered without further incident.

Scanlon is undeniably one of the best negotiators in the Midwest, perhaps even the nation. From what I've heard, his larger-than-life reputation is dwarfed only by the size of his ego.

Introductions are made. Too much urgency for niceties. The negotiator pulls up a chair and straddles it, facing us. "You left your phone inside?" he asks.

I nod. "I told him to talk to you."

We're interrupted when the door swings open. I glance over to see a tall, heavyset man wearing a Geauga County Sheriff's Department jacket enter. I've met Jeff Crowder several times since I've been chief. He's in his late fifties with a thick head of blond hair and the physique of a linebacker.

His bloodshot eyes sweep the room. He doesn't bother with introductions. "What's the situation?"

"We just started the debriefing." Ryan pulls out a chair. "Have a seat. We're going to want your take on this guy."

Crowder crosses the room, pulls out a chair, and lowers himself into it with an exhale.

Ryan turns his attention back to me. "King's armed?"

"He's got my sidearm," I tell him, trying not to wince. "A thirty-eight. City issue. I believe there's a long gun in the house, too."

Rasmussen shifts uncomfortably. Tomasetti looks away. Having your weapon commandeered by a previously unarmed suspect is the consummate rookie mistake. In the eyes of my counterparts, and regardless of the circumstances, indefensible.

Crowder makes a sound of thinly veiled disgust.

Ignoring all of it, I tell them about discovering

the stolen vehicle. "I'd just called for backup when he ambushed me."

Ryan snags a legal pad from a shelf behind him and pulls a pen from his breast pocket. He drops both onto the table between us. "Did King say what he wants? Did he make any demands?"

I recap the highlights of everything that was said, including the fact that I'd known him when we were kids. "King is claiming he didn't murder his wife," I tell him.

"Yeah and Jack the Ripper didn't gut eleven women," Crowder mutters.

"He wants someone to look into his case," I say. "Give the evidence a second look."

Ryan scrubs a hand over his jaw. "Of course he does."

"What's his frame of mind?" Scanlon asks.

"He's on edge. Nervous. But not out of control," I reply.

"Suicidal?" the negotiator asks.

I shake my head. "He said nothing to indicate he wanted to hurt himself. Or anyone else for that matter. He did, however, state he wasn't going back to prison."

Ryan and Scanlon exchange looks.

"That doesn't sound good," Crowder mutters. Mr. Helpful.

"Tell me about the hostages," Ryan says.

I give him the names and ages of the children and he jots them on the notepad.

"Where are the children?" Ryan asks.

"Upstairs," I reply. "They'd just gone to bed a few minutes before I left."

"They have the run of the house?"

"Yes."

Ryan snatches up his phone, thumbs a button, and speaks to someone on the other end. "See if you can find blueprints of that house. I know it's old. Just do it." He pockets the phone and turns his attention back to me.

"One more time, Chief Burkholder," Ryan says. "Take us through everything that happened from the get-go."

I start at the beginning and run through it to the end, recalling the conversations to the best of my memory. When he asks, I offer my impressions. Mostly, I stick to the facts. "I asked King multiple times to release the children, but he refused."

"Are the children afraid of him?" Scanlon asks.

I shake my head. "Not at all. In fact, they seem quite content to have him in the house. King has fed them. Put them to bed. After seeing the way he interacted with them—and the way they responded—I don't believe he means to harm them. I don't believe they're in imminent danger." I shrug. "They seem more worried about all the police activity."

"Well, that's cozy as hell," Crowder says.

Ryan jots something on the pad of paper. "He

get any extra ammo with that thirty-eight?"

"Just what's in the cylinder."

A pause ensues. Everyone absorbing the information, trying to come up with a strategy.

"You grew up with King," Scanlon says.

"His family lived next door to our farm for about six years," I reply.

As I speak, I sense Tomasetti watching me intently from across the table. He's been unusually reticent. I'm not sure if it's the result of his earlier worry about me, or because he doesn't like seeing me on the hot seat.

Ryan looks at Scanlon. "Any way we can use that to our advantage?"

Scanlon nods. "Might be helpful to keep Chief Burkholder around as a resource in case we run out of ideas on this thing."

"I'll help any way I can," I tell them. "But honestly, I tried appealing to him while I was inside and he wasn't receptive."

Ryan glances at his watch. "Anything else, Chief Burkholder?"

I tell them about the little Amish girl's assertion that there was a man with a long gun in the house the night Naomi King was killed.

"Now we got the one-armed man," Crowder grumbles.

I take them through the girl's account, leaving nothing out. Ryan scribbles onto a pad. Scanlon types into a tablet. All the while I'm aware of dispassionate eyes on me, and I know the information is falling on deaf ears.

"Let me get this straight." Crowder crosses his arms over his barrel chest and leans back in his chair. "So that fucking King marches a five-year-old into the room, puts her in front of you, and has her tell you that she witnessed the murder?"

"She didn't witness the murder," I tell him. "She claims she saw a man with a rifle in the house that night."

"You're aware the murder was over two years ago," Crowder states. "She was only three years old at the time."

"I did the math," I tell him.

"He coached her," Crowder says.

"It has been my experience that a witness that age is unreliable." Ryan looks from Scanlon to Crowder. "Jeff, were those kids interviewed by Children Services?"

"The sheriff's department talked to all of them. So did social workers from Children Services," Crowder replies. "I do recall one of them mentioning a man with a gun, but the kid was too young and the psychologist deemed her unreliable."

"What's your take, Chief Burkholder?" Tomasetti asks. "Did the girl seem credible?"

Leave it to Tomasetti to prod the elephant in the room.

"She's five years old now," I tell them. "She

relayed the story without input from King. I'm no expert, but if King coached her, he did a good job. She seemed credible. Confident. She gave details that would have been difficult for a five-year-old to fabricate."

"Details like what?" Crowder asks.

"For one thing she said the intruder was clean-shaven. Her father, being a married Amish man, had a full beard at the time of his arrest. She also said the intruder wasn't dressed in Amish clothes."

"Doesn't seem too complicated," says Crowder.

"She also said the man pointed the long gun at her," I say. "She claimed to have heard a 'click,' as if he'd pulled the trigger but for whatever reason the rifle didn't fire. If King had coached her, why would he ask her to say something like that? It doesn't make sense."

The men fall silent. Rasmussen and Tomasetti are looking down at their notes. Crowder, Ryan, and Scanlon are staring at me as if trying to decide if I've sided with the enemy.

"What are you saying exactly?" Ryan asks.

I meet his gaze head-on. "I'm telling you what was said."

"We had a shitload of evidence against that son of a bitch," Crowder says. "We're talking fingerprints. Blood. Gunshot residue. His fishing story was full of holes."

Ryan intervenes. "The children will certainly be interviewed again when this is over." He looks around the table. "We're not going to retry King tonight so let's deal with the crisis at hand. We need to get those hostages out of there unharmed and get King to lay down his weapons and turn himself in."

Rasmussen addresses Ryan. "Did you talk to the warden at Mansfield?"

Ryan nods. "They know how he got out, but they're still trying to figure out if he had help." He turns his attention to me. "Did King mention anything about the escape? Did he have help? Was it was planned? Or did he take advantage of an opportunity?"

"He didn't mention the escape at all," I tell them.

"Considering you used to know King, do you think it's possible he targeted you in some way?" Ryan asks.

"There's no way he could have known I'd be in those woods," I say.

"Did he know you're a cop now and living in Painters Mill?"

"He mentioned he had read about it."

The beat of silence that follows sends a string of tension through me. I try to quiet the unsettled little voice whispering things I don't want to hear, but I know how cops think. They're a suspicious lot, me included, and I know I'm just a step or two away from being accused of sleeping with the enemy.

"Any idea why he released you?" Scanlon asks. "I mean, you're a cop. Seems like you'd be a high-value hostage."

In unison, Ryan and Tomasetti lean in.

"I think he released me because he wants me to look into his case."

"So you agreed to look into it?" Crowder asks.

"I explained to him it's out of my jurisdiction, but I'd see what I could do."

"Good answer." Scanlon looks around the table. "If worse comes to worse, we can use it, dangle that carrot."

"Let's take advantage of any leverage we can get." Ryan turns his attention back to me. "Did he at any point threaten you?"

"He pointed the gun at me. I took that as a threat."

"Did he threaten the hostages?" Scanlon asks.

"No."

"Did he physically assault you or anyone else inside the house?" Ryan asks.

"Just when he jumped me in the woods. Even then, I don't believe his intent was to cause bodily harm. He wasn't unduly violent. No punching or hitting. It was more like he just wanted to overpower me, gain access to my weapon, and get me inside the house."

Crowder sneers. "That's when he got your

weapon? When he jumped you in the woods?"

"Correct."

"You'd called for backup at that point, though, right?" he asks.

I give the sheriff a pointed look. "I was on the phone with my dispatcher when he came at me, tackled me to the ground."

"You'd been notified there was an escapee in the area, hadn't you?" Crowder says.

"I'd received a notification call from ODRC, but I didn't believe King would show up in Painters Mill."

Crowder shakes his head with flourish. The sentiment behind it isn't lost on me—or anyone else. "With the Amish being so . . . family-oriented, I assumed you'd realize there was a high probability he'd return to them."

Another jab aimed at me. I don't jab back. No one knows more clearly than me that I screwed up. "He's from Geauga County," I point out. "Not Painters Mill. I didn't expect him to come into a community in which he isn't a member of the church district. That's not to mention he's estranged from his family. The Amish here in Painters Mill want nothing to do with him."

"Evidently ODRC thought the threat of him turning up here was great enough to put you on the notify list," the sheriff shoots back. "I mean, the guy's *kids* are here. That's a big deal."

I stare at him, fingers of anger poking me,

irritating me, goading me to poke back. But I know it would be counterproductive. Crowder may be an asshole, but I'm the one who got myself ambushed and my sidearm taken. So I suck it up and keep my mouth shut.

"Maybe you should have taken that call from ODRC a little more seriously." Crowder skewers me with a nasty look before adding the coup de grâce. "I hear that happens a lot with you."

I stare back at him. My heart is pounding. My hands are beginning to shake. But I give him nothing. "If you have something to say, maybe you ought to just say it."

He takes me up on it. "You knew there was an escaped felon in the area, and yet you were out in the woods, in the middle of the night, alone, and without backup. As a result of your poor judgment, he disarmed you, took five minor children hostage. He keeps the kids, but *you* get sent on your merry way. Now, not only do we have to deal with a hostage situation, but a crazy shit who's armed with *your* service revolver."

It's a cheap shot, but I don't defend myself. As angry as I am about being raked over the coals in the presence of my peers, the bottom line is he's right.

"King had actually taken those hostages before ambushing Chief Burkholder," Tomasetti points out.

Ryan intervenes. "I believe she's well aware of the situation at hand, Jeff."

"In case you're not reading between the lines, Sheriff," Tomasetti adds, "that means keep your extraneous commentary to yourself."

I risk a glance at Tomasetti. Outwardly, he appears calm and in control. But I know him too well. He's one more word away from launching an all-out assault on Crowder.

Crowder isn't deterred. "Don't tell me to keep my commentary to myself. I know what this motherfucker is capable of. I saw what he did to his wife." He glares at me. "I saw Naomi King lying in her bed with her goddamn chest laid open and her intestines all over the sheets. I saw all them poor kids with blood all over their hands." He looks at Ryan. "Joseph King is a dangerous son of a bitch and every single one of us would be wise not to forget it."

CHAPTER 9

The words are damning—worse than damning—especially coming from the sheriff of the county in which the murder happened. Not for the first time I wonder if I'm wrong about Joseph. If I'm looking for something that doesn't exist. That he murdered his wife in cold blood, he coached his little girl to lie for him, and I'm a fool for entertaining any possibility other than the one that's been established by solid police work, a copious amount of evidence, and an impartial jury.

No one speaks. No one looks at me. Except Crowder. He's staring at me; his face is red, the capillaries in his nose and cheeks standing out like ink on leather, his lips drawn tight over clenched teeth.

"That's enough, Crowder." Tomasetti's voice is like steel.

The two men stare at each other for the span of several heartbeats. Finally, Crowder rises. "Excuse me," he says, and strides to the coffeemaker.

I feel my credibility slipping away. These men are losing faith in me, in my competence as a cop. In their eyes I've become something I detest. A novelty because I'm female. A figurehead because I'm formerly Amish in a town where that matters. I'm not sure how it happened so quickly, but I know that no matter what I say from this point forward, it will be met with skepticism.

Ryan moves to break the tension. "For now we need to figure out how to best deal with King and get those kids out of there."

Scanlon looks at his watch and addresses Ryan. "I need to get a dialogue started with this guy. See if I can get a read on him. That'll help us get some kind of strategy in place."

Ryan glances my way. "I'm assuming there's no electricity in the house."

I nod. "He's got lanterns."

Crowder returns to the table, a cup of coffee in hand. "Can't even cut off the fucking electricity," he grumbles.

"Does he have family in the area?" Scanlon poses the question to Crowder. "Parents? Grandparents? Close relatives can be helpful in terms of negotiation."

"Seems like all of those Amish are related somehow," the sheriff says. "We got four or five families with the same last name in the area. I'll put one of my deputies on it, see what he can find out."

I look at Ryan. "Joseph King has two brothers, Jonas and Edward. His parents are dead." I look at Crowder. "Are either of them still in the area?"

"There's an Edward King lives out to

Huntsburg Township. Everyone calls him Stink Ed. Raises turkeys and the place smells to high heaven." He looks around the table, his eyes skipping over me as if I'm not there. "Problem is Stink Ed's one of them Amish that don't like dealing with the rest of us."

He realizes quickly the words were a mistake. Before he can rephrase, Tomasetti jumps on it. "Chief Burkholder used to know the family. She knows the Amish culture, the language." He looks at me, his expression deadpan. "Maybe you ought to run up there and see if either brother is willing to help."

"We've got a good relationship with the Amish," Crowder says. "I'd rather send one of my guys."

"I'm betting Chief Burkholder would be plenty effective," Tomasetti maintains.

"I figure she'd be even more effective if she called it a day," Crowder says.

Ryan groans. "Come on, people. Cut the crap. We need to take advantage of all our resources here." He looks at me. "Go talk to Ed King and his brother." He frowns at Crowder. "I need you here."

Crowder holds his gaze, stone-faced, saying nothing.

"Any idea where his other brother, Jonas, lives?" I ask Crowder.

Crowder doesn't even look at me. "No idea."

Ryan calls me over to where he's sitting. "We're probably not going to get blueprints on that old house. Can you give me a rough idea of the layout? Kids' bedrooms? Is there a basement? It'll be helpful to know where the doors and windows are, and where the people are inside."

Spying a pad on the table, he slides it over to me.

I pick up the pen and draw a crude outline of the house. "The kitchen is on the west side," I tell them. "There's a window above the sink here. A door off the mudroom that probably leads to the basement. Stairs to the second level are between the kitchen and living room. No windows there. I'm pretty sure the bedrooms are upstairs. That's where the kids were when I left."

"Where's King?"

"He spent most of his time at the kitchen table." I indicate the general position.

I study the crude sketch, recalling a few outside details as I left. "There are cellar doors on the east side, here." I draw an arrow to the windows. "Living room windows face north. Front door is here and faces east."

"Lots of trees on the east side," Rasmussen says offhandedly.

Crowder sits up a little straighter. "We got SWAT on scene."

Scanlon slides his chair back and rises. "I'm going to make contact."

155

Ryan crosses to the counter and addresses Scanlon. "Phone's here. It's set to record." He indicates a button on a small electronic console. "Mute here. Speaker. I'll be on the line with you and the only person in the room who has a mike besides you."

"Got it," Scanlon says.

"You're mobile." Ryan clips a wire and small device onto Scanlon's jacket and they take a moment to test the sound.

Ryan glances at me over his shoulder. "We're going to need a written statement at some point, Chief," he says to me, and then offers the remaining headset to Tomasetti.

"I'll get on it right away." I'm keenly aware that Ryan has dismissed me; my counterparts are largely ignoring me.

Crowder rises from his place at the table without looking at me and goes to the coffee station for another refill.

Rasmussen gives me a reassuring smile that isn't all that reassuring. "You did good, Kate."

I return the smile, but it feels stiff and unnatural.

Scanlon adjusts his mike, and—for God's sake—fluffs his hair. A radio personality an instant before airtime. "Test. Test. Test," he says in his radio announcer's voice.

"We're good to go." Ryan pulls on his headset.

"Let's roll." Scanlon makes the call.

• • •

The trailer falls silent. Even the rumble of the diesel engine, the swarm of law enforcement outside, and the intermittent crackle of police radios fade to background noise. I can practically hear the thrum of blood through veins, the zing of anticipation.

Crowder has taken up residence in a chair a few feet away and turned his back to me. Tomasetti stands next to the console, headset on. I can tell by the way his eyes skitter away from mine that he doesn't like what's going on. Of course, there's nothing he can do about it. Ryan and Rasmussen are fiddling with the console, talking in low tones. Scanlon hovers over an iPad, reading and making notes. Gearing up for contact.

The phone trills over the speakers, seeming inordinately loud in the confines of the trailer. One ring and King's voice comes over the line.

"Hello?"

"Mr. King?" Scanlon identifies himself, giving his full name and title. "It's me again." His voice is amicable, but firm. The kind of voice that seems to shout: I care about you. Talk to me. I'm your friend. I'm here to help. Let's do this together. "Are you all right in there?"

"I'm fine."

"How about the kids?"

"They are fine, too."

"Thank you for keeping them safe. And I want to thank you for releasing Chief Burkholder. We appreciate that."

King says nothing.

Scanlon says quickly. "Do you go by Joseph?"

"That's fine."

"Joseph, I want to talk to you tonight so you and I can work through this. I'm here to help you so we can get everyone out of there safe and sound, including you. Do you understand?"

"I didn't kill my wife," King tells him.

Scanlon shoots me a look. "Chief Burkholder relayed that information to us. Of course, we're going to look into it. All of us out here are very concerned."

"She said she'd look into my case," the Amish man tells him.

"This would be a lot easier if you came out here and talked to me in person, instead of over the phone."

King laughs, but the sound is fraught with tension. "I'm not going back to prison."

"I understand. For now we just want to talk to you so we can get things straightened out. Okay?"

No response.

"I know you may not believe this considering the circumstances, but we all want the same thing here. The truth. It's probably going to take some time."

The statement is met with silence.

"Joseph, while I have you on the line: Do you need anything? Do the kids need anything? Food?" Scanlon scribbles something on the iPad and lifts it to me with a question. *What else?*

I say quietly, "Flashlights. Candles. Lanterns. Phone battery."

Scanlon repeats all of it. "How's the phone battery? We don't want to lose communication with you."

"All I need is the truth. You're wasting time with all this talking."

"Fair enough," Scanlon says easily. He's found his stride now and is heading toward the zone. "I do need just one thing from you, Joseph. All I ask is that you keep me on the line. Stay with me. Talk to me. Will you do that?"

"You need to look at my case. I didn't kill my wife."

"Like I said, we're working on that now. Not all of us are familiar with your case, so it's going to take a little while."

"Katie Burkholder knows about the case. She knows the truth. She will tell you."

At the use of my first name, Crowder gives me a consorting-with-the-enemy sneer.

"Chief Burkholder told us everything you discussed with her, Joseph. Like I said, we're working on getting our hands on your case file now."

"My daughter saw the man who came into the house that night. No one believed her."

"We know that, Mr. King. That interview with Sadie is one of the things we're trying to get our hands on. She's your youngest, right?"

"Yes."

Scanlon hesitates, seems to take a moment to gather himself. "Listen, Joseph, since she's so young—and more importantly, since she might have information that could help your case—why don't you send Sadie out here to talk to us? We'll get the Children Services folks out here to talk to her right away."

"Katie already talked to her," the Amish man replies.

"I understand," the negotiator says patiently. "Will you work with me on this? Man-to-man? Meet me halfway? Send Sadie out here in good faith. I promise I'll take good care of her. I'll listen—"

The line goes dead. Scanlon hits END and sighs. "That went better than I expected."

"If that was good, I'd hate to bear witness to a bad one," Crowder mutters.

Ryan goes to the console on the counter and makes an adjustment. "You think he's stable?"

"I do, actually," Scanlon tells him. "For now."

"Hostages safe for now?" Tomasetti asks.

Scanlon nods. "I think so. From what I'm gathering it's all about the kids for him. Not as hostages, but because he wants them there with him. Even though he turned down my first request, it's still early in the game."

"At least he hasn't shot anybody yet," Crowder says.

"This is going to be a long process." The negotiator shrugs. "He's comfortable. He's got food, water, and shelter."

I catch Scanlon's eye. "Since King is Amish, do you think it would be beneficial to appeal to some of his religious sensibilities or Amish tenets?"

Tomasetti nods. "Might be an angle worth consideration."

"The more tools we have in our arsenal the better," Rasmussen puts in.

Crowder makes a sound of incredulity. "How religious can a man be who cuts his wife in half with a fucking shotgun?"

Ryan shoots him a warning look. "What do you have in mind, Chief Burkholder?"

"Maybe bring in the bishop or one of the preachers of his church district. They're influential members of the Amish community and they might be able to help talk him into giving himself up or at least releasing the children."

"This guy is no more Amish than I am," Crowder says. "He has no moral compass." He motions in the general direction of the Beachy farmhouse. "If we play nice with this guy he's going to snap and massacre everyone in that house."

Ryan doesn't defend me. Rasmussen looks down at his boots. Tomasetti makes eye contact with Scanlon. "What do you think?"

The negotiator grimaces. "One thing we don't want to do is make King feel as if he's taken things too far and there's no going back. We do not want to back this guy into a corner. If he feels all is lost, that he has no recourse, he might do something rash."

"Like what?" Tomasetti asks.

"If he feels there's no way out of the hole he's dug for himself and he's facing life in prison, he might consider suicide a better option. Worst-case scenario, he takes the hostages with him."

"Look," I say, "I knew King once. I was in there with him. I do not believe he's a threat to himself or those kids."

The silence that follows lingers a beat too long. Ryan shoots Scanlon a direct look. "What do you think?"

"Let's give this some time," the negotiator responds. "Let's not push him yet. Maybe get a family member in here and see how he reacts."

I glance at Tomasetti, find his eyes already on mine. A silent communication passes between us. *You've done all you can. Let it go.*

I know he's right. The last thing I want to do is

leave. But there's a distinct chill in the air here inside the command center. Not only have I become ineffectual, but I've worn out my welcome. Might be more productive to talk to Joseph's brothers and see if they'll help us out.

The command center door opens. I glance over to see a man dressed in full SWAT gear enter. About thirty years of age, he's tall and fit with a cocky countenance that's tempered by an air of military discipline. He's wearing Kevlar, and military-style boots, and carrying a rifle case. Eyes the color of a deep lake beneath a brooding sky sweep the room, landing on Crowder.

"Unit is on scene," he says.

Quickly, Crowder makes introductions. "This is Deputy Wade Travers, team leader of our SWAT unit." He says the words like some kind of proud papa.

The men shake hands. When it's my turn, Travers looks at me as if he's met me before. "Kate Burkholder." He recites my name slowly and thoughtfully, as if searching his memory. "You're the ex-Amish chief."

"Guilty as charged," I tell him.

"I've heard a lot about you."

"I categorically deny all of it."

He grins, showing a mouth full of perfect white teeth. His grip is firm. Not a knuckle squeezer. I try not to ponder the "heard a lot about you" comment.

Travers clears his throat, addresses the group, but his eyes are on Ryan. "You want me to get a couple of guys in position?"

Ryan looks at Scanlon. "Curtis?"

"I don't expect things to go south this early in the game," the negotiator says. "But we've got to be prepared for any scenario, including worst-case."

Crowder looks at me, as if expecting me to voice some objection. I train my eyes on Wade Travers, and I keep my mouth shut.

"I did a quick recon," Travers says. "We've got a lot of trees. Low-light conditions. But there's a decent-size window in the front with a clear line of sight. Not so great at the rear."

"Good to know." Ryan nods at Scanlon. If King needs to be moved to a location where he will be in plain sight, it will be up to Scanlon to get him there.

I'm fully aware that in a situation like this in which lives are at stake, it's always better to be overprepared than to get caught in a last-minute scramble. Still, I don't believe Joseph King presents that level of danger. But there will be no convincing my peers.

Nodding, Travers takes a step back, and then turns and leaves the command center.

Suddenly, I need to get out of there. Away from colleagues who've made it clear they don't trust my judgment or my capabilities. Rising, I turn to Ryan. "I'll call you with a number as soon as I get a phone."

"Absolutely." He says the word with a tad too much enthusiasm, offers his hand a little too quickly. Glad to be rid of me. "Thank you for all your help, Chief Burkholder. I'll let you know if the situation changes. If we need you, I'll give you a call."

I nod at the other men, but no one makes eye contact with me.

I walk to the door and let myself out.

The Amish are fond of proverbs and wise sayings, especially if there's a lesson attached. When I was a kid, one of my *mamm*'s favorites went something like "Think ten times, talk once." It means to think before you speak, something I didn't put into practice until long after my *mamm* passed away. The last twenty-four hours have demonstrated that I'm still a work in progress.

I'll be the first to admit I screwed up. I didn't take the threat posed by King as seriously as I should have. I walked into an ambush, got my sidearm taken away. It happens; cops are human, and they make mistakes just like everyone else. If they're lucky, it doesn't cost them their lives— or someone else's.

The eastern sky is ablaze with color when I descend the steps. Standing outside the command center, I take a good look at the area. The road in front of the Beachy farm is a parking lot of law enforcement and emergency vehicles. I see sheriff's department cruisers from Richland, Holmes, and Geauga counties, a big SUV adorned with the BCI logo, a couple of ambulances, personal vehicles, even a fire truck from the Painters Mill volunteer fire department. Down the road, a second news van has arrived to join the first. Thankfully, a uniformed deputy has cordoned off the area to keep the media at bay.

"Chief!"

I turn to see Glock trotting toward me. "Mona told me what happened," he says upon reaching me. "You okay?"

"I'm fine." I offer a wry smile. "Pride's a little bruised."

"Been there, done that. We all have."

"I'm unduly grateful you said that."

"What happened?"

I recap the incident in the woods with King. "He ambushed me. Took my weapon. Not my finest moment."

"Hey, it happens." He glances toward the command center. "Did it go okay in there?"

"They pretty much cut me loose."

"Nothing worse than a bunch of asshole cops."

I laugh. "Look, I'm heading up to Huntsburg to talk to King's brothers. You want to come along?"

He grins. "Someone's got to keep you out of trouble."

"I gotta get my vehicle and swing by the station to pick up a phone, a lapel mike, and my spare sidearm."

"Roger that."

Glock follows me to the station in his cruiser and parks while I go inside. I unlock the bottom drawer of my desk and pull out the old .38 that had been issued to the chief before me. By the time I make it back out to reception, Mona is off the phone and Lois has taken over.

"Hey, Chief."

"Didn't you get off an hour ago?" I ask.

"Phones are ringing off the hook with this King thing going on so I thought I'd stick around and lend a hand."

"I appreciate that. But you and Lois have to cut out the overtime."

"Sure, Chief."

I sigh, knowing she has no intention of complying with my wish. "I can pay a couple hours' OT, but no more." I'm not sure where I'll come up with the budget, but I will.

"Whatcha need?"

One of many reasons I've come to love Mona. "Run Edward King through LEADS and check for outstanding warrants." LEADS is the acronym for the Law Enforcement Automated Data System. "Get me his address. See if he has a phone."

"I'm on it."

"While you're at it do the same for Jonas King. They're Joseph King's brothers."

"Got it."

I'm nearly to the door. "Oh, and I need you to contact Records at the Geauga County Sheriff's Department and get the CCH on Joseph King." "CCH" is copspeak for "criminal case history." "Tell the clerk I need everything, including all accompanying documentation."

"When do you need it?"

"Is yesterday too soon?"

"Hopping into my time machine now."

Huntsburg Township is about two hours northeast of Painters Mill. During the drive, I fill Glock in on some of the details and tell him about King's little girl and her assertion that there was an armed stranger in the house the night her mother was murdered.

"It's problematic on so many levels I don't even know where to start," I tell him. "The murder was two years ago, which means the kid was only three years old at the time."

"That's pretty young," he says. "Kids that age still believe in the Easter bunny and tooth fairy."

"That puts things into perspective."

"But, Chief, that's not to say it isn't possible for a three-year-old to understand the concept of an intruder. I don't think it's out of the realm of possibility for her to remember the event as a five-year-old. My youngest is four and I'm telling you that kid remembers every single Christmas present Santa brought her the last two years right down to the color of her Barbie's dresses."

I look at him, trying to discern if he's attempting to make me feel better. Then again, backchat isn't his style. "I don't know anything about kids. But this little girl . . . Glock, she seemed utterly certain of what she'd seen. She went into details that would have been difficult to fabricate."

"You may not know kids, Chief, but you have good instincts when it comes to people. I say trust your gut."

I feel him looking at me, so I glance away from my driving. "What?"

"You think there's something to it or we wouldn't be talking about it."

"It's a little more complicated than that."

"Always is."

Frustrated, I sigh. "King is no model citizen. He's got a history of violence. A rap sheet for drugs and domestic violence. I'll be the first to tell you he fits the profile of a man capable of murdering his wife."

He considers that a moment. "Maybe all of that's true, but you still think there's something to what that little girl said."

"I could be way off base."

"But that's why we're on our way to Huntsburg Township."

"Exactly."

CHAPTER 10

It's nearly ten A.M. by the time Glock and I reach Huntsburg Township. Up until now, I'd been running on adrenaline, but two hours in the car served as a keen reminder that I've been up all night. I swing by a McDonald's in Middlefield for coffees and two breakfast biscuits to go, and then we're back on the road.

Edward King, aka "Stink Ed," lives on a dirt track off Burton-Windsor Road in the southern part of the township. It's a predominantly Amish area, with few telephone poles or power lines. We pass two buggies and a group of women selling bread and pies at a roadside stand before reaching the King residence. The lane is long, with more dirt than gravel, and bracketed on either side by two low-slung poultry barns. I park the Explorer at the side of the house. The stench of manure offends my olfactory nerves as we take the buckled, narrow sidewalk to the front porch.

Glock lingers on the steps while I cross the porch and go to the front door. Standing slightly to one side, I deliver a hard knock. A dog begins to bark somewhere in the house. Judging from the pitch, a small one, and I remind myself it's usually those cuddly little stuffed-animal look-alikes that bite.

I'm about to knock a second time when the knob rattles and the door creaks open. I recognize Edward King immediately. He's an older version of his brother. Same eyes and facial structure, but without the troubled eyes. He's wearing a blue work shirt. Dark trousers with suspenders. Straw flat-brimmed hat. No facial hair, which tells me he's not married.

He blinks at me, his eyes widening as recognition kicks in. "Katie *Burkholder?*"

"Hi, Edward." He's staring at my uniform with a shocked expression, so I add, "This is an official call."

"You're a *policeman?*"

"Yes."

His eyes flick to Glock and then back to me. "What's going on?"

I have my badge ready and show it to him. "I'm chief of police in Painters Mill now. I need to talk to you about your brother," I say over the barking of the dog.

"My brother?" He shushes a small, wire-haired pooch, nudges it aside with a booted foot. "Joseph?"

"Yes."

"Is he dead?"

"No, but he's in trouble," I reply. "Can we come inside and talk for a few minutes?"

He leads us through a living room jammed with what looks like handcrafted furniture. I feel the dog sniffing the backs of my ankles as we enter a small, cluttered kitchen. Edward ushers me into a ladder-back chair and pulls out the one across from me. Glock chooses to stand at the door.

"What happened to Joe?" he asks, settling into the chair.

Remembering Crowder's assertion that Edward is reluctant to speak with non-Amish, I switch to *Deitsch* and give him the condensed version. "He's barricaded himself in the house with all five children. He's armed with a rifle and a handgun."

"A *handgun?*" The Amish use rifles for hunting, but they generally have no use for a handgun. I don't tell him the gun is mine.

Edward looks down at where his hands twist on the table in front of him. "*Er is ganz ab.*" He's quite out of his mind.

"It's an extremely dangerous situation," I tell him. "As you can imagine, I'm concerned about the kids. Joseph, too. I don't want to see him hurt."

"I haven't seen or spoken to him since the trial," he tells me.

"Did you have a falling-out? I mean, after the trial?"

"Joseph has changed a lot since you knew him."

"In what way?"

"You remember how it was when we were young." His smile is a sad twisting of his mouth. "Back then he was all fun and games. Happy-go-lucky. A prankster. But, Katie, after Datt died . . ." He shrugs. "Joe changed. It wasn't for the better."

"How so?"

"It was as if the devil came up from hell and climbed into his head. During *Rumspringa*, Joe went heavy on the drinking. Started smoking cigarettes. Dope, too, I think. He stopped attending worship. Had a lot of girlfriends, most were not Amish. He'd disappear for days. Mamm worried herself to an early grave. Then he met Naomi."

For the first time, his smile is genuine. "She was the light to his darkness. And she had such a pretty face. A smile that could light up a room. A kind soul, but she was strong inside, too." He hefts a laugh. "Joe didn't stand a chance. He fell hard for her. She whipped him into shape in a matter of weeks. He forgot all about those other women. The alcohol. He changed and this time it was for the better." He grimaces, shakes his head. "They married shortly after they met. The babies came pretty quick. I thought they were happy."

I'm aware of Glock standing in the doorway, watching us. The dog sniffing my feet. The clock on the counter ticking like a metronome.

"But you know how the Amish are." His smile is knowing and sad.

I nod. "If there are problems in the marriage, we don't speak of them."

"Oftentimes to our own detriment."

"Did they fight?"

"Not at first, but later . . . I think so."

"What about the domestic-violence charges against Joseph?" I ask.

"I never would have believed Joe would hurt Naomi. I figured it was some kind of mistake. I thought the police had overreacted or somehow misunderstood. But now . . ."

"Did you attend the trial?"

"Every day." Grimacing, he lowers his head and shakes it. "Every word was like the fall of an ax. I couldn't believe the things I was hearing. About my own *brother.*"

"Was Joseph close to the children?" I ask.

"He doted on them." A sad smile curves one side of his mouth. "We used to make fun of him because it was such a turnaround for him. He'd been irresponsible for so long. By the time the babies arrived, he was a different man. A *good* man. For a while, anyway. At some point, things just sort of fell apart for them. Joe went back to his old ways."

"Edward, do you think Joseph murdered Naomi?" I ask.

Raw pain flashes in his eyes. "At first? Never.

But during the trial . . . the things I heard."
Grimacing, he shakes his head, looks down at
the tabletop. "*Gottlos.*" Ungodly.

"Did he ever mention Sadie seeing an intruder
in the house the night Naomi was killed?"

"I might've heard something about it."

"What did you think?"

"I think my brother is a liar. I think he told that
little child to say what she did."

I deflect a wave of disappointment, forge
ahead. "Edward, do you think you could help us
convince Joseph to give himself up?"

He raises his gaze to mine. "How would I do
that?"

"Come back to Painters Mill with me. Talk to
him. On the phone."

"Katie, after everything that's happened.
Everything he's done." He looks away, shakes
his head. "I've washed my hands of him."

"Edward, he's your brother."

"He's no brother of mine. Not anymore. I prefer
not to speak with him."

I try another tactic. "If you won't do it for your
brother's sake, will you do it for your nieces and
nephews?"

He stares at me, his eyes filling with tears. "No."

I nod, trying not to be irritated with him. "Do
you think Jonas would help?"

"Jonas was one of the few Amish who didn't
lose faith in Joe. Even after . . . Naomi."

"Do you have an address for him?"

"He lives over to Rootstown now. He's more English than Amish these days. Runs one of them Amish tourist shops with his buddy." He rattles off an address. "Big house off Tallmadge. Can't miss it."

I rise and start toward the door. I'm aware of Edward rising and trailing us. Upon reaching the door, I stop and turn. "Is there a way for me to contact you, Edward? Does the bishop have a phone? In case the situation with Joseph changes?"

He instantly translates the meaning of the question. *In case Joseph is killed.* "If it's about my brother, I'd prefer you didn't contact me at all."

"For a religious guy, he was pretty hard on his brother," Glock says as we slide into the Explorer.

"When you're Amish it's sometimes the people you love most you're toughest on."

"Tough love."

"It's brought more than one wayward soul back to the fold."

It's nearly noon by the time we pass the corporation-limit sign for Rootstown Township. Mona ran Jonas King through LEADS to check for outstanding warrants. Little Brother has kept his nose clean.

King's residence is located off Tallmadge in the heart of the township. A large sign dominates the manicured front yard: AMISH COUNTRY GENERAL STORE AND ANTIQUES. The house is a massive Victorian set among towering trees. It's the kind of neighborhood that was once residential, but is slowly transitioning to commercial, prompting some homeowners to sell out or transform their residences into businesses. That's exactly what King has done, and in high style.

"Nice digs," Glock comments as I park in the small rear lot. "I think LaShonda bought a baby quilt here right before Jasmine was born. Lasted through both kids and still looks brand-new."

"Nice to pass down an heirloom like that when they grow up." We disembark and take the sidewalk to the front door.

"Yeah, well, we're going to be needing it again in about six months."

I stop and swing around to face him. The grin feels silly on my face. "Seriously?"

He grins back. "Number three."

"Congratulations." I smack him on the shoulder. "You can look at the baby stuff while I talk to King."

"Thanks, Chief."

We ascend concrete steps to a large wooden deck that's part porch, part café. Two tables with umbrellas are on my right. A large sago palm juts from an equally large terra-cotta pot engraved with an interesting design. To my left is a fountain from which water trickles merrily over artfully arranged river rock.

The place hasn't yet opened for business, but the lights are on. I can see someone moving around inside. I cross to an antique-looking door and ring the bell. Glock stands a few feet away, checking out the pottery in the display window.

The door swings open, jingle bells chiming. "We're just opening—"

An attractive young man in a partially buttoned plaid shirt blinks at me. He wears a beard that's vaguely Amish, but a tad too manicured to be authentic. I don't recognize him, and I don't think this is Jonas King.

His eyes flick over my uniform. "Is everything all right?"

I have my ID at the ready. "I'm looking for Jonas King."

"Has something happened?"

"It's about his brother," I tell him.

"Oh shit. Joe." Looking concerned, he opens the door wider. "Jonas!" he calls out while simultaneously ushering Glock and me inside. "Come in. I'm Logan, by the way." He shakes both our hands, speaking rapidly. "Is Joe okay?"

Beyond him, I see a second male trot down the stairs, buttoning his shirt as he goes. He's a younger version of Joe, clean-cut, less the hard

179

edges and desperation. A lot more hipster than Amish.

He enters the foyer with a great deal of caution. "What's this all about?"

"It's Joe." The other man touches his arm.

The color drains from his face. I see him mentally brace. "Is he dead?"

"He escaped," I tell him. "He's taken his children hostage and he's holed up at his sister-in-law's house in Painters Mill."

Jonas gasps. "Hostage?"

"Oh my God, those poor children," Logan says. "Are they—"

"Joe won't hurt the kids," Jonas says without hesitation.

The words seem to calm Logan. He collects himself, and looks at me. "Jonas and I were just there, visiting with Daniel and Rebecca and the kids. On Easter Sunday. Those kids are so sweet and they've been through so much losing their mom the way they did."

Jonas meets my gaze. "Anyone hurt?"

"So far, everyone's okay," I tell him.

"What can he possibly hope to accomplish?" Logan asks no one in particular.

Jonas is looking at me closely. Now that the shock of learning what his brother has done is over, he's realized he knows me. "Katie? Burkholder?"

"It's been a while." I smile. "You're taller."

"I hope so." Despite the circumstances, he smiles back. "I think I was seven years old last time I saw you."

"I wish I were here under different circumstances." I pause, give him a moment to digest the news about his brother.

He glances past me and looks at Glock. "Do you guys want to sit? I can make coffee."

I shake my head. "Just a few questions and we'll get out of your hair."

"Sure. Whatever you need."

"When's the last time you saw Joe?" I ask.

"I went to the prison to see him," he tells me. "Six weeks ago."

"How was he?" I ask.

"The same way he's been for the last two years. Hopeless. Depressed. Pissed off."

"Did he give you any indication that he might do something like this?"

"No. I mean, of course he hates it there. Said it was a violent hellhole. But escaping? That's so crazy I can't even get my head around it."

"He's put himself in an extremely dangerous situation," I tell him. "The kids, too."

"This is so bad." Jonas raises his hand, bites at a nail. "I don't know what he's thinking."

I tell him about my conversation with Joseph, leaving out the details of how I ended up in the house with him. "Jonas, he insists he didn't kill Naomi."

His eyes snap to mine. "He's been saying that since day one. No one will listen to him. No one believes him."

"Do you?"

"With all my heart."

"Are you close?"

"Before all of this happened we were as close as brothers could be. Especially after Datt died. I mean, he was my best friend. Even when he was a teenager and getting into trouble, I always looked up to him. He always made time for me." He gives a wan smile. "We raised a lot of hell for a couple of Amish boys."

"I take it you left the fold?"

"Joe was one of the few who didn't condemn me when I told him about Logan." He nods toward the other man, and for the first time I understand. The men are partners, a relationship that would be frowned upon by the Amish.

"Did you remain close with Joseph as an adult?" I ask.

"We stayed in touch as much as we could. It wasn't always easy with him being Amish. I mean, he got his hands on the occasional cell phone and we talked. For the most part, I'd go see them, at the house."

I cover some of the same territory I did with Edward. "How was his marriage to Naomi? Did they get along?"

"They had some issues. Money troubles. Right

before . . . it happened, she took a part-time job at a restaurant in town. Joseph didn't like the idea of her working. Hurt his pride, I think. But they needed the money so he let it go. To tell you the truth, Katie, he wasn't always a good husband."

"How so?"

"He can be impulsive and irresponsible. Blows money like it's going out of style. Naomi's frugal, but Joseph was always buying things he didn't need. A few years ago he used his whole paycheck to buy a boat. She was furious, and rightfully so. Once, he went fishing up to Lake Erie for two days and didn't even bother to tell her. He had a temper, too. He never quite got a handle on it.

"Don't get me wrong; Joe's a lovable guy." He gives me a small smile. "You remember how charming he was. Especially if he wanted something. That's never changed. But let me tell you something: If he got pissed it wasn't pretty. He'd yell at Naomi over stupid stuff. The kids, too. I think part of the problem was that he thought she was too good for him. He felt like he didn't measure up."

"Did he tell you that?"

"It's just an observation. Frankly, she was a saint for putting up with his crap."

"What about the other trouble Joseph got into? The DUI? Drugs?"

"Hell if I know." Jonas shakes his head.

"Trouble just seemed to follow Joe. Yeah, he liked to have a good time; he drank too much sometimes. Smoked a little dope. He just had a penchant for handling things wrong. Never learned to use the good judgment God gave him. Rubbed people the wrong way. The harder he tried, the more he seemed to screw things up."

"How were things between you and Joseph after his arrest?" I ask.

"Our relationship took a beating those first few months after Naomi was killed. I mean, the evidence against Joe was overwhelming." His expression turns pained. "I found myself doubting him. I mean, I'll be the first to tell you Joe isn't perfect. He's screwed up so many times I lost count. Even the Amish gave up on him." His smile is wry. "But I knew he could never hurt Naomi. She was everything to him. The glue that held his life together."

I nod, not liking the knot that has taken up residence in the pit of my stomach. "You attended the trial?"

"Every excruciating day." He gives me a weighty look. "It was heartbreaking. I mean, I was close to Naomi, still mourning her. I sat there day in and day out, listening to a whole litany of how and why he shot his wife to death. The prosecutor was polished and credible and laid it all out so convincingly. I felt . . . betrayed by Joseph."

He sighs. "It wasn't until a few weeks later that I was able to look at the trial with an objective eye."

"And?"

"Frankly, the public defender didn't do a very good job of defending him. Of course, *Joe* didn't help his case. He was sullen and stoic and that's not to mention all the bad-husband stuff that came out about him in the course of the trial. But a bad husband does not a murderer make."

"Did any of the children testify?" I ask.

"No." Something flickers in his eyes. "But a couple weeks after the trial, Logan and I went to see the kids. They're good kids, Katie. I mean, they lost their *mamm*; their *datt* had just been convicted of her murder and sentenced to life in prison. And here they are putting on a brave front." Blowing out a breath, he shakes his head. "They were so sad, it broke my heart. Anyway, Rebecca invited us to stay for dinner. Later, when I was tucking the youngest into bed, Sadie told me something that chilled me to the bone."

I wait, knowing what's coming next, hoping for it and dreading it at once.

"She said there was a man in the house the night Naomi was killed. At first, I figured she'd just made it up. You know, because she couldn't accept the truth about her *datt*. But the way she told the story . . ." He shakes his head. "Katie, I couldn't stop thinking about it. I mean, she was

185

only four years old, but I swear to God she was telling the truth."

I stare at him, aware that the hairs on my forearms are standing up. "What did you do?"

"The next morning I called the public defender's office. He basically told me Sadie would be deemed unreliable because of her age."

"It seems like the defense attorney would be all over that," Glock says.

"He wasn't the least bit interested."

"What's his name?"

"Leonard Floyd." He frowns. "He's not going to be much help."

"Why not?"

"Killed in a car crash six months ago down in Bainbridge."

"Did anyone follow up?" I ask.

"I made a few calls. Talked to several attorneys."

"Four to be exact," Logan puts in.

"To make a long story short, they all said that while Sadie could be questioned as a possible witness, because of her age and the inability to cross-examine, her testimony would be disallowed." Jonas grimaces. "But I couldn't get it out of my head. I mean, I *believed* her. And I started thinking about some other things that had happened to Joe during and even *before* the trial. Things that just didn't add up."

"Like what?" Glock asks.

"A few weeks before the murder, the sheriff's department busted Joseph with some meth during a traffic stop. It's true that Joe had been drinking; he admitted it. But he swore the meth wasn't his. Said he'd never tried it. But in usual Joe fashion, he screwed up and ended up pleading no contest for a lesser sentence. Then there was the domestic-violence charge for when he"—Jonas makes air quotes with his fingers—" 'hit' Naomi.

"Joe always denied it, but he'd been in so much trouble I didn't know whether to believe him. I mean, everyone knew he had a temper. I saw him put his fist through a window once, the asshole. So I never really questioned the charge. He did time in jail for the domestic-violence charge, by the way.

"Anyway, while he was in jail, I went to see Naomi and the kids, just to check on them and see how they were doing. I'm sitting at the kitchen table with Naomi and she told me Joe didn't hit her."

Jonas makes a sound of exasperation. "I'm, like, *what?* Then it's confession time for her. Naomi starts crying and told me the police got it wrong. She told me the deputy who responded to the call just started putting words in her mouth. And get this: Because she was Amish, there were no photos taken, so they didn't even have *that* as evidence." He sighs. "In the end, Joe was convicted. He denied it from the start, but by then he had zero credibility and no one believed him."

"Did Naomi go to bat for him?" I ask.

"She was big into the whole separation thing. She didn't like the cops or the whole legal system. She didn't understand the legal process. Didn't want to get involved. Frankly, I think she didn't realize how serious the charge was, and she wanted to be rid of Joe for a few days."

"So she let her husband go to jail?" Glock presses.

Jonas and Logan exchange a look. "That was our reaction, too," Logan says. "But yeah."

"And of course, Joe was Joe." Jonas rolls his eyes. "I mean, here's Joe, facing jail time for the meth—serious as hell, right? So he's out on bond, he goes *fishing* up to Lake Erie and misses his court date. But that's Joe for you and, believe me, it didn't help. But, Katie, he *always* maintained that someone planted that meth. I figured one of his friends had left it in the buggy or something. Now, I'm not so sure."

"When people get into trouble with the law, they say all sorts of things to try and get out of it," Glock says.

"I get that," Jonas says. "I do. And I know how all of this must sound. I mean, Joe isn't exactly a Boy Scout, right?"

Logan steps in. "At that point Jonas took his concerns to the sheriff's department."

"And?" I ask.

"They jerked me around for a couple weeks," Jonas explains, "wouldn't return my calls. In the end all I got was a rash of patronizing bullshit and pat answers."

Jonas stops speaking, slightly breathless, and divides his attention between me and Glock. "No one knows better than me that Joe didn't help his cause. He's the only person on this earth I've ever come to blows with. But I'm absolutely certain he did not murder Naomi."

The words echo, their meaning as cold and heavy as steel.

"Someone did," Glock says.

"If not Joseph, then who?" I ask.

"I've racked my brain." Jonas gives an adamant shake of his head. "I have no idea."

"Anyone we should talk to?" I ask.

He looks at me, a slow smile touching his mouth. "Salome Fisher might be able to shed some light."

"Who's she?"

"The bishop's wife," he tells me. "She was Naomi's best friend. She won't speak to me, because I'm . . . well." He nods toward Logan. "But Naomi and Salome were close, Chief Burkholder. If anyone knows anything about what was going on in her life, it's Salome."

I pull out my pad and write down the name. "Where can I find her?"

"She lives south of here, off Wilkes Road. Got

a farm out there with her husband." His mouth curls. "From what I hear they weren't very helpful when the cops were there after Naomi died."

I'm still digesting everything that's been said when my phone vibrates against my hip. I glance down at the display and see DISPATCH pop up. "I have to take this." Turning away from the men, I answer with my name.

"Chief, I got shots fired out at the Beachy farmhouse."

"Shit." I reach down and turn up the volume of my radio, the hiss and bark of traffic jumping at me. In the back of my mind, I'm wondering why I didn't get the call from Ryan or even Tomasetti. "Anyone hurt?"

"Details are sketchy. The story I'm hearing is that King fired on a deputy. Deputy returned fire."

"I'm on my way."

CHAPTER 11

I use my emergency lights and siren and make the trip back to Painters Mill in an hour. All the while my mind runs the gauntlet of scenarios that could have played out. Did King panic and fire on law enforcement? Were the cops overzealous? Did it somehow involve the children? Was it an accidental discharge? The most troubling question of all: Am I wrong about King?

Using his cell, Glock tries to gather information, but no one seems to know exactly what happened. Just that gunfire was exchanged. Or else no one's talking.

The scene hasn't changed much in the hours since I left, but there's a frenetic energy now that wasn't there before. The road in front of the farm is jammed with law enforcement vehicles from as far away as Cleveland now. The media presence has tripled to include *The Columbus Dispatch*, a television station out of Akron, and another out of Cleveland.

Rather than fight my way through the crush of vehicles, I park a distance away and hoof it to the command center. A white van emblazoned with WAYNE COUNTY SPECIAL REACTION TEAM is parked a few yards behind the command center. A young deputy in full riot gear is leaning against the front grille, talking on his cell.

I fly up the steps and go through the door without knocking. Jeff Crowder is standing in the center of the room, looking at me as if I'm some undesirable that's wandered in off the street. Curtis Scanlon is sitting at the table, the headset looped around his neck like a noose. A deputy clad in SWAT gear sits at the table across from him, watching me with dispassionate eyes.

"Is anyone hurt?" I ask.

"No," Scanlon replies, but the word doesn't jibe with the way he's looking at me.

"King? The kids?"

"Haven't been able to get him on the phone."

"Shit." I take a breath, make an effort to dial it down and look around the room. "What happened?"

"King fired on one of my deputies," Crowder says. "The deputy returned fire."

The words jam a knot into my gut. Now that there's been an exchange of gunfire, it's only a matter of time before SWAT makes a crisis entry.

The temperature inside the command center is uncomfortably hot despite the blast of the air conditioner. Tension lies heavy in the air. No one's talking. There's no place for me to sit, so I move to the hallway that leads to the cab. It's the only place left that won't interfere with the flow of the RV or obstruct any of the electronics, and not for the first time I feel as if I'm in the way.

"Is Ryan around?" I ask Crowder.

"Yep."

He doesn't elaborate, so I glance toward the front of the RV, thinking he may have gone into the cab. "I need to speak with him."

Crowder smirks. "If you're in that big a hurry I reckon you could drag him out of the toilet."

Chuckles erupt. I smile, but my face heats.

Careful, a little voice warns.

I wait for a span of several heartbeats, but no one speaks. No one makes an effort to bring me up to speed on the situation. No one makes eye contact with me.

What the hell?

The restroom door swings open. Jason Ryan steps out, a newspaper tucked beneath his arm. He doesn't look pleased to see me.

Aware that all eyes are on me, I cross to him. "What happened?"

"Evidently King isn't in the mood to chat so we're kind of stuck in a holding pattern for now," Ryan says, and then, "Excuse me." Turning away, he tugs his cell from his pocket and just like that, I'm dismissed.

I glance at Crowder. Looking pleased by the exchange, he sneers and turns away. Scanlon is hunched over his iPad, brows knit, suddenly absorbed. Even the other deputy gives me the cold shoulder, which tells me he was present for at least one conversation in which I was the topic.

They're shutting me out. Cutting me off. Letting me know in no uncertain terms that I'm not needed. I'm not part of the team. This isn't my gig.

The door swings open. I glance over my shoulder to see a grim-faced Sheriff Mike Rasmussen come through, a folded newspaper in his hand. I've known Mike for about three years now. He's a solid cop and an apolitical sheriff with a laid-back personality, a wicked sense of humor, and truckloads of good judgment. There was a time—before he knew that Tomasetti and I were together—when he wanted to be more than professional counterparts. I consider him a friend and I know I can count on him to give it to me straight—even if he knows it's something I don't want to hear.

"You look like someone just shot your dog," Crowder tells him.

Rasmussen ignores him; his eyes are fastened to mine. In their depths I see an unsettling combination of discomfort and irritation. His mouth is pulled into a thin, hard line. He thrusts the newspaper at me. "You seen this?"

Perplexed, I take the paper, unfold it. The floor tilts beneath my feet when I see the front page.

For an instant, I can't believe my eyes. It's a color photo of me standing in the doorway of the Beachy farmhouse. King is leaning in to me, too close, his mouth a scant inch from mine. The headline reads SLEEPING WITH THE ENEMY.

My heart does a sickening roll and begins to pound. I can't look away from the photo. It's damning. Easily misconstrued. I'm aware that everyone is staring at me.

"I didn't want to spring this on you like this," Rasmussen tells me. "But it's out. I thought you should know."

I hear Rasmussen's voice as if from a great distance. I'm aware of the blood rushing to my face, heat on my cheeks, that I've gone breathless.

"It's not what it looks like," I say.

Ryan approaches, his eyes on the newspaper. Something sinks inside me when Rasmussen hands him another copy. "I bought up all the newspaper in the machine outside the diner. But there's no stopping it. It looks bad, Kate, and we're probably going to have to deal with some kind of fallout."

Ryan actually recoils when he sees the photo. He blinks twice and then his eyes find mine. "You didn't tell us King made . . . inappropriate advances toward you."

"He didn't. Not really." I flick my finger against the photo, refold the newspaper, and lower it to my side. "That's not what it looks like." I add a good bit of attitude to my voice, but the fact that I'm being forced to defend myself belies the bravado.

Ryan scrapes his hand over his hair, but he's still looking at the photo. "All right." He doesn't know what else to say.

"That photo is extremely misleading," I say, struggling to keep my cool.

Crowder laughs outright when he sees the photo. "For God's sake!"

I look at him, saying nothing. But I know he's not going to remain silent.

"Looks pretty damn cozy to me," Crowder mutters.

There's nothing I can say that will explain or excuse the photo. If I remain silent, I risk my counterparts filling in the blanks with speculation. No matter what I say, the words will be the wrong ones.

"As you can imagine, the situation was intense inside the farmhouse," I say. "King and I grew up together. When I left, he moved to embrace me. It wasn't appropriate so I stopped it." I motion toward the newspaper. "That photo was shot in that instant before I turned away from him."

"I believe you, of course." Ryan says the words a little too quickly, his eyes flicking to Rasmussen; he isn't sure what to think. What to say. "No one is questioning your conduct."

Crowder laughs. "The media are going to have a field day with that."

Rasmussen takes the newspaper from Ryan's hands. "If you have nothing productive to add, Crowder, I suggest you keep your mouth shut. That kind of commentary isn't helping."

Crowder doesn't take it personally. Shaking his head, he walks back to the table and reclaims his chair.

Rasmussen slants a look at Ryan. "Is this going to be a problem? I mean PR-wise?"

"It doesn't look good." Ryan shrugs.

Scanlon finally speaks. "I don't want King to see that."

"No reason why he could," Rasmussen says. "Unless he's in there, Googling himself."

"I'm assuming the newspaper is online, too," Ryan growls.

"Checking now." Rasmussen thumbs the Website address into his phone and utters a curse. "Yup."

"Circulation can't be much," Scanlon says.

"People are still going to notice," Rasmussen puts in. "Especially if it gets picked up by a larger outlet . . ."

Though I did nothing wrong, something akin to shame slinks through me. The hard truth is that I've compromised the credibility of the operation. I look at the men, hating the way their eyes slide away. Suddenly I've become one of

197

those female cops. The ones who aren't respected. Who aren't to be trusted. The ones who aren't part of the team.

"Look, we're all on the same page here," Ryan says diplomatically. "The photo looks bad. It's going to be misunderstood. We're going to be criticized. People are going to talk. If there's even a hint of impropriety or misconduct, things could get complicated. I mean, legally, but—"

"Could get dicey if we have to take this guy out." Crowder watches me, hoping I'll bite, waiting for a reaction.

I don't give it to him.

Rasmussen passes me the newspaper. "I don't think there's any way we can work this to our advantage."

No one responds. No one looks at me. No one knows what to say. What *can* they say?

"Kate, look, you've been the consummate professional through all this and everyone knows it," Ryan tells me. "You've been a tremendous help and I mean it. But that photo is going to undoubtedly complicate an already complicated situation. Look, no reflection on the good work you've done here and the hours and energy you've put into this thing. But this might be a good time for you to take a step back."

He phrased it as if I have a say in the matter, but of course I don't. I'm poison and I'm being told to butt out. Stay away from the case. Stay away from King.

Rasmussen finally makes eye contact with me. "I'll keep you posted on how things are going."

"I appreciate that." I look at Ryan, but he's already turned away. I want to shout at them that I didn't do anything wrong. There was no misconduct on my part. But I know there are times when perceptions outweigh facts, and this is a prime example.

I stand there another minute, watching the men work. But I've been effectively dismissed. It rankles. They're treating me as if I crossed some invisible line. As if I did something unscrupulous. I think about Tomasetti and how he might see this, and another layer of misery washes over me.

Ryan looks away from his phone call and makes eye contact with me. "We'll give you a call if we need you again, Chief Burkholder." His gaze slips to the door and back to me. "Thanks again for everything."

Fury sizzles beneath my skin, but I don't give it voice. "Sure thing," I tell him.

Eyes burn into my back as I make my way to the door. Then I'm through it, too much pride to slam it, and I take the steps to the scene outside.

I'm standing at the base of the stairs, trying to convince myself that my ego isn't bruised and smarting, when I spot Tomasetti striding toward me.

"You calling it a night?" he asks.

All I can think is that he doesn't know. He hasn't seen the headline. "We need to talk," I say.

He reaches me and stops, tilting his head to catch my eye. "You okay?"

"No." I pass him the newspaper.

He unfolds it, his eyes scanning. His expression reveals nothing as he takes in the photo and skims the accompanying article. When his eyes meet mine they're as hard and sharp as a scythe. He hands it back to me without speaking.

"Did Ryan see this?" he asks.

"They all did. Just now."

"What did he say?"

"He wants me gone."

"Diplomatic of him."

"I thought so." I close my eyes. "Goddamn it."

I take the newspaper from him, lower it to my side. I feel his eyes on me, but I don't look at him. I can't. I don't want to see condemnation or disappointment. "I did not behave inappropriately with King," I say after a moment.

"I believe you."

The words stop me cold. It's the one thing I didn't expect him to say, and I have to close my eyes against an unwelcome wave of emotion. I'd had my defense laid out and I was prepared to shout it out if I had to. As usual, Tomasetti was one step ahead of me.

When the silence becomes awkward, I manage,

200

"You have no idea how much I needed to hear you say that."

"Just for clarification purposes, I'm not some insecure high school boy. I know you too well to believe you'd engage in that kind of behavior."

"I'm sorry I doubted you."

"Kate, that's not to say it doesn't look bad. It does, especially if King forces our hand and we have to do something we don't want to do. You're a cop. To all of those unfortunate individuals who don't know you as well as I do, it might appear as if you were conducting yourself in a manner unbecoming a chief of police."

I have a sudden mental image of the photo hitting the front page of every newspaper in northeastern Ohio or trending on social media, and I groan inwardly. "It's going to damage my reputation. Take a chunk out of my credibility."

"People will think what they will. Probably doesn't help that you're female. Formerly Amish. In a position of authority. Any of the above could make you a convenient target."

"So what do I do?"

"Fuck 'em."

None of this is even remotely funny, but I laugh. It does nothing to dislodge the stone of dread that's taken up residence in the pit of my stomach.

"Kate, where this could get serious is this

current situation with King. If worse comes to worse and there's a fatal outcome, for King or any of the hostages, it could get ugly."

The words actually make me nauseous. Not because of any potential fallout due to the photo, but because the thought of someone getting killed—Joseph or one of the kids or a cop— offends me on both a personal and professional level.

"Tomasetti, there's got to be another way."

"That's up to King."

"There's got to be something I can do. Look, I knew him. I could talk to him. On the phone. I might be able to get him to listen to reason. If I could just talk to him—"

"You already did. You did your best and he didn't listen."

Quickly, I tell him about my visits with Edward and Jonas King. "Joseph's younger brother doesn't believe Joseph killed Naomi." I tell him about Jonas's exchange with Sadie. "Tomasetti, there's no way that little girl made up that story."

"Kate, are you saying you believe King is innocent?"

"I think it warrants a second look."

He sighs unhappily. "Kate . . ."

I relay what Jonas told me about his conversation with Naomi. "After Joseph was arrested, Naomi admitted that he didn't assault her."

"Look, I'm playing devil's advocate here, but how many times has a cop walked away from a suspected domestic-violence situation without making an arrest only to learn later it was a mistake because someone ended up dead? Cops make the best calls they can. The situation isn't always cut-and-dried. And they don't always get it right."

"Jonas doesn't believe King was ever violent with his wife."

"Sometimes loved ones are the last to accept the truth."

"Tomasetti, I don't know if I'm right. But none of this is adding up."

"Kate." Tomasetti lowers his voice. "Guilty or not or somewhere in between, the bottom line is we have a barricaded gunman with five minor hostages and he's refusing to cooperate or give himself up. He's fired on officers."

I start to turn away, but he sets his hands on my shoulders. "Listen to me. The situation is a powder keg and it's only a matter of time before someone gets hurt. He's not left us with much in the way of options."

I look away, fight off a wave of emotion I don't want to feel. "What are they going to do?"

"If he hadn't fired on that deputy, we'd simply wait him out."

"And now?"

He grimaces. "Ryan is waiting to hear back

from the AG. With the kids inside they can't do a tactical assault. If they're forced to move, I suspect they'll take him out with a sniper. I know you don't want to hear that, but unless something changes, it's probably going to happen."

"I hate this."

"I know you do. I'm sorry." His hands fall away from my shoulders. "Look, I have to go." He tilts his head, catches my gaze. "Don't beat yourself up over this."

I nod, heft my best phony smile. "See you at home later."

"I'll do my best."

Tomasetti disappears inside the command center without looking back. I stand there, trying to pull myself together. I know he's right. I did my best. It's all anyone can do. The knowledge doesn't help, because if someone gets hurt tonight, it won't have been enough to make a difference.

It's past time for me to leave. All I'm accomplishing by hanging around is torturing myself with the weight of my own mistakes and the knowledge that this is probably not going to end well. *It's out of your hands, Burkholder. Go home. Get some sleep.* I start toward my vehicle.

It's midafternoon. Around me the day is

overcast and cool with a hint of rain in the air. I find myself thinking about Joseph King and his children. Is he having second thoughts about what he's done? Are the kids frightened? Did they have breakfast? Do they have any idea how horribly this could turn out?

God, I hope not.

I don't speak to anyone as I walk along the road's shoulder. I concentrate on shutting down my thoughts, trying not to think of anything more complicated than the prospect of a hot shower and eight hours of uninterrupted sleep.

I'm midway to the Explorer when the *thwack! thwack! thwack!* of gunshots slices through the air.

CHAPTER 12

For an instant the sound freezes me in place. A thousand thoughts assail my brain at once. Vaguely, I'm aware that the tempo of the police presence has intensified. Shouting and movement and the bark of radios. I break into a run, pause at the caution tape demarking the police perimeter, look toward the Beachy house. Shock sweeps through me when I spot two SWAT officers moving toward the house through the trees.

And I know.

The rest of the world falls away. I feel as if I've been plunged into a sealed bottle from which all the air has been sucked. There's no sound or light, just the thrum of my heart, the hiss of my breaths tearing from my throat, and the knowledge that someone has been killed.

I don't remember ducking beneath the tape. Then I'm sprinting toward the house. Weaving through the trees. I'm aware of movement to my right. The flash of lights behind me. Someone ordering me to get the hell back.

I don't stop.

The high-pitched scream of a child cuts through all of it. I hear terror in the voice. The kind no child should ever experience.

Then I'm in the front yard. Grass wet beneath

my feet. I'm out of breath, partly from the physical exertion, partly from adrenaline. I scramble up the hill. I'm thirty feet from the house when the front door bursts open. The children pour out, faces ravaged, eyes crazed. I see blood on bare feet as one of the girls flies down the steps.

I spot Sadie, running across the grass. Arms outstretched. Blood on her dress. Her hands. She looks at me, but doesn't see. I dart left, drop to my knees in front of her. She flings herself into me so hard the breath is knocked from my lungs.

"Sadie."

Her arms scrapple at my shirt, tiny hands fisting the fabric, clinging as if some unseen force is trying to rip her away. "Datt! Datt! He's bleeding!"

I wrap my arms around her, pull her close. "It's okay," I tell her. "It's going to be okay."

She's tiny and shaking so hard I can barely hold onto her. "I want my *datt*!" she screams. "I want him!"

"We've got her! We've got her!"

I glance over my shoulder to see two women rush toward us. Expressions taut and grim. One's a cop. The other is wearing a blue blazer and skirt. I get to my feet. Sadie clings to me, but I pry her fingers from my shirt, shove her toward the woman who reaches us first.

"I'm with Children Services," the woman pants.

"Go with her, Sadie. It's okay, sweetheart. It's okay."

A sheriff's department deputy jogs toward me. He's shouting words I can't discern, gesturing angrily. Sadie screams again as I spin toward the house. I cross the sidewalk, take the steps two at a time to the porch, yank open the door.

"Joseph!" I don't recognize the voice that rips from my throat. *"Joseph!"*

I rush through the living room, past the stairs. Dim light from the window slanting into the kitchen. At the doorway, I spot an ocean of blood slicked across the floor, stark and red and surreal. There's an overturned chair. A spray of blood on the wall. Joseph is lying on his back, arms thrown over his head, one leg bent at an unnatural angle. A hole the size of my fist on the right side of his forehead. His left eye stares right at me. The other is rolled back white, the lid at half mast . . .

A second bullet tore through his throat. The source of the blood . . .

I've seen death more often than I care to recall in the years I've been a cop. Traffic accidents. Shootings. Stabbings. Death from natural causes. It's always a terrible sight to behold. This is worse. I knew this man. I spent my formative years with him. He impacted my life. The way I see the world. I spoke to him less than twenty-four hours ago. He was anxious and despondent, but he wanted to live his life.

I hear myself utter his name. But I know he's gone. Killed instantly, more than likely. I know better—*damn it, I know better*—than to go to him, but I do. Avoiding the blood, I kneel beside him. A cacophony of noise and movement all around. Shouting punctuated by the thud of boots, the jingle of tactical gear.

Joseph is wearing the same clothes as when I sat at this table with him. His shirt has ridden up. I see a white belly, the waistband of his underwear. A thin layer of male hair.

"You! Ma'am! *You!*"

A hand slams down on my shoulder. I catch a glimpse of a gloved hand, an officer in tactical gear. Helmet and flak jacket. He knocks me off balance and then I'm being hauled backward, dragged away from Joseph, toward the doorway. I scramble and twist, try to get my feet under me, finally succeed.

"Get the hell off me," I snarl. "I'm a cop."

"You can't be here," he barks. "What the hell are you doing?"

Wrenching my arm from his grasp, I grapple for my ID, yank it out. "SWAT took him out?"

"Yes, ma'am." His eyes flick to my badge and he relaxes marginally. "Look, you're not supposed to be here. We're securing the scene."

"Who gave the order?"

He blinks at the question. "I'm here to clear the house and secure the scene. You'll have to take that up with the guy in charge." He raises his hands, tries to herd me away from the scene as if I'm some dense animal.

"Kate! *Kate!*"

I glance right, see Tomasetti striding through the living room, his phone against his ear, his face grim.

"Come with me," he says.

When the SWAT officer doesn't back off, Tomasetti shoves his ID in his face. "I fucking got this," he growls.

The officer raises his hands, but holds his ground, watching us.

"He's dead." I glance at the river of blood, the spray on the wall, and I see Joseph the way he looked at me that final time. "The kids . . ."

"They're fine." Then Tomasetti's hand is on my biceps and he's guiding me through the kitchen doorway, into the living room, toward the door where half a dozen cops are coming through. "Let's go. They've got to secure the scene and we're in the way."

It feels wrong leaving Joseph like that. Bloody and sprawled on the floor. He'd hate that, I think. Wouldn't want anyone to see him that way.

I make a halfhearted attempt to free myself from Tomasetti's grasp. He doesn't release me.

"Kate." He says my name in a low voice as we go through the door. "You okay?"

"I'm fine, damn it."

He frowns. "Uh-huh."

I plant my feet, stop and turn to him. "Who gave the order? Why wasn't I told?"

"Ryan and Crowder worked it out. You weren't part of it."

"Did you know?"

"The order came down fast, Kate. Once King fired on law enforcement and they were able to take a clean shot, the decision was made. A sniper was put in place and he waited for the opportunity. Took the shot through the kitchen window."

"Tomasetti, King wasn't armed—"

"Yes, he was, goddamn it. He had a rifle. He had your fucking handgun. He fired on deputies."

"No, I mean . . . just now." The words tumble out of me; I'm fumbling them, my brain is misfiring, and I warn myself to calm down.

"He set down the handgun. So what? It doesn't matter. He's down. The children are safe. It's over."

"I don't think it's over. . . ."

He looks at me as if he wants to lay into me. Instead, he scrubs a hand over his face and softens. "You're not okay."

Only then do I realize he's right. I'm a mess. My entire body is shaking. My legs. Hands. My voice isn't steady. Worst of all, I feel the threat of tears, the one thing I will not allow at this moment.

Setting his hand against the small of my back, he motions toward the command center. "Remind me later to bitch you out for going in there, will you? Kill hadn't even been confirmed. If he'd been—"

"He wasn't," I cut in.

We arrive at the command center. A few yards from the stairs, I plant my feet and stop. "I don't want to go in there."

"You need a minute?"

"I'm not going in there. Not like . . . this."

Glancing left and right, he takes me around to the rear of the vehicle and leans me against the side of the trailer. "I just want to sit you down, get a look at you. Make sure you're all right."

"I'm okay," I tell him. "I'm just . . ."

"Hurting." He sweeps a tuft of hair from my face, and then says more softly, "Yeah, I get that. I'm sorry."

"I didn't want this to happen," I tell him. "Not like this."

"No one did."

I think about the children. Annie and Levi. Becky and Little Joe. And sweet Sadie . . . So young and innocent and yet they've endured so much, lost so much. I wonder who'll explain this to them. If someone will be there to comfort them, to hold them, wipe away their tears.

Through the throng of cops from a dozen jurisdictions, I see the Holmes County Coroner's van take the gravel lane toward the house.

I take a deep breath, blow it out, reach for a calm I can't quite get to. "Are you going to stay?"

"I need to stick around until the CSU is finished. Probably going to be a few hours."

"I need to go home," I tell him.

"You're still shaky."

He'll know if I lie, so I fess up. "I'm sick to my core about this."

He tilts his head, looking at me a little too closely. "Give me a few minutes. I'll get things tied up and drive you."

"No. Finish up. I'm fine." More than anything I want to lean into him, feel his arms around me, absorb some of his strength, because at this moment I need it desperately. Of course, I can't do any of those things; there are too many people around.

Offering up a smile, I take a step back. "I'm not very good company right now, anyway."

"You're always good company." He's not buying into it, but I know he can't get away.

"Don't stay too late," I tell him.

We touch hands, a brushing of fingertips, and then I turn away and start toward my Explorer.

PART II

❧   ❧

Every heart has its secret sorrows which the world knows not, and oftentimes we call a man cold, when he is only sad.
—Henry Wadsworth Longfellow, *Hyperion*

CHAPTER 13

I'm twelve years old and it's a beautiful summer day full of promise and adventure and, unfortunately for me, chores. My sister, Sarah, and I spent the morning picking raspberries down by the creek on the north end of our property. We ate nearly as many as we picked, but the berries were plentiful and we still managed to harvest eighteen pints. Yesterday, Mamm made a dozen loaves of yeast bread. Add to that the eggs I've collected over the last week—the brown ones that the tourists fawn over—and a dozen or so jars of apple butter, and I know it's going to be a lucrative afternoon.

At ten A.M., my brother, Jacob, loaded all our goods into the buggy and drove Sarah and me to the stand Datt built down by Hogpath Road where the English tourists have to drive past to get into Painters Mill. While Sarah smooths the red-and-white-checked tablecloth over the plywood surface, Jacob and I carry the last of the bread and eggs and raspberries to the table.

"Stop your pouting, Katie," Jacob says as he sets the last crate on the tabletop.

"I'm not pouting," I tell him.

He pulls the wooden sign from the back of the buggy and sets it against the front of the stand so it's visible from the road. "Pride in your work puts joy in your day," he says in *Deitsch*.

A little free time would have put plenty of joy in my day. I don't tell him that, of course. I simply hadn't planned on spending my birthday working our produce stand. All I'd wanted to do was finish my chores and hoof it down to the creek to go swimming with my siblings. We'd recently discovered a deep spot just past the rapids where the water runs fast and clear and cold. Our neighbor, Joseph, who's my brother's age and oftentimes swims with us, claims to have spotted a wood trunk half buried in the gravel bottom. I'm not sure I believe it, but the story has aroused the explorer inside me.

"It's my birthday," I snap.

"It's just another day to everyone else."

"Shush, you two." Sarah arranges the loaves alongside the pints of berries. "We'll have all this stuff sold in no time," she says. "We'll get down to the creek this afternoon when it's nice and hot."

Sarah, always the diplomat. The peacemaker.

Jacob sets the box of change on the tabletop. "I think our Katie is just anxious to see Joseph."

"I am not," I say, but my face heats, revealing the truth.

"Or maybe she just wants to do something fun on her birthday," Sarah soothes.

Smirking, Jacob goes to the buggy and climbs onto the seat. "I'll be back in a few hours."

Sarah waves. I don't bother, instead leaving him with a glower.

Clucking to the horse, Jacob snaps the reins and starts toward home.

I make my way behind the table, trying not to notice the car that speeds by, the face in the passenger window staring at me as if I'm some kind of exotic livestock.

"At least there's a breeze," Sarah says as she rearranges the eggs and berries. "A cake or two would have been nice. Or some pies."

"Nice to eat, maybe." But I have to admit, she's created an attractive display. The red berries. The rustic bread Mamm wrapped in cellophane. The brown eggs in the big wire basket. And those pretty little jars of apple butter.

"You did a good job on the sign, Katie. I like the blue."

I look at the sign and, despite my sour mood, a sense of pride moves through me. I found the old piece of wood in the barn last week. Datt sawed it to size and I spent most of last evening penciling in the letters and then filling them in with the paint Mamm had left over from the kitchen cabinets.

Sarah pulls out the paperback novel she's been reading and leans back in the lawn chair. Not for the first time I wonder how she can always be so content. It's not yet noon and already the back of my neck is wet with sweat and I'm pretty sure

I've got a mosquito bite or poison ivy on my ankle.

"Oh, look, our first customer!"

I glance up to see a silver car with wide tires and a loud engine pull onto the gravel shoulder. In the back of my mind, I'm hoping it's a large family and they'll buy two of everything. My heart sinks when I see the two teen-aged boys. When they shut down the engine, I hear the radio blaring some rock-and-roll music that's all the more tantalizing because it's forbidden.

They get out and start toward us. They're older than Sarah and me. Probably sixteen or seventeen. Both boys are wearing blue jeans and T-shirts. Reflective sunglasses. The one with long blond hair is smoking a cigarette.

"Hi, girls." The blond guy grins, revealing crooked teeth. "Whatcha selling today?"

The second boy hangs back slightly, but he's eyeing Sarah and me with a little too much interest. He's got dark, curly hair and a gold hoop in his earlobe.

"We have eggs, bread, and raspberries," Sarah tells him.

"And apple butter," I add, hoping they'll buy.

Curly Hair laughs. "Wow. Did you hear that, Mike? Eggs, bread, and fucking raspberries. Shit."

I glance at Sarah. "I don't like the look of them," I tell her in *Deitsch*.

She shrugs. "It's okay, Katie."

"*Si sinn net kawfa*," I tell her. They're not going to buy.

"*Ruich*," she says. Quiet.

I start to go around to the back of the table, but the blond guy steps in front of me. "It's rude to talk Amish to people who ain't Amish."

Heat flushes my face. Keeping my eyes on the ground, I try to go around him, but he steps into my way.

"I think she called you a homo, dude," says Curly.

The blond grins at me. "You call me a homo?"

My heart rolls and begins to pound. "No."

"I think she said *fucking* homo," says Curly.

The blond dips his head, so his face is only a few inches from mine. "You wouldn't lie to me, would you?"

I shake my head, unable to look at him. I don't even care if they buy anything now. I just want them to leave.

"She's kind of cute for an Amish girl," Curly says.

"Except that dress."

"Yeah, but it's what's *under* the dress that counts."

Again, I try to sidestep the blond so I can reach the relative safety behind the table, but he blocks me, grinning. He's standing so close I can smell the stink of cigarettes on his breath.

221

"You are kind of cute," he whispers. "How old are you?"

Curly makes his way to the table and looks down at our display. "Hey, can we try these berries before we buy?" Without waiting for an answer, he snatches a handful of raspberries from one of the containers and crams them into his mouth.

"Damn! Those are tasty!" he exclaims, chewing messily so that the red juice dribbles down his chin.

The blond boy points at his friend's chin, laughing, then picks up the container, tips his head back, and empties the remaining berries into his mouth.

Sarah shoots me a worried look. "Come around here, Katie."

Again, I try to go around the boy. This time he grasps my arm. "Where do you think you're going, *Katie?*"

"You owe three dollars for those berries." I'd intended the words to come out strong, but my voice is shaking.

"Three bucks?" The blond boy spits out the mouthful of berries. Red juice sprays the front of my dress, specks of it hitting me in the face.

Curly bursts into raucous laughter.

"Don't speak with them, Katie," comes my sister's voice.

The pounding of my heart nearly drowns out

her voice. I'm frightened of these two boys, but I'm also angry, because Sarah and I spent all morning picking those berries and now these two are going to ruin everything.

"You owe three dollars." I didn't intend to say the words; they just came out. Surprisingly strong this time.

The curly-haired boy laughs harder. "Dude, I think she's going to kick your ass."

"Naw, she just wants my body." The blond boy turns away and strolls along the table, running his fingertips over the tablecloth where Sarah displayed the bread and eggs and raspberries with such care. He pretends to accidentally knock one of the loaves of bread to the ground. "Aw, hell, look what I did!" he exclaims.

I go to the fallen loaf, snatch it off the ground. "Go away and leave us alone."

"Or what?" The blond boy snags an egg from the basket and hurls it at our sign. Yolk and shell splatter, yellow dripping down its face.

"Damn, those are some fresh fuckin' eggs!" Curly says, slapping his knees.

I make a grab for the basket, but he shoves me away with his forearm. I reel backward, land hard on my rear in the grass and dust. My temper kicks, and I'm on my feet in an instant. My vision narrows until all I see is the blond boy's face. He reaches for another egg. Vaguely, I'm aware of the sound of shod hooves against

223

asphalt. The boys hear it, too. They turn. I look over to see our neighbor Joseph King climb down from his *datt*'s old hay wagon.

An egg flies toward the horse, smacks it hard in the chest. The animal startles, snorting and stomping its hooves.

Curly and the blond boy double over with laughter.

Joseph gets an odd look on his face. Reaching into the wagon, he grabs the buggy whip and stalks over to the blond boy. Air whooshes as Joseph swings it like a bat. Leather cracks against the blond boy's chest. The boy yowls, puts up both arms to defend himself. The curly-haired boy takes a step forward, but Joseph is ready. He swings the whip a second time, strikes the boy's arm.

"That fuckin' hurt!" Curly screams.

Joseph swings the whip again, rakes it across the front of his thighs. Curly raises his hands and dances away.

The blond boy turns tail and runs.

"Get out of here!" Joseph swings the whip again, nicks the blond boy's back. "Both of you! Go on! Git!"

The curly-haired boy lurches toward the car, his sneakers sliding in gravel as he rounds the front. The blond boy yanks open the door, scrambles into the car. Once behind the wheel, he gives Joseph the finger. "Fuck you, Amish freak!"

Joseph darts to the vehicle, flips the whip around, and brings the heavy butt down on the hood hard enough to leave a crease.

"Fucker!" the blond boy leans out the window, his mouth open and flapping. "Look what you did to my car!"

The vehicle jets backward. Gravel shoots out from beneath the tires, striking the produce stand like a hail of bullets. Gears grind and then the car lurches forward. The tires squeal on the asphalt and then they're gone.

Sarah has already come around the table with a napkin to wipe raspberry juice and spittle from my face and dress. I'm brushing grass from my skirt. But I can't take my eyes off of Joseph. I can't believe he did what he did. That he did it to protect me.

He takes the time to check his gelding before coming over, running his hands over the animal's chest, scraping off the egg and shell with his palm and slinging it to the ground. Securing the whip in its holder, he pats the animal's rump and then strolls over to Sarah and me as if nothing happened.

"You girls okay?" he asks.

"We are fine." Sarah actually sounds a little miffed about what Joseph did.

Not me. "Is your horse okay?" I ask.

"Sonny don't take things too personal," Joseph says. "Can't see someone doing that to him. He's old and still works hard. I think he deserves a little bit more respect."

"Me, too."

I'm aware of Sarah looking at me. Probably thinking I'm being too friendly with Joseph. But I can't look away.

Joseph motions in the general direction in which the car drove off. "Those two are trouble."

"We know," Sarah says.

"I don't think they'll be back, though," he says.

"We're glad you came by when you did," I tell him.

His eyes smile, but his mouth doesn't follow suit. "Datt and me are going to bale hay this afternoon. Tell Jacob I won't be down to the creek till later."

Sarah and I exchange glances. We both know he's not asking about Jacob.

"I'll tell him," Sarah says.

"We're going to find that trunk and pull it out today." Joseph's eyes land on me. "You, too, runt."

I can't stop the grin that overtakes my face. "I'm not a runt."

"That's a likely story." Turning, he climbs into the buggy and drives away.

I haven't thought of that day on Hogpath Road in years. The event made one hell of an impression on my twelve-year-old psyche. That was the day I fell in love with Joseph King.

We never found the trunk in the creek that summer, but it wasn't for lack of trying. Sarah, Jacob, Joseph, and I swam every afternoon we could get away. We dove as deep as we dared. We dug in the gravel and mud. I suspect we knew there was no trunk; it was just another one of Joseph's tall tales. But what an adventure it was to search.

Joseph became my hero that summer. I never told anyone. I knew nothing about the ways of the world, but even at that tender age, I sensed that if the subject had been broached, something I wasn't quite ready to understand would have tarnished our relationship. And so we swam. We played tag and hide-and-seek and baseball. That winter was a cold one and we spent hours out on the ice playing hockey.

Joseph's *datt* was killed in the buggy accident that next year, along with the old gelding Joseph was so fond of. Joseph was never the same after that. Nothing was the same for any of us.

CHAPTER 14

I'm generally pretty adept at keeping a healthy emotional distance from cases that affect me personally. I've learned to compartmentalize, cram all those gnarly, self-defeating emotions in a box and deal with them at an appropriate time and in a manner that doesn't include three glasses of wine or, God forbid, that bottle of vodka we keep in the cabinet above the fridge. According to Tomasetti, it's all about perspective and moderation—and not necessarily in that order.

My feelings about the death of Joseph King are complex. The sense of loss is surprisingly keen. Some small part of my heart is broken because my childhood friend is dead, five children have been left without a father, and a piece of my past is gone forever. By all indications Joseph's life was fraught with bad decisions heaped atop poor judgment, and both of those things ultimately played a role in bringing it to a violent and early close.

It's the lingering sense of injustice that grates on my cop's sensibilities. The knowledge that the whole truth hasn't been told, will probably never be known, and the accused isn't around to set the record straight.

It's been twenty-four hours since the SWAT

sniper took the shot. The children are expected to be reunited with Rebecca and Daniel Beachy sometime today. Once the crime-scene unit was finished at the Beachy house and Joseph's body was removed by the coroner's office, half a dozen Amish women descended and cleaned up the mess. That's the thing about the Amish. When one of their own—or anyone for that matter—gets sick or is hurt and in need, they drop everything and rush in to help.

Joseph's death hit me harder than I expected. The truth of the matter is I went for years without thinking of him. When I did, it was just in passing or when I was feeling nostalgic or maybe when I drove past that old roadside stand on Hogpath Road. Until yesterday, that was the extent of my recollection. I'd only known him for five years after all. In the scope of a lifetime, a drop in the bucket.

But they were formative years. A period in which every experience is a first and you feel every little thing all the way to your soul. If an Amish girl could have a superhero, a playmate, and a big brother all rolled into one, Joseph King was mine. He was my friend. My coconspirator. My partner in crime. And, later, my first big crush. He was larger than life, and for a short span of time, I worshiped the ground he walked on.

Now, when I think of him, I won't wonder what

he's done with his life or if he's happy with the way things turned out. I'll think of the way he died and the role I played.

In the last twenty-four hours, everything that was said and done inside that house has replayed in my head a hundred times. I see the expression on Joseph's face when he told me he didn't kill his wife. I hear the truth in Sadie's voice when she relayed the story about the stranger in the house the night her *mamm* was killed. Was someone there that night?

It's nine A.M. and the Painters Mill police station is swarming with media when I arrive. A white SUV bearing the Channel 16 logo has taken up residence in my reserved parking spot. I park next to it and watch a cameraman unpack equipment from a van while a petite blond in a fuchsia-colored jacket and skirt sprays a cloud of something on her hair.

Apparently, several media outlets have caught wind of the photo of Joseph King and me, and they've come here in the hope of obtaining some juicy morsel. I get out of the Explorer, take the time to write a parking citation for the owner of the white SUV, and tuck it beneath the windshield wiper.

I cross the street at a fast clip. By the time I go through the door, my cop's suit of armor is securely in place. The usually quiet reception area is occupied by several young reporters and a photographer who has a striking resemblance to a wildebeest.

Eyes turn my way. Once I'm recognized, they rush me.

"Chief Burkholder!" A journalist in stilettos makes a beeline toward me, moving with awe-inspiring speed despite the pencil skirt and heels, and thrusts a microphone in my face. "Chief, can you tell me what transpired inside the house between you and Joseph King?"

"No comment," I say without looking at her.

"We'd like to hear your side of the story," she presses.

Ignoring her, I make tracks to the reception desk, barely managing to avoid another reporter in a neon green dress with the tattoo of a dragon on her right ankle.

"Chief Burkholder!" she screeches. "Tell us about your relationship with Joseph King."

Skid is standing outside his cubicle checking out her legs. Despite my mood, I smile as I pluck messages from my slot.

"Chief!" Lois gets to her feet. The headset she's wearing is askew. Her hair is sticking out on one side as if she's run her hands through it and never bothered to smooth it back down. She's holding a fistful of pink message slips.

"Thanks." I take the slips from her.

"Oh, almost forgot." She shoves two purple folders at me. "Mona left these for you."

Taking the folders, I motion toward the reporters. "How long have they been here?"

"Forty-five minutes or so."

Behind me, I hear the shuffle of shoes, the clanging of equipment. I turn to see four reporters and two cameramen standing inside the door. Two are on the phone. The other three shove microphones at me, shouting out questions.

"Chief Burkholder, can you tell us what happened in that farmhouse?"

"Is it true that you and King were once lovers?"

"Were you romantically involved with Joseph King?"

"Did he sexually assault you while you were being held hostage?"

"Was it consensual?"

Dear God.

I bring my hands together sharply several times. The room goes silent. Even the phone quiets. "The good news is," I tell them, "I'll be sending out a press release. The bad news is you have five minutes to leave the premises."

A hipster guy in skinny jeans and a neat little goatee shakes the press ID hanging around his neck. "Um, hello? We have a right to be here, Chief Burkholder."

"This is a non-public-forum public property." I send a pointed look at the clock on the wall, aware that there's at least one camera rolling, so I keep my tone cool and professional. "You now have four minutes to vacate the premises or I will begin writing trespassing citations. Do you understand?"

"That's a violation of our First Amendment rights," hipster dude tells me.

"You are free to pursue that avenue if you wish." I motion toward the wall clock. "Less than four minutes now."

I hear the rattle of paper and glance over to see Lois brandishing the old citation book. It's old as the hills; we haven't used it for years. But it's an effective prop.

I open the book and snag a pen off Lois's desk. "You can call me anytime to set up an appointment."

"That's a crock of shit," a heavyset cameraman in a Hawaiian shirt mutters.

"You'll be hearing from legal by the end of the day," a serious-looking young man calls out.

"Our main number will be included in the press release," I tell him. "You now have three minutes to vacate the premises. Let's pick up the pace, people."

The woman in the pink skirt is already on her phone, her eyes shooting daggers in my direction. I hear her hiss the word "bitch" but I let it go.

Skid moves toward them, his arms spread as if he's herding sheep. "Watch your step," he says to no one in particular.

When the last journalist goes through the door, Lois chuckles. "Well played, Chief."

"Thanks."

"Can you do that?"

"I hope so," I tell her.

Now that it's quiet, I realize she's looking at me as if seeing me in a whole new light. "I take it you've seen the photo."

"I'm sorry, Chief, but I think everyone has. Made the front page of *The Weekly Advocate*, and folks have been calling all morning."

Skid comes back inside. He's trying not to stare at me, but he's not doing a very good job.

I motion him over. "You saw it, too?"

He nods. "It's all over the Internet. I guess people are into the whole Amish-police-misconduct thing."

"Just so you know, there was no misconduct," I tell them.

"Never doubted it," Lois says.

Skid grins. "Next time I catch Steve Ressler speeding?" Ressler being the publisher of *The Weekly Advocate*. "I'm going to ticket the fucker."

I spend twenty minutes fielding calls, most from curious citizens, wanting to know about the photo. Some call to complain. A few call fishing for juicy details that don't exist. I return every message, assure all of them it's a nonissue, that there was no misconduct, but if they wish to lodge a complaint they're free to contact the mayor or town council. Judging from the tone of a few of the local merchants, I suspect they'll take me up on the offer.

As I wrap up the final call, I find myself eyeing the folders Mona left for me. Since the start, I've assured myself I wasn't going to get involved in a cold case that's already been investigated, gone to trial, and closed. A case in which the perpetrator was convicted and is now dead.

I open the top folder anyway.

This one contains all the information she could dig up on Joseph King before the murder of his wife. As usual, Mona's work is thorough, but the file is sparse in terms of documentation. I'd been hoping for a comprehensive criminal case history, arrest or Spillman reports, offense reports, citations, complainant and witness statements. Instead I have a summary report containing a list of charges along with dates and locations, a single summons to appear, four incident reports, a copy of a citation, and a mug shot. Considering King's lengthy list of infractions, it's far from complete.

I put the incident reports in date order and hunker down to read. His troubles began nearly four years ago when he received a DUI. According to the deputy's report, a vehicle clipped the rear quarter panel of his buggy while passing. Evidently, King veered left of center and made contact with the other vehicle. The driver overcorrected, lost control, and hit a tree. He was transported to the hospital via ambulance with minor injuries. The deputy who made the stop smelled alcohol on King. When he searched the buggy, he found an open container of alcohol. The deputy administered a sobriety test, which King failed. He was arrested on a DUI charge. A Breathalyzer test indicated that his BAC (blood alcohol level) was .108 percent, well over the legal limit. King paid a $250 fine and spent six days in jail.

Six months later, a Geauga County sheriff's deputy stopped him for operating a buggy after dark without lights. According to the report, King was trying to conserve his battery. Again, the deputy smelled liquor on his breath and arrested him on the spot. King's BAC was .110 percent. King was convicted, spent twenty-two days in jail, and paid a $500 fine.

Just two weeks later, an unnamed caller reported a "loud argument" between King and his wife, Naomi. The deputy arrived to find the couple embroiled in "a heated argument." Naomi "appeared disheveled, shaken, and frightened of her husband." The scene inside the home was in "disarray." The officer spotted a bruise on Naomi King's neck and, over her protests, arrested her husband on a domestic-violence charge. The charge was later reduced to the threat of domestic violence, which is a second-degree misdemeanor. King spent eight days in jail and paid a $250 fine.

Three months later an anonymous caller reported hearing gunshots and "rapid fire" at the King farm. A Geauga County deputy arrived to find Joseph King "intoxicated" and firing a rifle at "targets" he'd set up. According to the deputy's notations, King became combative and assaulted the deputy. King was arrested and charged with battery upon a public servant, which is a fourth-degree felony. This time, he did four months in jail.

King had only been out of jail for a week when, in the course of a "domestic violence situation" at his residence, a Geauga County deputy discovered a bag containing marijuana and a small amount of methamphetamine in the Amish man's coat. King was charged with a second-degree felony. The case went to trial and the charge was ultimately knocked down to a misdemeanor drug possession.

I'm paging through the docs for the third time when it strikes me that there are no witness statements included. Nothing from any of the complainants, including Naomi King. The "unnamed caller" is never identified. There are no photographs accompanying any of the domestic-violence incidents. Most cops are fanatical about recordkeeping, me included. Not because they enjoy truckloads of paperwork, but cops know all too well that in a litigation-run-wild society you cover your ass. That means meticulous documentation.

"So where is it?" I mutter.

I page through the file again, searching for things I missed, but there's nothing there. It's true that for religious reasons, most Amish would not be required to have their photographs taken; most police officers are trained to comply. That said, if the photo is only of a bruise somewhere on the body, it's likely the majority of Amish would allow it. Had Naomi King refused to let them photograph her? While that would explain the lack of photos, it doesn't explain the sparse information.

I go to the e-mail from Mona and read, *Hey Chief. Hope you're surviving all the craziness re J. King. Clerk at Geauga Records Dept sent everything he had and I printed for you. Hope it helps! See you tomorrow!*

The homicide file includes more in terms of documentation. There are pages of detective notes, crime-scene photos, logs, the autopsy report, lab and ballistics reports, and various computer-generated printouts. I read the ballistics report first. I'm midway through when a passage stops me cold. ". . . evidence that an attempt was made to fire the second shell present in the shotgun. A visible indentation on the primer made by the firing pin indicates the primer failed to ignite, possibly due to improper seating."

I flip the page and find myself staring at a computer-generated image of a primer that's been magnified twenty times. Even to my proletarian eye, the mark where the firing pin struck is clearly visible. I think of the story Sadie told about the armed intruder inside the house the night her *mamm* was murdered and I suppress a shiver. . . . *he raised the long gun like he was going to shoot us. I heard it click, but he must've been playing.*

Dear God, is it possible the shooter tried to kill a three-year-old little girl because he feared she might be able to identify him?

The lead detective was Sidney Tucker. I reach for the phone, knowing I'll need to be careful with my approach. No law enforcement agency wants some cop from another jurisdiction sniffing around about an old case or questioning their work. I dial the main number for the Geauga County Sheriff's Department and ask for Detective Tucker.

"There's no one here by that name," the receptionist tells me.

I ask her to put me through to the detective unit. A gruff-voiced detective tells me Sidney Tucker retired two years ago.

"Any idea how I can reach him?" I ask.

"I don't have his contact info. Last I heard he lives out by Mosquito Lake."

At two P.M. I grab my keys and head to reception. Lois is embroiled in a mound of salad heaped in a Styrofoam container. She looks up at me when I pass by her desk.

"That looks good," I tell her.

"Tried that new little shop down the street, Chief." Blotting her mouth with a napkin, she grins. "Don't tell the folks at the diner."

"When you get a minute, I need contact info for a retired detective with the Geauga County Sheriff's Department by the name of Sidney Tucker," I tell Lois as I head for the door. "Last known address was Mosquito Lake."

She jots it down. "I'll see what I can find."

"If you need me I'll be up in Geauga County."

"Joseph King stuff?"

"Just tying up a few loose ends. If anyone asks, I've packed up and moved to Key West."

She grins. "You and me and Jimmy Buffett."

"And that stray bottle of rum."

CHAPTER 15

According to Jonas King, Salome Fisher, the bishop's wife, was Naomi King's best friend. *If anyone knows anything about what was going on in her life, it's Salome,* he told me. I'd been planning to pay her a visit the day I talked to Edward and Jonas King, but I'd gotten the shots-fired call from Mona and had to cut it short. I figure the best friend is probably going to be a good place to begin, so I check the address and head toward Rootstown Township.

Salome and her husband live just off Wilkes Road. It's a rural area dotted with quaint farms festooned with the iconic silos and bank barns prevalent in this part of Ohio. The mailbox at the end of the lane isn't marked and I drive past it twice before realizing through process of elimination that it is, indeed, the place I'm looking for. There's a sign next to the mailbox that reads BROWN EGGS NO SUNDAY SALE. The lane itself is little more than a winding dirt track with a hump of weeds in the center. I follow it a quarter mile before the old white farmhouse looms into view. In the side yard, a garden striped with rows of baby corn, fledgling green beans, and a single row of caged tomato plants. A clothesline is strung next to the house and contains children's clothes—boys' trousers, work shirts, and little girls' dresses—all flapping in the breeze.

I follow the lane around to the rear of the house and park against a railroad timber where a dozen or so guineas and a lone peacock peck at the ground. Outside the barn to my left, two draft horses are hitched to a wagon loaded with hay. I wave at the Amish man watching me from the doorway. He doesn't wave back.

I take the stone walkway to the front of the house, ascend the steps, and cross to the door. The house sits atop a low hill with a pretty view to the north. In the flower bed next to the porch, a fat hen and a dozen or so chicks peck and scratch at a patch of irises, and I can't help but remember all the times my *mamm* burst from the door, armed with a broom, and swatted at the marauding chickens.

"Can I help you?"

I turn to see the Amish man who was in the barn come around the corner of the house. He's clad completely in black—slacks, vest, and jacket—and a white shirt. I guess him to be around fifty years of age. Pale blue eyes behind wire-rimmed glasses. A salt-and-pepper beard reaches nearly to his belt. The Amish don't work out or belong to gyms. But physical labor is often part of the lifestyle and this man has the physique of a man half his age. Shoulders the size of tires. A thick neck corded with muscle. Large hands with callused palms and nails worn down to the quick. He makes for an imposing figure as he stops at the base of the steps and squints up at me.

"Mr. Fisher?" I ask.

"That's me," he drawls as he ascends the steps. "Who wants to know?"

I extend my hand and introduce myself. "I'm the chief of police of Painters Mill."

"Police?" He ignores my hand. "What do you want with me?"

I relay the basics of the Joseph King situation. "I'm actually looking for Salome. I understand she was friends with Naomi."

"She knew her."

"Is she home? I'd like to speak with her if she has a few minutes."

He doesn't look happy about the request and takes a moment to look out over the pasture to the north. "She's been trying to put that business behind her," he says after a moment.

"I wouldn't be here if it wasn't important," I add in *Deitsch*. "I won't take up too much of her time."

"Burkholder, you say?" His eyes narrow.

"My parents were Amish." I've no idea if it will get me in the door, but I'm not above using my roots to get things done, especially when it comes to a case.

"I don't know if she will speak to you. About Naomi, I mean." He brushes past me. "I'll go get her."

He disappears inside, the screen door slamming behind him.

I spend a few minutes watching the chickens move from the now-mangled irises to massacre a beetle that dared trespass onto the sidewalk. I'm wondering if the Fishers forgot about me and thinking about knocking again when the door squeaks open.

To my dismay, it's not Salome Fisher. "She doesn't want to talk to you," he tells me in *Deitsch*.

"Mr. Fisher, I'm just trying to find the truth. Your wife may be the only person who can help."

He starts to close the door, but I set my hand against it. "Did you know Joseph?"

"Good-bye, Miss Burkholder." He glares at the place where my hand is preventing the door from closing, so I let it slide away. "I hope you find what you're looking for."

The door clicks shut.

I stand on the porch, disappointment sizzling beneath my skin. "It's *Chief* Burkholder," I mutter.

I take the steps to the sidewalk and make my way toward the rear of the house, where I parked. As I walk past the window, I see the curtains flutter. I wonder if Salome is inside, watching

244

me leave. I wonder if she's curious, if she feels guilty for not helping me. I slow my pace, hoping she changes her mind, but no one emerges from the house.

Upon reaching the Explorer, I yank open the door, climb behind the wheel, and start the engine. I make a U-turn and start down the lane. My mind is already forging ahead. I've just picked up my cell to see if Lois was able to find an address for Sidney Tucker, when I glance in the rearview mirror. Through the billowing dust, I see the figure of an Amish woman running after me, waving her arms.

I hit the brake so hard the tires slide. By the time I get out she's just a few yards away, breathing hard, her cheeks pink from the exertion of the run.

"Salome?" I call out.

"*Ja.*" She reaches me, bends at the hip, and takes a moment to catch her breath. "Couldn't make up my mind if I wanted to talk to you or not." She straightens. "You're that Amish police?"

"Yes." I introduce myself.

Salome Fisher is a pretty woman with a face full of freckles and eyes the color of a summer storm. I guess her to be at least ten years her husband's junior, but that's not so unusual among the Amish.

"I knew something bad was going to happen

when I heard Joe got loose from jail." The Amish woman cocks her head. "How are the children?"

I tell her what I know. "They'll be reunited with their aunt and uncle today, I think."

"Poor little things." She closes her eyes briefly. "I've been praying hard for them."

"Jonas told me you were friends with Naomi," I say.

The Amish woman looks away, but not before I discern the quick flash of emotion. When she finally turns her gaze to mine, her face is serene, her eyes soft. "Friends?" She hefts a laugh. "More like *shveshtahs*." Sisters. "Naomi was the best friend I ever had and probably ever will. I know she's with God now, but I miss that woman every day."

"You knew her well?" I ask.

"Better than she knew herself." Salome's mouth curves into a melancholy smile. "She was a good friend. A good mother. Wife." She gives a short laugh. "Naomi King was a force to be reckoned with. So full of life. And a little bit of vinegar, too."

"Did you know Joseph?" I ask.

"Not to speak ill of the dead, but I was no fan of Joseph King." She spits out the words as if they're chunks of rotting meat. "Everything that's happened to him was his own doing. The man was dense as a log."

"Did you know him well?"

246

"Well enough to know he was a brute and a drinker. Men like him?" She hefts another laugh. *"Sie scheie sich vun haddi arewat."* They shrink from hard work. "Joseph King was a lazy fool with a cesspit for a mouth and a head full of rocks. He had no business having all those children. Always yelling at them. Naomi, too, like she was some dense animal. He liked them to do their share around the farm, but never held himself to the same standard."

"What kind of relationship did he have with Naomi?" I ask. "Did they get along?"

"They had their differences," she tells me. "Naomi had a spine on her and a sharp mouth to boot. She put both to good use on that no-good husband of hers."

Up until now I'd been under the impression that Naomi King was a browbeaten wife who'd had little in the way of a support system. I amend my opinion. "Naomi stood up to him?"

Salome sets her hands on ample hips. "I seen her put him in his place a time or two. I reckon she should've taken a buggy whip to him. Doubt that would've helped, though." Her mouth twitches as if she's remembering something particularly amusing, but there's pain behind the smile, too. "No one knew it, but *sie hot die hosse aa.*" She wore the pants in the family.

"Was he ever abusive to her?" I ask. "I mean, physically?"

"Never saw it. I mean, not outright. But Naomi was private that way. Especially when things weren't going well. She never complained, though I suspect she had plenty of grievances." She shrugs. "But we talked like women do, you know. Too much if you ask our husbands, but then what do they know?"

"Were you aware of the domestic-violence charge against Joseph?"

"Naomi told me about it the day after they took Joe away. Everyone was talking about it—you know how the Amish are. They might be pious, but they like their gossip."

"What did she say?"

Salome takes her time answering. "I got the impression she didn't understand exactly what was going on when the policeman came to the house. She didn't mix much with the *Englischers*, you know. She didn't even realize it was a serious thing until she read about it later in *The Budget*. By then it was too late for her to do anything about it, so she just let Joe deal with it on his own."

"Salome, did Joseph hit her?"

Grimacing, she shakes her head. "Joe might've been as dense as a stump, even a little mean at times, but he never hit her. Not that I ever heard about, anyway."

A frisson of titillation zips through me. The kind that comes with a new tidbit of information on a case that's been stingy with facts. "Naomi let them charge and convict her husband when she knew he was innocent?"

"Joe wasn't exactly innocent now, was he? He was drinking and spoiling for a fight so the police came out and did what they do." She knows what I'm getting at and frowns. "We are separate, Chief Burkholder. Naomi didn't understand exactly what the police were doing. It didn't help that the policeman didn't explain. All she knew was that they took Joe to jail because he'd broken some English law."

Her expression turns troubled. "This is just me talking, but I suspect she was glad to be rid of him. Maybe she thought spending a little bit of time in jail would teach him a lesson. Give him some time to think and give her and the kids a few days of peace."

Her eyes slide toward the house and then her voice drops to a whisper. "My husband is the bishop. Naomi had come to him before, talked to him about Joe. Once, when she told him Joe had been taken to jail, he told her it was God's way of getting him off the road he'd been traveling."

If I didn't understand the Amish mind-set so well, I might've experienced a moment of indignation. But this isn't the first time I've seen something like this happen; I'm not surprised. In their quest to remain separate from the rest of the world, some Amish will stick their heads in the sand. They learn the hard way that ignorance is no protection from the law.

I move on to my next question. "Did Joseph get along with the kids?"

"Oh, he loved them. In his own way, I suppose. Always had a way with them because they loved him right back."

"Did Naomi and Joseph have a phone in their home?" I ask.

"Joe had a cell phone a time or two. Never was one to follow the *Ordnung*. But they didn't have one in their home. If Naomi needed to make a call she used the pay phone at the end of the road."

"Do you have any idea who called the police?" I ask. "Or how the police knew Naomi and Joseph were arguing?"

She blinks as if the question hadn't occurred to her, but should have. "I don't know."

For a moment I think she's going to say more. I wait, but she doesn't.

"How did you find out Naomi had been killed?" I ask.

"Stink Ed drove the buggy over and told us. I'll never forget the look on his face. He was just beside himself. Didn't go into much detail. Could barely speak. Just enough to tell us she was gone." She presses her hand against her chest. "I went to pieces. Couldn't believe it." She shores

250

up her emotions with a smile. "The only comfort came with knowing she was with God."

"Did you suspect Joseph?" I ask.

"I figured there'd been some kind of accident with the buggy or maybe something medical. Then I heard Joseph was in trouble and . . . I don't even know what I thought."

"Do you think he did it?" I ask.

She locks her gaze on mine. "I reckon he did if the law says so." Her voice drops to a whisper. "Much as I disliked Joseph, I never thought him capable of something like that. Shooting his own wife while she slept? With all them kids in the house?"

"Is there anyone else you can think of who might've wanted to hurt Naomi?"

"Someone *else?*" She looks at me as if my hair is suddenly peeling away from my scalp. "But . . . I thought Joseph was . . . I mean, he had a trial and it was decided."

I wait and she finally gives an adamant shake of her head. "Everyone loved Naomi."

"What about Joseph? Did he have any enemies that you know of? Any ongoing disputes? Over money or—"

My words are cut off by a male voice. "*Ich bin sell geshvetz laydich!*" I'm tired of that kind of talk. "*Die zeit zu cumma inseid is nau!*" The time to come inside is now.

I look past Salome to see her husband standing

251

in the gravel lane twenty yards away, his hands on his hips, staring at us. I didn't hear him approach.

Knowing our time is limited, I repeat my question. "Did Joseph have any enemies?" I ask quickly.

She glances over her shoulder at her husband, then back at me. "I believe I've said enough. Got to get back to work now."

She starts to turn away, but I reach into my pocket and pass her my card. "Call me if you think of anything else or if you just want to talk."

She takes the card without looking at it and drops it into her apron pocket. Without bidding me good-bye, she turns and starts toward the house.

It's almost always helpful to see the crime scene, even if the case is cold. Photos and sketches and notes are beneficial, but a walk-through can add perspective, scope, and clarity. The farm where Naomi and Joseph King lived with their five children is just fifteen minutes from the Fisher home, so I head that way.

The house is abandoned now. After Naomi King's death—and Joseph's incarceration—the children moved in with Rebecca and Daniel Beachy in Painters Mill. The eighty acres they left behind was leased to the Amish family next door, and they use it to farm hay and corn, and run a couple of dozen head of cattle on the pasture. The money, which probably doesn't amount to much, goes to the Beachys.

The gravel lane is overgrown with weeds and lined on both sides by blackberry bushes that will undoubtedly bear copious fruit by summer's end. As I zip past, I can't help but wonder how many times Naomi King sent her children down the lane to pick berries.

I pass a row of blue spruce trees; then the lane curves right and the old farmhouse materializes. It's a plain house with white siding and a red brick chimney. There are no shutters or landscaping. Rusty tin shingles on a steeply pitched roof. The lawn is a tangle of knee-high grass, patches of thistle not yet in bloom, and a thousand other unidentifiable weeds. I can just make out the rusty frame of a swing set with an attached slide that's been twisted by summer storms and the weight of winter snow.

I pull around to the back of the house and park adjacent to a tumbling-down chicken coop. The door stands open, giving me a view of the nesting boxes and a roost that's broken in half. A sapling tree has taken root in the coop yard and pushed through the chicken wire covering the top. And I'm reminded of how quickly Mother Nature reclaims what is rightfully hers.

I get out of the Explorer and make my way to the back door. I find the key where Daniel

Beachy told me it would be, beneath the nearest rock of the flowerbed, and I let myself into the mudroom.

Abandoned homes have a distinctive smell. But it's more than the redolence of mildew and dust and uncirculated air that defines it. It's an intangible sense of abandonment, of loneliness, a sort of vacuum left behind when the final person walked out the door with the knowledge that he or she would never return. And I'm reminded of ghosts.

The mudroom is oblong and small with an ugly plywood floor. Two small windows to my right, but not much light makes it through the grime. There's a small workbench to my left, its surface covered with dust and droppings. Something was once clamped to the edge with a metal plate, but the bolts are long gone. The only thing left is an odd-looking steel arm. It's about a foot long with a foam roller handle that's been chewed up by rodents. On impulse, I pull out my phone and snap a photo. There's an old propane refrigerator in the corner. The door stands open, and through the gap I can see where some industrious mouse has built a nest of cardboard and dried grass.

I stand in the mudroom and for an instant I try to imagine the voices of children as they played in the backyard. The squeak of the swing set as little legs pumped with all their might. The echo of laughter. The lingering aromas of cured ham and bean soup for supper. The clang of pots and pans as Naomi King washed and dried the dishes. Joseph standing at the workbench tinkering with some project . . .

The kitchen is still intact. Plain cupboards painted white, the hinges just beginning to rust. An old-fashioned Formica countertop marred with a brown ring where someone set a too-hot skillet. I look at the window above the sink, where a terra-cotta pot sits on the sill, a long-dead plant crumpled and brown. There's a chipped porcelain sink and stainless-steel faucet crusted with hard-water minerals. An old propane tank lies on its side on the floor. The place where the stove once was is bare.

The floor creaks beneath my feet as I walk into the living room. There's no furniture. To my left is a side door with a broken pane. Water stains on the hardwood floor that's started to warp. A wasps' nest hangs down from the ceiling in the corner; I can hear the buzzing from where I stand, so I back away and move on.

The stairs are to my right. A narrow, darkened stairwell and steep wooden steps. I know from the police reports that the murder happened in an upstairs bedroom. I take the steps to the top. There's a small round window to my right. A narrow, tall-ceilinged hall to my left. Four doors stand open, dim light slanting into the hall. I see a half dozen or so nails in the walls, probably where a baby quilt or macramé wall hangings once hung. Farther down, the arm of what was probably a gas light angles down from the ceiling.

I go to the first room, glance inside. It's a small space with a single window. Typically Amish, with no closet, no frills. Rough-hewn wood plank floors. Homemade wood pegs set into the wall for hats and clothes.

I continue down the hall, pass a bathroom. Grimy window. Old-fashioned claw-foot tub. The sink has been disconnected from the wall, leaving the pipes exposed, and sits at a cockeyed angle on the floor, its white porcelain striped with rust the color of blood.

The next room is also a small bedroom. Same setup as the first. One of the windowpanes is broken. Beneath it the hardwood planks are misshapen and starting to rot.

The master bedroom is at the end of the hall. The door is ajar. I push it open the rest of the way, the squeak of the hinges inordinately loud in the silence. I feel something brush against my head and, thinking of spiders, I swipe at it with my hand. But it's only the steel arm of the gas ceiling light.

I peer into the bedroom. Two windows are swathed with homemade curtains that are caked with dust and cobwebs. The room is devoid of furniture. Blue paint on the walls, darker where a tall headboard must have been. I wonder about the things this room has witnessed. I wonder about its secrets.

Recalling the police photos, I look at the place where the bed used to be—against the wall to my left—and I realize I'm probably standing in the exact place where the killer stood the night he murdered Naomi King.

"Who are you?" I whisper.

I think of Sadie and the story she relayed about the stranger in the house that night. I step back into the hall and glance at the room she shared with her sister. Two doors down. She said she got up to use the bathroom, which is next door to her parents' room. Of course, it would have been very dark. But if the bedroom and bathroom doors were open, if the curtains had been parted, there would have been enough light for her to see someone standing here, at least in silhouette.

A sound from downstairs interrupts my thoughts. A door closing. Footsteps against the hardwood floor. They're not trying to be quiet. Still, it gives me a start. Setting my hand over my .38, I go down the hall and look down the stairwell. No one there, but I can hear someone moving around.

Quietly, I descend the stairs. Midway down, the step creaks. I'm nearly to the ground level when an authoritative male voice calls out.

"Stop right there."

I reach the base of the stairs to see a Geauga County sheriff's deputy standing in the living room, his hand on the butt of his Glock, looking at me as if he's trying to decide if he's seen me on the FBI's most wanted list.

"I'm a cop," I tell him.

He's an attractive man of around thirty years of age. Not much taller than me, but he's got the physique of a professional wrestler. I can see the cords in his thick neck above the crisp collar of his uniform shirt. Short sleeves revealing biceps the size of Thanksgiving turkeys. Expensive sport sunglasses at his crown over buzz-cut hair.

Eyeing my uniform, he starts toward me. "You got ID on you?"

"I'm Kate Burkholder." Slowly, I reach for my shield and hand it to him. "Chief down in Painters Mill."

"Painters Mill, huh?" He takes my ID and looks at it carefully. "You're a long way from home."

I offer my hand and a smile. "Out of my jurisdiction, too."

"Nick Rowlett." We shake and he hands my ID back to me, his expression thoughtful. "One of the neighbors called, said she saw a vehicle out here. Figured I'd find teenagers looking for ghosts or smoking dope." His eyes narrow on mine. "Your name's familiar."

"I was involved in the standoff with Joseph King."

"Nasty situation." He shakes his head. "You got business up this way?"

The last thing I want to do is reveal to local law enforcement that I'm here looking into a case they closed two years earlier. Especially when Sheriff Crowder made it abundantly clear he's no fan of me or Joseph King. Still, a deputy sheriff could be a good source of information.

"After the standoff with King, I just wanted to drive up and take a look around."

"You find what you're looking for?"

"I haven't quite figured that out yet."

"I just remembered where I heard your name," he says. "You're the one who used to be Amish. You knew King back when you were kids."

"That's right." In the back of my mind I wonder if he saw that damn photograph, but he's too polite to mention it. "His family lived on the farm next to ours."

"Personal connection makes it even tougher." He offers a slightly apologetic look. "Hated the way all that turned out."

I'm not sure if he's talking about the takedown of King or the murder of his wife.

He sighs, his eyes scanning the room, and then shakes his head. "Our department took a lot of calls out here that last year or so before he killed her."

I think of the skimpy file and ask, "What kinds of calls?"

"Ran the gamut. King was one of those guys that was always getting into some kind of trouble. If he wasn't drunk and disorderly, he'd get himself pulled over—in the buggy of all things—and we'd catch him with alcohol or drugs. Later, we started getting domestic-violence calls. Honestly, I think he'd been beating the hell out of her for some time. No one knew about it and she never told anyone. I can't help but wonder . . . if we'd done something sooner she might still be around." He shrugs. "But then you know what they say about hindsight."

"Who was it that called the sheriff about the domestic disputes?"

"Neighbor, I think."

I wonder if it's occurred to him that the neighbors on both sides are at least half a mile away. "What was Naomi King like?"

"Only met her a couple of times. Nice woman. Pleasant. Pretty, too. I always wondered what she saw in King. From what I hear, the guy was a thug and a bully."

"You know what they say about love being blind."

He laughs. "Ain't that the truth."

"Were you involved in the homicide investigation at all?" I ask.

For the first time he doesn't look quite so cocky; his eyes flick away from mine. "I was one of the first responders. It was my first homicide

260

and let me tell you, it was a bad scene." He gives a self-deprecating laugh. "Learned I wasn't such a tough guy that morning, I guess."

"Anyone who doesn't feel that way probably shouldn't be a cop," I say.

"Hated to see things turn out the way they did, but we're not going to miss Joe King around here. I figured that son of a bitch was out of our hair for good when he got sent up to Mansfield. No such luck."

An awkward silence ensues, but he takes ownership of it. "Sorry if you were a friend of his."

"It's okay," I tell him. "No offense. I hadn't seen Joseph in over twenty years."

"Well, I hope I'm not overstepping, Chief Burkholder. But I had multiple run-ins with that guy. He might've been Amish and all that, but he was a bad egg. When the mask came off, he was like any other piece of shit I'd ever dealt with. Worse, because you weren't expecting it from an Amish dude. Hell, even the bishop figured Joe did it."

The statement gives me pause; I'd just talked to the bishop and he hadn't mentioned any such thing. "The bishop said that?"

The deputy doesn't notice my surprise. "In the course of one of the interviews. I mean, for King's own *bishop* to deem him guilty? I think it says a lot about what the Amish thought of him."

Deputy Rowlett cocks his head, studies me a moment. "You interested in the murder, or what?"

Careful, a little voice whispers.

"I just wanted to get a few things straight in my head, I guess."

"Did you?" he asks.

"Enough so that I can put it to rest."

A call comes over his radio. He responds via his shoulder mike and then turns his attention back to me. "I've got to get back to work," he says. "Look, if you need any information on any of this stuff, let me know and I'll send it your way."

"Do you have any idea where I might find Sidney Tucker?" I ask.

He looks surprised that I know the name of the detective who worked the homicide of Naomi King. "Last I heard he was living out to Mosquito Lake." He pauses, ignoring his radio. "Haven't seen Tuck since he retired. If you talk to him, tell him I said hello, will you?"

"Honestly, I'm probably not going to make it over that way. If I do, I'll tell him." I offer up my best sheepish smile. "At some point I'm going to have to get back to work, too."

He's staring at me as if he isn't quite sure whether to believe me; then he motions toward the stairway. "Feel free to finish what you were doing, Chief Burkholder. Look around as much as you like." He grins. "Be careful, though. I hear there are ghosts out here."

After tipping his hat, he turns away and disappears through the mudroom.

CHAPTER 16

There's not much a cop dislikes more than to receive conflicting information in the course of a case. Precious time is wasted sorting through the half truths or outright lies to get to the facts. Then you waste more time figuring out who's feeding you false information and why. I'm not even officially working on the Naomi King murder case and yet that's exactly what's happening.

After my conversation with Salome Fisher I have to wonder: Is it possible the domestic-violence charges against Joseph King were, at least in part, the result of some kind of disconnect between Naomi King and the sheriff's department? Is it possible that neither she nor Joseph fully understood the seriousness of the charges and therefore made little effort to fight them? Was he charged and later convicted because no one stepped forward to set the matter straight? It seems implausible. But having grown up Amish, I understand the attitude that might put such a scenario into play.

The Amish community's disdain for litigation could have dissuaded both Joseph and Naomi from eliciting the services of an attorney. The separation tenet could have discouraged them from asking questions that should have been asked. As a whole, the Amish seem to hold themselves to a higher level of accountability. While they'll be the first to forgive, that forgiveness doesn't always lend itself to tolerance, especially when it comes to a man like Joseph King, who repeatedly found himself on the wrong side of all those Amish rules, not to mention the law.

But while the domestic-violence conviction was a crucial part of the prosecution's case, it wasn't the only evidence presented against Joseph King in the course of the trial. The shotgun had been recently fired. There was gunpowder residue on his clothes. Naomi's blood was on his jacket. There was circumstantial evidence as well as the dubious timeline of his fishing trip to Lake Erie.

I'm about to call Lois to see if she was able to get an address or phone number for Sidney Tucker when a call comes in from Auggie Brock.

"Hey, Auggie. What's up?"

"Kate, I'm glad I caught you." He pauses with a little too much drama. "The town council asked me to call you."

"If this is about the covered bridge, I got sidetracked by the King situation and——"

"This isn't about the bridge. It's about that photograph of you and Joseph King."

The initial fingers of uneasiness press into the back of my neck. "All right."

265

"Look, it's all over the Internet, Kate. Did you see the headlines? 'Sleeping with the Enemy'? 'Kiss of Death'? Good Lord. Three newspapers have picked up the story two days in a row now. If the *Plain Dealer* or *Columbus Dispatch* jump on the bandwagon, the shit is going to hit the fan. We're going to have some fallout."

"Auggie, I can assure you there was no misconduct—"

"Kate, the council members want to see you."

Silently, I count to ten. "When?"

"Now would be great."

He starts to say something, but I hang up on him.

The Painters Mill City Building is on South Street half a block from the traffic circle. The two-story brick structure was built in 1901 and has gone through several renovations since. It housed a post office in 1954. There was an elementary school on the first and second floors in the 1960s, while the new school was being built. The Painters Mill town council moved in after a fire gutted the top floor back in 1985. Citizens can pick up city permits, vote on issues, pay traffic citations, and attend council meetings.

I'm running later than I intended, so I opt for the stairs in lieu of the notoriously slow elevator. By the time I reach the outer chamber I'm breathless. The administrative assistant is already

266

gone for the day, so I cross to the double doors and let myself in without knocking.

Six sets of eyes sweep to me when I enter the room. Mayor Auggie Brock sits at the head of the cherrywood conference table, a stack of folded newspapers in front of him. Councilwoman Janine Fourman sits next to Auggie, bejeweled fingers pecking on a sleek laptop. She owns several of the Amish tourist shops in town. She's the most vocal of the group, has political aspirations to become Painters Mill's first female mayor, and would like nothing more than to replace me with someone a bit more malleable.

The remaining council members are part-time volunteers. Dick Blankenship is a local farmer. Bruce Jackson owns a tree nursery on the edge of town. Ron Zelinski is a retired factory worker. Neil Stubblefield teaches high school algebra and coaches the football team.

"Chief Burkholder." Auggie rises and motions me to the only vacant chair. "Thank you so much for coming. I know you're busy wrapping up the Joseph King fiasco."

I don't take the chair. "What can I do for you?"

Auggie reaches for the newspaper, snaps it open, and turns it so I can see the photo and the headline. KISS OF DEATH. "I take it you've seen this?"

I glance at the paper, cringing inwardly at the sight of Joseph trying to kiss me. "I've seen it."

Ron Zelinski looks down at the coffee cup in front of him as if suddenly fascinated by its contents. Bruce Jackson shifts uncomfortably, his chair creaking beneath his weight. I don't miss the smirk on Janine Fourman's face, a teenager watching her favorite slasher film, and I'm the one who's about to venture into the basement.

"We're getting . . . calls," Auggie tells me. "Lots of them. Citizens wanting to know how their police chief was caught in such a . . . compromising position."

Janine Fourman jumps in. "They want to know how it is that a city employee, the chief of police at that, is engaging in such inappropriate conduct." She flicks the newspaper with her finger. "The man kissing you murdered his wife and took five children hostage, for God's sake."

"A man who was later shot dead by the police," Blankenship adds.

"It looks bad, Kate." Auggie eyes me as if it pains him to say the words. "We're fielding calls from reporters as far away as Cincinnati. I'm sure they're calling your office, too. If this thing catches fire, we could be in for a shit storm."

I want to point out that he's mixing his metaphors, but I know it would only make the situation more contentious, so I bite my tongue and remain silent.

"What exactly are we supposed to tell the folks?" Auggie asks.

"In all fairness, we thought we should hear from you," Zelinski says. Mr. Reasonable.

"We have city leaders calling for your resignation," Janine interjects.

"That's not to mention the prisoner-rights groups," Auggie adds. "I hate it, but this thing could conceivably get pretty ugly."

I take a moment to make eye contact with each council member. Auggie is having a tough time meeting my gaze. Stubblefield and Jackson look as if they'd rather be getting colonoscopies. As usual, Janine has blood in her eye. I'm pretty sure Auggie was railroaded into this.

"With that photo making the rounds, I believe we need to do some damage control," Auggie says.

When no one says anything, Janine jumps in. "Do you have an official explanation you'd like to share with us, Chief Burkholder?"

This is my chance to defend myself. That's why I'm here. Why I've been waylaid by these people I've worked with for over four years now. But as I look from face to face, the reality of the situation becomes clear, and the anger I'd been experiencing gives way to a deep sense of disappointment.

"Apparently, all of you have already made up your minds about what happened," I say.

"We asked you to come here because we'd like an explanation from you," Auggie says, trying to

269

sound diplomatic, but it comes across as whiny and insincere.

"All right." I motion toward the pile of newspapers lying on the tabletop. "Regardless of what you or anyone else might think, I did not engage in any form of misconduct while in that house with Joseph King."

"We believe you, of course," Stubblefield says quickly. "But that photograph is . . . damning."

"One of the prisoner-rights groups has called for an investigation," Jackson puts in. "A couple of the shop owners in town have already weighed in on this."

"Kate, Painters Mill is a tourist town," Auggie adds, as if I'm somehow not aware of the fact. "You know how important that is to our economy."

"We don't want tourists thinking our police department is . . . engaging in any kind of . . . dubious behavior," Stubblefield adds.

My temper stirs in earnest. This is a witch hunt and I've had enough. "In that case I suggest you put your heads together and figure something out." I take a step back and reach for the doorknob. "I've got to get back to work."

Looking alarmed by the possibility that I'm going to walk out, Janine stands. "We've already come up with a solution."

Ron Jackson looks at the mayor. "For God's sake, Auggie, tell her."

All eyes turn to Auggie, including mine.

"Kate, I hope you know we're on your side," he says. "You have a lot of fans in this room."

"I can see that." Out of the corner of my eye I see Janine Fourman roll her eyes.

"But that photo presents a problem for Painters Mill and the image we want to project. As mayor, it's my responsibility to deal with it and make the hard decisions. We've looked at that photo carefully. While you may not have done anything inappropriate, it *appears* you did. Appearances are important when you're in the public eye."

He pauses dramatically. "After much discussion, the town council and I decided to place you on restricted duty."

I tamp down another rise of anger, keep my voice level. *"Restricted duty?"*

"That means you can continue with your duties as chief, but you can't be on patrol," Auggie explains.

"I know what it means," I snap.

"With pay," Stubblefield adds quickly.

I ignore him, focus my attention on the mayor, saying nothing.

He's one of those people who can't bear silence. "Come on, Kate. Don't look at me like that. You'll be back to full duty in no time. A few days. This is mostly for appearances. You know, until this thing blows over. Think of it as a vacation."

I barely hear the final sentence. I'm not sure which is worse, the sense of betrayal or the humiliation.

Without a word, I turn and open the door. Auggie calls out to me, but I leave the room and cross through the outer chamber without looking back.

Knowing Auggie will come after me if only to make nice, I take the stairs two at a time to the ground floor. He calls my cell twice on the way down, but I don't answer. I like Auggie; he's a decent mayor. Before this, I'd begun to think of him as an ally—and a friend. The problem is he doesn't have the fortitude to stand up for what he believes is right when he's outnumbered. This isn't the first time he's let a self-interested town council or group of merchants browbeat him into throwing me under the bus.

I jog down the hall and smack both hands against the exterior door. It swings wide and crashes into the wall with a satisfying *bang!* Hitting the fob, I slide behind the wheel of the Explorer, slamming the door a little too hard. It helps.

Anger is such a waste of time and energy. It takes a monumental effort, but I shove my temper aside, put the vehicle in gear, and pull onto the street. I'm not going to let this sidetrack me. I'm not going to let it stop me. And I'm sure as hell not going to let it keep me from getting to the truth.

"Damn it." I rap my fist against the steering wheel.

By the time I reach the first traffic signal, I'm calm enough to call Jodie, my second-shift dispatcher. "Do you know if Lois left contact info for Sidney Tucker?"

It's too late for me to drive back to Geauga County this evening. But at least I'll have the address; I'll be able to make the trip first thing in the morning.

Papers rattle on the other end. "Got it right here, Chief." She recites a Cortland, Ohio, address along with a phone number. "How'd it go with the mayor?"

"Don't ask."

"Oh boy."

"Thanks for the address."

"Hang in there, Chief."

My anger drops off on the drive to the Beachy farm. I want to check on the family, on the children, and it won't help if I walk in foaming-at-the-mouth mad. This is about Joseph King's kids, not me. By the time I turn in to the gravel lane, I've composed myself.

There are indelible reminders that just forty-eight hours ago, the farm was the scene of a barricaded-gunman-and-hostage situation. At the height of the standoff, there were a couple of dozen vehicles parked along the road, and on either side of the lane. The traffic left tire ruts on the shoulder and the grass trampled to dirt.

I park at the rear of the house and take the flagstone path that's overgrown with henbit and clumps of fescue to the front. I ascend the steps, cross the porch, and give the door a firm knock. The door flies open. I glance down to find myself face-to-face with Little Joe, and I'm struck anew by how much he looks like his father.

"Little Joe," I say. "*Wie bischt du?*" How are you?

"*Ich bin zimmlich gut.*" He looks over his shoulder. "*Mir hen Englischer bsuch ghadde!*" We have another non-English visitor.

I heft a smile. "Been getting a lot of them?"

"Too many, according to Aunt Becca."

"Chief Burkholder?"

I look past the boy to see Rebecca Beachy come out of the kitchen, her hands busy with a raggedy dish towel. "What brings you here this evening?"

"I just wanted to see how everyone is doing," I tell her.

Reaching over the boy, she pushes the door open and ushers me inside. "Come in."

The house smells slightly of bleach, some kind of pine cleaner, and freshly brewed coffee. I brace as Rebecca takes me into the kitchen, half expecting to see some sign of the shooting's aftermath, but the room is tidy and clean. There's no sign of the carnage I saw last time I was here.

"I made coffee if you'd like some," Rebecca says. "Date pudding, too."

"That would be great." I don't want either, but I need something to occupy my hands. "Thanks."

I'm trying not to look at the place on the floor where I found Joseph when movement in the doorway catches my attention.

Levi and Sadie are standing just inside the living room, hiding behind the wall, peeking out at me. Levi grins and turns away, his little feet pounding up the stairs as he flees. Sadie grins and starts toward me. "Hi, Katie."

The instant I lay eyes on the little girl, something melts inside me. She looks fragile and sad, her eyes far too old for a five-year-old. I don't know if she's been told about her father, but I can tell she knows something.

Cradling her doll against her chest, Sadie stops a couple of feet away and looks at me expectantly. "I was wondering if you'd come back."

"I had to check on you to see how you're doing."

"You mean after what happened to Datt?"

"Yes, baby," I say quietly. "You doing okay?"

She nods vigorously. "Aunt Becca made date pudding and let me lick the bowl. That helped a bunch."

"It doesn't get any better than that." I turn my

attention to the doll she's holding against her. "How's Dottie doing?"

Another grin emerges and I catch a glimpse of tiny baby teeth. "She's doing good, too." She uses a little fingernail to scrape at a stain on her doll's dress. "Did you know my *datt* went to heaven and now he's with my *mamm*?"

The question knocks me off-kilter. Such a sad comment from a five-year-old kid. For a moment, I'm not sure how to respond. I look at Rebecca; the Amish woman gives a somber nod.

"I know, sweetie. I'm sorry."

"I think he'll like it there." Her brows go together as she gives the notion serious consideration. "I mean, he gets to be with Mamm *and* Jesus."

At a loss for words, I glance at Rebecca, but she just shakes her head. "I think you're right about that."

The little girl is still thoughtful; she's looking at me closely, studying my face as if she's going to have to recall every detail later. "My *datt* liked you, too, even though you're an *Englischer.*"

"The feeling was mutual," I say.

Rebecca sets two small bowls of date pudding and two mugs of coffee on the table. "Sadie, why don't you run out to the barn and tell your brothers to come in and wash up for bed?"

The little girl eyes the pudding. "May I please have one, too, Aunt Becca?"

"You already did." The woman punctuates the statement by brushing her hand over the girl's cheek. "You're like a little bottomless pit."

The child grins. I see those little baby teeth again and I'm reminded of just how young she really is. How much she's suffered and lost . . .

"Go on now. Gather up your brothers and tell them to get washed up. I want teeth brushed, too. Scoot."

Giving me a final smile, the girl heads to the back door and lets herself out.

"Poor little thing," Rebecca says, shaking her head.

I take the same chair Joseph used just two days ago. I still feel the energy of him in the room; I can't seem to stop looking around. At the wall where there was blood spatter. The floor where he died. The table where we sat together and remembered.

"How much did they see?" I ask.

"Too much." She settles into the chair across from me. "Sadie and Becky saw all of it. They'd been sitting at the top of the stairs when the police shot him down."

Her voice breaks. Her face screws up. She presses her hand to her mouth, unable to speak. After a moment she composes herself. "Don't know why they had to do that."

I don't respond.

"The social worker people told Daniel and me

that the two girls came down to 'wake him up.' *Mein Gott.* They had his blood all over their little hands." She shakes her head. "Honestly don't know if I'll be able to forgive Joe for putting them through that."

"What about the other kids?" I ask.

"They saw Joe lying there on the floor like a shot deer. But they didn't see it happen, which is a blessing for them I guess." She closes her eyes tightly. "I can't imagine the things that went through their little minds."

"I'm sorry, Rebecca."

"It's all part of God's plan." She says the words because it's what she was taught to believe. But she's not convincing.

"The social worker people kept the kids away from us for almost two days," she tells me. "Acting like Daniel and I did something wrong. Those kids needed to be home with their family."

I pick up my mug. "I'm glad they're home with you now."

"The police talked to us a lot. Asked us all sorts of questions about Joe. Now that he's dead, they don't come around much."

"How are you and Daniel holding up?" I ask.

She softens at the question and reaches out to pat my hand. "We're all right. Still trying to get used to the idea of Joseph being gone. Hurts my heart the way it happened. Even after what he did. The poor lost soul." Her eyes flick to the floor where he'd lain dead. "Just knowing what happened here. Feels . . . strange."

"It's going to take some time." I sip some of the coffee, trying to get my words in order. "Rebecca, when I was here that night with Joseph and the kids, Sadie told me she saw a stranger in the house the night Naomi was killed."

The Amish woman's eyes jerk to mine. "We've heard the story," she says. "That's all it is. A story told by a little girl who shouldn't be thinking of such things."

"I'm sure you know I spent a couple of hours with Joseph that night, Rebecca. We talked a lot during that time. I realize this isn't a good time to bring this up. I know all of you are still hurting. But do you think it's possible there *was* a stranger in the house that night?"

The Amish woman takes her time answering, twirling her spoon in the date pudding, but not eating. Finally, she looks at me and sets her napkin on her lap. "I think whatever happened that night is done and over with, Kate Burkholder. I think those poor babies have been through enough. Enough blood. Enough death. Enough pain. Enough lying. I know you were fond of Joe and all, but I'd appreciate it if you didn't go dredging all of that up again."

"Don't you want to know the truth?"

"The truth." She says the word as if it's a vile thing. "What will your precious truth accomplish?

Will it bring back Naomi? Will it bring back Joe? Will it change any of what's happened?"

"Rebecca, if there's a possibility Joseph didn't murder your sister." Leaning forward slightly, I lower my voice. "If that's true; if I find proof, that means whoever killed her is still out there."

"I don't believe it." She stares at me for an interminable moment. "Not for one minute."

"What if you're wrong?"

"Were all those police wrong?" she snaps. "Was the jury wrong?"

"I think mistakes were made."

"It's over and done. Finished. I'd just as soon not revisit any of it. I sure don't want those children having to relive it."

"Don't you care about justice?" I say.

"Justice for whom exactly, Kate Burkholder?" For the first time she looks angry. "Will Naomi get justice? Will she get her life back? Will those children get their mother back? I think not."

I'm about to say something about the reputations, the legacy that will be left for the children, but Rebecca gets to her feet and motions toward the door. "I think it would be best if you left before the children come back inside."

"Rebecca—"

"I'll walk you out."

I'm standing at the stove, pushing stir-fried vegetables around in a skillet, when Tomasetti

280

arrives home. I've already broken the seal on a bottle of cabernet. I'm midway through my second glass when he comes up behind me and puts his arms around my waist.

"Tough day?" he asks, pressing a kiss to my neck.

I tilt my head, giving him access, trying to decide how to break the news about my being placed on restricted duty. Of all the people in the world, Tomasetti will understand. He knows me inside and out. And while he knows better than anyone that I'm fallible and sometimes I push too hard, he also knows that I'm a good cop, a good chief, and that I will pursue justice to the end.

"Want a glass?" I ask.

"You bet."

I can tell by the way he's looking at me that he knows something is awry. Better to just lay it out and get it over with. "They put me on restricted duty."

He makes a sound that's part disappointment, part sympathy. "The King thing?"

"The photo." It's not like him to mince words. I say it because I know he didn't want to.

"And a little politics." He picks up the bottle and fills his empty glass with a little too much wine. Topping off mine, he goes to the table and pulls out a chair. "Sounds like it might be a two-glass kind of night."

I follow him over and sink into it.

He sits across from me. "Lay it on me."

I tell him about the scene in the town council chamber. "I handled it poorly and walked out. Tomasetti, I didn't do anything wrong."

"I know you didn't. Auggie knows it, too." He takes a sip of wine, sets down the glass. "That said, you *have* rankled a feather or two over the years."

"Apparently, that's my specialty."

"One of many reasons I'm crazy about you."

I frown. "You're not making it easy for me to be miserable."

He fingers the glass stem, swirls wine. "So what else is bothering you?"

I pick up my glass and sip. "It's scary how well you know me."

"I think that's supposed to happen when two people who care about each other live together for an extended period of time."

Reaching across the table, I smack him on the arm. He smiles at me and we fall silent. He's waiting for me to continue. I'm procrastinating, because I'm pretty sure he's not going to like what I have to say.

"I'll go first," he says after a moment. "You don't believe Joseph killed his wife."

"The more people I talk to and the more I learn about the case, the more convinced I am that something is not right."

"Have you decided what you're going to do about it?"

"I thought I might poke around a little, talk to some people, see what I can find out."

"People like who?"

"The lead detective, for one." I tell him about Sidney Tucker.

"He still with the sheriff's department?" he asks.

"Retired."

"And you're going to do all of this while you're on restricted duty."

"You know how it is with me and rules."

"They just get in the way anyway," he says dryly, and then eyes me over the rim of his glass. "Kate . . . look, I know you don't want to hear this, but I wouldn't be doing my due diligence as the love of your life if I didn't, so I'm just going to put it out there."

"Okay."

"Bear in mind . . . when Joseph King was killed, you lost a big part of your childhood. We see things differently when we're young. We see people differently."

"I'm aware," I say.

"Maybe your opinion of him is skewed because of your past with him. Because he was a big part of your life and you cared about him."

"Tomasetti, it's been a long time since I was thirteen years old. I'm a cop and I'm pretty sure

I've got a handle on any bias I might be experiencing."

"I guess that means you're not going to let me talk you out of this."

I take my time answering, knowing it's important to get the words right. "Five children are going to grow up without their parents; they're going to grow up believing their father murdered their mother. I think there's a good possibility someone out there got away with murder."

"Will you do me a favor?"

"If I can."

"If you have to walk into the lion's den, watch your back, especially around Crowder."

"I will. He wasn't exactly subtle about his opinion of me."

"Or King."

We fall silent, both of us caught up in our thoughts.

"I wish I could let this go," I tell him. "I wish I could walk away and forget about it. Tomasetti, I can't."

"If you did, you wouldn't be you and I probably wouldn't love you as much as I do."

I nearly choke on my wine. "I think that's the corniest thing you've ever said to me."

"You could be right."

"But it's working."

He grins. "Maybe you should set down that glass."

I do. "Turn off the stove."

Dinner forgotten, I pull him to his feet. He takes me into his arms and presses his mouth to mine.

CHAPTER 17

There are certain moments in which time stands still. Moments when every emotion, every physical sensation—the breeze on your face, the smell of fall foliage, or the refrain of a song on the radio—is imprinted on your mind and remains crystal clear through the decades.

The spring storms came with relentless fury the year I turned thirteen. Four days of driving, torrential rain filled the gullies and turned even the smallest streams into raging rivers the color of creamed coffee. Painters Creek swelled to three times its usual size, the swift water tearing hundred-year-old trees from the earth and sending them downstream.

One of our mama cows and her newborn calf went missing that third day. Daisy was everyone's favorite—sweet and personable with a star the shape of Ohio on her forehead. Datt and Jacob spent the morning looking for her. I wasn't allowed, which I took as a personal affront because it was me who'd cared for her since she was just a calf. I knew Daisy better than anyone; I knew her favorite grazing spots, and I couldn't bear the thought of something happening to her, or God forbid, her calf. And so while Mamm was busy scrubbing the upstairs bathtub, I pulled on my jacket and slipped out the back door to look for her.

Daisy preferred to graze in the low area near the creek where the grass was lush and green and she had plenty of shade on sunny days, so that's where I began. I almost couldn't believe my eyes when I caught my first glimpse of the creek. It had transformed from a meandering stream to a raging brown torrent that cut into the bank and tore around the trees like a writhing, churning serpent.

I'd only walked along the bank a couple of hundred yards when over the roar, I heard Daisy bawling. I could tell by the pitch that she was scared. I ran toward the sound, which seemed to be coming from somewhere downstream. I knew about the dangers of high water. Instead of getting closer to the creek, I headed toward the high area we called "the cliffs," where I would have a clear view and hopefully pinpoint her location.

I plowed through saplings and bramble, the stickers from the raspberry bushes tearing at my face and clothes. Finally, I was standing on the edge of the cliff, a place where the water had carved out a muddy cave right beneath me. Thirty feet down, the tops of the saplings swayed as brown water swirled past.

"Daisy!" I cupped my hands over my mouth. "Daisy!"

Through the saplings, I caught a glimpse of movement. The black and white of the cow's coat. Squinting, I sidled closer to the edge of the cliff, and I got my first good look at her. Daisy and her calf were standing on a small rise surrounded by fast-moving water. Usually, the sandbar-like rise is an extension of the bank. The flooding had turned it into an island that was quickly being consumed by swift water. Both cow and calf were in danger of being swept away.

It hadn't occurred to me to bring Daisy's halter or even a rope. I had no way to get across the water. No way to reach her.

"Datt!" I looked around, but there was no one in sight. "Jacob! I found them!"

The next thing I knew the ground collapsed beneath my feet. One moment I was standing on the edge of the cliff in knee-high grass, the next it crumbled beneath me. I made a wild grab for solid ground, but I wasn't quick enough. Dirt and grass flew at my face as I tumbled down the cliffside. Mud found its way into my mouth and eyes. Sapling trees punched me, their spindly branches tearing at my clothes and kapp. Then I plunged into the churning, ice-cold water, stinking of mud and fish and rotting foliage. My knee scraped the gravel bottom. The world went silent. Water in my eyes and ears and nose.

The current tumbled me end over end. Cold fists punching. I inhaled water and began to choke. Panic jetted through me. I kicked and my face broke the surface. I caught a glimpse of treetops and sky. A tree slammed into my shoulder, spun me around. Something scraped my leg. A tree root protruding from the bank banged into me. I grabbed for it, but the current ripped it from my grasp.

My feet lost purchase as I entered deeper water. A hard rush of panic clutched at me.

"Katie!"

I looked up, water streaming into my eyes. I couldn't believe it when I saw Joseph King running along the bank, arms pumping, eyes on me. He hurdled a fallen trunk. Hands tearing through brush.

"Swim to the bank!" he shouted. "Go with the current! Don't fight it! Let it carry you!"

I barely heard him over the roar of water. I floundered, my dress tangling around my legs, catching on submerged branches and roots. Water washed over my face. I sucked in a mouthful, choked it out. The current dragged me over a rock, knocking hard against my shin.

Please God. I don't want to drown.

I clawed toward the bank. I lost sight of Joseph.

"Here!"

I looked over my shoulder. He was just a few feet away, standing in water to his waist, hand outstretched. "Come on! Swim! You're a fish, remember?"

His name tore from my throat. "I can't!" But I did. I swam as I'd never swum before, kicking, kicking.

Then my hand was in his. Fingers grasping my arm, strong and warm and safe. "I got you."

He hauled me from the water, my knees and the tops of my feet scraping gravel and rock. He tripped over a large rock and landed on his behind. The water tried to take me again, but I crawled toward him, grabbed on to his pants leg. I lay there, facedown in the gravel and rocks, choking and gagging and trying not to cry.

I wake with a start, the smell of creek water and mud in my nostrils. The warmth of Joseph's hand closing over mine. The knowledge that I'm not going to drown warming me from the inside out.

"Kate. Hey. Wake up."

I open my eyes to see Tomasetti gazing down at me. "You okay?"

I push myself to a sitting position, shove the hair from my eyes, half expecting it to be wet, and I try to get my bearings. It's still dark outside. I glance at the alarm clock to see it's not yet five A.M.

"Sorry I woke you," I say, but my voice is hoarse.

"Must have been a bad one."

"It was . . . vivid."

The back of my neck and my T-shirt are damp with sweat. I'm still breathing hard, so I make an effort to dial it down. When I let out a breath, it shudders. "Didn't mean to scare you."

"Stop apologizing."

I toss him a smile, grateful he's there. "Yes, sir."

He scoots back, props himself against the headboard. "You want to talk?"

Taking a fortifying breath, I relay the events of that long-ago day. "I hadn't thought of it in years. Looking back as an adult, I honestly don't know if I would have made it out of that creek if it hadn't been for Joseph."

"He saved your life?"

"I think so. But . . . we were so young . . . we didn't know anything. Tomasetti, we didn't know what a momentous act it was. We didn't realize it was a big deal. We didn't even tell anyone it had happened." I laugh. "I think we were more worried about the cow and calf."

"Did you get them out?"

"We did."

"So it had a happy ending."

Smiling, I snuggle against him and my nerves begin to smooth out. I set my head against his shoulder and listen to the slow and steady thrum of his heartbeat.

"Just so you know," he says after a moment, "my opinion of Joseph King just went up a couple of notches."

Even though I'm still shaken from the dream, I chuckle. "That's something."

Leaning closer, he kisses my temple. "I'm sorry for what happened, Kate. I know you cared for him. I know it hurts that things played out the way they did."

"Thank you for saying that."

"If it's any consolation, I believe Ryan and Scanlon did the best they could."

"I know. I just . . . I wish they'd listened to me.

I *knew* King. I knew the good side of him. There was a possibility I could've talked him down or defused the situation. Tomasetti, they wouldn't listen to me."

"I know." He hugs me against him. A beat of silence and then he asks, "Did you love him?"

The question makes me smile. "I'm not sure that's the right word. I mean, I had no concept of love when I was thirteen years old. Puppy love, maybe."

"When you're that age puppy love doesn't feel like puppy love."

"Tomasetti, you're not jealous, are you?"

"Should I be? I mean, there was that kiss . . ."

I elbow him. "There was no kiss."

For the span of several minutes we lie against each other. Then Tomasetti says, "Look, I may not agree with what you're doing. I don't have as much faith in Joseph King as you do. But will you let me know if you need help? I may not have what it takes to save your favorite cow, but I have resources."

We both fall into laughter and I put the moment to memory, knowing it's precious, a snapshot in time that will stay with me the rest of my life.

"Have I told you I love you recently?" I ask.

"Not recently," he says.

"Well, I do."

"In that case . . ." Setting his hands on either side of my face, he lowers his mouth to mine.

CHAPTER 18

The *graabhof* lies on a stretch of road lined with quaint farms southeast of Burton, Ohio. It's a small cemetery filled with neat rows of plain headstones and surrounded by a three-rail wood fence. A solitary maple tree stands sentinel on the left side of the entrance gate. It's a bucolic scene made all the more melancholy because of its beauty.

The Amish generally turn out in droves when a member of their community passes away, sometimes traveling for miles to pay their final respects. Usually, there's a funeral service at the home of the family. The minister or bishop will give a sermon that oftentimes includes some type of moral lecture. There's no singing, but Bible passages are recited and at the end of the service an obituary is read, usually in *Deitsch*.

The plain casket is then transported to the *graabhof*. Family members and friends follow in what is usually a long line of buggies. Most funerals garner so much in the way of buggy traffic that I sometimes dispatch an officer to deter any disputes between the slow-moving buggies and impatient drivers.

There was no funeral service for Joseph King this morning. As I make the final turn onto Jug

Street, I pass only three buggies and a lone couple walking alongside the road, and I realize with a deep sense of sadness that, in light of recent events, few have turned out to mourn him.

I pull onto the narrow gravel shoulder and park behind a buggy. A few yards away, half a dozen men and women clad in black stand among the neat rows of pale headstones. Next to them, the wagon containing the casket lies in wait. More than likely the grave was dug by hand last night or early this morning—well before the mourners arrived—by two or three young Amish men.

I leave the Explorer and walk through the gate. Curious eyes descend upon me as I approach the group. There are no children present, just three couples and a group of men who are probably the pallbearers. I'm midway to the gravesite when the sound of tires on gravel draws my attention. I turn to see a silver Toyota pull up behind my Explorer. A bittersweet pang sweeps through me when Jonas King and his partner, Logan, get out and start toward me.

I stop and wait for them, extending my hand to both of them when they reach me. "I'm sorry about Joseph," I tell him.

"Thank you, Katie. And thank you for coming. I'm still trying to process it." Jonas blows out a breath and I realize he's quite upset. "I knew something like this could happen. I just . . ." He lets the words trail as if not sure how to finish the sentence. "I still can't believe it. I mean, Joe was always such a fixture in my life. Even while he was in prison. I can't believe he's gone."

I nod, understanding that unexpected punch of grief, of disbelief, all too well. "Does Edward know?"

He nods. "I told him but . . . He's not coming."

"How did you find out?" I ask.

"Sheriff sent a couple of deputies out to the house right after it happened." He looks at me. "Were you there?"

I nod and for an instant, I'm back at the Beachy farmhouse with Joseph and the kids, and I can't meet his gaze.

"I saw the photo," he says.

"Jonas, I'm sorry—"

He notices my reaction and chokes out a laugh. "It's okay," he says easily. "Joe was. . . . a rascal." He hefts another laugh, but it comes out with a sob. "He never said it, never said anything, but I think he was always a little bit in love with you."

Feeling more than is prudent, I wait a beat, and then change the subject. "I saw your nieces and nephews last night."

He flashes a smile at Logan. "We're heading that way next. How are they doing?"

"Good. Rebecca and Daniel are taking good

care of them and getting them back into a normal routine."

"They were there, too, that night, weren't they?"

"Yeah."

"Shit. Poor kids." Jonas brings his head forward and pinches the bridge of his nose, but quickly regains his composure. "The thing is, those kids have already been away from their *datt* for two years. Sad as it is, it'll probably make their adjustment easier."

It's true, but we both know their scars will run deep.

"Jonas, I know this isn't a good time to talk, but I want you to know I went to see Salome Fisher."

His gaze jerks to mine. "You did? What did she say?"

I take him through my visit with her. "She doesn't believe Joseph was physically abusive to Naomi."

"I thought that would be the case." He shakes his head. "But if that's the truth, why didn't she speak up? I mean, during trial?"

"I was left with the impression that the bishop thought it might a good lesson for Joseph to spend some time in jail."

He scrubs a hand over his face. "You know, Katie, those two domestic-violence charges played a big role during the murder trial. The prosecutor hammered it home every chance he got." He shakes his head. "I just don't see how Joe was *convicted*."

"The one thing I can tell you is that domestic violence doesn't always mean someone got punched," I explain. "According to Ohio code, if you put your hands on someone, you're probably going to jail. There are gray areas. Cops make judgment calls."

Sighing, he looks past me at the group of Amish that have congregated around the gravesite. "I don't believe he put his hands on her. My brothers and I weren't raised that way."

An awkward silence descends. I can tell by the way Jonas is fidgeting, not meeting my gaze, that he's got more to say, but he's debating whether he should.

"If you've got something to tell me, I think now would be a good time," I say.

Jonas tightens his lips, but says nothing.

Beside him, Logan sets his hand on Jonas's arm. "This has been eating you alive for two years. This is your chance. Tell her."

Jonas takes a deep breath, like a free diver about to descend into the depths, and then the words start to pour out. "I don't know how or why, but I think Joseph was railroaded. I think the meth was planted. I think the domestic-violence charges were . . . exaggerated."

"By who?"

"I don't know. But I knew Joe. He did not do meth. If you knew him . . . Katie, that's just crazy."

"Look, when someone has a problem—with drugs or alcohol or whatever—sometimes loved ones are the last to know. Some people are good at keeping secrets. They're able to function even when their life is spiraling out of control."

"He didn't have a drug problem," Jonas says testily.

I don't respond.

"And who called the cops the times when Joseph and Naomi were supposedly arguing?" he asks. "They didn't have a phone. They lived too far away for the neighbors to overhear them, if, indeed, they *were* arguing. How did the cops know to show up?"

I stare at him, silently acknowledging that the question has been bothering me as well. "I thought of that."

"I can tell by the look on your face."

I take a moment, look past him at the group of mourners. I wonder how many of them knew Joseph. How many of them are here simply because he was Amish and they are bound by duty.

I turn my attention back to Jonas. "Did Joseph have any enemies that you know of?"

"Pissing people off was one of his specialties."

"Can you be more specific?" Now it's my turn to get testy.

He gives me a tired smile. "He'd ticked off a few people in his day, but nothing serious that I recall." He thinks about it for a moment. "The only people who hated Joseph were the cops."

"What about Naomi? Did she have any enemies?"

He laughs at the notion. "God no. The woman was a saint."

Movement where the graveside service is about to be held draws my attention. I glance over to see four young Amish men removing the casket from the wagon with two long poles.

"We'd best get over there," Logan says.

The two men start toward the gravesite.

"Jonas?" I call out.

He turns and raises his brows.

"I'm going to talk to the detective who handled the murder investigation."

Tears fill his eyes, but he doesn't let them spill. "Joe never had anyone to look out for him when he was alive. Not me. Not Edward. Now it's too late. What an epic fail."

I hold my ground, watching as the two men join the rest of the mourners.

"It's not too late," I whisper.

I stayed for the graveside service, watching most of it from a distance. It left me feeling depressed and unsettled. It was too brief, the minister reading just a single hymn. By the time the first shovel full of dirt was tossed onto the casket, the mourners were already heading to their buggies. Duty done. Time to call it a day. Good-bye, Joseph.

It's not yet noon when I climb into the Explorer and pull onto Jug Street. I'd decided to heed my own good judgment and head back to the farm. Maybe take a nice, long, exhausting run to work off some of the melancholy that's been dogging me. But my mind isn't on home or running or even my job. I can't stop thinking about Joseph King, the circumstances of his life and death and those final hours we spent together in the farmhouse.

Joseph never had anyone to look out for him.

Jonas King's words ring hard in my ears as I head toward Wooster.

"Shut up, Jonas," I mutter.

I'm southbound on Ohio 44 when I realize I can't go back. I make a sudden turn into the parking lot of a heavy equipment dealership. I sit for a moment, reminding myself I'm on restricted duty; it doesn't help. Gravel spews from beneath my tires as I make a U-turn and head east instead of west.

The last thing any cop welcomes is some yahoo from another jurisdiction coming in and questioning his work. Of course, I'll do my best not to be obvious about it, but that's exactly what I'm going to do.

Forty-five minutes later I'm idling down Lake Shore Drive on the west side of Mosquito Lake near Cortland when I spot the street number on the mailbox. I make the turn into a neat asphalt drive and park in front of the attached two-car garage. The house is a split-level brick built back in the sixties. It's quiet and nicely kept with a dozen or so massive maple trees in the front. A row of lilac bushes that will be covered with blooms in the summer delineate the property line to the south. A hedge of barberry bushes runs the length of the driveway and adds yet another layer of privacy.

I go to the front porch, walk past two Adirondack chairs, and knock on the storm door. I wait, listening for a radio or television, but no one answers.

"Crap," I mutter, wishing I'd called before making the drive. But I know why I didn't; I wanted to catch the former detective off guard and unprepared. So much for best-laid plans.

I'm nearly to the Explorer when I decide to check the backyard. I'm pretty sure this property backs up to the lake. With Tucker being retired, there's a decent chance he might be outside working in the garden or something.

I go around to the side, walk past a gazebo and a shed. The backyard is huge and backs up to a wooded area. It's unfenced, so I start across the grass toward what looks like a trailhead. It takes me just a few minutes to reach the lake. It's a pretty spot with an abundance of birds and sixty-foot-tall trees. The water is as smooth as glass. A corpulent man wearing khakis, a fishing hat, and sunglasses is standing on the bank, fishing.

"Catching anything?" I ask as I approach.

He glances at me over his shoulder and continues reeling. "You should have seen the largemouth bass I just tossed back in. Had to be six pounds of him."

Sensing a fish story, I smile. "Why'd you throw him back?"

"Never liked fish," he tells me. "But I damn sure like to catch them."

Upon reaching him, I extend my hand. "I'm Kate Burkholder, the chief down in Painters Mill."

Eyes narrowed, he wipes his hand on his pants. "Nice to meet you, chief of police Kate Burkholder. I have a feeling you're not here to check my fishing license."

We shake. His grip is firm, but not too tight. Hands callused and dry. Slow, easy release. He's about sixty years old with a kindly face and grandfather eyes. I can tell by the way he looks at me that while he possesses the countenance of some harmless senior citizen, the part of him that is a cop is alive and well.

"If you have a few minutes, I'd like to talk to you about the Joseph King case," I tell him.

"Joe King, huh? Read about what happened." Holding the line with his left forefinger and thumb, he draws back and casts beautifully. "You're the cop spent some time with him in the house with the kids?"

I nod, watch the spinning lure catch the sunlight a couple of feet beneath the surface. "Joseph asked me to look into his case."

"Did he now? Huh. So that's why you're here."

"I'm here because I know some cases have two files: a sanitized file and a street file."

That gets his attention, like a dog that's been deemed too old to fetch, but still can't take his eyes off the ball. Tucker finishes reeling in the lure, leans the pole against a tree, and goes to the small cooler at his feet. "Want a beer? It's cold."

"No thanks."

"I know it's only noon, but I'm retired, so . . ." I wait while he pops the top on a Budweiser and drinks deeply. "Geauga County not share the file with you?" he asks.

"Some of it," I say vaguely. "Wasn't much there."

He slants me a look, a sly smile overtaking his expression. "That photo of you and King didn't help, did it?"

I look out over the water, embarrassed, saying nothing.

"Then again, cooperation and the sharing of information isn't exactly a hallmark of the detective unit."

"Mr. Tucker, I just want to get your take on the investigation. Your observations about the case as a whole. If you're pleased with the outcome."

He takes his time answering, seeming to consider every word before speaking. "Joseph King was a son of a bitch. He was a drunk. Irresponsible. Spent money like it was going out of style. Treated his wife and kids like shit. Didn't deserve any of them if you ask me."

It doesn't elude me that none of those things have anything to do with the actual case. My curiosity piqued, I wait.

"I was a sheriff's deputy for thirty years, Chief Burkholder. I was ready to retire long before I actually did. But I took the time to get my finances in order and all that." He grins. "Get all that gnarly love-for-the-job crap out of my system."

His grin falters and he turns thoughtful. "I wanted three things to happen when I retired. I wanted to do so with a clear conscience. I wanted to wake up every morning and have breakfast with my wife. And I wanted to spend my afternoons fishing this lake.

"My wife died of cancer right before I retired." Shaking his head, he looks out over the lake. "One out of three ain't exactly great."

He shrugs. "Still get to fish every day, anyway."

I give him a moment to say more, but he doesn't. He finishes the beer, reaches down and pops the tab on another. In the distance, I hear the whistle-like call of some large water fowl. He looks toward the sound and tells me, "That's the tundra swan. Been watching them all spring. Beautiful animals."

"Why didn't you retire with a clear conscience?" I ask.

He looks down at the can in his hand. When he raises his eyes to mine, his kind grandfather demeanor has darkened. "I don't think he did it."

After everything I've heard about Joseph King—from the cops as well as the people who'd known him—I almost can't believe my ears. "You don't believe he murdered his wife?"

He looks at me, saying nothing.

"But it was your investigation," I say.

"Was it?"

I feel myself blink. "I don't understand. What are you saying?"

"I'm saying shit runs downhill and unless you've got some kind of fecal fetish you'd better get out of the fuckin' way."

"Mr. Tucker, are you telling me someone somehow influenced your investigation? Did someone try to intimidate you in some way?" I press. "Someone in the sheriff's department?"

He hefts a bitter laugh. "Look, I've got two

306

daughters left. Six grandkids. I'm retired now. I'm old and tired. I drink too much beer. Talk to myself." He looks down at the can in his hand as if he's lost his taste for it. He upends it and swigs again anyway.

"Look, Chief, I suspect you're a good cop since you've driven all the way up here to ask me about Joseph King. But listen, it ain't your deal and it ain't your fuckin' case. If you're smart, you'll let this go. Joseph King is dead. His wife is dead. Nobody gives a shit about either of them now."

"I do," I say fractiously.

"Excuse me if I don't get out my violin."

"Mr. Tucker, I know Joseph King wasn't perfect, but he deserved to live his life."

He sighs tiredly. "Do yourself a favor and walk away while you still can."

Now it's my turn to laugh. "What do you mean, while I still can?"

He dumps the rest of the beer onto the ground and crushes the can. Bending, he tucks it into the cooler; then he picks the cooler up and grabs his pole. "It was nice talking to you." He starts toward the house.

"But . . . wait." I fall into step beside him, having to walk at a fast clip to keep up. "If Joseph King didn't murder his wife—"

"No one said that—"

"Who did?"

"I wouldn't fuckin' know."

"But you said—"

"What I said was this and it's the only thing you need to hear: If you're smart you'll leave this alone. Go back to your loose cows and jaywalkers and Saturday-night drunks and have yourself a nice, long, peaceful life."

"Mr. Tucker, you can't drop a bomb like that and then walk away."

"Really?" Stopping, he swings around to face me, giving me a red-eyed glare. "Try this on for size then: Take your badge and your attitude and get the fuck off my property. Don't come back. Is that clear enough for you?"

It takes me forty-five minutes to make the drive to Chardon. All the while, my conversation with Sidney Tucker churns in my brain like shards of glass, cutting and grinding.

I don't think he did it.

I can still feel the low-grade thrill the words induced. He's the first cop I've talked to who believes Joseph King didn't murder his wife. But how could he make a statement like that when he was the lead detective? And why wouldn't he talk to me about it? It doesn't make sense.

Walk away while you still can.

What the hell did that mean? Were the words some kind of threat? From who? And why?

The Geauga County Safety Center is located on

Merritt Road south of Chardon. The low-slung white building is a large complex that houses the sheriff's department, the county jail, dispatch, and Records. The coroner's office is located within the complex as well. One-stop shopping for a small-town cop who's light-years out of her jurisdiction.

"Not to mention her mind," I mutter as I park in the lot and leave the Explorer.

I use the crosswalk and pass the flagpoles where the wind whips the flags into a frenzy, the halyards clanging against the mast. I go through a set of glass doors to a sleek reception area and approach the information window.

A young woman in a Geauga County Sheriff's Department uniform snaps open the sliding glass. "Help you?"

Since I'm on restricted duty, I'm wearing civilian clothes. Hoping my being a cop will garner a bit more in terms of cooperation, I set my badge on the counter and identify myself. "I'd requested some records a few days back. I was in the area for a funeral so I thought I'd stop in and pick them up in person, save you guys the trouble."

She looks at my badge. "Painters Mill. You talking about the Joe King stuff?"

"Yes."

She glances at the clock on the wall. "Let me call Records." She motions to a sofa set against

309

the wall, just below a framed color photo of Sheriff Jeff Crowder. "Have a seat."

Fifteen minutes later, I hear the lock on the door click. I look up from my phone to see a young African American man wearing creased khakis, a crisp white shirt, and a coordinating tie standing in the doorway, his eyes on me. "Chief Burkholder?"

I rise and cross to him, stick out my hand. "Kate."

He grins. "Dylan."

He's attractive, with a quick smile and intelligent eyes tinged with good humor. Too young to be a cop. College student, maybe. The wire-rimmed glasses give him a studious appearance.

"I'm closing a case down in Painters Mill," I say easily, "and wondering if I can pick up some records."

"Usually we need some time to pull files, but since you're law enforcement and you're here . . ." He ushers me into a hallway. "You need copies? Or just a look-see?"

"Both if possible."

"I'm not that busy this afternoon, so I'll see what I can do."

He takes me down a series of well-lit halls, past a couple of glassed-in offices. Two uniformed deputies approach, giving us cop's nods as they pass. Though the Safety Center is a good-size building, home to multiple county agencies, I find myself hoping I don't cross paths with Jeff Crowder.

"You civil or law enforcement?" I ask as he punches a code into a door and ushers me through.

He grins, pleased by the question. "Civil. For now," he adds quickly. "I'm hoping to get into law enforcement one of these days. Preferably federal. You know, Homeland or the bureau. I'm a full-time student over at Kent State. I work here part-time two afternoons a week."

"Good place to get some experience under your belt." I'm trying to charm him in case I need help with something; so far I think it's working.

"Hope so."

"When do you graduate?"

"Spring."

I dig into my pocket, hand him my card. It earns me another grin.

We go through another door and enter a large, slightly shabby office with four open cubicles loaded up with desktop computers and landline phones. An old-fashioned microfiche squats atop a steel desk in the corner. Two glassed-in interview rooms along the wall look out over the parking lot. The opposite wall is lined with floor-to-ceiling file cabinets.

"Which case you looking for?" Dylan asks as he takes me to his cubicle.

"I'd like to see everything you have on Joseph King."

"I heard what happened down there in Painters Mill." But my request seems to give him pause. "Someone from your department called. Mirna . . ."

"Mona."

"That's it." His brows knit. "I thought I sent everything your way already. . . ."

"We received some of it, but I'm not sure everything was there."

"Huh." He looks perplexed. "Let's see what we can find."

He slides into a chair and jiggles the mouse to wake up the computer. "Kind of odd for a police chief to make a trip in person," he says as he pulls up a menu. "I mean on old cases that aren't really related."

"Since it was a hostage situation, I want to make sure I have everything on file. I was in the area for a funeral, anyway." I shrug, nonchalant, keeping it light, my eyes on the monitor. "I always like to make sure I dot my i's and cross my t's. A small town like Painters Mill can't afford any kind of litigation."

"Better to have too much documentation than too little. Someone sues, and you can't cover your butt, you're sunk." He taps a key. "Here we go. King, Joseph. Let's see . . . I've got several cases . . ."

"I'd like to see all of them."

"Okay." He hits another key. "I've got booking files, including booking sheets, criminal history, court papers, inmate records, fingerprint scans."

I recognize the reports as the same ones I already have back at the station. "What about incident reports? Witness statements? Especially on the two domestic-violence cases."

"I can check. Didn't think you'd want to see those since they're not related to the standoff." He types in a command. "I've got complaint files and some incident reports."

"What about LEADS? NCIC?"

"Protected."

I knew those records would be unavailable, but I thought it might be worth asking about.

"Hmm." His brow furrows. "Wait a sec."

His fingers fly over the keyboard. "That's odd . . . it looks like some of the records were . . . purged."

"Purged?"

He's staring at the screen as if his life depends on his figuring it out. "They should be here, but they're not."

"What kinds of records?"

"Looks like . . . whoa . . . just about everything."

Record-retention laws exist in the state of Ohio. Generally, the statute of limitations on a misdemeanor is two years. Seven years for a felony. When it comes to a sex offense or homicide, all law enforcement agencies are required to keep the records forever. Still, if a particular agency is lax or doesn't have a policy in place, things can and do fall through the cracks. That's not to mention the accidental or inadvertent purging of records. It's dangerous, particularly when it comes to documentation for arrests and court cases with the possibility of future litigation.

"What *do* you have?" I ask.

"Just what we sent you guys down in Painters Mill."

"Any idea what happened to the rest?"

"It looks like some of the records were purged accidentally when we computerized everything last year." He looks away from the monitor and makes eye contact with me. "You want me to print these records for you?" He motions toward a Hewlett-Packard printer the size of a large suitcase.

"Since I'm here." But I have a sinking suspicion I've already seen everything. "Any chance I can get my hands on the autopsy report?"

"You mean for Naomi King?"

I nod. "Just for my file."

"I'll request everything and print it, let you take it with you and sort through it at your convenience. That okay?"

"Perfect."

CHAPTER 19

I was blessed with good mentors during the early years of my law enforcement career. Men and women who generously shared their knowledge and experience with a cocky young rookie who wasn't always as receptive as she should have been. When I made detective, my sergeant paired me with a veteran who had more years on the force than I'd been alive. Francis Rosiak was just six months away from retirement when we worked our first case: the discovery of human remains from a homicide that had occurred a decade or so earlier.

It was my first big case and as cold as Lake Erie in January. Information was scarce, and I had absolutely no idea where to begin. Francis did. In fact, I'd never seen him stumped, and one of the best pieces of advice I've ever received came from him in the course of that case. "Figuring out where to start is easy," he told me. "You start at the beginning."

The advice has served me well over the years.

I make the drive to Rootstown despite the pouring rain and reports of flash flooding in Portage County. A renewed sense of urgency dogs me as I turn in to the lane of the Fisher farm. The rain is coming down so hard I can barely see the overgrown two-track as I make my way toward the house. I park in the same place I did last time I was here. As I shut down the engine, I notice the barn door standing open. Since it's Bishop Fisher I want to speak with this time, I put the Explorer in gear and pull up to the barn.

Swinging open the door, I sprint through the rain, my feet sinking ankle deep in spongy gravel, mud, and standing water. I'm soaked to the skin by the time I enter the barn. Rain pounds the tin roof in a deafening roar. The smell of horses and hay and damp earth fills my nostrils. A nice-looking little bantam rooster sits atop the top rail of a horse stall, crowing his ass off. There's no one else in sight.

"Bishop Fisher?" I call out. "It's Kate Burkholder."

The rooster eyes me warily as I take the wide, dirt-floored aisle more deeply into the barn. I hear a horse whinny over the din of rain, glance left and see a sorrel looking at me over the gate to his stall. An ancient-looking manure spreader is parked in the aisle outside a second stall.

I sidle between the manure spreader and the façade of the stall and catch a glimpse of the bishop inside. He's using a pitchfork to muck manure and toss it onto the spreader.

"Bishop Fisher?"

He turns. "I thought I heard someone out there."

I make a show of shaking water droplets from my jacket. "We're getting some good rain."

"Corn sure isn't going to complain. Been a dry spring so far."

I stop at the stall door and watch him work. "I've mucked more stalls than I care to count," I tell him.

"If you're feeling nostalgic, Kate Burkholder, I have another pitchfork hanging in the tool shed."

I smile. "I wanted to talk to you about Joseph King."

"I thought we already did that."

"Actually, I have a bit of new information I want to run by you."

"Good news, I hope."

"I'm not sure." I pause before continuing. "I was told by one of the deputies that in the course of an interview you told him you believe Joseph killed his wife."

"I don't recall saying anything like that." The bishop shovels another pitchfork of manure and wood shavings into the spreader.

I can't tell if he's lying and I have no way of knowing if the deputy who talked to him misspoke or misunderstood. Still, I press on. "It was in the course of an interview you did with one of the Geauga County sheriff's deputies after the murder."

The bishop sets down the pitchfork and leans on it, giving me an assessing look. "What exactly is your intent with these questions, Kate Burkholder?"

"All I want is the truth," I tell him.

"Or maybe you have an ax to grind against the Amish?"

"I have nothing but admiration and respect for the Amish." I meet his gaze head-on. "Unless they break the law."

"It's always a little bit more spectacular when it's the Amish, though, isn't it?"

"Not for me."

He contemplates me thoughtfully, as if seeing me for the first time. "There are times when the truth is a painful thing. Times when it will hurt people. There are times when silence is best."

"My *mamm* was fond of *glay veis leek.*" Little white lies. "She used them to keep the peace," I tell him. "To keep people from getting hurt. Police don't have that luxury."

"Luxury?" The Amish man's eyes are cold. "Joseph King is dead. Naomi is dead. What does it matter now?"

"It matters because if I'm right, someone got away with murder."

"You know nothing," the bishop hisses. *"Nothing."*

"Enlighten me."

"Aeckt net so dumm." Don't act so dumb.

"Why are you so certain Joseph killed his wife, Bishop?"

318

"Joseph King was no innocent." He looks at me as if I'm something to be pitied. "I believe the devil climbed into his heart and left the black stain of evil. I believe he killed his wife in a fit of rage. And I believe he thought he had reason to do so."

"What reason?"

For the first time the bishop looks uncertain. "Naomi is not here to defend herself."

That's the last thing I expected him to say. "Why would she need to defend herself? She was the victim."

He looks at the pitchfork as if he'd forgotten it was in his hands, jabs it into the trampled manure and wood shavings, and tosses it into the spreader. "What exactly are you going to do with this information?" he asks.

"I'm going to stop a killer."

"And if it hurts someone? Innocents?"

"Would you rather someone get away with murder?"

He sets down the pitchfork, leans on it. "I have struggled with this. I've asked God for guidance." Clenching his jaw as if against a powerful wave of emotion, he shakes his head. "Naomi came to me. For counsel. A few weeks before she was killed."

"What happened?" I ask.

He stares at me for a long time, as if he's trying to come to a decision. I wait, staring back, aware that my pulse is up because I'm pretty sure I'm about to hear something that's going to change everything.

"She was tearful and troubled and . . . deeply ashamed," he whispers.

"Ashamed? Of what?"

"Naomi King had gone down a dark road." He pauses, looks away, his mouth quivering. "She'd been unfaithful to her husband. Betrayed her vows. Not once, but . . . many times."

It's the first I've heard of infidelity on Naomi's part and the words shock me. "Naomi was unfaithful?"

"Yes."

"With who?"

"She wouldn't say. Just that he was not *Amisch*. She came to me seeking guidance. And forgiveness." He shakes his head. "Normally, with a transgression, I would ask the person to confess before the congregation and ask God for forgiveness. But with this . . ." The Amish man shrugs. "Knowing what I did about Joseph and all the trouble he'd caused with his infidelities and the law . . .

"Naomi and I prayed. I told her to ask God for forgiveness. I asked her to confess her sin to her husband and from this point on to remain faithful to him. She assured me she would do those things. A week later, she was dead."

He closes his eyes tightly, trying to hold back

tears, not quite succeeding. In all the years I've known the Amish, lived with them, lived apart from them, I've never witnessed a bishop breaking down.

"Naomi must have done as I advised," he whispers. "She must have confessed to her husband that she had broken her vows, that she'd been unfaithful. Because of my counsel . . . I believe Joseph flew into a jealous rage and took her life."

The rain continues in a relentless deluge, pounding the roof and slapping against the ground. The noise inside my head is every bit as deafening. I don't know what to think. I'm not sure how to feel. The bishop's theory makes perfect, terrible sense. The weight of the guilt I see in his eyes is crushing. Have I been wrong about Joseph? Did I let my past, my feelings for him, blind me to the truth?

"That's why you told the police you thought Joseph had done it," I say after a moment.

He nods. "I still do."

In the dim light slanting in through the open Dutch door behind him, I see tears on his cheeks and I'm moved by them. "This was my doing," he says. "At least in part. But I am just a man. Imperfect. Flawed. Unworthy."

"The only person responsible for Naomi's death is the person who pulled the trigger," I tell him.

He considers that for a moment. "That may be true. But if I hadn't told Naomi to confess her sin to Joseph, would she still be here?" He offers a sorrowful smile. "Neither you or I will ever know, of course. It's a question I'll take to the grave."

"Not if I have a say in the matter." Surprising myself, I reach out and set my hand over his forearm. "Thank you for telling me. I know it wasn't easy. I'll safeguard the information to the best of my ability."

"Be careful in your search for the truth, Kate Burkholder." Easing his arm away from me, he goes back to his mucking. "You may not like what you find."

CHAPTER 20

Be careful in your search for the truth, Kate Burkholder. You may not like what you find.

The bishop's words follow me as I take the Explorer down the lane and start toward home. If he's telling the truth—and I have no reason to suspect a lie—he just handed me a motive for murder. Jealousy over an illicit love affair.

Maybe Tomasetti is right, and I'm seeing Joseph King through the eyes of the young Amish girl I'd been. An innocent girl with a bad case of hero worship and in the throes of her first crush. Is it possible? After all this time and after all of my law enforcement experience, I'm unable to look at this with an objective eye? The thought makes me feel like a fool.

I rap my palm against the steering wheel hard enough to hurt. "What the hell did you do, Joseph?" I whisper.

I'm passing through Parkman, deep in thought, when I drive past a small restaurant called the Sweet Rosemary Café. I recall Jonas telling me that Naomi King had worked part-time at a restaurant in town. On impulse, I hit the brake, turn around in an alley, and pull into the gravel lot.

I don't expect to learn anything earth-shattering, but you never know when some nugget will come your way. Besides, it's been a long day. I could use some caffeine.

The Sweet Rosemary Café is part bakery, part restaurant, and part Amish tourist shop, all of it housed in an old two-story house built into a hillside. I take the sidewalk around to the antique-looking front door and enter to the enticing aromas of cinnamon, yeast bread, and fresh-brewed coffee. There are three other customers in the dining room. Two elderly men sit at a small corner table, embroiled in conversation, and a woman in a denim skirt and blouse sits at another table sipping iced tea and tapping a message into her phone. The waitress, a middle-aged Mennonite woman, is behind the counter, drinking coffee and watching a soap opera on the television mounted above the kitchen pass-through.

Four stools line the counter, so I slide onto the nearest one and upend the mug in front of me.

Tearing her eyes away from the TV, the waitress glances my way and grins. "They're about to kill that guy for the third time this year. Damien Rocco aka bad dude."

I laugh, game for the topic. "He deserve it?"

"Oh yeah. He's offed so many people I lost count." Snagging the coffeepot, she treads over to me and pours. "My husband thinks I'm a hard worker. He has no idea I come here to watch

TV." She taps her *kapp*. "We used to be Amish so we don't have one at home."

"Your secret is safe with me," I say in *Deitsch*.

Arching a brow, she shoves a tiny stainless-steel pitcher of cream toward me. "You *Amisch* or what?"

"Used to be." I offer my hand and introduce myself, letting her know I'm the chief of police from Painters Mill.

"Leah Yoder." She wipes her hand on her apron and we shake. "You miss it?"

"Sometimes." I pour cream into my coffee. "Not the rules so much."

"I hear that."

I sip the coffee and sigh. "I think that's the best coffee I've ever had."

She beams. "The owner, Mrs. Kresovich, gets it from a roaster up in Cleveland. Fancy stuff, let me tell you. We got some lemon custard pie left if you want a piece. On the house since you're a cop."

"Let me pay and you have yourself a deal."

"Never argue with the fuzz." She goes to a small refrigerator, pulls out a plate, and removes the plastic wrap. Snagging a napkin and fork from another place setting, she slides them over to me and sets the pie in front of me. "What brings you to this neck of the woods?" she asks.

"I'm tying up a few loose ends on a case."

Her eyes meet mine, her expression sobering. "You talking about the Joe King thing?"

I nod. "Did you know him?"

"I knew Naomi," she tells me. "She worked here for a time."

"Were you close?"

"We were. I considered her a friend. I liked her a lot and I sure hated to see her go the way she did. Such a tragedy, especially for the kids."

Emotion flashes in her eyes, so I give her a moment before asking, "What was Naomi like?"

"Quiet. Kept to herself at first. But I'm a talker. You give me enough time and I could carry on a conversation with a tree. I got the gift of gab, or so my husband tells me. So, yeah, we talked. She was a real nice gal. A good woman. Better than most. She liked to laugh, but didn't do it enough." She sighs, thoughtful. "She loved them kids, that's for sure."

"Did she talk about Joseph much?"

"Complained about him plenty."

"Did they get along?"

She huffs. "Like cats and dogs."

"Any idea what they argued about?"

"A lot of ground to cover, how much time you got?"

Grinning, I sample the pie, find it tart and creamy and delicious. "Till the end of this fine slice of pie at least."

"Not to speak ill of the dead, but Joe was

impulsive and lazy. Spent too much money and they didn't have much to begin with." She chuckles. "That Naomi. She'd come in slamming things around and grumbling and I knew they'd been at it. Heard her actually cuss him a couple of times and believe me, she wadn't a cussing kind of girl." Her brows snap together. "Always got the impression Joe didn't like her working. That set her off a couple of times because he was always buying stuff he didn't need with money they didn't have."

I think about my conversation with Bishop Fisher. "Was he jealous?"

She gives me an odd look, the meaning of which I can't quite decipher. "Never met a man who wasn't. Some just hide it better than others." She lowers her voice. "Don't tell my husband I said that." She punctuates the statement with a conspiratorial wink, but she's trying a little too hard to keep it light.

Sighing, she shakes her head. "I never thought it would end up the way it did. I mean, with her dead. One day we're complaining about rude customers, the next she's just . . . gone. I don't even think I said good-bye to her that last day. Figured I'd see her soon enough. I guess you never know."

I fork a piece of the pie. "You heard Joseph is gone, too?"

She nods. "That standoff thing was all over the news up here."

"I'm working to close the file," I tell her. "I've talked to a lot of people in the last couple of days. Interestingly, I'm getting quite a bit of conflicting information."

"About who?"

"Joseph." I shrug. "I talked to him the day he was killed."

The waitress's eyes widen. "You're the one who was in that house with him for a bit."

I nod. "He was adamant that he didn't murder his wife." I glance left and right and then lower my voice. "One of his children, the little girl, corroborated it. I wasn't sure what to make of any of it, so I decided to look into a few things before I closed the file for good."

When she doesn't respond, I add, "I'm not here to dig up dirt or ruin anyone's reputation. I'm trying to find the truth. That's all."

Suddenly Mrs. Gift-of-Gab isn't quite so talkative. Picking up a small box, she begins stocking postcards in a rotating countertop display rack. "I don't see how that matters now. I mean, with both of them dead."

"The truth always matters," I tell her.

She doesn't respond, but continues to slide postcards into slots.

"Did Naomi ever mention the Amish bishop?" I ask. "Bishop Fisher?"

She goes still, a machine that's gone into a stall, and in that instant I know there's something

328

there. Something she doesn't want to discuss.

"Don't think she ever did," she says breezily.

"What about his wife, Salome? I heard she and Naomi were friendly."

Rather than answer, she spins the rack, stuffs another stack of postcards into a slot.

"I know Joseph wasn't a good husband," I tell her. "If Naomi turned to someone else, no one would blame her."

She stops and turns to me. "Is that what you think she did? You think she two-timed her husband?" She hefts a short laugh.

"I don't think anything. I'm asking."

She waves off the statement. "I don't know what kind of fishing expedition you're on, but I ain't biting. You damn cops are all the same. Well, let me tell you something: Naomi King was a saint. She was a good wife. And a good mom. You got it?"

"Someone murdered her in cold blood," I say quietly. "I don't think it was Joseph."

"Bullshit."

I push the pie away and sigh. "I'm not judging her for what she did or didn't do. I don't care about that. All I want is the truth. And to get a killer off the street. You're not helping."

Finally, she picks up the box, shoves it beneath the counter, and glares at me. "She was my friend. Maybe I know something about her. Maybe I don't. All I can tell you is that if she was keeping some secret, she wouldn't want anyone to know. Especially the Amish. And those kids."

I lean closer to her. "I *didn't* know her, but I'm pretty sure she wouldn't want her husband's legacy to evolve around a murder he didn't commit. Or for her killer to get away with it."

She stares at me, shocked to silence. Her eyes sweep the dining room, as if checking to see if anyone is listening, then come back to me.

"I know she was seeing someone," I say quietly.

Leah Yoder starts to move away, but I reach out and set my hand on her arm, stopping her. "I promise not to be careless with whatever you tell me. If I can protect Naomi's reputation, I will."

The woman eases her arm from beneath my hand, looks down at the counter. "I don't know who it was. She never said."

"Was he Amish or English?"

"English."

"First name? Last name? Is he married? Do you know where they were meeting?"

She shakes her head. "She was careful. But I saw her getting out of a car once. That's all I know."

"What kind of car?"

Leah looks down at her hands, sets them against the countertop as if to keep them from shaking. "A police car."

CHAPTER 21

It's fully dark by the time I arrive at the station. The rain has returned with a vengeance, the weatherman announcing new thunderstorm and flash-flood warnings for Stark, Wayne, and Holmes counties. Welcome to northeastern Ohio in April. At least the media have gotten bored and left.

Parking in my usual spot, I use my jacket to cover my already-ruined hair and hightail it inside. I find my second-shift dispatcher, Jodie, reclined in her chair, her sandal-clad feet propped on the desk, blue-tipped toes wriggling to Phantogram's "Fall in Love." The sight bodes well for the possibility of a blissfully quiet evening.

She sits up upon hearing the door close and turns down the volume. "Oh, hey, Chief."

"Looks like everything's quiet on the home front," I say, plucking messages from my slot.

"Just the way we like it."

Skid is usually on second shift, but he took a couple of days off to see his parents in Ann Arbor. Normally I'd cover for him, but since I've been placed on restricted duty, Glock has stepped in to take up the slack.

"Any dry uniform tops lying around?" I ask her.

"Got a medium right here."

"It'll do."

She reaches into her file drawer and pulls out a neatly folded shirt with PAINTERS MILL PD embroidered on the sleeves. "There you go, Chief."

I take the shirt. "Since it's just us tonight and the phone is quiet, you can turn the radio back up if you want to."

She flashes a grin. "Roger that."

In my office, I change into a dry shirt. While my computer boots, I call Tomasetti and tell him about my trip to Geauga County.

"You've been busy for a chief on restricted duty," he says when I'm finished.

I recap my conversation with the bishop. "Naomi confessed to him that she was unfaithful to her husband."

"That doesn't bode well for Joseph King's innocence."

"It also brings someone else into the equation."

"Do you know who she was seeing?"

"The waitress she worked with thinks it might be a cop."

He sighs. "Well, shit."

"That's exactly what I was thinking."

"Look, Kate, I'm not saying I'm on the same page with you, especially when it comes to Joseph King. From all indications, he's guilty as hell. He found out his wife was unfaithful and he killed her. Wouldn't be the first time." Tomasetti pauses. "Enter that second person and the possibility that he's a cop and . . . maybe he's not the only one who thought he had reason to kill her."

"Tomasetti, this changes everything." Even as I recoil at the thought of someone in law enforcement committing such a heinous crime, another part of me relishes the prospect of an alternate suspect.

"It makes the situation a hell of a lot more complicated," he says.

My mind is already forging into a shadowy corner I don't want to look into. I tell him about my trip to the Geauga County Safety Center. "The records clerk told me the records had been purged. Even here in Painters Mill, we have a retention policy in place. We keep everything for a minimum of seven years. Not just felonies, but misdemeanors."

"I'm well aware of Ohio's retention laws."

"I know, but—"

"Kate, are you telling me you believe those records were purged or altered to conceal evidence? Do you think there was some kind of official misconduct going on? Some kind of cover-up or conspiracy to convict King?"

"I think all of those things are a possibility."

"That's a damn serious allegation."

"I'm aware."

"If we make this official . . ."

"We're not there yet," I say quickly. "I don't have proof. I don't have enough."

"But you're just getting started." He sighs, an unhappy, impatient sound. "Do me a favor and stay under the radar, will you?"

"That's the plan."

"Kate, look, if this gets to be too much or your gut is making you uneasy about something, will you let me know?"

The burst of gratitude in my gut is tempered with the knowledge that he's putting enough weight in the information I've unearthed to be concerned. "I will. Thank you."

He shifts the conversation away from work. "You going to make it home tonight?"

"I've got a few things I need to tie up here first."

"Uh-huh." He sighs. "Don't poke that stick of yours into too many dark holes. You may not like what runs out."

"Hey, I'm on restricted duty, remember?" But I'm thinking about Sidney Tucker's parting words. *Walk away while you still can.*

He makes a sound that's part laugh, part growl. "As if that's going to stop you."

I start with the Geauga County Sheriff's Department, collecting the names of current and past deputies, key administrative staff, and the higher-ups. I'm so embroiled in my task, I don't notice the shift change when Mona comes in—early as usual—and Jodie goes home.

At eleven P.M., Mona peeks her head into my office. "Want a pizza, Chief?"

I look up from my monitor. "LaDonna's is closed."

"There's that new place on Main. They're open until midnight. The pepperoni-and-mushroom is to die for."

"We're speaking the same language."

Glock comes up behind her. "Make it a large, will you?" He digs into his pocket and pulls out a twenty.

"I got it," I tell him. "Chief's treat."

Neither of them moves and I look up to find them staring at me. I give them a *what?* look.

"We hate that the town clowns put you on restricted duty." Mona looks at Glock, then back to me. "All of us."

"I appreciate that."

"Um . . . we were wondering . . ." She motions at the paperwork spread across my desk. "Need a hand?"

Glock shrugs. "It's a quiet night. We're here. May as well put us to work."

I give both of them a long, assessing look, wondering if they have any idea how deeply they've touched me. "This is . . . sensitive," I tell them. "Off the record. Way off the record."

Mona grins. "Off-the-record is our specialty."

I hesitate, considering the repercussions of involving them. But I trust them, I realize. I absolutely trust them. To keep the project confidential. That they will do a thorough job. And that nothing they see will go beyond the walls of the police station.

I pass my notes to Mona. "I need the names and contact info of every officer who currently works for the Middlefield Village Police Department. I need the same for anyone who has left the department or been terminated in the last two years. Check to see if any of them have pending misconduct cases or reprimands over the last two years. I need details of any misconduct issues, official or otherwise."

The look Mona gives me is worth a thousand words, and I realize I've touched her just as deeply. "I'm *so* all over this." She rips the paper from my hand and leaves my office.

I turn my attention to Glock. "Aren't you supposed to be on patrol?"

"It's raining cats and dogs out there, Chief. Thieves and drunks aren't even venturing out tonight." He pats the radio strapped to his belt. "If the zombies swarm, I'm on the ready."

I pass him two sheets of paper containing the names of the Geauga County sheriff's deputies I've already collected. "Run them through LEADS, see if anything pops. When you're finished, have Mona take a look at social media."

"You got it."

Half an hour later, I hear the outer door open and someone walk into the reception area. I'm assuming it's Glock bringing the pizza when Pickles appears at my door, aforementioned pizza in hand.

"I'm going to have to pick off all his pepperoni," he tells me. "Gives me heartburn something awful."

I withhold a smile, trying not to look surprised—or moved—by his presence. "You work the crosswalk this morning, Pickles?"

He hikes up his uniform trousers. "Didn't have to draw my sidearm once."

"I'm glad our grade-schoolers are so well behaved."

He frowns. "No one agrees with the restricted-duty crap, Chief."

"I appreciate your saying that."

"Pencil-necked sons of bitches. Excuse my language, but it's just a bunch of political horseshit." He lowers himself into the visitor chair across from me and takes in the paperwork spread out on my desk. "What do you have for me?"

"It's confidential."

"Figured as much." His eyes narrow on one of the documents. "Since we're dealing with a bunch of fuckin' cops."

Movement at the door to my office draws my attention. I look up to see T.J. standing there, his jacket dripping rain. He raises a six-pack of pop and a bag of ice. "Where do you want this?"

I frown at him. "T.J."

"Chief." He hands me a shit-eating grin.

"I thought you had a hot date tonight?" I ask.

"She had something come up with her folks." He shrugs, but his eyes skitter away and I know he's lying.

For a moment, I'm so overwhelmed I can't speak. By their loyalty. Their commitment to their work. Their dedication to this department and law enforcement as a whole. I'm incredibly lucky to have such a remarkable group of police officers working for me. Most of all, I'm thankful to call them not just friends, but family.

Sitting back in my chair, I look from T.J. to Pickles, try to find my voice. "You guys don't have to do this."

"Yeah, we do," Pickles says.

"We do." T.J. strolls over to my desk and takes the other visitor chair. "I take it this is confidential?"

"Nothing we talk about tonight leaves this room," I say.

Both men nod.

"What do you have?" T.J. asks.

"A mess." I pick up a sheet of paper and hand it to him. "Here's what I need."

By two A.M., the words on my computer screen are beginning to blur, and I find myself having to read passages twice just to comprehend them. I'm running out of steam. Glock has been called out twice. Once for a fight down at the Brass Rail Saloon. The other for a domestic dispute out at the Willow Bend Mobile Home Park. Otherwise, the night has been inordinately quiet—and frustratingly unproductive.

I'm thinking about calling it a night when T J. strolls into my office and takes one of the visitor chairs. "This is kind of interesting."

I look up, glad for the interruption. "What do you have?"

He passes two sheets of paper to me. "Last summer, a Geauga County deputy filed a lawsuit against Sheriff Jeff Crowder and the Geauga County Sheriff's Department claiming she was targeted for retaliation after reporting that drug evidence was tampered with."

"That *is* interesting." I look down at the newspaper story and read.

DISGRACED GEAUGA COUNTY DEPUTY FILES SUIT

Twenty-seven-year-old Vicki Cascioli, who was terminated last year for "insubordination, multiple unexcused absences, and sexual harassment," has filed a civil lawsuit against Sheriff Jeff Crowder and the Geauga County Sheriff's Department. Cascioli, who'd only been with the sheriff's department for eight months, claims sheriff's deputies regularly tampered with evidence and engaged in other unlawful activities. According to Cascioli, she was a "whistleblower" and was "targeted for retaliation" by her superiors and her counterparts. Sheriff Crowder could not be reached for comment. No court date has been set.

I look at T.J. "Get me everything you can find on Cascioli, will you?"

"You got it."

"Run her through LEADS, too. Have Mona take a look at her social media posts. See if anything pops."

A little over an hour later, Mona rushes into my office, looking bright-eyed and a little too excited. "I think I found something."

"Since the rest of us are striking out, lay it on me."

She looks down at the printout in her hand. "I found an interesting archived story from two and a half years ago in the Russell Township daily newspaper." She begins to read. " 'Nineteen-Year-Old Ohio Woman Allegedly Raped by

340

Geauga County Deputy.' " She glances up at me. "That's just the headline."

"You have my undivided attention."

She reads, " 'The victim claims she was pulled over by Deputy Wade Travers around three A.M. on a desolate road southwest of Chardon. When she failed a sobriety test, he arrested her and placed her in his car. Instead of taking her to jail, the victim claims, he offered to let her go if she had sex with him. When she refused, she alleges he pulled her from the car and raped her. The situation is under investigation by the Geauga County Sheriff's Department.' "

"Wade Travers?" Exhaustion forgotten, I get to my feet. "I've met him."

"Don't get too excited," she tells me. "There's a twist."

Mona looks down at the paper. "This story came out of the same newspaper four days later. 'Nineteen-year-old Kelly Dennison admitted to detectives that she lied about being sexually assaulted by Geauga County sheriff's deputy Wade Travers in the course of a DUI arrest. Travers, who had been detained and was facing termination and arrest, was reinstated yesterday.' "

"That's interesting as hell," I say.

"But it's a false alarm, right? I mean, he was exonerated."

I think about Joseph King and the purged

records, the alleged affair between Naomi King and a cop. And I wonder . . .

"Get me everything you can find on Kelly Dennison, including contact info. Social media. Ask Glock to run her through LEADS to see if she's got a record or warrants."

"Will do."

She starts to leave, but I stop her. "Oh, and Mona?"

"Yeah, Chief?"

"Nice job."

CHAPTER 22

I was fourteen years old the last time I saw Joseph King. He'd been on my mind a lot that cold and rainy spring. All winter, I'd pined for summer. To endless afternoons spent at the creek, fishing or swimming or wading where the water ran clear and fast. I could just see the roof of the King house from my place at the kitchen sink, and while I washed the dishes in the evening, I'd find myself straining my eyes, just to catch a glimpse of him. I'd daydream that he'd emerge from the woods between our farms the way he used to with that I-don't-have-a-care-in-the-world grin on his face and that old bamboo fishing pole at the ready.

But he never came. Things had changed over the winter. I hadn't seen him much since his *datt* was killed in a buggy accident last fall. He didn't come over anymore. When he did, it was only to help Jacob or Datt with some big project. I was never included.

Our family attended the funeral. Even at such a solemn occasion, I'd secretly watched Joseph, hoping he'd come over and talk to me so I could offer my condolences. But he'd been stone-faced and sullen and didn't even look my way.

That had been months ago and I was still young

enough, naïve enough, to believe things could be the way they were before the accident. I wanted to see Joseph laugh again. I wanted him to say things that would make my *mamm* frown. Most of all I wanted to go on another grand adventure—like our search for that trunk buried in the gravel bottom of the creek, or the exploration of some mysterious Indian burial ground.

It wasn't to be.

I was in the horse stall mucking when I heard the barn door slide open. I glanced over the gate to see Joseph silhouetted against the daylight. My fourteen-year-old heart leapt so hard I had to put my hand to my chest. But I'd known he would come back. Now, I thought, everything would be the same and we could get back to the way it had been before.

"Joseph!" Dropping the pitchfork, I rushed from the stall, almost forgetting to close the door behind me.

He'd stopped ten feet inside the sliding door. He didn't speak as I crossed to him, just watched me with a sort of quiet intensity, as if he didn't quite remember who I was. He was taller now. His face had grown lean. An odd sense of self-consciousness assailed me. "I was wondering when you were going to come over," I said, a little too breathlessly.

"Katie." His voice was deeper. It was the voice

of a man, not the boy I'd splashed in the face with water. Certainly not the boy I'd beat in a footrace the day he walked me home from school.

I didn't know how or when it happened, but he was a stranger to me. I didn't know him. I didn't know what to say to him.

"How are you?" I asked.

"Fine." He angled his head. Relief swept through me when I thought I saw the hint of a smile. "*Du gucksht gut.*" You look good. "You've gotten pretty."

"You, too."

He smiled then, but it was a fleeting twisting of his mouth that wasn't reflected in his eyes.

It was a silly thing to say. Boys weren't pretty. My face heated, but I forged ahead. "I haven't seen you much."

He shrugged. "Been busy. Is Jacob around?"

"He's putting new chicken wire on the coop. Something got in and killed two hens last night. Our best layers."

He nodded. "Damn coyote probably."

I was inexplicably nervous and reminded myself this was Joseph. But it was as if there were another person in the room with us. A person I didn't understand and didn't necessarily trust.

"What are you doing here?" I blurted.

"I came to tell you good-bye."

"Good-bye?" I choked out a laugh. "You're not going anywhere."

It was a stupid thing to say, but he laughed. "We're moving to Geauga County."

"But . . ." I couldn't finish the sentence. I couldn't grasp the meaning of what he'd said. He couldn't move away. It would ruin everything. All my plans for summer. "When?" I managed, hoping against hope he was kidding.

"We're leaving tomorrow," he told me.

The words hit me like a sucker punch. I actually took a step back, brought my hand up to my stomach. "But . . . why?"

Glancing toward the door, he shrugged. "Mamm has family there. My grandparents. An aunt and uncle. After Datt . . . She wants to be with them."

I blinked at him, overwhelmed with an emotion I couldn't identify. "But . . . what about us?" Realizing how that sounded, I quickly added, "I mean, all of us. Jacob and me and . . ." I ran out of breath, struggled to get oxygen into my lungs. "We're your family, too."

"I don't have any say in the matter."

"But . . . we were going to spend the summer together. Like before. You and me and Jacob. We were going to swim and . . . what about the trunk? I mean, in the creek? We have to find it, bring it out, and find out what's inside."

His smile was so sad it brought tears to my

eyes. "There is no trunk," he said after a moment. "I made it up."

That he would lie about something so important infuriated me. He was making fun of me, I realized. Purposefully hurting me and getting a good laugh out of it.

"I'm not a kid anymore," he said.

I stood there, mortified and humiliated because at some point I'd begun to cry. I'd never let him see me cry. Not even the time I ran into the barbed-wire fence and cut my arm and Mamm had to take me to the doctor for stitches. I always made sure Joseph knew I was tougher than that. Crying was for girls and I wasn't just any girl.

"Katie."

I knew it was irrational to be angry with him. I knew better than to feel so betrayed. But when you were fourteen, it wasn't easy to hold those kinds of emotions inside. "Why don't you just go ahead and go then," I told him.

"You don't mean that."

Rolling my eyes, I brushed the tears from my cheeks. "I never liked you anyway."

"I can tell." He shifted his weight from one foot to the other. "Same here."

"I have to get back to work." I backed toward the stall, bumping my leg on the wheelbarrow full of muck.

He started toward me. "I didn't make it up."

I sidestep the wheelbarrow and stop. "You mean about the buried trunk?"

"It's there. In that deep pool. You're going to have to find it on your own this summer."

He stopped a scant foot away from me. Somewhere in the back of my mind I was aware of a hissing sound. I almost couldn't believe it when I realized it was my own quickened breaths.

He looked down at me and smiled.

A thrill like I'd never experienced before in my life rushed through me, from the top of my head all the way to my toes. It was like an electrical shock that short-circuited my brain so that I couldn't formulate a single, rational thought.

Then his hands were on my shoulders. I looked at him, a small part of my brain disbelieving he could be so tall. My heart breaking because we wouldn't be spending the summer together and I cared a lot more about Joseph King than I did that stupid buried trunk.

He looked at me in a way I'd never been looked at before. In a way that thrilled and alarmed in equal measure. Raising his hand, he cupped the side of my face. "I'm going to miss you, runt."

The words brought another round of tears. I couldn't imagine not seeing him again. I stood there, humiliated, fighting the deluge, but failing.

"Shush."

He leaned close, angled my chin up with his

palm. The next thing I knew his mouth was on mine. Tentatively at first and then his lips were pressed hard against mine. I tasted the salt of tears. I squeezed my eyes shut, torn between running and trying to absorb the moment, because I knew it was somehow momentous.

His arms went around me. "I'll write—"

"*Katie!*"

Jacob.

I shoved hard against Joseph's chest, reeling backward with so much force I stumbled over my own feet and nearly fell.

My brother stood just inside the door, fists clenched at his sides, staring at Joseph. "What are you doing?"

Joseph stepped back, shoved his hands in his pockets. "Saying good-bye to Katie."

Jacob's eyes flicked from Joseph to me, but the energy was all for Joseph. "Go inside, Katie."

I barely heard him over the wild rush of blood through my veins. My heart pounded so hard I was dizzy. I could still feel the warmth of Joseph's lips against mine. The guilt of what I'd let happen pressing down with such force I could barely breathe.

I didn't respond; I couldn't move. I stood my ground, trying not to cry, not succeeding.

Jacob tightened his mouth and strode over to me. "Go on." Setting his hand on my shoulder, he nudged me toward the door.

Joseph moved so quickly I barely noticed him coming. One moment I was thinking about arguing with my brother, the next Joseph grasped his arm, spun him around, and punched him hard in the face.

"Joseph!" I screamed.

Jacob's head snapped back. He went down hard on his back, his arms flying over his head. For an instant he didn't move. I heard myself cry out his name. Then he sat up, shook his head. Blood streamed from his nose, dribbled over his mouth, and pattered against the front of his shirt.

It was the first time I'd ever witnessed a fight; the first time I'd been exposed to any kind of violence. The ugliness, the utter wrongness of it, frightened me on a level so deep I felt sick.

Using his sleeve, Jacob wiped blood from his nose. He got to his feet, his eyes on Joseph. "I think you should leave."

I couldn't stop staring at them. In some small corner of my mind, I kept expecting them to crack up with laughter, turn to me and laugh even harder because the joke was on me. But these two people I thought I knew so well, people I trusted and loved, suddenly seemed like strangers.

My legs were shaking so hard, I wasn't sure I could stand on my own power, so I went to the stall door and leaned. I watched as Joseph crossed to my brother and stuck out his hand for a shake. Jacob held his gaze, but did not accept it.

The parody of a smile spread across Joseph's face.

Stepping back, he turned his attention to me.

There were a thousand things I wanted to say to him. But Jacob was watching and the words tangled on my tongue. The only sound that emerged was the cry of a puppy spending its first night alone.

"See you around," Joseph said, and stalked from the barn.

Wu schmoke is, is aa feier.

It's an old Amish saying that translates to: Where there's smoke, there's fire. I'm a firm believer in the axiom, which is why I was up early despite a late night, and am now on my way to talk to twenty-one-year-old Kelly Dennison, whose last known residence was in the township of Novelty, Ohio.

It's not yet noon when I make the turn off of Sperry Road and head north on Ohio 105. The narrow stretch of beat-up asphalt is rural and crowded with trees, the branches thick enough to turn the otherwise bright morning to dusk.

Glock ran Dennison through LEADS last night. She has no warrants, but did thirty days in the Geauga County jail on a first-degree misdemeanor of making false allegations against a peace officer. She works second shift at a nearby retirement home. I'm hoping to catch her this morning before she leaves for work.

Normally, I'd be in uniform and have another officer with me. The problem is this is not an official investigation; I'm basically working on a hunch and I'm outside my jurisdiction. That's not to mention my restricted-duty status. However you cut it, I'm treading on thin ice.

Dennison's residence is a rusty tin box of a trailer set atop a hill with a dead pine tree in the front, a yard that's gone to weeds, all of it surrounded by a chain-link fence that's slowly being pulled down by honeysuckle. An old Honda Civic with bald tires squats in a narrow driveway that's more mud than gravel. I park behind the Honda, my tires sinking in too deep, and step out. I check the fenced area for a dog, then let myself in through the gate, keeping one eye on the window as I take the trampled path to the raised front porch.

Opening the screen door, I knock. "Kelly Dennison?"

No answer. Stepping back, I glance at the window, but the curtains are drawn tight; I can't see inside. Using my key fob, I knock again, louder this time. "Hello? Kelly?"

I'm thinking about going around to the back when I hear the snick of a lock. The door squeaks open and I find myself looking at a pretty young woman with wavy blond hair and last night's mascara smeared beneath large, crystalline eyes.

She's wearing a Detroit Red Wings T-shirt and cut-off denim shorts.

Looking as if she was forcibly dragged from her bed, she gives me a not-so-friendly once-over. "Who are you?"

"I'm Kate Burkholder, chief of police down in Painters Mill, and I'd like to talk to you for a few minutes," I tell her.

She looks past me to see if there's anyone else around. "About what?"

"The incident two and a half years ago with Deputy Wade Travers."

A quiver runs the length of her. She opens her mouth, but doesn't speak. Then her face goes cold. "What are you? Some kind of reporter or something? I wish you people would leave me the hell alone."

She starts to close the door, but I put my hand against it and stop her. "I'm not a reporter."

"Yeah, well, I still don't want to talk to you," she says dismissively. "Now get the fuck off my porch, man."

"I need your help," I tell her. "It's important."

"Do I look like I care?"

"After what happened to you? You should."

"I lied about that. Made it all up."

"Kelly, I know you don't know me. You have no reason to trust me. But this is extremely important. I need to know the truth about what happened that night."

Her raccoon eyes narrow. "Who *are* you?"

Now it's my turn to hesitate. This is where things get tricky. "Look, I'm a cop, but I'm off-duty so this is sort of an unofficial visit."

"No offense, but I'm not a big fan of cops. They don't like me much either. That's all I got for you, lady."

She starts to close the door, but I put my foot in the jamb.

"You're a persistent bitch, aren't you?" she snarls.

"You have no idea."

A tinge of amusement melts some of the ice in her eyes. "Why would I even give you the time of day?"

"Because I don't think you lied," I tell her. "I think someone persuaded you to change your story. I think you were willing to do jail time to protect yourself."

She gapes at me and for the first time I see a sliver of vulnerability beneath the brass. I pounce on it. "I'm trying to get to the bottom of . . . something else. Another case that may be related. If you help me, maybe I can help you, too."

"What do I have to lose, right?" Bad attitude back in place, she swings open the door. "Welcome to FUBAR. Want a beer?"

A few minutes later we're seated in a small living room with threadbare carpet and curtains the color of mustard. I'm sitting on a sofa that smells of cigarette smoke and mold. Kelly Dennison sits cross-legged in a recliner that looks relatively new. An old REO Speedwagon song about olling with the changes wafts out from somewhere down the hall.

"So, you're a cop?" she asks, digging a cigarette from a pack.

"I'm not here as a cop," I reply. "I'm here as a private citizen."

"And I should know what to make of that?"

"Look, all I can tell you at this point is that whatever we discuss here today is off the record, okay?"

"Whatever floats your boat." She follows up with an I-don't-give-a-shit shrug.

There's a playpen in the corner. A baby bottle half full of something red on the counter in the kitchen. A child's plastic key ring on the floor at the mouth of the hall.

"You have children?" I ask.

"My daughter's three."

"She's sleeping?" I ask.

"Just leave her out of this, and get to the point," she snaps.

"I need to know what happened that night in Chardon two and a half years ago."

She lights the cigarette and takes a long drag. "Jesus."

I wait.

"I'd been out with one of my girlfriends." She

slants me a hard look. "Yeah, I'm gay. Bi really. I have girlfriends and boyfriends. So what?"

She's trying to shock me; it doesn't work. "You were on your way home?"

"Yup. Karen and I went to dinner and hit a couple of bars in Cleveland. I think I had three or four drinks. Dropped her off at her apartment and started for home around two thirty A.M. I was out in the middle of bumfuck when a Geauga County sheriff pulls me over."

"You were alone?"

"Yup."

"Where exactly?"

"I don't know. Some lesser road off Caves Road. I'd been drinking so I took the back roads, thinking that would keep the cops off me." Her smile is bitter. "Didn't help."

"What happened?"

She glares at me, letting me know her discomfort is my fault for bringing this up. "He started out all professional like. Asked me how much I'd had to drink. I told him one beer." Another hard smile. "So he gives me a Breathalyzer. He asked me to get out of the car and gives me a field test, you know where I had to walk the line. I thought I'd passed." Shrugging, she falls silent and concentrates on her cigarette.

"Did he arrest you?" I ask.

"He handcuffed me. Said he was going to call for a female deputy. Then he put me in the backseat of his car." She stubs out the cigarette and lights another. "By then I was upset and crying. I figured I was going to jail for DUI. I'd have fines and a lawyer to pay, neither of which I could afford." She makes a sweeping gesture that encompasses the interior of the trailer. "As you can see, I don't have a lot of money. So, yeah, I was upset.

"Anyway, after a few minutes he gets me out of the car. I knew something was up because he was . . . different. Not quite as professional. He was being, like . . . *nice.* He started asking me all kinds of questions. I told him where I worked. That I had a daughter. He let me smoke a cigarette. The whole time I thought he was trying to keep me calm while we were waiting for that female deputy." She shrugs. "It wasn't until I told him I was gay that he . . . I don't know, he got kind of . . . excited."

"What did he do?"

"He asked me if I liked oral sex and then he told me if I gave him a blow job, he'd let me go home." She sucks hard on the cigarette. "Gotta be honest with you. I was tempted. I seriously couldn't afford a DUI. But the thought of . . . I mean, I didn't exactly handle it right, but how the hell do you handle something like that? Anyway, in the end I said no.

"It didn't go over very well. I mean, it was like someone flipped a switch in that dude's head.

He got all pissed off. Started pushing me around. The next thing I know he throws me over the hood of his car, slams my face down, and starts yanking down my pants."

The young woman shrugs as if she's immune, as if remembering that dark moment doesn't affect her. But I wasn't born yesterday. Despite the bad attitude and foul mouth, I see the rise of humiliation, fear, and rage.

"He must've had a rubber with him. I don't remember him putting it on. But he just . . . clamped his hand over the back of my neck, bent me over the hood, and stuck it in. Started humping me and grunting like some kind of animal. Lasted a minute maybe and he was done."

A wave of revulsion grinds in my gut. Sexual assault is a hideous crime. In this case, the ugliness is made even worse because it was perpetrated by a cop. A cop who has never been punished.

"He told me if I told anyone he'd hunt me down and kill me. He'd kill my family." Her voice falters. "My little girl." Her face splits into that bitter smile again. "Then he let me go."

"What did you do?"

"I went home. What else would I do? I was a fucking mess. I called Karen. She came over and picked me up. She told me to go to the hospital, but I'm like . . . fuck that. So she took me back to her apartment and I spent the night. The next day she talked me into calling the newspaper."

She looks down at her cigarette, rolls it between her fingers. "They send out this . . . college girl. She's, like, younger than me. But she seemed serious, so I told her everything—every sordid detail—and she writes this huge story. I mean, this girl's thinking Pulitzer Prize and a promotion. I'm thinking it's going to get the son of a bitch arrested."

"What happened?"

"The night after it was published? Prince Charming came to my trailer. I was sleeping. Alone. Just me and my daughter. And he was . . . furious. I mean foaming-at-the-mouth pissed off. He put a gun to my head. He picked my daughter up by her *foot,* held her *upside down,* and put the gun against her *head.*"

For the first time, she chokes back tears. "He told me if I didn't tell that reporter and the cops that I made the whole thing up, he'd come back and kill us both. He said he'd get away with it because he's a cop."

She turns those blue eyes on me. "I believed him."

"What did you do?" I ask.

"What do you think? I called the fucking reporter and told her I made it up. A couple days later, the cops came out and arrested me for making false allegations against a police officer.

It was a felony, but my attorney got it knocked down to some lesser misdemeanor." She looks down at the cigarette burning in her hand. "My parents had to mortgage their house to pay for all this shit."

"Mama."

Kelly startles with so much force that she nearly drops her cigarette.

I glance left to see a little girl standing in the hall. She has mussed blond hair and cherub cheeks. She's wearing a T-shirt that's too big—her mom's, probably—and dragging a doll by its hair behind her.

"I'm hungry," she says.

"Come here, baby." Kelly Dennison opens her arms and the little girl goes into them, snuggles against her.

"Thank you for telling me," I say. "I know it wasn't easy."

Hugging her child against her, she kisses the top of her head and then looks at me. "Why are you asking me about all this crap, anyway?"

"I think this is one of those rare occasions where the less you know, the better."

"Since that's the case, try this on for size: You tell anyone what I said and I'll deny every word. You got that?"

"I got it," I tell her. "Loud and clear."

CHAPTER 23

In the years I've been in law enforcement, I've been lied to more times that I can count. Some people are good at it. Others not so much. I'm no slouch when it comes to discerning one from the other. Kelly Dennison might be rough around the edges; she might even be a capable liar. But I don't believe she's lying about what happened the night she was pulled over by Deputy Wade Travers.

The last thing I want to believe about a cop is that he is corrupt. If my suspicions are correct, Wade Travers is a violent sexual predator—and maybe worse. He's used his position of power to find victims—women in trouble with the law. He assaults them and then he uses his position as a cop to intimidate them into silence. The next logical question is: What else has he done?

I call Tomasetti as I pull out of the driveway and head south. "I have a name for you," I say without preamble.

"Lay it on me."

"Wade Travers. He's a Geauga County dep—"

"I know who he is," Tomasetti cuts in.

"You know him?"

"I know his father-in-law is the goddamn sheriff."

"Jeff Crowder?" Shock renders me speechless; despite my foray into the sheriff's department personnel, no one had uncovered that information. When I find my voice, I say, "That explains a lot of things."

"It explains why you need to be careful."

"I'm not wrong about this."

"Kate, I'm not saying you're wrong. And I will help you, but I need something concrete before I can pursue this on an official level. You understand what's at stake."

"I understand." My mind spins through everything I've learned, the things I suspect, and I struggle to put them in order in terms of provability. "Two and a half years ago Travers was accused of sexual assault."

"I looked at it," he tells me. "The victim retracted her story. She was charged and did jail time. Travers was vindicated. Kate, there's nothing there."

"There's nothing there because he intimidated her into keeping her mouth shut." I tell him about my visit with Kelly Dennison. "He threatened her. He threatened her infant daughter."

"We need proof."

"She's too frightened to come forward."

"And she has a small credibility problem."

I think about my trip to the Geauga County Records Department. "What about the purged records?"

A pensive silence ensues, and then, "If we can come up with something concrete that shows Travers or anyone else inside the sheriff's department has altered official records to cover up misconduct or corruption or to alter evidence, I can get involved and make this official. Without some proof of wrongdoing . . . the best we can hope for is the initiation of an audit based on the missing or purged records. I'd prefer not to go that route."

"An audit now would just give them a heads-up and ample time to cover their tracks," I murmur.

"Look, Kate, we have to bear in mind here that we're talking about a man's life, his character, his career."

"Or a dirty cop," I snap.

"We have to be sure." Another thoughtful pause. "You think a cop inside the Geauga County Sheriff's Department was involved with Naomi King. You think there was some kind of falling-out between them. You think he murdered her and then framed her husband for it? Kate, do you have any idea how that sounds?"

"I know how it sounds," I retort.

"We need something substantial before I can begin any kind of investigation. Even then it's probably going to take some time to get things rolling."

"I guess I'd better get started then."

"In the interim, I'll dig around a little on my end, see if anything pops."

"Thank you."

"Don't thank me yet," he says. "We're a long way from bringing this thing to a head."

Vicki Cascioli lives in a Victorian-style duplex just north of Auburn Corners. I'm still mulling my conversation with Tomasetti when I take the steps to the porch and knock.

I hear at least three locks disengage. The door opens and I find myself looking at a striking woman with black hair pulled into a ponytail, a flawless olive complexion, and the cheekbones of a runway model. Dark eyes fringed with sooty lashes and full lips are set into an oval face. No makeup, but then she's one of those women who doesn't need it. She's tall and large-boned with a muscular build. All two hundred pounds of her is packed into snug jeans and a faded Ohio State sweatshirt.

I show her my badge. "Vicki Cascioli?"

"Maybe." She takes the time to scrutinize it. "What do you want?"

"I'm Kate Burkholder, chief of police down in Painters Mill."

"Yeah, I can read."

"I'm not here in an official capacity."

"Then you probably got the wrong house."

"I want to talk to you about the Geauga County Sheriff's Department."

"In case you're not up on your news, I don't work there anymore."

"That's why I'm here."

Tilting her head, she looks at me a little more closely. She may not be a cop any longer, but she's still got the look. Direct gaze with that inherent hint of suspicion. Straightforward demeanor. No-nonsense approach. A little bit of bad attitude thrown in for good measure.

"All right." She steps aside. "I'll bite."

I keep a close eye on her as I brush past. I'm pretty sure that's the outline of a pistol tucked into the waistband of her jeans. She takes me into a good-size living room with high ceilings and a bay window that looks out over the street. The room smells of paint and turpentine. Country music pours from a set of speakers set up on a sofa table. A half-dead ficus tree in the corner. Threadbare sofa and chair. No TV. A well-used leather punching bag hangs from a hook set into the ceiling. An easel in the next room—the dining room—holds a large canvas soused with oil paints in magenta and purple and blue.

"You're a painter?" I ask.

"I dabble." She gives me another once-over, curious now. "All right. You're in. You want to tell me what this is all about?"

I'm going to have to be cautious. I don't know

this woman. I have no idea where her loyalties lie or what kind of person she is. If she has an agenda that has nothing to do with right or wrong. As far as I know she's a wannabe rookie cop who couldn't cut it and now she's looking for some easy money to pay her rent.

"I was involved in the Joseph King standoff a few days ago," I tell her.

"Yeah, I heard about that. Tough break. SWAT got him, didn't they?"

I nod. "I understand you used to be a deputy with the Geauga County Sheriff's Department."

"Once upon a time."

"How long were you with them?"

"Eight months."

"Were you involved in the Naomi King murder case at all?"

"Before my time."

"You ever make any stops out at the King farm?"

"Never did."

Nodding, I turn my attention to the punching bag, the set of gloves lying on the hardwood floor beneath it. "You box?"

A smile touches her eyes, but she says nothing.

"Ms. Cascioli, I read about what happened to you."

"Yeah, well, so did everyone else." Bitterness laces her voice.

"What are you doing for a living now?"

"I'm unemployed. Shocking, right?"

"You looking to get back into law enforcement?"

She sneers. "What do you think?"

"I think it depends."

"On what? The tooth fairy?"

"On the information that comes out in the course of your lawsuit. On the truth."

Her eyes narrow on mine. I've got her undivided attention now. She's staring at me, wondering why I'm here and where all of this is going.

"Your lawsuit alleges that while you worked for the sheriff's department, your fellow deputies and Sheriff Jeff Crowder were regularly tampering with evidence and engaging in other unlawful activities."

"I know what my lawsuit is about," she says.

"You claim you were terminated because you were a whistleblower."

"Look, Chief Whatever-the-fuck-your-name-is, my lawyer told me not to talk to anyone about the lawsuit."

"Probably good advice."

Sighing, she crosses her arms, unimpressed, saying nothing.

Vicki Cascioli is a tough cookie, and I struggle to find the right words. Some angle that will compel her to buck her better judgment and give me something I can use. I'm coming up short. "I know this is a sensitive situation, but I need your help. It's about the Naomi King murder case and Joseph King. It's important."

"Can't help you."

"Ms. Cascioli, I believe we want the same thing."

"You have no idea what I want."

"You're right. I don't." I stumble over words that aren't quite right, not sure how to best proceed. "I think the King case went to trial without all of the evidence ever coming to light. There's something going on. I'm trying to figure out what it is."

"Are you recording this?" For the first time she looks angry. "You wearing some kind of fucking wire?"

"If you're that paranoid, you can check." Maintaining eye contact, I raise my hands to shoulder level.

Her mouth curves. Never taking her eyes off mine, she quickly and impersonally gives me a thorough pat-down, leaving the pockets of my jacket and jeans turned inside out.

"Lift up your hair," she says.

Rolling my eyes, I do, and she runs her fingertips around the back of my neck and beneath the collar of my jacket.

Finally, she steps away.

I hold her gaze. "What are they doing?"

"I've seen them plant dope. Pot. Meth. Coke. I know at least two deputies have acted improperly with females during DUI arrests. I know at least one deputy has taken cash off a drug dealer and kept it. The information never made it into any report or file."

"How deep does the corruption go?" I ask.

"All the way to the top," she says in a low voice.

"Who's involved?"

She shakes her head. "I'm not going to go there with you."

"How did you find out about it?"

Her mouth twists into something ugly. "Sleeping with the enemy."

"Who?" I repeat.

"Time's up." She strides to the door and opens it. "Hit the road."

There's an old saying in the annals of law enforcement. It goes something like this: When a case stalls, get off your ass and canvass. Any cop worth his salt knows it's one of the most effective tools a cop has. Of course, the best time to canvass is immediately after the crime. It's been over two years since Naomi King was murdered; the case is as cold as the bones of her decomposing body.

Still, in terms of the good old-fashioned canvass, there are a couple of things that might work to my advantage. The area is rural—fewer homes to cover—and it's predominantly Amish. The Amish tend to stay in one place longer than their English neighbors. And while members of the Amish community may have been reluctant to come forward for the local police, they may be more likely to speak with me.

The King farm is just half an hour from Auburn Corners. Garnering any useful information from the neighbors is a long shot, but since I'm already in the area it's worth the trip. I cruise past the abandoned King farm. Of course there's no one there.

Just us ghosts, a little voice whispers.

I continue on to the next farm. The name Nisley is hand-painted on the mailbox. I start down the gravel lane and realize quickly that this is a large farm. The lack of telephone poles and the general appearance tell me it's Amish-owned. I idle past a loafing shed and a pen to my right, where half a dozen Hereford cattle mingle with some spotted hogs. The lane cuts between two massive white barns and a corn silo to my left; then the lane veers right and the house comes into view. It's a two-story red brick with a big elm tree in the front yard and a flowering cherry tree at the side. I park a couple of yards from the cherry tree and take a narrow sidewalk around to the front of the house and knock.

An Amish woman in a dark blue dress opens

the door and looks at me as if I'm some vermin that's wandered in out of the woods. I can tell by her *kapp* and dress that she's Swartzentruber, one of the most conservative of the Amish sects. She's wearing wire-rimmed glasses and holding a threadbare dish towel in her hand. I estimate her to be about sixty years of age.

I move quickly to get this off on the right foot. "*Guder nammidaag.*" Good afternoon. "Mrs. Nisley?"

She arches a brow, not impressed with my knowing her name or my use of *Deitsch.* "What can I do for you?"

I introduce myself. "I'm the chief of police over in Painters Mill." This woman is no pushover, so I launch into my spiel. "I'm closing out the case on Joseph King. I don't know if you heard, but he's dead."

"I heard. Everyone's been talking about it since it happened." She doesn't invite me inside. "What do you want?"

"Did you know the King family when they lived next door?" I ask. "Naomi and Joseph?"

"Knew both of 'em. Rode to worship with the family every now and again. When he bothered to go, anyway."

"I'm trying to . . . understand what happened, Mrs. Nisley. What were they like?"

"Naomi was nice as could be. *Demut.*" Humble.

371

"A good *mamm* to her children. A good wife, too."

"What about Joseph?"

"My *grossmuder* told me once that if you don't have something nice to say about someone, don't say anything at all. I have nothing to say about Joseph King."

"Did you ever hear them arguing or anything like that?"

"From here?" She laughs. "Don't think so."

"Did you ever call the police? Ever have a reason to?"

She looks at me as if I'm crazy. "Why would I do something like that?"

"I'm wondering if you ever heard or saw something that gave you cause to be concerned or worried."

She sets her hand on her hip and stares at me. "No."

"When's the last time you saw them?"

"I saw them the Sunday before it happened. The whole family. We all rode to worship together and—"

"*Veah is datt?*" A gruff male voice calls out from inside the house. Who goes there?

I look past Mrs. Nisley to see an Amish man hobbling toward us on crutches. He's wearing typical Amish clothes—blue work shirt, black trousers, suspenders, and a flat-brimmed hat. He's an amputee, missing his left leg at the knee.

His trousers are folded up and pinned to keep the hem from dragging.

He doesn't look pleased by my presence, so I heft a smile, hoping to charm him into answering a few more questions. "I hope I'm not disturbing your lunch."

Grimacing as if his missing limb is causing him pain, he glares at me. "*Vass du vella?*" What do you want?

I identify myself and tell him the same thing I told his wife—in *Deitsch*. "I'm closing the case and I was hoping you might answer some questions about Joseph and Naomi King."

"We don't know anything about them." He looks at his wife. "We've much to do." Then he turns his sights to me. "*Die zeit zu gay is nau.*" The time to go is now.

"Mr. Nisley, did you ever become concerned about Naomi or the kids and call the police?" I ask.

He closes the door in my face.

I hit every house within a three-mile radius of the King farm, venturing into chicken coops, a slaughterhouse, and within smelling distance of manure pits, all to no avail. Most of the Amish answered my questions without qualm, but none of them offered anything new. I'd hoped to find some busybody who liked to spend his or her time looking out the window and gossiping about what she'd seen, but no such luck. So far the afternoon has been a big, fat strikeout.

I'm westbound on Nash Road when I come upon a group of five Amish boys walking along the shoulder, two in front and three in the back. They're talking and gesturing, probably on their way home from school. On impulse I slow and stop next to them.

"*And wie bischt du heit?*" I begin. How are you today?

The boy nearest me slows. The others look away and keep going. I keep the Explorer in gear and idle along beside them. "My name's Kate Burkholder. I'm the police chief in Painters Mill and I'm wondering if you guys would mind answering a few questions for me."

The group slows. I've snagged their interest. Bored, I realize, and probably not too anxious to get home and start chores. Pulling the Explorer slightly ahead of the group, I shut down the engine and get out.

"I won't keep you too long," I say in *Deitsch* as I approach.

The boys stop walking, exchanging glances, all ears now. I guess them to be in their early teens. They're not sure why an *Englischer* woman has flagged them down, but they're curious. The boy nearest me eyes me from beneath the brim of his straw hat. "*Kannschtr du Deitsch schwetze?*" Can you talk Dutch?

"I used to be *Amisch*," I tell him. When no one says anything, I jump into my first question: "You guys live around here?"

Heads nod.

"Did any of you know Joseph or Naomi King?"

Another look is exchanged, this time fringed with uneasiness.

A tall blond boy with a bowl haircut and green eyes steps forward. "I knew 'em," he says. "What do you want to know?"

"Did you ever see or hear any trouble out at their place?"

"Heard talk about it," the blond boy says.

"What kind of talk?" I ask.

He doesn't answer, but a shorter, heavier boy chimes in. "That there was all kinds of hanky-panky going on out there."

The boy beside him giggles. When he notices me looking at him, he sobers.

"What do you mean by that?" I ask.

The heavyset boy looks at me as if he wished he hadn't mentioned it. "Never mind."

"It's okay," I say quickly. "I'm not from around here. I'm closing a case and trying to . . . understand what happened."

The heavyset boy backs away. "I gotta get home." He turns away and starts walking. Two others join him. I call out, but they wave me off and keep moving.

I look at the two boys who remain. "What about you guys? You ever hear anything about the Kings?"

A skinny, sandy-haired boy with acne on his cheeks replies. "Maybe."

"I'm Kate, by the way." I stick out my hand and shake hands with both of them.

"I'm Roy," says the sandy-haired boy. "This here's Emery." He squints at me. "Are you really a cop?"

"Yes, but I'm off-duty."

Evidently, Roy's the talker of the group. "Me and Emery done some work for Joe a few times."

"What kind of work?"

"Mucking horse shit, mostly." He smirks at his audacity, trying to be cool, testing the waters. "Cleaned out that old manure pit once. Paid us ten bucks an hour."

"Not bad," I say.

"Mr. King didn't have the money to pay us once, so he took us pheasant hunting," Emery adds. "We helped him reload a bunch of shells and shit."

"You got any cigarettes?" Roy asks me.

I barely hear the question; something the other boy said caught my attention. "What did you say?" I ask with a little too much intensity.

Emery's eyes widen. "Uh . . . nothing."

"About reloading," I clarify.

The Amish boy's eyes flick from me to his friend and back to me. "Just that Mr. King was a reloader."

"He reloaded ammo?" I ask. "For his shotgun?"

"Yeah."

Reloading basically means the gun owner assembles his own cartridges or shells as opposed to buying factory-loaded ammo at the store. I don't know much about the process, but I've been around enough cops and shooting enthusiasts to know that if it's not done with meticulous care, misfires can and do happen. I think of the workbench in the mudroom of the King home, the steel arm I hadn't been able to identify. That was where he'd done his reloading. And for the first time the misfire that occurred the night Naomi King was killed makes sense. More than likely Joseph King improperly seated the primer.

The boys are looking bored again. They're about to blow me off, so I launch back into my original line of questioning. "You were about to tell me something about the Kings."

Emery drops his gaze to the ground. "We don't really know anything."

Roy looks at him. "What about that one time?"

Judging by the look on Emery's face, the statement requires no clarification. Emery looks embarrassed, can't meet my gaze. "I dunno . . ."

Both boys look uncomfortable. As if they want

to tell me something, but aren't sure they should share.

"What happened?" I press.

Emery casts a covert look at Roy and shakes his head. The silent message is clear: *Don't tell.*

"I'm trying to get to the truth about some things that have happened," I tell them. "That's all. Please, if you know something . . . tell me."

"We don't know anything." Emery looks at his friend. "I gotta go."

The boys start to walk away. I watch them go. Frustration is like a fist in my chest, twisting. I'm standing there, shaking my head, when I notice Roy lagging behind, looking at me over his shoulder.

I call out to him. "If you know something, even if you think it might not be important, you should tell me. You won't get into any trouble."

The boy stops walking. I cross the twenty feet between us. "I want to make sure the truth comes out," I tell him.

Though we're on a back road that doesn't get much in the way of traffic, the boy's eyes dart left and right. He cocks his head as if listening for the hiss of tires on pavement. Then he looks down at the ground. "I think I know why he killed her," he whispers.

"You know why *who* killed her?"

He looks at me as if I'm dense. "Mr. King."

"Why?" I ask.

He glances over his shoulder to see how far his friend has gone. Emery has slowed down, but isn't close enough to hear. Roy leans toward me anyway. "I saw . . . *her.* I'd been to a singing over to the Miller place." He motions east. "It was dark. Real late. I was on foot. There she was. And she wadn't alone."

"Mrs. King?"

"*Ja.*"

"Who was she with?"

He looks away, wipes his hands on his trousers as if his palms have suddenly gone wet. "A policeman. They were . . . you know. Doing it. Right on his car."

"Having sex?" I ask once I find my voice.

Color climbs into his face, but he nods. "I was just walking along, not paying much attention. And I heard this *sound.* I thought it was . . . an animal. You know, a dog that had been hit by a car or something. I went to check and . . . there they were."

"Are you sure it was Mrs. King?"

"I looked right at her."

"Did she see you?"

He shakes his head. "They were . . . too busy."

"Did you recognize the policeman?"

"Couldn't really see his face, just . . . you know."

"Where did this happen?"

He points. "There's a two-track pulls into a

hayfield, half a mile or so down the road. There're lots of trees." He shrugs. "It's private. Not much traffic."

"What did you do?"

He lets out an are-you-kidding-me sound. "I kept walking."

"How long ago?"

"Couple months before she . . . died."

I think about that a moment, my mind grinding out a dozen different scenarios. "Did you tell anyone?"

He looks sheepish. "Naw. What would I say?" He looks past me at his friend. "I didn't even tell Emery until after she was killed. Emery's real smart. He thought it would be best if I just kept my mouth shut, so I did."

CHAPTER 24

I leave Roy to catch up with his friend. Reluctantly, he gave me his last name and address, both of which I write down in case I need to contact him later. I don't know if he would be a willing witness if, indeed, this pseudo case I'm building comes to fruition. And of course there's the issue of his being a minor; I'd need permission from his parents.

Dusk has fallen, but it's still light enough for me to try and find the two-track. Turning the Explorer around, I head east, keeping my eye out for the place where Roy claims to have seen Naomi King and a cop having sex. Sure enough, a mile down the road, a dirt track cuts through the trees on the north side and opens to a large hayfield. Roy was right; it's well hidden. The perfect spot for a covert rendezvous, especially under cover of night. The question is, who was Naomi King with?

Two adults engaging in consensual sex isn't a crime. But in light of Naomi King's murder—and the possibility that she was having an extramarital affair that was never revealed in the course of the trial—it's worth a thorough look. Enter the dark rumblings about Wade Travers into the equation, and a disturbing picture begins to emerge.

I believe Kelly Dennison's story about the rape. I believe Vicki Cascioli's assertion of shady goings-on inside the sheriff's department. And I believe Roy saw Naomi King having sex with a cop. None of those potential witnesses are as credible as Wade Travers. Dennison has a record; she's done time in jail. Cascioli has been painted as a disgruntled ex-cop. Roy is a minor—and Amish. Joseph and Naomi King are dead. How do I go about investigating Wade Travers without raising suspicion?

"Good question," I mutter as I pull the Explorer into the two-track, turn around, and head west.

I call Tomasetti as I make the turn onto Tavern Road. "Who says good old-fashioned police work is outdated?" I recap my conversation with the two Amish boys. "They saw Naomi having sex with a cop."

"A deputy?"

"Don't know."

"Did they recognize him? Get a name?"

"No and no. Even so, I think this opens up some possibilities."

"Including the possibility that Joseph King found out his wife was screwing around and flew into a rage."

"If that's the case," I say, "the information should have come out in the course of the trial."

Vaguely, I'm aware of a vehicle behind me. I'm driving the speed limit, which is fifty-five miles per hour. I drift slightly right, hugging the white line so he can pass, and I turn my attention back to my conversation.

"Tomasetti, I talked to Joseph at length the night I was in the house with him. I don't think he knew about Naomi's affair. I sat there and listened to his daughter tell me there was another man in the house that night. A man with a long gun, standing outside her mother's bedroom. The deeper I get into all of this, the more strongly I feel that Joseph King did not kill his wife."

Even though I'm alone and in my own vehicle, I find myself lowering my voice. "We need to look at Wade Travers."

"All right. But if we're going to—"

The Explorer jolts with so much force my head snaps against the seat rest. Headlights flash behind me. I catch a glimpse of a hood coming up fast on my left and I think, *Drunk driver.* A pickup truck. White.

Vaguely I'm aware of Tomasetti's voice coming over the Bluetooth. "Kate?"

"Hold on," I grind out.

The truck hovers for an instant, too far back for me to see the driver. Quickly, it veers right and slams into the Explorer. Steel clangs against steel, screeching as my vehicle is shoved right. I'm jerked left, my head bouncing off the driver's-side window. "Shit!"

The steering wheel is nearly wrenched from my

hands. Both right wheels, front and back, leave the asphalt, swerve onto the gravel shoulder. I grab tight, yank it back, feel the back wheels skid, then catch.

"Kate, what's going on?"

"Crazy driver running me off the road."

The truck's engine groans. A lot of power. Big engine. Tall hood. Souped up. The grille looms outside my window. Too close. Can't see the plate. I hit the brake hard. Down to forty miles an hour. The truck surges ahead, swerves right. I'm not fast enough to avoid it. The truck's rear bumper crashes against my left quarter panel.

The fender buckles. My tires lose purchase. The road curves left. I'm not going to make the turn. The Explorer goes into a spin. I brake hard, steer into the skid, but my efforts are fruitless. I try to get a look at the truck's license plate, but it's too far ahead and moving away fast.

The Explorer crosses the road. Tires screeching. Dirt and gravel fly outside my window. I'm thrown hard against my safety belt as the vehicle nose-dives into the ditch. The airbag explodes, punching me in the face and chest like a giant boxer's glove.

Abruptly everything goes still. I'm so stunned that for a moment I'm frozen in place. The Explorer has stopped at a steep angle. Engine no longer running. Something hissing. I'm being held in place by my shoulder harness and seat belt. I'm aware of the airbag slowly deflating.

Pain in the general area of my chest where the strap cut into me. The windshield is cracked. The hood buckled. Through the glass I see mud and grass and yellow cattails.

I lift my hands, set them on the steering wheel; I'm shaking violently. I shift, move my legs. No pain. No serious injuries.

"Shit." I groan the word and look around for my phone. It had been in the cup holder in the console; I'd been using my Bluetooth. It's probably somewhere on the floor now.

I set my right forearm against the steering wheel and unlatch my safety belt. With my left hand I reach for the door handle. Relief slips through me when it creaks open. The Explorer has come to rest nose-down in a six-foot-deep ditch. The grille is submerged in a couple of feet of water. I climb out, set my feet on the ground, sink into mud up to my ankles. Last year's cattails scrape my legs as I wade through them. The bank is steep and I have to use my hands to traverse the incline. Slowly, I make my way up to the road's shoulder.

It's almost fully dark now. No one around. The truck that hit me is long gone. I feel alone and exposed, more shaken than I want to admit. *This was no accident,* a little voice whispers, and a chill that has nothing to do with the temperature sweeps through me.

I'd been on the phone, not paying attention.

The truck seemed to come out of nowhere, approaching me at a high rate of speed. Was this a case of drunk driving? Of road rage? An impatient driver who became angry because he thought I was driving too slowly? I don't think so; I'd given him ample opportunity to pass. No, this is something else. But what?

Realizing I need my phone, I slide back down the incline and crawl into the Explorer. I grapple around inside, finally locating my cell on the passenger-side floor.

I dial 911 as I make my way back up the slope and report the accident. Then I dial Tomasetti.

"What the hell happened?" He doesn't bother trying to conceal his concern.

"Someone ran me off the road. Took off."

"Are you all right?"

"I'm fine." I glance over at the wrecked Explorer. "Auggie's not going to be too happy with me."

He's not amused. "Where are you?"

I look around. There's a farm about a quarter mile down the road. A church across the street. "Ohio Eighty-eight," I tell him. "A few miles south of Parkman."

"Don't go anywhere. I'm on my way. Keep your goddamn sidearm handy, will you?"

I've investigated dozens of traffic accidents over the years, from routine fender benders to fatality wrecks and everything in between. Even with all that experience, it's different when you're the one behind the wheel.

It takes ten minutes for the Portage County sheriff's deputy to arrive on scene. Deputy Chaney is a no-nonsense African American guy with a professional demeanor and a keen sense of humor, both of which calm my frayed nerves. I let him know right off the bat that I'm a cop—which earns me a little bit more in the way of regard. He listens carefully when I tell him about the white pickup truck running me off the road.

"Drunk driver?" he asks.

"I don't think so. It seemed intentional."

"Road rage?" he asks.

"I was going the speed limit, gave him ample room to pass."

"You never know what's going to set someone off," he tells me.

I don't offer another explanation despite the one pounding at the base of my brain. I don't know who the driver was. I don't know his intent. Because of the sensitive nature of my suspicions about a neighboring jurisdiction, I hold my silence.

When I'm finished with my statement, the deputy puts out a BOLO for the truck to the state highway patrol and surrounding law enforcement agencies.

I'm kicking myself for not noticing more

details about the truck or the driver. All I recall is that it was an older white pickup truck. Possibly a Dodge. I think it had big tires because it was quite a bit taller than the Explorer. I couldn't swear to any of it.

Way to go, Kate.

It takes another half an hour for Peck's Wrecker Service to arrive on scene. "Pecker" is a colorful guy who wears a cowboy hat and boots, and has me laughing despite the circumstances as he goes about attaching the wench to the undercarriage.

I'm standing on the road's shoulder, trying not to look as shaken as I feel, when Tomasetti rolls up in the Tahoe, turns on his flashers, and parks behind the cruiser. He exchanges a few words with the deputy who's taking photographs of the scene and then starts toward me, his gaze intent, his expression grim. "I let you out of my sight for more than a few hours and look what happens."

"I wish I could say you should see the other guy, but he got away."

I see restraint in his expression. The sharp edge of concern cutting through a thin layer of irritation. I remind myself he was on the phone with me when it happened. He tried to hide it but when I finally called him back he was frantic with worry. He was pissed off and scared, two emotions he did not want to feel. I can tell by the way he's looking at me that he wants to touch me, run his hands over me to make sure I'm not hurt. But that need is tempered by the urge to bitch me out for poking around where I shouldn't have been poking around.

He settles for a light brushing of his fingertips against my cheek. "You're sure you're all right?"

"I'm sure."

He frowns, yet softens at the same time. "You're bruised. Maybe you ought to get yourself checked out in the ER."

The knot on my left temple is just starting to make itself known. Probably from my head knocking against the driver's-side window. "Seriously, I'm fine," I tell him.

He doesn't look convinced, but walks away to take a good long look at the Explorer. "What happened?"

I tell him everything. "It was no accident, Tomasetti. And it wasn't random. That son of a bitch came out of nowhere. He came at me fast and hard, hit me twice."

"You tell the deputy that?"

I nod. "I didn't tell him who I suspect."

His expression goes dark. He glances over at the deputy, who's still photographing the scene, and lowers his voice. "Kate, do you think a cop did this? Someone with the Geauga County Sheriff's Department?"

"That's exactly what I'm saying."

"You get a look at him?"

"No. Damn it." I sigh. "But I'm telling you this

was no accident. Whoever was driving that truck purposefully tried to run me off the road."

"To accomplish what exactly?"

I shoot him an are-you-serious look. "I've been sniffing around, asking questions. Maybe he caught wind of it. Maybe he got nervous and decided to do something about it."

"So he tried to kill you by running you off the road?"

"Or shut me up." I think about Kelly Dennison. "Intimidation is part of it. That's his modus operandi."

Shoving his hands into his pockets, he looks over my head at the wrecked Explorer, sitting cockeyed behind the wrecker. "I'm sure he has no idea how hard your head is," he mutters.

Shaken as I am—or maybe because of it—I laugh. "You always manage to say just the right thing."

"I don't like it that you're on his radar."

"Neither do I. Nothing I can do about it."

"Yeah, well, I can."

I look at him, wait.

"It's time I got involved, Kate. Make this official. Start an investigation."

"You said we don't have enough. That we should wait until we have something significant."

A small shrug. "We'll see."

But I know Tomasetti too well to think he won't get it done.

The emergency lights of the wrecker flicker off the façade of the church across the street. We watch as the driver pulls the Explorer onto the road.

"I'm sorry I scared you," I tell him.

"If you want to make it right, you could sit the rest of this out. At least until BCI can get a fingerhold on this thing."

"There's not much more I can do," I tell him.

He nods, his expression softening. "You want a ride home, Chief?"

"I thought you'd never ask."

CHAPTER 25

I dream of Joseph King, a disjointed collage of memories tinged with nightmare imagery. We're in the woods and we're running from someone or something. The sense of danger is keen and I'm terrified. I can hear our pursuer behind us, breaking through brush, deadfall cracking, branches waving as it crashes through the forest. Joseph and I have reached the limits of our endurance. We can't run any farther. But I know the cliffs are up ahead. Somehow I know we'll find shelter and safety in one of the caves.

"Keep running," I tell him. "Come on! If it catches us, it'll tear us to shreds!"

"You go on, Katie. I'm spent."

That's when I notice the blood streaming from a gaping hole in his chest, streaming down to soak his trousers. "You're bleeding!" Panic laces my voice because I know the thing pursuing us will smell the blood.

"Run!" I scream.

Joseph smiles, that familiar twisting of lips that's mischievous, knowing, and kind. But there's blood on his teeth. Blood in his eyes, dripping down his cheeks like tears.

"They think I killed her," he tells me.

I catch a glimpse of something dark moving

through the brush. Coming toward us. So large I feel the ground shudder beneath my feet. "It's coming!" I tell him. "Run! *Run!*"

"Already here," he says.

The beast reaches us unseen, and yet it's there right in front of me. I see Joseph yanked from his feet. The spray of blood against the foliage. The creek running red with it.

Joseph.

I turn and run, leaving him, guilty but too terrified to stay. I run as fast as I can. Arms pumping. Feet pounding. Horror ripping through me with every thrust of my heart. I sense the beast behind me. I feel its claws scrape my back. The sound of fabric ripping, and then I'm being pulled backward into space . . .

I wake in a cold sweat, my breaths rushing in and out, the smell of blood in my nostrils. I sit up, look around. On the nightstand next to the bed, my cell phone is vibrating.

I snatch it up. "Burkholder."

"If you want to talk about that street file, take a drive up to my place."

Even in my befuddled state I recognize Sidney Tucker's voice. "Tell me what you know," I say.

"Not over the phone. If you're interested, come on."

"Mr. Tucker, if—"

The line goes dead.

"Shit."

I swing my legs over the side of the bed, set my feet on the floor, take a moment to settle my nerves. It's not yet fully light outside, but Tomasetti's already gone. The window is open and I can hear rain falling. The rumble of thunder in the distance makes me think of the beast in my dream.

It's not until I'm behind the wheel of my rental car that I acknowledge the achiness that settled into my muscles overnight. I felt fine after the crash yesterday; this morning it feels as if my car had been sent through a crusher with me inside.

Because of the possibility of an official investigation, Tomasetti had my Explorer towed to an impound garage not far from his Richfield office. Sometime today, a crime-scene technician will go over the damage with a fine-tooth comb in an effort to retrieve paint or marks that might help identify the vehicle that hit me.

I swing by LaDonna's Diner for a to-go coffee, down half of it before leaving the parking lot, and make the drive to Cortland in an hour. All the while I wonder about Tucker's change of heart. What made him change his mind about talking to me? And what information does the so-called street file contain that the official, sanitized file does not?

Rain sweeps down from a cast-iron sky when I pull onto Tucker's asphalt driveway. There's no car in sight, but then that was the case when I was here two days ago; it doesn't mean he's not home. Around me, the treetops bend and twist with frenetic energy in the near-gale-force wind. I hightail it through stinging rain to the front porch and knock.

It's so chilly this morning I can see my breath puffing out from my short sprint. When the retired detective doesn't answer the door, I pull open the storm door and use my key fob to tap on the wood.

"Mr. Tucker?" I call out. "It's Kate Burkholder."

I wait for a full minute. Leaning left, I glance at the big front window, but the blinds are tightly closed. I knock again, using the heel of my hand. "Sidney Tucker? Are you there?"

Annoyance rises in my chest. Did he change his mind about talking to me? Or did he jump in the shower, thinking I wouldn't get here so quickly? Step out for a quick errand? Did he run me all the way over here for nothing?

I leave the porch and walk around to the rear of the house. There's a good-size deck with a grill and a table and chairs. A bird feeder full of millet and sunflower seed mounted on the rail. As I ascend the steps and cross to the door, the whistle of a tundra swan sounds in the distance. It's a forlorn sound that echoes off the treetops only to be lost in the din of rain, the low roar of the wind.

I'm a few feet from the door when I notice it's

standing open several inches. It occurs to me that if Sidney Tucker had stepped onto the deck earlier and didn't close the door properly, the wind could have pushed it open. Still, the hairs at the back of my neck stand up.

"Mr. Tucker?" I call out. "It's Kate Burkholder! Can you come to the door please?"

I look around for neighbors, but there's no one there. Not only is the weather atrocious this morning, but the house is tucked into the trees and isolated from view.

Turning back to the door, I push it open. The hinges creak. I call out to him again. "Hello? Mr. Tucker? Are you there?"

No response.

"Shit," I mutter, and step into the kitchen. There's a round dining table straight ahead. Four chairs with frilly cushions. Cluttered counter-tops. Two pans left atop the stove. There's a TV on somewhere in the house. The air smells of popcorn and coffee, all laced with the unpleasant aroma of garbage that should have been taken out a day ago.

"Mr. Tucker?"

I glance down, notice wet footprints on the linoleum. Someone has, indeed, been outside in the rain. Where the hell is he?

Pulling out my phone, I scroll through incoming calls and redial the number of the last caller, which was Tucker. I'm about to turn around and go back outside when I hear a cell-phone ring-tone somewhere in the house. I hold up my phone. Two rings. Three rings. Four . . .

I let it ring half a dozen times and hit END. The ringing stops. "Well, shit."

I stand there a moment, trying to decide if I should continue on or go back to my vehicle and leave. I venture to the doorway between the dining room and kitchen, peer into the living room. The lighting is dim with the blinds pulled tight. I see a sofa against the wall to my right. A morning news show blares from a small TV on a stand.

Sidney Tucker is laid out on a recliner. At first glance, I think he's sleeping. Then I realize the pattern on the wall behind him isn't some bad wallpaper print, but blood. Copious amounts of it.

I fumble for the switch. Terrible light floods the room. Sidney Tucker's head is thrown back. An ocean of blood on his shirt. His eyes are on me, terrified and blinking. Somehow, he's still alive. His chest rising and falling, keeping time with the sound of a sucking chest wound.

For the span of several heartbeats I'm so shocked, I can't move. I'm aware of my heart thrumming hard in my chest. The copper-methane smell of blood offending my olfactory nerves. Then my cop's mind clicks back into place.

"Who did this?" I rush to him, my every sense honed to my surroundings, reaching for my phone. "Who did this to you?"

His eyes roll back white. He makes a sound that ends with wet gurgle deep in his throat.

"You're going to be okay," I tell him. "I'm calling an ambulance now."

It occurs to me this could be an attempted suicide, but I don't see a weapon. And most often a suicidal man will put the weapon to his head, not his chest. I'm reminded that Sidney Tucker had been about to tell me something about the Naomi King murder case.

I yank my cell from my pocket.

"Get your hands up! Sheriff's Department! Get them up! Right fucking now!"

A hard rush of adrenaline. Jamming my hands in the air, I glance over my shoulder to see a deputy sheriff come through the back door, a Glock leveled on my chest.

"I'm a cop!" I tell him. "I got a man down!"

"Keep your fucking hands where I can see them!" He enters the living room. His eyes flick to Tucker. "Don't fucking move."

I raise my hands higher, keep my palms toward him. "I'm a police officer."

"Shut up." He's young and jumpy. Keeping the Glock trained on me, he approaches. "Turn around and place your hands on the wall. Do it now."

I set my hands against the wall. "He needs an ambulance." My heart is pounding, but I remain calm. "I'm armed," I tell him. "I'm a cop."

"Don't look at me," he snaps. "Keep your eyes on the wall. And don't you fucking move. You got that?"

He sweeps his left hand over me, quickly and impersonally, and finds my .38 immediately. He slides it from its nest. I hear him check the barrel and then he says, "Step back from the wall. Put your hands behind your back."

I do as I'm told. I hear him remove handcuffs from his belt compartment. He snaps one bracelet over my right hand, cranks it down tight, and then grasps my left wrist and does the same.

"This is for your safety and mine," he tells me, calmer now that I'm restrained. "You're not under arrest, but you are being detained until we can figure out what's going on here. Do you understand?"

"Yes."

He motions to one of the chairs at the kitchen table. "Sit down and do not move."

I lower myself into the chair, motion with my eyes toward the living room. "He needs an ambulance now. He's hurt bad."

When he looks at me I see sweat on his forehead despite the chill. He looks nervous, his eyes repeatedly going to the back and front doors.

I guess him to be just under thirty. Light brown hair and eyes. For the first time I notice his Geauga County Sheriff's Department uniform jacket, and an odd sense of uneasiness slips through me. This is Trumbull County; Geauga County has no jurisdiction here. What the hell is going on?

"What's Geauga County doing here?" I ask in my cop's voice.

He ignores me and he doesn't holster his weapon. He makes no move to render aid to Sidney Tucker.

"Please," I say. "That man in there's a cop. He's been shot."

He pulls a cell phone from his uniform pants. That's when it occurs to me he has yet to use his radio. At this point he should have already called for backup, for an ambulance; he should have let his dispatcher know he'd encountered an unknown individual inside the home of a gunshot victim.

He thumbs a button on the phone and puts it to his ear. "I got her," he says, and drops the cell back into his pocket.

I got her.

A tingle goes through my body. I tamp down a rise of foreboding. Something is off about the way this is playing out. He hasn't even checked on Sidney Tucker yet. It's almost as if he'd already known what he would find . . .

"I'm a cop," I say again. "My ID is in my wallet. Back right pocket."

"I know who you are."

I'm still trying to get my brain around that when movement at the back door draws my attention. Uneasiness transforms into cold hard shock when I see Nick Rowlett and Wade Travers come through. Both men wear civilian clothes. Ski caps. Black leather gloves. Disposable shoe covers . . . What the hell?

The realization that I've walked into a trap hits me like a brass-knuckle punch. I look at Rowlett. "Get these cuffs off me. *Right now.*"

He turns his attention to the young deputy. "Tuck?"

The other man nods. "Alive. Barely. Better hurry."

"I owe you, man."

The deputy shakes his head. "I'm out of here." Giving me a final look, he goes through the back door without looking back.

I turn my attention to Rowlett. "What the hell is going on?"

He doesn't respond.

My heart begins to pound, a metronome flying out of control. A precursor to panic stabs claws into me, taking hold, but I shove it back in its deep, dark hole. I try to get a sense of how secure the cuffs are, find them snugged down tight.

Vaguely, I'm aware of Travers going into the living room.

Rowlett holds his ground, dividing his attention between the two of us.

"If you don't get Tucker help, he's going to die," I say.

Rowlett doesn't respond.

"Nick," I say. "What is this? You're a cop. What are you *doing?*"

"The official term for it is covering our tracks," he tells me.

"I don't know what that means."

One side of his mouth curves. "Yes, you do."

"Who did that to Sidney Tucker?"

He looks amused. "Why, *you* did, Kate Burkholder."

I blink, bewildered. The one thing I am certain of is that the situation is about to get much, much worse. Rowlett is staring at me intently, a starving dog eyeing a piece of meat. I try to control my breathing, but I don't manage. They're coming too fast, betraying my mounting fear. "I don't understand."

"Sure you do." Pulling out the chair next to me, he straddles it, sets his elbows on the back, his chin on his hands, and gives me his full attention. "You were obsessed with Joseph King. Everyone knows that. Look at the way you were at the standoff that night. So you went to Old Tuck, armed, out of your jurisdiction, out of control,

402

and you started making a bunch of wild accusations. Tuck, being the good detective he is, documented everything. Put it all in a file for safekeeping."

I stare at him, my heart pounding. "No one will believe that."

"We'll make sure they do. I mean, we're cops after all. It's what we do. And for fuck sake, we'll have Tuck's body to explain, right?"

"He's already been shot. Ballistics will disprove whatever the hell you're trying to do."

"What? You've never heard of a throw-down weapon? The one you brought with you with the serial number filed off? The one that can't be traced and has your prints all over it?" It's a term used by cops for an unregistered gun they can drop at a scene to justify a bad shooting.

"You, by the way, are about to have gunshot residue all over your hands and jacket," he tells me. "From the throw-down *and* that trusty little thirty-eight you carry. Four slugs will be retrieved from Sidney Tucker's body in the course of autopsy and sent to the lab. One from the throw-down and three from your thirty-eight. We might even put one in the wall to make sure nothing hinky happens with the striations or whatnot."

"That's insane."

He only smiles.

"People know I'm here," I tell him. "They know I came here to see Tucker."

"That's why they're here, right?" He tilts his head, looking at me as if he's trying to figure out some intricate math equation. "What was it with you and that fucking Joseph King anyway? He was a loser, but you just wouldn't stop. None of this would have happened if you'd just kept your big mouth shut. If you'd gone back to Podunk and shut the hell up. If you'd done that one simple thing, Old Tuck would still be fishing the lake and everyone would be happy. But no, you had to keep pushing, pushing, *pushing.*"

Keep him talking, a little voice whispers. *Stall him. Buy some time. Someone will come.*

But no one is going to come. I didn't tell anyone where I was going. I had no cause to be concerned. I was so eager to get the information from Sidney Tucker, I was careless.

"Is this about the Naomi King case?" I ask.

Nothing.

"If Joseph King didn't murder her, who did?"

He glances into the living room, then turns his attention back to me. "Doesn't matter now, does it?"

"Travers," I murmur.

Though he'd been on my radar, I still experience a surreal wave of disbelief that this is happening, that a fellow cop is sitting a foot away from me, divulging it. "Why?"

"Oldest reason in the world. Travers and the

Amish bitch were fucking like rabbits every chance they got."

"That's hardly a motive for murder," I say.

"It is if you're married with four kids—and have your eye on running for sheriff. I told him to cut it out, but . . . you know how it goes. After a few months she started getting serious. I mean, it was like *Fatal Attraction* meets *Amish Mafia*." He laughs at his own joke. "She wanted to leave the Amish. Leave her kids. Her husband. Scared the shit out of Wade. I mean, that would have *destroyed* him. Ruined his career. His marriage. His future."

He shrugs. "He tried to reason with her, but she wouldn't listen. Kept pushing." He pauses. "Kind of like you, Chief Burkholder. I mean, she had this . . . obsessive personality. Who would have thought? A fucking *Amish* chick?" Another shrug. "Anyway, Travers knew if he didn't find a way to stop her, it would cost him his marriage. His children. His future. She was a nobody so . . . bang, bang, problem solved."

"He murdered her and framed her husband?" I ask.

Rowlett nods. "King was a fucking idiot and practically laid the framework. He was abusive. He had a temper. Liked his booze. All we had to do was pull him over a few times and plant some weed or meth or maybe just haul him in for a DUI. He made it easy."

"Bring her in here!" comes Travers's voice from the living room.

Another punch of adrenaline, tangling with the fear inside me. I'm helpless without the use of my hands, unable to defend myself or get away. I look down at my .38 on the table in front of Rowlett.

He notices and picks it up. "Get up."

I'm thinking about making a break for the back door, but he grasps my arm, pulls me to my feet, and shoves me toward the living room. Wade Travers is standing a few feet from the recliner where Sidney Tucker is fighting for every breath. It's such a macabre, surreal scene I can barely process it.

"We need to uncuff her for this?" Travers asks.

"No, just turn her around," Rowlett says.

Grasping my arms roughly, the two men turn me so that my back is to Tucker. I try to jerk away, but they're too strong, fingers digging into my biceps and forearms.

"What the hell are you doing?" I ask.

No one answers. Travers lifts my cuffed wrists. Rowlett holds the .38 snug against my hands and fires three times in quick succession. The gunshots deafen me. I jolt violently with each. In my peripheral vision, I see Sidney Tucker's body jerk.

Dear God . . .

Gunshot residue, I realize. On my jacket. My

hands. And now two slugs from my weapon are inside Tucker's body. These men—these *cops*—are going to frame me for the murder of Sidney Tucker and then they're going to kill me. Probably make it look like there was an exchange of gunfire and both of us sustained fatal wounds.

"The throw-down, too," Travers hisses. "Put one in the wall above him. We need her prints on it. Shells, too. Residue on her hands and jacket."

A pistol is pressed against my palm. A gloved hand crushes my fingertips against the cold steel in multiple areas, multiple times. Next come the shells; two of them are pressed against my fingertips. Another blast shocks me. My ears are ringing. Terror jangling every nerve in my body. Panic kicks in, mindless and ineffective. I twist, bring up my knee, try to ram it into Travers. He dances back and I only manage to brush it against his hip.

"Cut it out," he snarls.

I catch a glimpse of Rowlett's face, teeth clenched, lips peeled back. He comes at me. Twisting, I brace against Travers, bring up my leg, and kick him in the abdomen. He reels backward, and hits wall.

"Watch her feet," he growls.

"Help me!" I scream the words as loud as I can in the desperate hope that a passerby—a jogger or dog walker or someone out on the lake—will

hear me and intervene. But it's a hopeless last-ditch effort.

"Don't mark her up," Rowlett says. "We don't need any more complications."

They lower me to the floor, facedown. I bring up my knees, try to get my legs under me, but the men are too strong. With my hands cuffed behind my back, I'm powerless to help myself. I jerk my wrists against the cuffs brutally, hoping they'll bruise my skin. Evidence, I think, but it only fuels my fear because by the time any bruising is discovered I'll be dead.

The sound of a car alarm shrills over the cacophony of the struggle. Both men go stone-still, exchange a puzzled look.

"That's mine," Travers says.

"Turn that fucking thing off," Rowlett snarls. "The last thing we need is neighbors sniffing around."

I look up to see Travers jog to the back door, yank it open, and go through.

"Let me go and I'll help you," I say.

"Shut up."

The car alarm goes silent. I raise my head, look around. A few feet away, Sidney Tucker lies dead. Before they leave here today, they'll put one or more bullets in me from Tucker's weapon so it looks as if Sidney Tucker and I got into a firefight. Dear God, I walked right into it. . . .

I close my eyes against the fear crawling inside

me. I think of Tomasetti and what this will do to him. I think of the people I love. The ones I'll leave behind. The things I've left undone. Unsaid. The sense of outrage, of loss and absolute terror overwhelms me.

"Was Sidney Tucker in on it?" I ask.

"Tucker was a stupid old man. Went soft after his old lady bit it. We knew it was just a matter of time before he started talking."

"He told you I talked to him?"

"Fuckin' guy had a death wish, I guess."

He's waiting for Travers to return. When he does, they'll kill me, clean up the scene, plant any additional evidence, and go. Wait for someone to find our bodies.

I set my forehead against the hardwood floor and close my eyes. I'm shaking all over. My arms and legs. My teeth are chattering. I'm incredulous that my life will end this way. *I'm sorry, Tomasetti. . . .*

Renewed fear surges when I hear the back door open. Rowlett is kneeling beside me, his knee pressed against the small of my back. He's messing with the throw-down pistol.

"Hurry up," he says. "We gotta go."

I raise my head, glance toward the door to see Vicki Cascioli standing just inside the kitchen. She's assumed a shooter's stance, a nasty-looking Sig Sauer in her left hand. Is she part of this, too?

"Put the gun down," she calls out. "Get your hands up. Do not move."

Rowlett glances over and freezes. I feel a quiver run through his body. The weight of his knee shifts off my back. Out of the corner of my eye, I see the .38 in his hand. His finger making its way inside the trigger guard . . .

"He's armed," I call out.

Her eyes are focused completely on Rowlett. "Don't do it. You know I'll make the shot—"

Rowlett throws himself backward, brings up the .38. Gunfire erupts. An endless stream of explosions. A slug tears into the floor inches from my shoulder. Chunks of wood hitting my face and hands. Free of him, I curl, put my face to the floor to protect my eyes.

The gunfire stops. A shocking silence falls. The smell of gunpowder fills the air. I hear a groan, glance right to see Rowlett lying on the floor a few feet away, a red bloom spreading center mass. I swivel my head, look at Cascioli. She's down on one knee. Sig still up. But her head is angled down. Blood streams from a tear in her cheek.

I roll away from Rowlett, get my knees under me and rise. "Where's Travers?" I ask her.

"Outside. He's down . . ."

The words are garbled. She's been shot in the face. Her mouth is mangled, filling with blood.

"Cascioli, get me out of these cuffs."

She nods, spits blood on the floor. Moving gingerly, she rises, tucks the Sig into the front of her pants. "Tuck's got a key," she mumbles. "Back here."

She staggers down the hall and returns a minute later, the small key in hand. Turning, I offer my wrists. I can feel her hands shaking as she struggles to unlock the cuffs. She says something I can't understand.

When the cuffs fall away, she goes to her knees. At first I think she's going to pass out. Instead, she brings her hands up to her face and bursts into tears.

CHAPTER 26

Human beings are resilient creatures. That's a good thing, I suppose, when you take into consideration the things we do to ourselves. The things we do to each other.

Cops like to believe they're immune from all those gnarly emotions that plague the somehow lesser beings. They'll argue the point until they're blue in the face. Me included. We're a tough lot, after all. We've seen it all. Nothing can shock us.

It's all bullshit.

A number of psychological changes occur during and after severe psychological trauma. The shrinks have come up with all sorts of interesting terminology. Tunnel vision. Auditory exclusion. Inattentional blindness. And afterward, things like emotional numbing, post-traumatic stress disorder, and the big daddy no one likes to talk about: depression.

I don't remember calling for an ambulance. I couldn't tell you which phone I used or whether it was a cell or land line. I don't recall dialing 911 or giving the dispatcher an address. I don't remember relaying the situation or giving an address or explanation. I don't even remember calling Tomasetti or hearing his voice on the other end of the line, though later I would learn I did, indeed, do all of those things.

When the paramedics arrived, I was inside Sidney Tucker's house, sitting on the living room floor, holding Vicki Cascioli's hand. Both of us were trying pretty hard not to look at the two dead cops in there with us. I should have been relieved when the knock on the door finally came, but my perceptions were skewed. Instead of relief, I felt a burst of mind-numbing terror because I was utterly certain that someone else had arrived to finish the job started by Wade Travers and Nick Rowlett.

That was a little over an hour ago. I'm sitting in the backseat of a Trumbull County Sheriff's Department cruiser, trying to maintain some semblance of my cop persona, my dignity. Failing on both counts because I can't stop shaking. I've talked to two deputies and a detective so far. As you can imagine, everyone has a lot of questions about what happened inside that house. When I asked about Vicki Cascioli, I was informed she'd been transported to the hospital with a gunshot wound. While it's a serious injury, I'm told, it isn't life-threatening. Wade Travers had been found outside, cuffed to his vehicle, and was taken into custody. Nick Rowlett and Sidney Tucker were pronounced dead at the scene.

At some point, one of the paramedics gave me a reflective, insulated blanket. I'm sitting in the backseat of the cruiser, watching the scene unfold through the rain-streaked windshield, when I see someone approach. An irrational wave of fear ripples through me. Then the door swings open and John Tomasetti bends and looks in at me.

"Are you all right?" he asks. "Are you hurt?"

His expression is grim and intense, infused with an array of barely controlled emotions I couldn't begin to identify. Front and center is the slow simmer of fear and relief that he hasn't arrived to find me in a body bag.

There are too many cops around for me to act on my own emotions. The knowledge that I came very close to never seeing him again.

"I'm okay," I tell him.

He's already reaching for my hand, taking it in his. I can feel him shaking, the wash of fresh emotion cascading over his face. "Goddamn it." He closes his eyes, takes a moment. "What happened?"

I give him the condensed version. "I wasn't expecting an ambush."

"No cop ever is, Kate." He scrubs a hand over his face. "For chrissake."

"Has Cascioli talked to anyone?"

"She's got a facial wound, so she hasn't said much. Detective that talked to her said Cascioli and Tucker were friends. She rode with him when she was a rookie. She knew he was into some unsavory things. She knew some of what was going on and had been trying to talk him into coming clean. From what I've gathered Tucker called her this morning, too. He knew they were gunning for him." He shakes his head. "He was right."

"She going to be okay?"

"She lost some teeth and she's probably going to need some reconstructive surgery, but she's going to make it. She's damn lucky to be alive. So are you."

A rush of emotion surges. The last thing I want to do is cry. I fight it, but it's another battle I'm losing. "Tomasetti, they were *cops*. I never imagined . . . fucking *cops*."

"Cascioli said it's been going on the entirety of her career. When she spoke out, they smeared her and got her fired. They threatened her, tried to intimidate her."

I think of my visit to her apartment. All the locks on her doors. The punching bag. The pistol tucked into her waistband. "She's not the kind of woman easily intimidated."

He grimaces. "Look, Kate, BCI is taking over the investigation. This is going to be a big deal. They're moving now, going to try to figure out how deep the corruption goes."

"Cascioli told me it goes all the way to the top," I tell him.

He gives me a sage look and I realize he can't talk about it or say anything more. His silence has nothing to do with his trust in me, but is because of his strong ethics, his professionalism, and his code of honor. It's the kind of man he is. It's one of many reasons I love him.

"This was about Joseph King," I tell him. "The murder of Naomi King." I close my eyes against another round of tears. "Tomasetti, he was innocent. They destroyed him."

He nods. "It's going to take some time and a lot of unraveling, but I'll make sure the truth is told. All of it." He looks behind him as if taking in the scene, and I realize I'm not the only one whose emotions are running high.

"Joseph King's family," I say, "the Amish community . . . they need to know."

"Scoot over." Taking a final look around, he gets into the car with me and slams the door.

"Tomasetti . . ."

"Stop talking." He pulls me into his arms, holds me tightly against him, and presses his face against mine. His whiskers scraping my cheek, his lips brushing mine. "I couldn't handle it if something had happened to you. Kate, you came this close . . ."

"I'm sorry I scared you," I whisper. "I'm sorry I put you through that. I know how—"

He silences me with a kiss. It's too intimate and goes on too long. But I sink into it. I cling to him, absorbing his strength, taking comfort, putting the moment to memory.

After a minute, he pulls away. "Don't let this shake your faith. In cops. In law enforcement. I mean that."

"I won't." Still, I'm glad he said it.

"Tomasetti, there are two cops standing outside the car."

Sighing, he pulls away, gives my hand a final squeeze. "Stay put. Lots of people want to talk to you."

"I know the drill."

"You up to it?"

"I am now."

"Let me know if anyone gives you any shit."

He opens the door and gets out, leaving me alone with my thoughts, the ghosts of my past, and the knowledge that somehow everything is going to be all right.

EPILOGUE

Drizzle floats down from a sky the color of cast iron when I pull onto the narrow gravel shoulder in front of the *graabhof.* I sit there for a moment, watching the procession of buggies pull in and park, the young hostlers taking hold of the reins and leading the horses forward so that all the buggies are lined up neatly. It's a scene vastly different from the one that played out six days ago when Joseph King was laid to rest.

This is an unusual gathering. It's not a funeral, more like an after-the-fact memorial service. I'm profoundly moved that the Amish community turned out; some hired drivers and traveled from as far away as Painters Mill and beyond to pay their final respects.

Families with children, couples, the young and elderly alike leave their buggies and approach the plain headstones where Joseph and Naomi King will lay side by side for all of eternity.

Shutting down the engine, I get out of the rental car and make my way through the gate. I spot Jonas King, his brother Edward, and Logan standing apart from the crowd. Jonas raises his hand and I wave. I see Bishop Fisher and his wife, Salome, standing near the headstones. The bishop notices my approach and gives me a nod.

I stop before reaching him. This gathering isn't about me, and I remind myself I'm an outsider here. This is about Joseph and Naomi King, gone before their time. It's about their children, the Amish community as a whole, and setting the record straight.

The crunch of tires over gravel draws my attention. I glance behind me to see a white van pull up to the gate. The rear passenger door slides open. I recognize my brother, Jacob, and his wife, Irene, immediately as they disembark. I'm surprised to see that my sister, Sarah, rode with them as well. My chest swells at the sight of them as they start toward me. We shared so much in the years we lived next door to Joseph King. I wonder if their memories are as crystal and happy as mine, if their regrets as deep.

"Jacob." I nod at my brother as he and his wife approach. "Irene. *Wie geth's alleweil?*" I ask. How goes it now?

"*Mir sinn zimmlich gut,*" Jacob says. We are pretty good.

"I'm glad you came," I say.

"*Yaeder mon set kumma,*" Irene puts in. Everyone ought to have come.

"Knowing the truth about Joseph . . ." Jacob shrugs. "It was the right thing to do."

My sister joins us. "Hi, Katie."

"Sarah." I step forward and give her a hug. "Thank you for coming."

She eyes the small crowd standing near the headstones. "It's a *shay samling*, Katie." A nice gathering.

"Good turnout, too," Irene puts in.

I feel my brother's gaze on me and look his way. Our eyes meet and in that instant I know we're remembering the way it used to be. We're kids again and life was one big adventure. In the span of a few short summers, we learned so much about the way the world worked, learned even more about each other. It's a rare moment, *our* moment, one we haven't shared for a very long time.

"It's been too long since you and I have seen each other," Jacob says.

"I think it's time we remedied that," I reply.

He looks past me, at the mourners who've gathered among the headstones. "I walked past that old swimming hole yesterday," Jacob says in *Deitsch*. "That old dead tree we used to jump off of is gone, but the water's still deep."

"You didn't happen to see an old trunk sticking out of the gravel bottom, did you?" I ask.

"No." He smiles. "But I looked."

Raw emotion flashes on my sister's face. "I hadn't thought of that in years."

For the span of a full minute, we stand there, embroiled in our thoughts, remembering a thousand innocent summer days and friendships that transcend even death.

As if realizing he's ventured into dangerous territory, my brother looks down at the ground. "I'm glad you put all this together, Katie. It's good for everyone to know the truth." He nods at his wife, and the three of them start toward the place where the Kings are buried.

"Katie!"

I glance toward the line of buggies to see little Sadie King running toward me, her dress swishing around her legs. Behind her, the rest of her siblings and her aunt and uncle climb out of the buggy.

"Sadie." Kneeling, I open my arms and she flings herself into my hug. "I'm so pleased all of you could make it."

"Aunt Rebecca says Datt was a good man and we shouldn't miss this. She said everyone was wrong about him. And now that he's living with Jesus he can be with our *mamm* and finally be happy."

I don't know exactly what the children were told, but I'm glad their aunt and uncle put to rest any doubts they had about the decency of their father.

"Your aunt is a wise woman," I tell her.

The four remaining children approach tentatively. They're more reserved than Sadie, partly because we're in the *graabhof*. Amish children are taught from an early age that it's a solemn, sacred place and they are to be on their best behavior. No running or laughter. I think about Sadie's loose relationship with the rules and it makes me smile.

The oldest, Becky, moves closer and offers her hand. "Thank you for trying to save our *datt*," she says earnestly.

"It was the right thing to do," I tell her. "I wish I could have."

The girl's brows knit as she considers my answer. I find myself hoping she'll recall more good than bad when she remembers her father.

Sadie pulls away and smiles at me. "I'm going to say good-bye to my *datt* now," she says, and starts toward her parents' graves. "Bye, Katie."

"Bye, sweetheart."

Levi is next. Making eye contact with me, the little boy grins and keeps moving, too shy to speak, walking right past me. A man of few words, and I think he must take after his *mamm*.

Little Joe stops next to me and gives a serious, resolute nod. "I'm just like my *datt*," he says seriously. "That's what everyone says."

"You look just like him," I say. "*Beheef dich.*" Behave yourself.

He grins and turns to catch up with his siblings. "Katie."

I turn my attention to Rebecca and Daniel Beachy. They're both clad in black, their best church clothes. Despite the harsh words between us last time I was at their farm, they stop to chat and I'm pleased to see them.

We exchange handshakes. "I'm glad you came," I tell them. "I'm glad you brought the children."

"Thank you for finding the truth about Joe," Daniel tells me.

I nod. "Everyone needed to know."

"I wish we'd had as much faith in him as you did," Rebecca says. "We should have."

"You couldn't have known you'd been lied to by the police." I didn't tell them—I didn't tell anyone—about Naomi's indiscretions. Bishop Fisher and I discussed it and decided it's a secret best buried with her.

Rebecca's smile is fraught with what looks like regret. "We told the children he was a good man."

"They told me." I glance toward the kids as they make their way toward their parents' graves. "They've endured a lot and they've handled it with courage and grace. Joseph and Naomi would have been proud."

Daniel nods.

"Thank you," Rebecca whispers, her voice thin. "I'd best get over there before Sadie starts coaching the bishop on how best to deliver a sermon."

I watch them walk away, trying not to feel blue, but I know there's a good chance I may never see the kids again. They're part of Joseph

King. His legacy. And it's a part of my past that's gone forever.

The hiss of tires on asphalt draws my attention. I glance over to see Tomasetti's Tahoe pull up and park behind my Explorer. I wasn't sure he'd have time to meet me here; he's been working around the clock on the investigation into the murders of Sidney Tucker and Nick Rowlett.

Something goes soft in my chest when I see him get out. He rounds the front of the vehicle and opens the passenger door. Curiosity sparks when I see Vicki Cascioli slide gingerly from the passenger seat. The right side of her face is heavily bandaged. Even from twenty yards away I can see that her eye is blackened. She moves with the slow deliberation of a woman three times her age.

I hold my ground and wait for them to reach me.

Tomasetti speaks first, his eyes taking in the length of me. "Chief Burkholder."

The words are ridiculously formal, since we've been living together for over a year now. Despite the melancholy curling in my gut, I smile. "Agent Tomasetti."

I turn my attention to the woman beside him, taking in the pale complexion, the watchful, uncomfortable eyes. There are a few small cuts on the left side of her face. Bruising at her throat. Tension seems to emanate from her entire body.

The three of us exchange handshakes.

"Ms. Cascioli," I say. "How are you feeling?"

"One surgery down, a few more to go." Her voice is low, her mouth barely opening, and I realize because of her injuries it's difficult for her to speak.

"Kate, I hope it's not inappropriate for us to be here," Tomasetti begins.

I glance back to where several dozen Amish have gathered at the graves of Joseph and Naomi King. I'd wanted to stand with them, to pay homage in my own way, to say good-bye to Joseph King. But I know Cascioli just finished her initial deposition with BCI, and I'm hungry for news about the investigation.

"It's okay." I motion toward our vehicles. "Let's talk over there so we don't bother anyone."

We go through the gate to stand next to the Tahoe. "How did the deposition go?" I ask Cascioli.

"I told my story," she says. "What I knew. When I knew it. How I believe all of it went down."

I glance from her to Tomasetti and back to her. "What happened to Sidney Tucker?"

She squares her shoulders. A sigh hisses between her lips. She's shoring up her resolve, I realize, her emotions.

"He was a good man," she tells me. "A good cop. Not perfect, but . . ." She shrugs. "When

Peggy got sick he just stopped trying. He let himself get sucked into some things he shouldn't have."

"Things like what?" I ask.

"I rode with Tuck for four months, when I was a rookie. He showed me the ropes, taught me a lot. We butted heads the first week or so. In fact, I think he pretty much hated me." She starts to smile, but ends up wincing in pain. "The more time we spent together, the closer we became. I think he sort of saw me as his surrogate daughter or something. I loved Tuck. He was funny and competent and over the months he became like a father to me. I hated to see him retire, but . . . he wanted out.

"Anyway, I'd heard stories about Rowlett and Travers. You never know what to believe, so I asked Tuck about it. He wasn't a big talker, kept a lot to himself, but I think he *needed* to tell someone what he knew. I think he felt guilty because he'd looked the other way while Travers and Rowlett crossed the line. Tuck had violated his own code of honor and it wasn't sitting too well."

A smile lights her eyes. "He was one of those guys who doesn't talk about personal things or, God forbid, emotions. But he opened up to me. He was incredibly troubled by what was going on.

"At first it was just bits and pieces. The snippets

I heard felt more like gossip than reality. But I knew there was *something* going on. I knew it wasn't good." Absently, she touches the bandage on her face. "After Peggy went into hospice, I stopped by Tuck's place one evening to return his phone. He'd left it in the cruiser. I found him sitting in the dark, drinking, distraught, and he told me everything. And I do mean everything. Every ugly, damning detail.

"Rowlett and Travers were . . ." She struggles to find the right word then spits out, "Corrupt. They were abusing their power as police officers. They were shaking down local drug dealers, stealing cash or drugs or both, letting the dealers who'd roll over on their competitors operate unencumbered. When they stopped female drivers for DUI or some other serious offense, they'd offer to look the other way if the women had sex with them."

I find myself thinking about Kelly Dennison, one of the few who'd stood up to them, and how much it had cost her. She'd been forced to recant her story. She'd been silenced and disgraced and shamed. She did jail time for a crime she didn't commit, all to save not only herself, but her child.

"What could I do? I was just a dumb rookie." Cascioli shakes her head. "I wanted to keep my job. So I kept my mouth shut. It wasn't easy. When I couldn't take it anymore, I confronted them." Her laugh is a bitter sound. "They destroyed me. My reputation. My career. They got me fired and pretty much ruined any hope of me ever landing another job in law enforcement."

"Tuck knew and stayed quiet?" I ask.

Her eyes meet mine and she gives a reluctant nod. "They tossed him some money a few times. A hundred here, a hundred there. You have to understand, when Tuck found out Peggy only had a few weeks to live, he pretty much stopped caring about everything. He had a lot of her medical expenses to pay. We're talking tens of thousands of dollars—and he didn't have it." She shrugs. "So he accepted the cash Travers or Rowlett gave him and he kept his mouth shut."

The twist of her mouth is bitter. "Until you showed up asking questions. I suspect he was ready to come clean. He'd had enough and wanted to stop Rowlett and Travers."

"How did Naomi and Joseph King play into all of it?"

"According to Tuck, Travers pursued Naomi King. Charmed her. Made all these phony promises. He had a sexual relationship with her. Travers was manipulating her and laughing about it behind her back." She shakes her head. "I couldn't imagine with her being Amish and all but . . ." She lets the words trail. "Tuck said Naomi King got serious about Travers. She wanted to leave the Amish. Leave her husband. Her kids.

"Travers has four kids. He's married to the sheriff's daughter. Had his eye on becoming sheriff one day. If any of what he was doing came to light . . ." She shrugs. "He had a lot to lose."

"So he murdered her," I say. "He framed her husband. And if it hadn't been for Sidney Tucker, he would have gotten away with it."

"Tuck and you, Burkholder," Cascioli adds.

I wish I could take solace in the knowledge, but I can't. Joseph and Naomi King are still dead. Their children will still grow up without their parents.

"How is it that Joseph King was convicted of domestic violence?" I ask, bracing because I don't want to hear that Joseph had been abusive to his wife.

"From what I understand, Naomi had a cell phone her husband didn't know about. That's how she communicated with Travers. She'd call him sometimes when she and Joseph got into it. A few times, Travers or Rowlett showed up and took Joseph to jail. They embellished their police reports."

I find myself thinking about the footloose boy I'd known. Joseph King had had so many hopes and dreams for the future. All of it taken from him by a corrupt few.

"How deep did the corruption go?" I ask. "I mean, Wade Travers was Jeff Crowder's son-in-law."

Cascioli glances at Tomasetti.

"We're looking at Crowder," he tells me. "That's all I can say at this point."

I think about how Crowder treated me during the standoff and for the first time it makes perfect, awful sense. For now, it's enough.

I turn my attention to Cascioli. "I didn't have the chance to thank you for saving my life," I tell her. "If there's anything I can do to help you get back on your feet . . ."

"Once I'm through all these surgeries," she says, "I'm going to apply at a couple of police departments, maybe a sheriff's department. A reference would be nice."

"You got it."

Giving me her best tough-guy impression, despite the emotion I see in her eyes, she turns and starts toward the Tahoe.

I look toward the gathering of Amish, where Bishop Fisher is in the midst of a sermon that's rife with admonitions and ample references to the life and character of the departed.

"You and the bishop didn't tell them about Naomi King's indiscretions?" Tomasetti asks.

I glance over at him and shake my head. "We figured the King family had been through enough."

I watch Cascioli climb into the Tahoe and slam the door. "Are they going to put her before a grand jury?"

He shakes his head. "She still has her peace officer certification. When she walked into the scene with you, Rowlett, and Travers, she had a right to defend herself and an obligation to intervene."

We fall silent for a moment, both of us watching the service. "Crowder's going down," he says. "You didn't hear that from me."

"Hear what?" I smile, but once again my attention is on the service.

"Why don't you go over there and pay your respects?" Tomasetti says. "I'm going to drop Cascioli at her apartment and then I have to get back to Richfield."

Before I can stop myself, I reach for his hand and squeeze. "See you tonight?"

"Bet on it," he tells me.

I watch him walk away and then I start toward the service to bid a final farewell to my childhood friend and let go of another piece of my past.

Books are
produced in the
United States
using U.S.-based
materials

Books are printed
using a revolutionary
new process called
THINK tech™ that
lowers energy usage
by 70% and increases
overall quality

Books are
durable and
flexible
because of
smythe-sewing

Paper is
sourced using
environmentally
responsible
foresting methods
and the
paper is acid-free

Center Point Large Print
600 Brooks Road / PO Box 1
Thorndike, ME 04986-0001 USA

(207) 568-3717

US & Canada:
1 800 929-9108
www.centerpointlargeprint.com